W9-BNN-422

BT 3/14

# GIULIANA'S WAY

BERNARDS TOWNSHIP LIBRARY
32 S. MAPLE AVENUE
BASKING RIDGE, NJ  07920

# GIULIANA'S WAY

## Albert M. Parillo

authorHOUSE®

*AuthorHouse™ LLC*
*1663 Liberty Drive*
*Bloomington, IN 47403*
*www.authorhouse.com*
*Phone: 1-800-839-8640*

© *2014 Albert M. Parillo. All rights reserved.*

*Cover design—Barbara Lee*
*Cover photo—Tetyana Sadovenko*
*Author photo—Margit Erb*

*No part of this book may be reproduced, stored in a retrieval system, or transmitted by any means without the written permission of the author.*

*This is a work of fiction. The characters and events in this book are fictitious. Any similarity to real persons, living or dead, is coincidental and not intended by the author.*

*Published by AuthorHouse 12/27/2013*

*ISBN: 978-1-4918-3728-3 (sc)*
*ISBN: 978-1-4918-3705-4 (hc)*
*ISBN: 978-1-4918-3727-6 (e)*

*Library of Congress Control Number: 2013921753*

*This book is printed on acid-free paper.*

*Because of the dynamic nature of the Internet, any web addresses or links contained in this book may have changed since publication and may no longer be valid. The views expressed in this work are solely those of the author and do not necessarily reflect the views of the publisher, and the publisher hereby disclaims any responsibility for them.*

"For the deliberations of mortals are timid, and unsure are our plans."

*Book of Wisdom 9-13 (18)*

"There is no love sincerer than the love of food."

*George Bernard Shaw*

For my parents, Albert and Barbara

# PART ONE

# AMALFI

# Chapter 1

It was not unlike every other morning in Amalfi: a warm sun blanketed the town's craggy cliffs; the azure-blue waters of the Mediterranean gently lapped its rocky shoreline; stalls and food shops along its main shopping street readied their wares for another busy day of commerce; and high above the square in the majestic Sant'Andrea Cathedral a smattering of the town's faithful gathered for early morning Mass.

But in the seven-member dwelling of Antonio and Maria Landini it was anything but a typical Amalfi morning: a layer of sadness, thick as fog after an all-night rain, shrouded the once-happy household—the youngest member of the family was leaving.

On the night before the journey that would completely change her life, Giuliana Landini went to bed earlier than usual. But sleep would not come. In its place a steady stream of conflicting emotions and gut-wrenching questions wreaked havoc on her peace of mind:

*Am I going to be happy living in a strange new land with an uncle and aunt I hardly know? Are Mama and Papa going to be all right without me? And what about my friends . . . will they still be my friends even though I'll be five thousand miles away?*

Other painful reminders—of who would be missed and what would be lost—left her even more anxious and sleep deprived.

*Dear Father Di Pina . . . not having him around anymore is going to be hard for me to deal with. He's been my inspiration. He taught me so much about art. How many times did he say*

1

*to me that an artist was as close as one could get to being God-like?*

*And Maddalena Vertucci . . . I'm going to miss her so much. When I think of all the wonderful times I spent in her church rectory kitchen, I want to cry. She gave me my passion for food . . . most of all, her creative approach to preparing it.*

*But my biggest regret is leaving Nonna Dona. She's been at my side from the day she came to live with us after Nonno died when I was a little girl. She taught me more than anyone else. God only knows, will I ever see her again? Am I doing the right thing?*

The adrenalin rush from reflecting on these and other disturbing thoughts flooded Giuliana's head and sat her bolt upright. She got out of bed, and in the dense silence and darkness of early morning made her way to the kitchen. There she found her grandmother at the table, rosary in hand, her vacant hazel eyes staring into space.

Nonna lit a candle when she heard footsteps. Its flickering flames cast a soft glow, illuminating Giuliana's face and the swollen red eyes she couldn't keep from rubbing. "Please sit, my child," she said softly. She then rose from her chair and went over to the ice box and poured milk from a bottle into a small pan and placed it on the stove. "A warm glass of milk will help make you sleep."

Giuliana was grateful to have found her grandmother up. A little conversation, even at this hour, might help lessen the anxiety that engulfed her as the fast-approaching time to leave everything she held dear grew nearer. While Giuliana sipped her milk, Nonna Dona went to the alcove off the pantry. She brought out a hanger covered in a white sheet and handed it to her granddaughter.

"I made this dress especially for your trip," Nonna Dona said as Giuliana ran her hands over its soft surface. "I want you to look nice while you're traveling on the boat . . . you can wear it all summer long when you get to America." The dress was a colorful print that perfectly complemented Giuliana's slightly tinted olive complexion and dark hair. The next morning, everyone remarked how grown up and lovely she looked. While on the boat, whenever she appeared in her new dress, other girls her age and some older ones as well couldn't take their eyes off the stylish, beautiful young girl.

Giuliana couldn't stop kissing her grandmother, the one person everyone said she most resembled, not only in looks but in temperament and outlook. Reluctantly, but ever so gently, Nonna Dona eased her granddaughter away. "Now please go back to bed and try to get some sleep . . . you have an exhausting day ahead of you."

Giuliana, with heavy heart, glanced over her shoulder as she started to walk away. Nonna Dona rose from her chair and came over to the child and took her hand. "I know you've heard me say it a thousand times, Giuliana, but I'm going to say it once again . . . hold onto your dreams and don't let go of them. And don't be afraid to take chances or let anybody try to talk you out of doing what you want to do. Live your own life." She paused and let out a sigh. "Remember one other thing: life is full of surprises, it can change in a heartbeat."

\* \* \*

With these cautionary yet not unhopeful words indelibly etched in memory—they were the last ones she'd ever hear her grandmother say to her—Giuliana Landini, four months past her eleventh birthday, got on a boat the next day and sailed for America, leaving behind, in June of 1941, hearth, home and the *bella Italia* of her youth.

Conspicuously missing from the small party to see her off at the Naples pier was her grandmother, Donatella Teresa Fassano. She feigned over-exertion from too much excitement the last few days as reason for not accompanying her daughter, son-in-law and three grandsons on the long and uncomfortable bus ride from Amalfi to Naples when in fact she could not bear to bid Giuliana goodbye in the presence of others, including her own family. She officially performed that bitter-sweet task while they were alone picnicking on the beach in nearby Atrani, just the two of them, on the next to the last day before Giuliana was set to depart. They spent the better part of the afternoon reminiscing, mostly about Donatella's youth, of which Giuliana never tired of hearing, and discussing in general what life might be like in America. Just before leaving the beach, Donatella handed her granddaughter a brightly wrapped package. She had thought long and hard about what sort of going-away present she should give Giuliana and had discussed the matter with her daughter Maria on a number of occasions.

"Since Giuliana is starting a whole new life, she needn't carry anything with her but her ambitions," Maria told her mother, her voice cracking when she said it. "Let her start out totally fresh. So whatever you give her, make it small but memorable."

Giuliana excitedly unwrapped the package. Resting between nicely starched tissue paper was a shiny black leather-bound diary with gold-plated clasp and lock. Engraved on the front were Giuliana's name and the date, June 15, 1941, embossed in gold letters. "Keep this diary close to you, and write something in it every day," Donatella said. "When you fill this one start another, and then another. Who knows, by the time you're a grown woman you might have written a book or two. At the very least, you'll have a record of your life and adventures in the new world."

Giuliana was enormously pleased. She had trouble fighting back tears, but having inherited her grandmother's stoic disposition in addition to her other attributes, she was able to suppress the impulse.

After all other farewells had been dispensed with, Giuliana the next day—the last one she would spend in Amalfi—went with Nonna Dona to Santa Croce Church to have lunch with the pastor, Father Marco Di Pina, and his housekeeper/cook, Maddalena Vertucci, next to her grandmother and parents, the two people she most admired.

Maddalena's sadness over Giuliana's imminent departure did not prevent her from preparing a magnificent lunch for her young friend. With the serving of the main course—veal shank osso buco with saffron infused porcini mushroom risotto with flecks of black truffles in a rich flavored ragu—Father Di Pina poured a glass of his finest Brunello di Montalcino. "While the dish looks beautiful on the plate," he proclaimed, smacking his lips, "I promise it will taste even better on the palate." As a bow to the august occasion he insisted, over the not-too-strenuous objections of Donatella, "that Giuliana should be allowed to partake of this splendid potable." (Later on in life, as she perfected her culinary skills, Giuliana became a bona fide oenophile, owing much of her knowledge in the proper pairing of wine and food to what she had learned at the dining table in the rectory of Santa Croce Church in Amalfi, lorded over by the courtly, and portly, priest, Father Marco Di Pina.)

While coffee and desert were being served, the pastor announced that it was time for gift giving, and excused himself. When he was safely out of the dining room, Maddalena reached for a parcel sitting on the floor under her chair and handed it to Giuliana, who opened it with child-like anticipation. Inside the box was a beautiful hand crocheted shawl. "You'll need it on those cold nights in America," Maddalena said. Nestled among its folds was a cloth-bound booklet containing a sheaf of papers neatly tied together. On its frontispiece was written in perfectly formed letters: *For My Lovely Young Friend Giuliana Landini, Maddalena Vertucci's Favorite Recipes, June 12, 1941.*

Giuliana bolted from her chair into Maddalena's waiting arms. "This is the best gift you could have given me, Maddalena," Giuliana exclaimed with glee, hugging the housekeeper and not wanting to let go. "I will cherish these pages forever." Holding up the booklet, she added: "You can be sure I will be making every one of these recipes. When I do, I will be thinking of you. And when I put on this lovely shawl, it will be as though I have your loving arms wrapped around my shoulders."

Father Di Pina entered the room carrying a large rectangular cardboard box. He was delighted to see how happy Giuliana was with the going-away presents Maddalena had given her. Unlike Maddalena's brightly wrapped gifts, his present was drab in comparison. He placed it upright against the corner of the table, at the head where he customarily sat. While still standing, he asked Giuliana to open it from the top and gently lay the box flat on the floor.

"I'm afraid I didn't have time to wrap it," he said. Then as carefully as he could without hurting himself, he got down gingerly on all fours and in both hands secured the unopened end of the box. While pulling delicately at his end, he asked Giuliana to place her dainty hands into the other end and slide out its contents. When she saw what it was she was so overtaken that she remained on the floor, on her knees, for some time.

"Could this possibly be for me?" she asked.

"Yes it is," said Father Di Pina.

It was the St. Lucy painting hanging in the upstairs hallway; she fell in love with it the first time she saw it. Giuliana began to cry. The portly priest had by now pulled himself up from his kneeling position and lifted the girl gently off the floor. He took both her hands in his, and did not wait for Giuliana to say what she very much wished to say if only she had been able to speak. Donatella and Maddalena sat motionless, in tears.

"From the moment you first laid eyes on this picture, and your reaction to it as told to me by Maddalena," Father Di Pina proclaimed, "and after all the visits you've made here over the years without ever once failing to go upstairs to bask in the beauty of this exquisite work of art, I knew in my heart this painting one day would be rightfully yours. Well, Giuliana, that day has come."

# Chapter 2

That first night on the boat, as it sailed serenely out to sea, the protectively packed St. Lucy painting resting upright next to her bunk, Giuliana lay deep in thought, trying to recapture the circumstances of how, at the age of six, she had first come in contact with the painting, the most cherished possession she would ever own. This brought into focus, in the most loving way, the two extraordinary people responsible for her now having it in her possession: Father Marco Di Pina, for the gift itself; Maddalena Vertucci, for exposing it to her in the first place.

\*   \*   \*

It was late morning on a warm, sun-drenched August day when Giuliana stepped out of her bedroom onto the shaded patio that led to the cantilevered gardens that ran a full seventy-five feet along the highest point of the Landini property. There she met up with Nonna Dona who was inspecting the plum tomato plants staked all across the stone wall that sat at the top level of the gardens separating the Landini property from that of the Giordanos, which rested above. Just below the plum tomatoes was a long row of cherry tomato plants and, interspersed among the plants, fresh basil and oregano. On the third level were the most amazing cucumbers and small gourds, tiny orange chili peppers (sinfully hot) plus larger green and red chili peppers, and on the next or fourth level Giuliana's favorite vegetables—eggplant, zucchini, red and yellow sweet peppers and green beans. A variety of herbs grew like protected little offspring among the vegetables.

On ground level several feet adjacent to the gardens was a cave-like opening that had been fashioned out of the natural rock formation of the mountain from which the Landini house and all the other houses in that area of Amalfi had been carved. Running along both sides of the interior thick stone walls were heavy wooden shelves on which sat Donatella's canning treasures in different size mason jars—stewed tomatoes, pickled eggplant, string beans and beets. In one corner next to the shelves was a two-burner stove used for preparing the tomatoes and vegetables for the canning that took place every year in late summer. In the farthest corner was the rustic wine-pressing equipment Antonio and his sons used for making, in the fall, a year's supply of their home made wine. Dozens of erect, moss-covered bottles stood perfectly aligned, soldier-like and proudly, on the shelves above it.

Since coming to live with the Landinis after her husband died, Donatella Fassano, much to the delight of everyone in the family, had, in just over a year, completely revived the vegetable gardens as well as a small patch several feet from the entrance to the storage and preparation area where the most beautiful wildflowers and other indigenous plants embroidered the ground and grew in fragrant, colorful abundance. She tended her gardens at least an hour or two each day, explaining to her granddaughter in precise detail what she was doing and why she was doing it. Giuliana's parents and brothers were nowhere in sight to disturb her daily lesson in horticulture. Such precious moments would all but disappear in a few weeks when Giuliana would be starting elementary school.

But on this particular Saturday morning there would be no gardening lessons. After bidding Giuliana a warm good morning, Nonna Dona took her granddaughter by the hand and while descending the ancient stone staircase leading to the road in front of the house, told her that they'd be going off to La Chiesa di Santa Croce, a five-minute walk away, to meet with the pastor and several other guests in the church rectory.

When they arrived at noon, Donatella and Giuliana were ushered by Maddalena to the shaded arbor located between the church and the rectory, an exquisite setting for the wonderful meal she would soon be serving to the group. In the center of the arbor, seated at a large communal dining table that appeared to have weathered many years of liturgical as well as other gustatory feasts, were Father Di Pina; Armando Gallardo, Amalfi's much loved physician, and his wife, Matilda; and Francesco Montone, town solicitor, and his wife, Beatrice. A place had not been set for Giuliana, who was to remain in the kitchen with the housekeeper/cook while Father Di Pina and his guests, including Donatella, lunched and tended to the business for which the cleric had invited them: to discuss fund raising plans for the parish school.

Preparations for the elaborate lunch were well underway when the priest, after greeting his guests, brought Giuliana into the kitchen where Maddalena was busy at the stove stirring with a long ladle, then tasting with the delicate touch of one practiced and discerning finger, the delectable contents of several pots. The smell of simmering sauce mingled with the pungent aroma of beef braising in perfectly seasoned juices set off little Giuliana's salivary glands, and after an affectionate greeting from Maddalena she was seated at the end of the long kitchen table where she immediately began sampling each of the dishes Maddalena would be serving to Father Di Pina's guests: an antipasti of grilled vegetables, porcini mushrooms and fresh buffalo mozzarella; chicken consommé with tiny tortellini stuffed with ricotta, parsley and basil; homemade wide, flat fettuccini coated in just the right amount of ragu; and stuffed veal roast accompanied by long, thin string beans that had been marinated in olive oil, a touch of wine vinegar, a sliver of garlic and fresh mint. Dessert consisted of fresh seasonal berries in a mascarpone-based zabaglione cream, and thumb-sized just-baked biscotti.

Giuliana tried a little bit of everything, but not the meal's appropriate after dinner *digestivi* reserved for the adults—amaretto, Sambuca, grappa and, for those who required it after such a sumptuous meal, fernet. When she finished eating, she gladly helped Maddalena with getting things ready for lunch.

\*     \*     \*

Giuliana was acquainted with Maddalena Vertucci long before her grandmother came to live with the Landinis; everyone in town knew the kindly church housekeeper. But a deep friendship—a love no less, not merely an acquaintance—between the young girl and the older woman commenced on the day Giuliana was taken for the first time to the 7:30 a.m. Mass her grandmother attended daily since coming to live in her daughter's house. Whenever Giuliana accompanied her grandmother to church during the week thereafter she was thrilled to see Maddalena, but no more so than when they would often meet late morning in the square or in the markets along Flavia Gioia where most of the town's shopping was done.

Giuliana was much taken with how particular Maddalena was in choosing from the profusion of food carts and stalls until it was explained to her by her grandmother one day that in the person of Father Di Pina Maddalena was catering to the most refined and discriminating palate in town. And the priest made no bones about letting everybody know it, which, at times, left him rueful whenever he had to turn down a dinner invitation graciously extended to him by a parishioner. But such was Father Marco's inclination to remain in the rectory at meal times, except on occasions when it was absolutely impossible for him to say no—weddings, baptisms, funerals—that it became the source of great amusement amongst townspeople when they ascertained what new excuse he had conjured up as to why it was out of the question for him to dine elsewhere than at the table he never tired of describing as the best in the whole of southern Italy—his own.

As was the case throughout her life Giuliana's charm, intelligence, maturity and force of personality captivated everyone she came in contact with, young or old. Maddalena was no exception. Unmarried, with not a single Vertucci relative in the area, she made the church in effect her family: all of her attention, all of her loyalty—her whole life, in short—she gave to the church. And to a handful of close friends, first and foremost among them, Donatella Fassano and, as time went on, Donatella's granddaughter, the child, Giuliana Landini.

As their relationship grew Maddalena, quite surprisingly given their enormous age difference, made it a regular habit of seeking this exceptional six-year-old child's opinions, and approval. When asked by Giuliana whenever they were together in the church rectory kitchen how and why she did something, Maddalena wasn't satisfied merely to answer the child; she invariably went a step further, such was her desire to impart as much of her extensive knowledge of food and its preparation as she could to her young friend.

On one particular Friday visit, for example, Maddalena had marinating in a shallow baking pan two medium-sized *orate* suitably filleted, seasoned and dressed, ready to be grilled for Father Di Pina and his guest. Wanting to demonstrate for Giuliana the proper way to butcher and debone a whole fish, Maddalena took a third *orate*, which she said she would have for an early supper later that afternoon, and went through the entire procedure all over again, step by careful step. When she finished, Maddalena, without the slightest hint of braggadocio, said that she could de-bone a fish as well as or better than any fishmonger in Amalfi. Observing with saucer-like eyes the virtuoso performance, Giuliana never forgot the demonstration.

Giuliana's love affair with cooking really began when Donatella arrived in the Landini household. Her mother Maria, as with typical Italian women of her generation, knew her way around the kitchen, but a linen business she had started when Giuliana was hardly out of diapers had finally taken hold, affording little time for her to prepare all but the simplest meals. She left the more elaborate ones to her mother, which Giuliana savored with relish and was always eager to help in their preparing. Giuliana's food obsession was fueled to an even greater extent during the time she spent in the rectory kitchen with her grown up-friend Maddalena Vertucci, who made of cooking an art.

One evening Giuliana asked her grandmother if it were possible for her to go more often to the rectory to visit with Maddalena, giving as an excuse the housekeeper's need for company, not her own desire to learn all she could from such an outstanding cook. In making the request, she was careful to avoid any mention of cooking; she did not want to let on to Nonna Dona that she was in any way comparing her cooking skills with Maddalena's, which Giuliana, even at the age of six, was astute enough to recognize as being superior to either her mother's or her grandmother's, good as they were.

One day after church, Donatella asked Maddalena if she would be good enough to look after Giuliana in two days time. She said she needed to go to Salerno to attend to some urgent family business. "If you can do me the favor, Maddalena, I'll leave Giuliana off with you after Mass and pick her up at the rectory around 1 p.m."

"I'd be delighted to have the child," said Maddalena, "I'm sure Giuliana and I will find plenty to do to occupy our time together."

On Thursday, Dona dropped off Giuliana as planned, leaving Maddalena an entire morning to conduct for her more than willing young pupil a master class in the preparation of that evening's featured entrée, braised rabbit.

"The first thing one must do when preparing food . . . what do you think, Giuliana?" the housekeeper asked.

"Make sure you wash your hands really well," came the quick reply.

"Excellent. And do you know what the next most important thing is?"

Giuliana thought for several seconds, staring intently at her inquisitor. Then, reluctant to offer an answer she wasn't certain was right, shook her head.

"You must always have on a clean apron . . . not only to protect your clothes but more important to make certain your hands don't come in contact with anything but a spotless garment. Remember: in the kitchen cleanliness is next to godliness."

When Donatella picked her up that afternoon Giuliana couldn't wait to tell her grandmother everything she did and had learned during her visit with Maddalena. "Nonna, she has the most wonderful kitchen," Giuliana said brimming with excitement while taking her grandmother's hand as they started their five-minute walk home. "Over the long table in the middle of the kitchen are twenty pots and pans—I counted every one of them. They hang on hooks attached to the ceiling. In one corner next to the sink is a butcher-block table; it's where Maddalena prepares her meats. On the other side of the sink is another square oak table on thick legs. It has a marble top in the middle of the wood. Father Di Pina had it made for her because he said that was best for cleaning fish." She paused, then added, "Maddalena told me that her kitchen was a holy place. Is that right, Nonna?"

Donatella had spent countless mornings with Maddalena in the rectory kitchen and was familiar with its contents and layout, but she listened with fascination to every word Giuliana said as if she were hearing it for the first time. She never once glanced the child's way, staring straight ahead as they walked so as to conceal first the smile, then the almost painful effort it took to stifle the laughter that was slowly building up in her. To burst out laughing would have the effect of trivializing her precocious granddaughter's riveting account, and the older woman had no intention of submitting to that irresistible urge. So she allowed the child to continue her commentary without interruption.

"The dinner Maddalena is preparing tonight for Father Marco and his three guests is going to be wonderful. You'll never guess what she's making, Nonna." Before Donatella could venture a guess, Giuliana continued: "Braised rabbit. She even had me help her make it . . . in a big cast iron pot. She made it cook in the oven for almost three hours. The longer it cooks the better it tastes, Maddalena said."

Hardly drawing a breath, Giuliana went on to describe in meticulous detail—she appeared to have memorized every step of the process—how a woman in her sixties and her six-year-old companion had cooked a meal that Maddalena promised she and her grandmother would get to taste the next day, "God willing there are any leftovers."

"First she cut up some pancetta, in tiny pieces, and put them in a pot with a little olive oil. When the pancetta had browned just enough, she took the bacon out of the pot and put in the rabbit cut up in small pieces. She had me wash the pieces in cold water and pat them dry before she put them in the pot. Then she added carrots, celery, onions and a few pieces of fennel. She said fennel was her secret ingredient, it added more flavor to game . . . what's game, Nonna? She also put in the pot rosemary, thyme, salt, pepper and fresh chicken stock, then two full spoons of tomato paste; Maddalena said it added color and sweetness to the juices the rabbit braised in. Now here's the part I love the most, Nonna."

They had arrived at the house, but the girl held her grandmother back so that she could finish off her commentary, as well as finish off the dish. "Maddalena took a bottle of white wine . . . she opened it a half hour before she began putting everything into the pot . . . she said the wine needed to breathe . . . why is that, Nonna? . . . and poured two glasses of it into the pot. She then told me a secret about the wine, she said you were the only person I could tell it to. She said Father Di Pina likes red wine the best . . . he says true wine drinkers like red more than white, so he told Maddalena to cook with red wine, except when she was making fish. But Maddalena said white was better for cooking game . . . what's game, Nonna? She said that in all the time she cooked rabbit for Father Di Pina, as much as he knew about food and wine, he never noticed the difference." Grandmother and granddaughter both laughed heartily.

The next day at lunchtime, Giuliana went to the church rectory with Nonna Dona. Maddalena, as promised, served them the previous evening's leftovers, explaining that braised rabbit in fact tasted even better a day after it was actually cooked. "Aren't you lucky," she happily exclaimed to her guests.

That night, on her knees, saying her prayers before bed, Giuliana told the Blessed Mother that the meal she had that day was the best she had ever had, better than any of her mother's or grandmother's. While at it, she also asked God to give her the courage not to lie to either of them if she were ever asked who the best cook in Amalfi was. "Please, God, never make that happen." Before falling off to sleep, Giuliana vowed that "someday I'll be a great cook, just like Maddalena."

After Mass on the following Monday, Donatella met up with Maddalena and informed her that Giuliana had asked whether she could spend more time at the rectory. Maddalena was delighted. Anticipating such a request, she had already taken the matter up with Father Marco. He approved wholeheartedly since he, too, found the angelic child irresistible and always welcomed her visits. Moreover, he felt her presence in the rectory from time to time would provide companionship for his housekeeper, who often spent the better part of every day without having a single person, other than himself, to talk to.

It was thus settled between Donatella and her daughter, Maria, that Giuliana would spend Mondays and Fridays with Maddalena from after morning Mass until two in the afternoon. This arrangement would last through August, four weeks until Giuliana started elementary school, which she looked forward to with growing anticipation.

*     *     *

During her days at the rectory, Giuliana paid close attention to Maddalena's every move as the housekeeper went about preparing dish after dish from her extensive repertoire, with nary a note to guide her along her culinary peregrinations, only tasting as she went from pot to pot. Some of the dishes the young girl was not familiar with. They were of the northern Italian variety, many with Germanic influences.

This style of cooking Maddalena inherited from her parents, who were originally from the north of Italy where meat, not fish, was more often served; butter used more than olive oil; and pasta prepared in a white cream or meat-flavored brown, not red, sauce. Being able to deftly switch culinary gears between north and south—which Father Di Pina, with his far-ranging, eclectic tastes, found to be the acme of his housekeeper's considerable cooking talents—Maddalena had built up a body of Italian cooking few people in the Amalfi area were exposed to, the exception being the pastor, his guests and now Giuliana, who had the rare experience of observing firsthand the woman's remarkable cooking legerdemain, then oftentimes getting to taste the results.

Over time, Giuliana learned recipes of every kind, from the most basic to the more time consuming and elaborate: soups—meat-based, chicken-based, fish-based, vegetable-based; homemade pastas of every description (Giuliana's personal favorite—spaghetti carbonara); fish; fowl; game; roasts; stews; vegetables; risottos; cakes and pastries. There was little in the way of food preparation Maddalena, whose cooking was a clear manifestation of a farm-to-table predilection—an unflinching insistence on using only the freshest local ingredients—didn't expose her inquisitive pupil to. While the older woman was the apotheosis of cooking of the highest order, the child Giuliana became her most ardent acolyte. When she got home from one of her visits to the rectory she couldn't wait to describe to her grandmother, and to the rest of the family later that evening, the dish or dishes Maddalena prepared that day.

Later on in life, Giuliana often reminisced about the lessons she had learned as a child in Maddalena's sacrosanct kitchen. She found that her approach to cooking was inspired and informed by, but not taken directly from, Maddalena's recipes, most of which had been handed down for generations by various Vertucci family members and then modified or expanded to satisfy her own sophisticated tastes.

Giuliana, instead, chose a more methodical approach, one that called for the complete deconstruction of a dish and an analysis of each ingredient in relation to every other. She would then experiment by putting together a whole range of new and what she hoped would be harmonious combinations that few cooks, excepting those with her creative sensibilities, would ever have expected to work. In most every respect, Giuliana's cooking fell well outside the standard tropes usually associated with traditional Italian food, resulting in a cuisine that was new and original, perhaps even revolutionary, and one that most certainly would not have easily been embraced by southern Italians in the 1940s.

*   *   *

A few days before school started, which happened to be the weekend Father Di Pina was called to Naples on church business, Maria Landini invited Maddalena to be a guest at their Friday-afternoon luncheon, the one time during the work week the entire Landini family was able to gather together at table. This being Giuliana's regular day at the rectory, it was decided that she and Maddalena would leave the rectory no later than one o'clock in order to arrive home a few minutes later, lunch being served promptly at one-fifteen. On such occasions when Father Di Pina was away Maddalena, free from having to prepare her customary elaborate evening meal, made due with a light supper for herself—a small salad, some cheese and fruit—so there was no cooking to be done on this day except for the freshly baked semolina rolls, already rising in the oven when Giuliana arrived, that Maddalena was taking to the Landinis.

"We are going to devote the entire morning to housecleaning," Maddalena informed her young guest, an announcement that brought a frown to Giuliana's face. The thought of not getting to observe Maddalena prepare another one of her wonderful meals was a terrible disappointment. But she didn't say anything. She couldn't imagine what cleaning had to be done since there wasn't a day when visiting the rectory that she hadn't found the kitchen to be spotlessly clean. Perhaps Maddalena had in mind all the other rooms in the rectory, none of which Giuliana had ever been in.

"We'll start in the kitchen and thoroughly scrub every pot and pan, if that's alright with you, Giuliana," Maddalena explained, always attentive to her young friend's desires and wanting to make clear this was a request, not an order. "Then we're going to wash every eating utensil and all the glassware and tableware. Okay?"

As they went about their work, the woman washing, the girl drying, the subject of school came up in conversation. Maddalena told of her own brief education—her family took her out of school after the fifth grade—and how even to this day she regretted having been forced to leave at such an early age. Giuliana, for her part, described the mounting excitement she was feeling at the prospect of starting school the following week when classes at Santa Croce resumed, and how much she looked forward to learning about . . . well, everything. She told her older companion, as they emptied all the shelves in the pantry and washed down every surface, how much she had already been taught by Nonna Dona.

"I know the alphabet, how to add and subtract . . . I also know how to read and write. Every night before I fall asleep, Nonna reads to me. The next day we talk about the story we read the night before." She described for Maddalena some of the books Donatella read to her, "even though I don't understand a lot of what she reads. When Nonna goes some place, she always brings me back a book. Someday when my brothers get married, I'll give them to my nieces and nephews," she said proudly.

When the cleaning in the kitchen had been completed, Maddalena took her energetic helper to the other rooms in the rectory. On the first floor was Father Di Pina's small but neat office, a large parlor and a formal dining room, the latter two rooms containing many antiques, some quite rare, the prelate had accumulated over the nearly forty years of his priesthood. Maddalena said that she would handle the dusting of the *objets d'art* and Giuliana, if she didn't mind, the rest of the furniture.

Before proceeding to the second floor, Maddalena suggested they take a break. The housekeeper made a cup of hot steaming coffee for herself and put out a tray of cookies and a glass of milk for Giuliana, who sat at the very spot at the end of the kitchen table where only a week ago she had eaten the best meal she had ever had in her young life. Giuliana apprised Maddalena of that very fact as she sipped her milk: she never squandered an opportunity to thank the rectory cook for the experience in hopes that perhaps a second best meal would not be too long in the offing.

Giuliana resumed the conversation they had been engaged in minutes before about school and books, and then brought up a subject she always found fascinating—her grandmother's all too brief school career. She told the older woman about why and when it stopped, and about how its cessation had impacted her life. "Did Nonna Dona ever tell you, Maddalena, about the cheese-making business she and my great grandparents had many years ago?" asked Giuliana.

"Yes, Giuliana, your grandmother and I have been friends for many years . . . there is very little she hasn't told me about her life," Maddalena replied.

"Well, you know then that she thought she made the right decision to go to work and stop going to school. But she doesn't want me to do that. She wants me to stay away from my mother's business and stay in school. What do you think, Maddalena?"

"I completely agree with your grandmother. Look at me," said Maddalena ruefully. "As much as I love working for the church, there isn't much else I have in my life. People who are educated have a lot more to look forward to in life than a peasant woman like me." Maddalena paused for a moment, averting her eyes from Giuliana's intense, sad stare. "Don't misunderstand me, I am perfectly content with my lot. Father Marco is the most wonderful man you could ever know . . . and besides, if I were somewhere else doing some other job, I wouldn't have you and your grandmother as friends."

Giuliana listened intently to her friend, smiling gratefully for the compliment she had just received. She then asked, with a hint of concern in her voice, "Is Nonna Dona a peasant woman, too, Maddalena?"

"Oh no, Giuliana, your grandmother is a refined woman . . . one of the most knowledgeable people I have ever met, even though she doesn't have much formal education," Maddalena said emphatically, wanting to drive the point across to her young friend. "She is smart and wise . . . that's why so many people in town look up to her. I see a lot of her in you. I think you should heed your grandmother's advice . . . stay in school, get a good education, don't let anybody or anything deny you the opportunity, even though in the Italy of today a good education is not such an easy thing to come by."

After this exchange, Maddalena took Giuliana to the second floor living quarters, an area otherwise off limits to all but Father Marco's family and close friends. At one end of the corridor was the pastor's bedroom. It was a good size but pristine, with a bed and chest of drawers, on which sat pictures of his parents and other family members, the only furniture in the room. The walls were bare except for a crucifix that hung above the head of the bed. Opposite the bed was a door that led to a much larger room, the pastor's study. Giuliana, in recounting the day's events to her family later that evening, pronounced it to be the most impressive room in the house.

She tried her best to describe its delicacies and visual textures: The walls were of rich mahogany and rose fourteen feet to the ceiling; three were adorned with paintings, thirty in all, she counted.

Most were of sacred subjects, which gave the room an unmistakable sanctified look and feel. The floor was made of highly buffed wide wood planks covered in the center by a rich Bakara rug that, according to Maddalena, Father Di Pina had purchased in Pakistan some years back. In one corner was the softest, most comfortable looking easy chair and matching ottoman. Next to the chair was a tall brass lamp with a wide cloth shade on which was painted a lovely pastoral scene; golden tassels hung down from around its entire circumference. She had never seen one like it. In the opposite corner was a small narrow table with a standing crucifix, votive candles in cranberry glass placed on either side. Directly in front of the table, which had the appearance of a small altar, was a *prie-dieu* made of the same wood as the walls, with the arm rest and kneeler covered in rich red velvet. But what really caught Giuliana's attention was the fourth wall, a floor-to-ceiling built-in bookcase housing hundreds of volumes. *I wouldn't want to have to dust these shelves,* Giuliana said to herself.

At the other end of the narrow hall was the guest room. It was smaller, though not by much, than the pastor's bedroom and had a four-poster bed, a crucifix, a four-drawer dresser and a small sink with a mirror above it. In an opposite corner sat a table and lamp, and a few feet to the right a large window that was two feet shy of running floor to ceiling. While Maddalena changed the bed linens, Giuliana scoured and cleansed the sink. She then moved to the dresser, where with her right hand she ran a damp rag along the bottom and sides of the four empty drawers.

As she did so, the duster that was in her other hand dropped to the floor and when she turned around to pick it up the cone of bright light that streamed in from the window and into the hallway through the bedroom door that had been left ajar illuminated the darkened recessed alcove across the hall. It cast a soft, celestial glow on a large painting, which she had failed to notice before entering the room, hanging on the wall over a small wooden table with a hurricane lamp sitting on top. Giuliana looked up and instantly became transfixed by what she saw: it was a painting of Santa Lucia, St. Lucy, the patron saint of light, the saint people with vision problems normally prayed to. She remained rigid, not moving so much as a muscle, her head tilted back, eyes wide as saucers, lost in a reverie Maddalena dared not disturb, even though she was blocking the woman's exit.

After a minute or so Maddalena gently nudged the child aside. "Don't tarry too long, my sweet, we have only fifteen minutes before we're expected at your house," she said as she left the room.

Giuliana did not so much look at the picture as study it. As one would expect of a child of her impressionable age she was at once fascinated and at the same time repulsed by the image of two eyes, as realistic as though they had been plucked just moments ago out of someone's head, that rested on a pewter plate held in Lucy's delicate left hand.

When they were walking home a few minutes later, Giuliana asked Maddalena about the painting, but the housekeeper was unable to expound on its provenance, except to say that she knew it to be one of Father Di Pina's prized possessions. "If you are really interested in knowing more about it you are going to have to ask Father directly," said Maddalena. Giuliana planned to do just that.

# Chapter 3

Some weeks later, on a late Saturday morning—Giuliana was now full time in school so her visits during the week with Maddalena were permanently suspended—she and her grandmother arrived at the rectory. While the two older women remained in the kitchen, Giuliana went to the pastor's office just off the parlor in the front of the house. The door was open; he had been expecting the child. Standing by the window with a book in his hand, the priest motioned Giuliana to enter.

"I was looking for some inspiration for tomorrow's homily," he said, moving from the window to his desk. He then took the chair from in front of the desk and placed it directly next to his, and invited Giuliana to sit. "I'm afraid I shall have to look elsewhere," he said closing the book with a clap, laid it on the desk, then sat down. "By the way, do you happen to know what a homily is, my dear?" Giuliana shook her head. "Of course not," said the priest. "But while you may not know the word, I'll bet a smart girl like you knows what it is."

Giuliana thought hard for several seconds. Believing she had found the answer, she then blurted out exuberantly, "Is it when you get up and talk to the people in the church?"

"Precisely," a delighted Father Di Pina exclaimed. "It's my Sunday Mass sermon, another word for homily . . . the subject of which is normally taken from the day's gospel, and . . ." He stopped mid sentence. "But that's enough religious instruction for one day . . . I know that's not what you came to hear me talk about."

The priest rose uneasily from his chair and went back to the window. Much too heavy for his modest height he was, at sixty-six, as rotund as the overstuffed ottoman that sat beside the easy chair in his office he so much loved. The creases that ran across his worn rumpled clothes accentuated his corpulence and did very little to hide the wide swath of flesh strapped across a burly chest hidden under his cassock. No matter how much he was urged by doctor, family and friends to curtail his glutinous eating habits, the obdurate priest waved all protestations aside. Never one to let his praying get in the way of his eating, he readily admitted, "to anyone who cares to know, that my only serious temporal indulgences, thank you, are art and antipasti, the latter fueled by generous amounts of vintage Chianti and, at the culmination of one of Maddalena's sumptuous meals, the smoothest grappa from Tuscany's finest distillery."

Ordinarily the priest did not feel the need to spend time worrying about his avoirdupois excepting such times, which lately had been occurring with much greater frequency, when he was forced to endure painful attacks of gout. Whenever they came on he would adhere (religiously) to weeks of abstemious behavior, abandoning his Spartan diet only when he knew it was absolutely safe to resume his customary glutinous ways. All things considered, however, his health was better than one might expect, which continued to baffle his good friend and physician, Doctor Armando Gallardo.

Giuliana was happy to have successfully answered the priest's question. It was obvious he was also pleased. But that did not surprise her. She knew him to be, as did everyone in his pastoral care, the most accommodating man. Though far and away the town's most learned citizen, comfortable in a handful of languages beside his native Italian, he was sensitive to people's feelings (except, perhaps, when it came to dining at their tables), a true friend to all in his flock, young or old. And much loved.

He was also a bona fide raconteur. Giuliana had been duly forewarned by her grandmother before going off to see the gregarious

Father Marco that "he'll talk a person's head off on just about any subject, given half the chance." She had attended Sunday Mass often enough to have been exposed to his formidable preaching and storytelling skills, and like everyone else in the parish mesmerized by his sonorous voice. Parishioners described his sermons thusly: invariably loud, frequently melodramatic, sometimes humorous, more often serious, but always totally riveting. And never short. Perhaps in talking with me, Giuliana hoped, he'll show some compassion and not be so long-winded.

As Father Di Pina got more and more into the story of the St. Lucy painting, which he told in a quiet, modulated, and diffident tone of voice, conscious he was speaking to a child, albeit a very smart one, Giuliana wished he would never stop talking. He turned from the window and sat down in the high-backed Victorian chair whose winged arms appeared to embrace his portly body.

"The painting was done by a Roman artist and teacher by the name of Ottavio Colangelo," the pastor explained. He then recounted to his rapt listener how it came into his possession, pausing occasionally only to shift position in his chair or to take off and then put back on glasses that kept slipping down his crimson, bulbous nose.

"When I was studying for the priesthood I found the work, as did most of my fellow seminarians, to be enormously hard and intense. As a way of relieving some of the pressure, it was suggested by our guidance counselor, an enormously astute and wise man, that it might be helpful for those of us who wished to do so to take up painting during what leisure time we had. Having always been a lover of art, even at an early age, I was thrilled at the prospect of indulging in one of God's greatest gifts to mankind under the tutelage of someone as renowned as Professor Colangelo. But much to my disappointment at first, I found myself the only one who considered the idea to have merit. Luckily, it just so happened that our counselor was a close friend of Colangelo's, so arrangements were made for me to attend a painting class once a week for three hours in his studio, conveniently located within walking distance from the seminary.

"I must tell you, my child, I enjoyed this diversion more than I can possibly say: it did in fact take my mind off my studies while I was engaged in it, and I was all the happier for having this brilliant painter all to myself. But even more than that, something else happened to me in that studio beyond being a witness at the creation of great art. I found that my faith, and my desire to become a priest, deepened in that sanctified place." He paused for a moment and wiped his brow.

"Now as far as my own art was concerned"—the priest shook his head from side to side; it was his way of registering the disappointment he still felt after the passage of all these years—"sadly, I wasn't a very good painter. I had little talent. The paint brush in my hand simply would not do what my head and heart wanted it to." But quickly regaining his amiable, upbeat demeanor, he added, "but what I did discover about myself, thanks in large part to Professor Colangelo, was that I possessed a truly discriminating and natural eye. I was, how should I put it without sounding pompous, a real connoisseur of art. In other words, I could readily recognize whether a painting was any good, a not so small or insignificant talent, if I do say so myself. It was quite a revelation, Giuliana."

Father Marco rose from his chair and went to a table next to a bookstand. On it was the largest bible Giuliana had ever seen. Maddalena one day told her he knew every word of it by heart. Also on the table was a tray with a pitcher of water and two glasses. The priest poured himself a glassful, and asked his young guest whether she wanted some. She declined. He then returned to his desk, sat down and continued his story.

"There were so many excellent works of Colangelo's in every corner of his studio, wonderful pictures he had painted over the years. A lot of them were stacked tightly like thick slices of my mother's homemade bread. Another one of his paintings that caught my eye rested on an easel. It was a rather large painting . . . three feet by four feet . . . of St. Lucy . . . similar to the smaller one that hangs on the wall in the upstairs hallway. The inspiration for this picture was the famous Lucy painting done by the great 14th century Florentine artist Giovanni di Bartolomeo Cristiani."

He cleared his throat, wanting to make certain the emotion he always felt when describing the picture to anyone who showed an interest in it did not impede its telling. "I was taken aback by the painting . . . first and foremost by its beauty . . . but even more than that, by its subject matter. You see, my mother, God rest her soul, had a reproduction of a picture very similar to this one . . . an inexpensive paper print . . . in a cheap frame that sat on a night table next to her bed. Every night before falling off to sleep she prayed to St. Lucy. Did you know, Giuliana, that St. Lucy is the patron saint of light, and of sight? Well, let me tell you a little bit about this remarkable woman.

"The long and short of it is that Lucy was a Christian whose Sicilian father, an apostate—it's another word for someone who doesn't believe in religion—wanted to marry her off to a well-to-do pagan fellow. She refused. As a consequence of her defying his wishes he decided to make an example of her by having her killed, if you can believe it. In the course of this brutal martyrdom, Lucy lost her beautiful eyes, but her vision, miraculously, was later restored. Her feast is celebrated on December 13.

"Now, getting back to my mother. She, unfortunately, had lost her right eye to infection when she was a young girl, not much older than you. Every night she prayed to the saint to protect the one good eye she had left so that she would be able to see the beautiful faces of her children, and grandchildren . . . also to be able to gaze upon the beauty of God's other wonderful gifts."

Giuliana sat enthralled. Father Di Pina was motionless as well. He continued in a voice so muted that Giuliana had to move her chair closer to the priest: "The picture of the eyes resting on a plate affected me much as it did you the first time I saw it. But in my case, in a different more personal way. When I told Professor Colangelo this story about my mother, as I'm telling it to you now, he was much moved.

"On the day of my ordination into the priesthood," he went on, "my parents hosted a wonderful party in my honor. All of my family and friends were present to celebrate this joyous occasion. One of the guests, to my delighted surprise, was Ottavio Colangelo. At one point during the festivities the guests came forward and presented me with a gift, *la busta*, just as they do at weddings. Dear Ottavio, God rest his memory, gave me the best gift of all—the painting you see on the wall upstairs in the alcove. He had painted it just for me . . . almost an exact replica of the Cristiani masterpiece of St. Lucy. Now, my child, do you see why this painting means so much to me?"

That night Giuliana lay awake long after Nonna had left the room. One persistent thought kept her from the sleep that very often came long before her grandmother finished reading to her: *What would it be like to be able to paint a picture as beautiful and as moving as the St. Lucy in Father Di Pina's rectory? Or, if not to have painted such a picture, then to at least own a magnificent work of art . . . to look at it and study it to my heart's content anytime I wished. I'd give anything for either privilege.*

Apart from Father Di Pina's impressive collection and the great art in Amalfi's grand Sant'Andrea Cathedral, Giuliana, at this stage of her life—she had just turned seven—had not been exposed to what one might consider art of any enduring quality. The half dozen or so statutes in her own Santa Croce Church where she and her family worshiped were mere replicas, not originals, and the inexpensive prints of Jesus, the Blessed Mother and other saints found on the walls of shops in the piazza certainly did not qualify as high art. Moreover, there was no famous museum in Amalfi, other than the excellent maritime museum, to go to for inspiration.

It was thus left to Nonna Dona, when Giuliana apprised her grandmother of this sobering fact some days later, to help fill the void. From then on, whenever Donatella went on excursions to larger towns in the area she would bring back an art book or two for her grandchild. Giuliana was so taken with the books that she started to draw. Even if she wasn't ready quite yet to read the books, she would at least have reproductions of great Italian painters and sculptors to copy. Caravaggio was her favorite.

# Chapter 4

So much of what Giuliana learned she owed to her grandmother. Not all of it art related. That thought was in her mind as the ship sailed serenely across the ocean's waters to what would be for her not only a new destination, but a new beginning. While seated alone on deck one morning after breakfast, with nothing but memories and an album of pictures of family and friends to comfort her, Giuliana went back in time to consider those circumstances that had brought her to this seminal point in her life.

When, after a protracted and painful period of indecision, she had finally made peace with the notion that leaving Amalfi for America was best for her, Giuliana did not look back on her decision but turned her full attention to what lay ahead. The tug of leaving parents and three older bothers of course weighed heavily on her, but she was at the same time exhilarated at the prospect of what she hoped would be an exciting new life, albeit in a land she knew little about apart from what she had learned in school. Though knowledge of the "new world," as the Italians were wont to call it, was sketchy, there were sufficient accounts sent back to the motherland by many *émigrés* who had chosen to live in America that it was indeed the land of opportunity. They also told, and much was made of the fact, that women, when they chose to or needed to, were working outside the home, a phenomenon unheard of in the male dominated society from whence they came.

Giuliana was not aware of any of this. No one in her immediate circle of family and friends, save for her uncle and aunt, with whom she would soon be living, had ever expressed a desire to travel to the United States, let alone settle there permanently. But thoughts of another life in another world changed dramatically for Giuliana, then five, when her grandmother, Donatella Teresa Fassano, came to live with her daughter and son-in-law exactly one year to the day her husband, Alfonso Fassano, Amalfi's much respected stone mason, was killed instantly at the age of fifty-nine when the burro laden with bags of cement he was leading up a steep rocky incline lost its footing and fell, with enormous weight and pulverizing force, directly on top of him, crushing his spine.

Devastated by this horrific event, Donatella nevertheless bore her sorrow with dignity and did not allow even those closest to her, son Umberto and daughter Maria, to feel pity for her terrible loss, nor for their own. Friends as well marveled at her stoic demeanor and composure. Only when Donatella after just six months dispensed with the wearing of the black dress, emblematic of mourning Italian widows determined never to let the world forget their loss, did neighbors begin to question her behavior. But whatever their disfavor, or outrage, it affected Donatella not in the least. If anything, she continued to live life as she saw fit, and never looked back or questioned any decision she made.

It was no surprise, then, that as soon as this strong minded, independent woman came to live permanently in her daughter's home, Donatella, affectionately known in the family as Nonna Dona, assumed a pivotal role. As family matriarch it wasn't long in fact before she took over complete running of the house, leaving her son-in-law and daughter to pursue their own passionate interests: Antonio and his three sons, as did their ancestors for generations before them, trolling the rich fishing waters of the sparkling Amalfi coast; Maria pursuing a craft in which she exhibited from early childhood a growing competence—the sewing by hand of exquisite lace tablecloths, napkins and runners of such quality they were purchased by shops from Salerno to Positano and sold to appreciative tourists as soon as they came in. Demand for her lace was so strong in fact that shortly after Donatella came to live with the Landinis, Maria had her cousin Vincenzo Fassano, a master carpenter, erect a modest studio at the end of the garden, equipping it with a ten-foot-long cutting table, a new loom and seven feet of cabinets and storage bins.

With a quiet place away from the house to ply her trade, and with Giuliana in the caring and capable hands of her mother, Maria was now free to work from dusk to dawn, breaking only for the sumptuous weekly Friday lunch the family most looked forward to—the best of that morning's catch, delivered to the table by her husband, and prepared by Donatella, with an able assist from a delighted Giuliana.

Thus order was firmly established in the Landini household. More important, the job of caring for Giuliana became Donatella's paramount responsibility, which she dispensed willingly and embraced thoroughly. For the next two years, or until she reached school age, Giuliana thrived under her grandmother's looming presence. They did everything and went everywhere together: to markets to shop; to church to worship; to visit with friends who sought Donatella's counsel; to town hall meetings in which her grandmother was a key participant; to the maritime museum, town library and paper mills in the Valle dei' Mulini. Giuliana's favorite stop—the pasta factory across from the wharf.

Along with such useful tutorials, Donatella exposed her granddaughter to books—on art, music, architecture, literature. Such exposure to life beyond her parents' encapsulated world provided the underpinnings of an education well beyond anything Giuliana was getting from them, or in school. For in the person of her grandmother she now had a mentor who not only loved her unconditionally (not that her parents loved her any less), but also, from the moment Donatella became a permanent member of the household, the single most influential person in her granddaughter's life, teaching her in ways no

34

one in Giuliana's immediate world, including her parents, could possibly have done.

*   *   *

Even at sixty, Donatella Fassano was a striking presence. Tall in stature, impeccable in dress, confident in speech, she could easily have been mistaken for the town's pre-eminent female aristocrat rather than the wife of its best bricklayer. Her statuesque, imposing height (at 5'10" a veritable cypress among seedlings) and patrician good looks—long, angular, perfectly smooth face, wide-set almond-shaped hazel eyes, shining mane of wavy jet black hair with not a trace of gray or white, whisked into a tight, perfectly formed bun the size of a pomegranate— set her conspicuously apart from other women in the village of similar age or younger to whom *una bella figura* was an only now and then indulgence.

She also possessed, in addition to her commanding air and cool, confident demeanor, an active, inquiring mind, and was astute in matters that belied her limited schooling, politics being one of them. Though she entertained no political aspirations of her own—she was skeptical of position and power and those who lusted after either—she followed very closely the unsettling, not too subtle changes occurring in Italy at the time and was a relentless, outspoken critic of Benito Mussolini and his Fascist party, becoming even more vocal in her disdain after Italy, by now a full-fledged ally of Nazi Germany, declared war on France and Britain in June of 1940. At first her unabashed abhorrence of the Mussolini government was viewed with suspicion by many of her conservative and compliant neighbors unfazed by *Il Duce* and his Fascist ways. To them, he was the perfect antidote to Italy's economic ills, the brilliant innovator of much needed reforms, the "benevolent dictator." In short, a savior. Her contempt for Mussolini aside, she was still greatly admired and respected by townspeople who continued to seek her counsel on matters other than politics or war. She remained a fixture as one of Amalfi's most influential citizens throughout her life.

Donatella arrived at a crossroads in life at about the same age as Giuliana did when she left for America. It occurred when her father, Giuseppe Mancuso, started a cheese making business on the family farm. As she came of age, Donatella became so enamored with the business of making cheese and, like her father, so good at it, that when it came time for her to graduate from elementary school her parents were forced into making a heartbreaking decision: take her into the business permanently or have her give up schooling altogether.

It was not an easy decision for the Mancusos to make. For they had both been brought up by their own parents to cherish education and the benefits that flowed from its embrace. In the end, it was Donatella herself, bright and mature beyond her years, who resolved the issue by choosing, however reluctantly, work over school. Though Donatella sadly suspended formal schooling—but not education itself, which she characterized as a life-long pursuit best left to the individual—she told Giuliana that it turned out to be the wisest decision she ever made in her life. For if not for business, she and her future husband, Alfonso Fassano, whose family construction company was brought in by the Mancusos to build their new cheese making facility, might never have come together.

Giuliana had heard her grandmother tell the story over and over again, but never tired of it. "The cheese business changed my life," Donatella admitted to her granddaughter one day while working in the garden. "It not only took me out of school forever, it brought me together with your grandfather, a much more important happening in my life."

# Chapter 5

Giuliana loved hearing the story of her grandmother's youth as much as Donatella liked telling it, especially the part about her days in elementary school. When it came to the subject of her own schooling, Giuliana looked back fondly on the influential role Nonna Dona had played in shaping it.

When Giuliana finally came of age, she couldn't wait to start school. But with its onset arose a thorny problem. Her restless, inquiring mind, coupled with the at-home instruction she was regularly getting from her grandmother, put her considerably ahead of the other children who did not have the advantage of someone like Nonna Dona to teach them. Just as Donatella had feared, school was not the edifying experience she had hoped it would be for her granddaughter. Giuliana needed to be stimulated, pushed, challenged. Donatella appealed to Sister Carolina, the school's headmistress, to see what, if anything, could be done to make that happen. While the nun was aware of the problem, she seemed at a loss as to what to do about it.

Donatella next thought of approaching Father Marco but almost immediately dismissed the idea, believing it to be an imposition on his time and more weighty priorities. Then an idea came to her in a flash: The following week the committee formed to help raise money for the school was scheduled to meet. Donatella thought this would be the perfect time to broach the subject of the school's academics and teaching methods. Once considered the shining light of elementary schools on the Amalfi coast in Donatella's time, Santa Croce's star had considerably dimmed. The time had arrived to do something about that.

In a report submitted by the lawyer Signor Montone, he stated that fund raising so far had been a surprising success: enough funds had been raised to cover construction of two new classrooms, and even provide a surplus, not insubstantial, to underwrite other pressing school necessities, at the very least the purchase of new books, supplies and other learning materials. Father Di Pina, who delighted in finding any excuse to celebrate, uncorked a bottle of his finest Prosecco. He poured a glass for each of his guests and, raising his own full-to-the-brim flute, offered in a lengthy toast his "heartfelt thanks and congratulations to my dear friends for achieving such commendable results."

Then the committee got back down to work. Members spoke openly about the overall quality of education at Santa Croce, and its limited resources. They covered at length the curriculum, instruction, lack of modern teaching materials, and the pressing need for at least one new teacher. There was a lot to be done in the way of improving standards, was the unanimous consensus. Apropos, was the subject of Donatella's concern for Giuliana's academic progress, or lack there of.

It was at this point that Dr. Gallardo introduced into the deliberations a letter he had only days before received from a young Scottish woman known to everyone in the room from summers she and her well-to-do family had spent vacationing on the Amalfi coast some years back, one Camilla McDonough. Donatella knew the young girl well, and her mother Grace even better: Mrs. McDonough was one of Maria's best cutomers.

"Camilla said in her letter that her life in Glasgow had taken an unexpected turn; she did not elaborate," Dr. Gallardo reported, "and that she very much wanted to come back to the area to live . . . permanently. I don't know whether you're aware of the fact that she's an elementary school teacher. She said in her letter she's prepared to give notice where she's now teaching, informing them that she will not be returning next term. She said she hoped that something could be worked out here. Of course, she's a lay person not a nun, but from her lengthy and rather convincing letter I wouldn't be surprised if Camilla might not be just the person we need to help put life back into Santa Croce. She asked if there was anything I could do to intercede on her behalf in securing a teaching position here. She indicated a willingness to immediately send along a resume and references. She also said that if something could be worked out, she would accept whatever salary the school deemed appropriate."

# Chapter 6

Camilla McDonough was twelve when her family took up summer residence in Amalfi. Her father, Liam, a high-up executive with the Glasgow-based banking conglomerate, Europa Bank Ltd., had been relocated to Naples to open a branch office from whence Europa, in partnership with Banco Napalitano, planned to extend its formidable banking arm through the south of Italy. In late May of that year, 1925, just after school had been let out, Liam moved his wife Grace, and children, Camilla and twin brother Connor, to Naples. Mother and children were to spend the summer in Italy and return to Scotland when school resumed in early September.

On a weekend motor car sojourn out of Naples one Friday shortly after the family had arrived, the McDonough clan headed for the Amalfi coast. They chose to explore this destination at the suggestion of a company bank official who knew the area well and was conversant with its once formidable history. The McDonoughs were intrigued by what they learned.

During the Middle Ages Amalfi was one of four powerful maritime republics; Naples, Genoa and Venice the other three. Through strong sea-faring skills and an astute business sense Amalfi established successful and very profitable links between east and west, with the Byzantines and Arabs. In the 11th century the Normans conquered much of southern Italy, stripping Amalfi of its trading along with its very independence, thus robbing the area for centuries of its once thriving economic viability.

What eventually saved the Amalfi coast was something its citizens always took for granted—the area's natural beauty. Capitalizing on it, however, didn't happen until well into the 18th century when Amalfi became a much sought-after destination for foreign visitors, thus paving the way for the establishment of a thriving international tourism market. Once renowned for its maritime prowess, Amalfi was now a town better known for its paper and pasta—and spectacular beauty. Beginning in the early 1920s, it became an oasis for intellectuals and artists and writers from all over the world—Longfellow, Cocteau, Picasso, Victor Hugo, Ibsen, Wagner, John Steinbeck, among many others, all drew inspiration from the place. Even Adolph Hitler was smitten with the area: he once remarked that had he not been elected chancellor of Germany he would have happily gone to live in Amalfi for the rest of his days.

The plan was for the McDonoughs to enjoy a leisurely weekend taking in the sights along the Amalfi coast, basking in the sun and getting away from, if even for only a few days, the noisy, bustling, overcrowded city of Naples. One look at the rugged, achingly beautiful *Costiera Amalfitana* from the narrow winding roads of the *Monti Lattari* that wound high above the shimmering emerald sea below, took their breath away. The architecture was astonishing and unique: sculpted into the natural rock formation were churches with high steeples that co-mingled with arcaded houses—sparkling white, cream-colored and pastel hued. All along cliff-hung coves, the houses were strung in craggy irregularity and embraced a wild munificence of thick vegetation, bougainvillea, a network of mini waterfalls and, as far as the eye could see, a panoply of green and gold olive and lemon groves. The trip immediately turned into a frantic reconnaissance mission: all four McDonoughs were enchanted by the area and in unanimous agreement that finding a place in or around Amalfi, high on a hill, overlooking the sea, but easily accessible to the beach, was an absolute necessity.

And so it was that the McDonoughs spent the next five summers in Amalfi, reluctantly giving up their dream villa on the hill only after Liam was posted back to Europa's Glasgow headquarters. During the time the McDonoughs spent in the region, they became friendly with many of its inhabitants, including Maria and Antonio Landini and their three sons (Giuliana had not yet been born), Dr. Gallardo and his family, and the Montones. It wasn't until the second summer of their stay in Amalfi that a friendship, which on its face may have at first seemed unexpected to say the least, but almost immediately turned out to be an exceedingly warm one, was forged between the McDonoughs and Father Di Pina.

Only when it came to ecclesiastical matters did the McDonoughs initially feel any sense of dislocation *vis-à-vis* their relationship with their new Italian friends. The elder McDonoughs were raised as strict Church of Scotland adherents but had long since abandoned their faith, Grace early in college, Liam long before. They were suspect of religion in general but most especially Roman Catholicism, their *bete noire.* What disturbed them most was the Catholic Church's insistence on allegiance to the Pope, for whom they shared a mutual antipathy. This understandably put them at odds with all Roman Catholics, but not nearly as much as with native Italians whose love for the Holy Father and unshakeable belief in his infallibility was genuine and irrevocable.

If the McDonoughs were fearful their lack of religious faith stood in the way of relationships they wished to cultivate with their new Italian neighbors, they needn't have worried. After all, they were well off, well bred, well traveled, well educated: Liam held a masters degree in business from the London School of Economics, Grace a doctorate in the history of eastern cultures from Dublin's Trinity College, a subject she planned to resume teaching once the children were at university. More important, they were genuinely nice people. Amalfitani welcomed them with open arms, particularly the town's intelligentsia: Dr. Gallardo, solicitor Montone and Father Di Pina.

Especially Father Di Pina. To him Liam and Grace McDonough were the ideal companions and dinner guests. Rather than take exception to, or be offended by positions they espoused on the subject of religion he was in fact welcoming of their arguments, for it gave him the rare opportunity to show off his own knowledge of not only his but other faiths. Even more satisfying from his perspective were those times he was able to engage the couple in the kind of animated, no-holds-barred, give-and-take discussions that inevitably ensued, which he relished with childlike glee.

As for the McDonough children, in the matter of religion and religious worship, they were left to fend for themselves. Camilla, more than her brother, found her parents' indifference to religious faith unsettling. For some time she had yearned for an outlet to express her innermost feelings—she said she always felt the presence of a force beyond what she could merely see and experience—but had so far been unable to find one. That is, not until she arrived in Amalfi.

Very often when she was in the town square, she and her new Italian friends would play a game of racing up the long flight of sixty-two stone steps leading to the magnificent Cathedral of St. Andrew that loomed over the town. One day just as they reached exhaustedly the last step, the magnificent bronze doors—cast in Constantinople in the 11th century with *bas*-relief depictions of Christ, the Madonna, St. Andrew and St. Peter carved into the façade—swung open and a young man and his female companion, each carrying a huge bouquet of flowers, exited the church, a funeral Mass and procession having concluded only moments earlier. Camilla asked one of her friends if it would be all right for them to go in. As they entered, the three Italian girls dipped their fingers in the small holy water receptacle on the wall next to the door, made the sign of the cross, genuflected, then proceeded down the aisle to the vestibule of the church, choosing the first pew, where they knelt in prayer, their non-Catholic companion watching with great interest their every move. Camilla did not sit with them. She chose, instead, a pew a few rows back and was just about to sit when she noticed the names engraved on small brass plaques on the back rest of each pew.

When the girls left the church minutes later, Camilla was anxious to learn the significance of the public display. She was told that families of deceased parish members chose this means of expression to memorialize and honor their dead loved ones.

The next morning after breakfast, Camilla decided to go into town and visit the cathedral on her own. As she was about to enter the church she ran into an out-of-breathe Father Marco, who had come to St. Andrew's to meet with Don Salvatore Gaetano, the cathedral's pastor. She told him of her visit to the church the previous day and of her desire to spend more time there, alone, without the distraction of friends. She said she had come to admire at leisure the magnificence she had been exposed to only briefly the day before. She also said she wanted to learn more of the cathedral's history. (Years later when she came back to Amalfi to teach, she accompanied Giuliana and her friends to the cathedral and conducted much the same tour for them.)

"I will be with Don Salvatore for only a few minutes," Father Di Pina told Camilla, "so if you'd like to wait for me in the church, I will personally show you around and explain to you as much as you'd like to know about this spectacular edifice."

In touring the cathedral, originally constructed in Byzantine, Arabic and Norman style in the 9th century, Camilla was deeply moved by its majestic Baroque interior: the sumptuous, richly carved, coffered ceiling; the stunning high altar anchored on either side by resplendent white marble Bernini statues of St. Stephen and St. Lawrence; the superb twin antique granite columns from Paestum supporting the triumphal arch of the main apse. Father Di Pina explained how the cathedral had undergone numerous renovations over the centuries: it was enlarged in the 10th, rebuilt in Arabic-Norman form in the 13th, remodeled in the 16th and 17th centuries and then again between 1701 and 1731. The last renovation took place in 1861, after the façade had been seriously damaged.

As she walked about, Camilla stood in awe of the large magnificent paintings inlaid into the ceiling and along the walls, the beautiful stained glass windows, and the enormous stunning candelabra made of exquisite Murano glass. "This is a beautiful sight to see when they're all lit at night," intoned Father Di Pina. In two side niches along the back right-side aisle were housed, in one, a reliquary bust of St. Andrew made of 16th century tooled silver and, in the other, the Coffin of the Dead Christ, removed from the church once a year on Good Friday and carried in poignant procession through the town.

Then Father Di Pina took Camilla by the hand and led her to the steps to the right of the main altar and down into the crypt, the heart and soul of Amalfi, where lay under the altar, covered by a heavy slab of marble, the preserved head and bones of St. Andrew, the town's patron saint, whose remains were brought to Amalfi from Constantinople in 1208. She stood transfixed before the central altar, adorned in precious marble carvings, overcome at the sight of the imposing eight-hundred kilo bronze statue of St. Andrew, whose massive proportions were not unlike those of the Moses sculpted by Michelangelo, who, appropriately enough, was the teacher of Michelangelo Naccherino, the Amalfitan artist who in the year 1604 created the statue of St. Andrew.

Camilla wanted to know more about St. Andrew. Father Di Pina told her that he was a fisherman, Jesus' first disciple and the patron saint of Amalfi. He evangelized Greece, which then ranged as far as present day Russia, and was crucified in Patras. From there Cardinal Pretas Capuano, Papal Envoy to the Fourth Crusade, took his body first to Constantinople and later to Amalfi, on the 8$^{th}$ of May 1208, and buried it in the crypt. The priest went on to explain that the bones of St. Andrew continually exude a liquid substance, called the "manna of St. Andrew," which is believed to have miraculous virtues. Father Di Pina reached down into the deep pocket of his cassock. He took out a thin white paper bag, approximately three-by-five inches. He handed it to Camilla. It had a picture of the statue of St. Andrew in the crypt depicted on its face. Inside the envelope was a pressed, flat piece of cotton, the size of a half-dollar, said to contain drops of a dense liquid that appears on the apostle's sepulcher six times during the year.

"The two most important dates to commemorate these events are the 30$^{th}$ of November, the feast of St. Andrew, and June 27, the day of the miracle," Father Di Pina explained as they left the crypt and went back into the main church.

"What is the day of the miracle?" Camilla wanted to know.

The prelate walked to the far end of the aisle that led to the back of the church. Near the door was a large canvas commemorating the miracle attributed to St. Andrew. "Legend has it that on June 27 in 1544 Amalfi was invaded by the Saracens," Father Di Pina explained. "The entire population was terrorized by the sight of ships arriving from afar, so they gathered in the piazza and prayed to St. Andrew to save them. Just as an attack was to take place, St. Andrew raised a tempest at sea. A sudden surge in the waves swept away and sank the ships of the pirate Ariadeno Barbarossa. It saved Amalfi and neighboring towns from certain destruction.

"The feat is solemnly commemorated every June 27, a feast day in Amalfi. Devout processions and celebrations take place, during which the statue of the saint is carried up to the sea on the shoulders of members of the Confraternity, all of whom are dressed in white. The silver statue, two and a half meters high and extremely heavy, is then handed over to fishermen who take it back to the cathedral. With great fanfare and enormous effort, they race up the sixty-two steps with the statue in tow. There is a tremendous sense of joy and collective gaiety on the part of the entire population. Everybody takes part in the celebration, with choirs and instrumental music and candlelight processions on neighboring mountains and on the beach. Once you've experienced this scene you won't soon forget it."

Clutching the packet containing the "manna of St. Andrew" in her left hand—she carried it on her person the rest of her life—Camilla dipped the middle finger of her right hand in the holy water receptacle and turned around to take in the splendor of the magnificent church one more time before leaving. At that very moment she told herself that she would have to learn more about Catholicism, with or without her parents' approval. It would take the better part of a decade: just before turning twenty-two Camilla McDonough was baptized into the Catholic faith.

# Chapter 7

Two important determinations were made by the parish school capital campaign committee as it deliberated: the raising of new funds was deemed encouraging; the hiring of a new teacher was deemed necessary. Everyone was delighted, no one more so than Donatella Fassano. Finally, someone with an inspired teaching agenda might well be arriving soon at Santa Croce. Dr. Gallardo sent a letter to Camilla McDonough informing her that, indeed, she would have to come to Amalfi for in-person interviews with committee members who hadn't seen her in years.

Sister Carolina and Father DePina, who together exercised all administrative responsibilities for the day-to-day running of the school, conducted the interviews with Ms. McDonough; they lasted the better part of two days. But it took a lot less time than that for the priest and the nun to arrive at a similar conclusion—Camilla was the ideal candidate for the school: her references were glowing, her university and post-graduate work outstanding, her teaching qualifications impeccable.

Much in her favor was that she knew Amalfi and many of its people intimately, spoke Italian fluently and, as an unmarried woman, would presumably be able to devote undivided attention to her work. In short, a perfect fit for Santa Croce. And most important, from Father Di Pina's and Sister Carolina's perspective, Camilla was a devout, worshipful Catholic who wasn't about to corrupt the children by espousing positions contrary to the teachings of the church.

At noon on that second day of interviews she went to the rectory to lunch with Father Di Pina. The two had had a friendly relationship during the time the McDonoughs vacationed in Amalfi so the priest was anxious to renew old ties and catch up on what Camilla and her family had been doing since he last saw her, and them, some ten years earlier.

"We speak often when all of us are able to get together about the wonderful summers we spent here," Camilla said, as soon as she had tucked herself comfortably into a chair to the right of the priest at the dining table. "Father and Mother talk about all four of us coming back for a holiday, but it obviously hasn't happened. What with our respective hectic schedules we never seem to be in the same place at the same time."

"What a pity," said Father Di Pina, thinking back to the challenging but always enjoyable times he had with the elder McDonoughs arguing religion, philosophy and politics. "Tell me about everybody . . . please do, Camilla."

She told of her father's increasing responsibilities at the bank: "He was appointed executive vice president of the bank a couple of years ago and he seems fairly certain that the position of president will be his in the not too distant future." She then went on to describe her mother's re-entry into the world of academia as she promised she would do once her children had gone off to college: "Mother's been teaching at Glasgow University these last several years . . . eastern history is her specialty. She's recently been offered the chair of the department but isn't quite sure whether she's up to all the internecine battles she keeps saying take place more and more inside the walls of academia. At any length she really does love teaching."

"I guess you're a chip off the old block," said Father Marco, raising a glass of his finest French claret to his lips.

"Perhaps," said Camilla, "but I don't think I have her absolutely first rate mind."

"Nonsense," said the priest, raising a forkful of sweet, tender octopus to his mouth. "Now please tell me about Connor."

"Well, Connor, he's the one, don't you know," Camilla said, in a voice bubbling with pride at mention of her twin brother. "I get to see him quite frequently, thank God . . . have him and his girlfriend, a lovely person I might add, over for drinks as often as possible. He sort of bummed around, I hate to say, for a few years in a number of meaningless jobs until his girlfriend put him on the straight and narrow and convinced him to go back to school. I'm happy to report he'll be getting his master's in economics at the end of the term. A job is waiting for him in the investment banking division at father's company as soon as he graduates. We're all delighted and very proud of him, especially Father."

"Well, so far so good," said Father Marco, quite pleased with what he had been told about the McDonoughs, all the while relishing the quickly disappearing plate of *penne amatriciano* Maddalena had placed before him. "Now tell me about your life, Camilla, everything."

"Well, there isn't much to tell, Father, that you don't already know. My letter to Dr. Gallardo and what's in my resume, I think, pretty much says it all."

"Oh, those," Father Di Pina said rather dismissively, "they're nothing but innocuous little factoids that can't possibly describe what a person's really like. And that's exactly what I wish to know, Camilla . . . what it is that's uppermost on your mind, and how you feel about things. But first, tell me . . . what's happened in your life since I last saw you?"

Camilla spent the rest of the meal, and through dessert, describing mostly her educational background: secondary school, college, graduate school, the required work she did for both her undergraduate and graduate theses. "Since my major was Medieval English literature," she explained, "my work inevitably gravitated to some of the great works in the field. I was especially taken with Shakespeare's sonnets and Chaucer's poems. I did my undergraduate thesis on the former and my post-graduate on the latter."

"What aspect of these works did you cover?" asked the priest, his interest peaked.

"I was certain you'd ask me that. I expounded on the role Christianity played in both the sonnets and then later in Chaucer's Canterbury Tales"

"I'd love to read what you had to say, but I suppose I'll have to wait for your exegeses to be published in Italian," said the priest, a broad smile crossing his face.

Having introduced the subject of religion tangentially, she sensed that Father Di Pina now wished to delve a little more deeply into the matter of her conversion to Catholicism, which she willingly volunteered before he had a chance to ask.

"From as far back as I can remember I had a yearning for a religious connection in my life, which was the exact opposite of that of my parents, as you know. I always felt I was in limbo when it came to the matter of faith. I was determined to do something about it. It all came together right here to Amalfi—on a day I'll never forget, during that wonderful morning you and I spent in Sant'Andrea's. It continued more intensely all through college and university. While I was writing my thesis on Shakespeare's sonnets—he was an Anglican Catholic as you well know—I found this to be the perfect time to learn more about the faith in order to do justice to the work I had undertaken.

"So I sought out the university's Catholic chaplain, a Jesuit priest, Father Nicholas McGregor, head of campus ministry. I found him to be an absolutely brilliant, first-rate theologian. In the course of our many discussions I got deeper and deeper into learning about Christianity in general, and Catholicism in particular. He kept emphasizing over and over again what to him were the three great pursuits that made human beings most like God—art, sex and religion. Or, to put it another way, the artist, the lover, the saint . . . each, respectively, was put on this earth to create art, to create human life, to create the bridge between God and man through sainthood. These are God's greatest gifts to mankind. I never forgot those words."

The priest sat motionless, taking in silently without interruption the young woman's every word.

"At first I was frankly more interested in learning as much as I could about Catholicism so that I could understand a lot better how the faith of these two giants of literature impacted their writings. But as my knowledge increased, so did my curiosity. I became quickly in awe of the Catholic faith—its traditions, its liturgy, its universality— as I knew in the back of my mind I would be if ever I were exposed to its teachings in more than a perfunctory way. In this regard, Father McGregor was indispensable, both to my work and to my ultimate initiation into the faith."

"When did you actually become a Catholic, Camilla?"

"In my senior year in college, six years ago," Camilla said, "I was twenty-one at the time, in the midst of writing my Shakespeare thesis, and taking instruction, both at the same time. On April 6, 1934, Easter Sunday, the holiest day in the Christian calendar, I was baptized, received my first communion, and was confirmed, all in the same ceremony . . . sort of like a triple win at the races. Father McGregor said Mass on that auspicious day and administered the three sacraments to me and six others, all younger candidates. As beautiful and uplifting as was the ceremony, what moves me still to this day was the presence of Mother, Father and Connor—my "bloomin'atheist family," I like to call it—present at my initiation into a faith they appeared, at least on the surface, to abhor."

Father Di Pina laughed heartily at Camilla's characterization of her family. "I would have given anything to have been there to see their faces."

"They even hosted a lovely dinner party in my honor, with many of my friends in attendance in a campus faculty dining room. It was quite a day . . . I shall never forget it."

Father Marco sat in silence several moments while meticulously peeling an orange. From the rind he carved a pair of eyeglasses that were perfectly shaped and emitted the most pungent, pleasant aroma. The innocuous diversion gave him ample time to form as delicately as he could the question that had been on his mind ever since he learned of Camilla's desire to come to Amalfi: "Why would an attractive, intelligent young woman like yourself even dream of coming to an impoverished oasis in the south of Italy, living amongst an overwhelming percentage of illiterate people, and teach, leaving behind family, friends, a promising career and a world teeming with all sorts of opportunities and intellectual stimulation?"

"I know it's been a question on everybody's mind," Camilla said. "I shall give you the same answer I gave Sister Carolina, Dr. Gallardo and the lawyer Montone: I need to start a new chapter in my life, in a different place than the one I have always known and . . ."

". . . need to or want to, Camilla?" Father Di Pina interrupted.

"I suppose both," Camilla said.

"Do I take it, then, that there might be something perhaps that has happened to you recently from which you wish to, how should I put it, escape?"

Camilla looked away from the priest's riveting stare and did not answer, believing she had reached a crossroads in the interview that could possibly dash any hope she might have of securing the teaching position at Santa Croce she so desperately coveted. Father Di Pina, sensing her unease, decided to delve into less sensitive areas, thus freeing at least momentarily Camilla's obligation to immediately answer his probing question.

"And what about your personal life here . . . what's to become of it? We all know you are eminently qualified to assume a teaching position at our school, over qualified I dare say if you ask me, so there's no question on that score. But any kind of a social life here would seem entirely out of the question. So what, then, if you were to come here, could you possibly look forward to except a stimulating conversation now and again with a certain tired old priest and perhaps a few others? Would these occasional diversions be enough to entice you and hold your interest?"

"I realize how odd it must seem to all of you for me to want to leave the safe comforts of home as it were and move here permanently. But that is precisely what I wish to do . . . at this stage of my life."

"But you still haven't answered the question, Camilla . . . why?"

"Because I strongly believe I can make a difference in the lives of the children . . . and frankly, it would be a wonderful challenge for me to see if I can."

"Do you consider coming here some kind of experiment that you need to get out of your system?" asked the priest, careful to conceal whatever frustration he was feeling at Camilla's less than forthright answer.

Camilla was put off by the priest's insistent probing. Her face flushed momentarily but she was as determined to hold her ground as resolutely as he was his. "Oh no, Father, I've stated it badly," said Camilla. "My every intention, if I am allowed, is to come here and give my all to these children. My motivations are genuine . . . to teach them, and I don't mean to be critical, in ways the school here cannot possibly imagine."

"That is commendable, my dear, and I do most certainly believe you are sincere in everything you say about what you wish to, and can, accomplish at Santa Croce." But the priest was far from satisfied. Intuition told him there was something more to Camilla's rather tepid and quite predictable explanation and he wasn't about to let up until he got at the heart of the matter. "Now think very carefully, my dear, before answering my next question. Is being a teacher in Amalfi your sole reason for wanting to come here?"

Their eyes locked. And held for what seemed like more than the second or two it took before Camilla pushed her chair back, rose, and without answering the priest's question, walked to the window that looked out onto the patio. Father Di Pina remained seated. With her back to him, Camilla commenced to give the following narrative:

"In the beginning of my senior year at university I met a graduate student two years older than I, and before the semester had ended I found myself madly in love with him. It was also at that same time that I was taking instruction in the church. We were perfectly right for each other on so many levels that when we broke up toward the end of the year each of us experienced a depression so profound that it affected our health, his as well as mine. You see, neither one of us was prepared or willing to renounce the intractable position we held vis a vis the one thing that eventually drove us apart—his abhorrence of the Catholic religion, and my complete and total surrender to it."

She turned from the window and faced the priest, but remained standing. "Had it not been for my more frequent meetings with Father McGregor, and for his consoling presence in my life at the time, I shutter to think what might have happened to me. Why is it, I kept asking myself, that the people most dear to me—father, mother, brother and now lover . . . yes, father, lover in all that the word implies—have all conspired in making me feel that my faith, instead of the glorious

55

force it had steadily become in my life, was in fact a major impediment in how each of these otherwise four precious people related to me. I literally became sick. All that summer I was like a zombie. I avoided my parents, Connor almost completely . . . and Jeffrey Fryer, my *innamorato*, totally."

Father Marco rose and went to Camilla. He took her by the hand and guided her to a chair at the opposite end of the table, away from the elaborate lunch she had just been served. Before seating himself at her side he brought her a glass of water, which she gratefully accepted.

"Go on," he said.

"In the fall, by the grace of God, having literally willed myself to get on with life, and feeling sufficiently recovered from this terrible ordeal, I commenced my graduate studies, which I once feared I'd have to put off, temporarily or perhaps even permanently. But school, as it has always been for me, proved to be an elixir. I dove into my work with a passion and inexhaustible focus, allowing nothing but my studies to consume my time and energies. As for Jeffrey, I must confess he wasn't ever far from my thoughts, though I hadn't seen nor heard from him in well over a year. I knew by this time he had earned his post-graduate degree, and learned subsequently that he was teaching freshman English at the university. One morning, during a class break, I was in the student lounge enjoying a cup of tea, engrossed in a book, when I looked up and standing directly in front of me, looking down at me with those soulful eyes of his, was Jeffrey. I was startled momentarily. He asked if he could join me . . . I found I couldn't very well say no."

"Need I venture a guess as to what happened next?" Father Di Pina asked. Camilla smiled slightly and paused for a second before assuming again her serious demeanor. "As you so astutely surmised, we took up again, as though nothing had ever happened previously . . . not within days, or weeks, or a month, but almost immediately, more torrid than even before." She hesitated, while casting a far-off look away from the priest. "You have no idea how ecstatically happy I was . . . more deeply in love than ever."

"Did Jeffrey feel as much?"

"Looking back, I'm not quite so sure. But during the remainder of that year, and a good part of the next, being in love with a man I adored was all that seemed to matter to me. And yet, during this seemingly idyllic period of our relationship, he would now and again bring up the subject of religion, even though at the time I had, for all intents and purposes, completely turned my back on it. I stopped going to church, and receiving the sacraments was of course totally out of the question. In effect I put God out of my life, I put Christ out of my life, I put the Catholic Church out of my life. For a short time it worked. But no matter what I did or said, he just wouldn't let the matter go. He said in his heart he was certain I was deluding myself . . . that I was accepting of the situation, in other words acceding to his wishes temporarily, that it was only a matter of time before I would turn my back on him and return to the wily clutches of the Church, is how he put it, and that if I were indeed serious about entertaining a long-term, permanent relationship with him, that I would have to once and for all renounce the Church. It was the only way.

"Lucky for me, at a time when I had put most everything sacred to me out of my life, thankfully I hadn't kicked Father McGregor out, as well. All through my affair I never stopped going to him. I was tormented, conflicted, I begged him to tell me what I should do, but he simply would not do it. All he kept saying was that I had to work it out for myself . . . that I had to let my conscience be my guide. Where had we heard that bromide before? But Father McGregor was absolutely right, of course: either I had to follow the tenets of my faith unconditionally, or I had to abandon it altogether.

"Jeffrey's refusal to accept who I was and what I believed in effectively ended our relationship for good almost two years ago. It came to a head when I told him that I wanted to have his baby. I felt a child would, despite our differences, draw us closer together. His child, our child, couldn't help but deepen our love for each other. He said it was a totally foolish thought on my part: 'Weren't things already bloody complicated enough,' he said. 'Besides, you'd insist on our raising the child Catholic, and I wouldn't dream of allowing you to,' is what he said. He kept insisting that's all the Catholic Church was interested in—converting people to their bogus faith.

"Then he turned to attacking what he called the notion of God. 'There is no God . . . no supreme being . . . no omnipotent force looking over the shoulder of every single person on earth, claiming to protect every one of us. If that were true, why would there be so much evil, so much senseless death, so much unhappiness in the world. No, Camilla, you can have your bloody faith . . . my faith is me, in the here and now, not the hereafter . . . what I can see with my own two eyes, experience with my own intellect and being. I don't need anything or anyone else to tell me whether my actions are good or bad. I'm perfectly capable of doing it myself.'

"When I suggested that such arguing was the height of intellectual arrogance, he became even more incensed. When I suggested to him that the very God who permitted so much that was wrong with the human condition was also the same God who allowed order and consciousness and, most of all, free will to exist . . . well, he could hardly contain himself. But I wasn't finished: I told him that he was holding himself up as a superior being who obviously knew, with unshakable certainty, just how matters stood . . . and that millions upon millions of people of faith, including some of the most brilliant people who ever walked the face of this earth, were wrong.

"Since I also happened to be a believer, I didn't see how we could ever work out our differences. I begged Jeffrey to try to understand that the faith I had fought so hard, for so long, to embrace, was simply much too strong for me to abandon, and that now that I'd found it I couldn't imagine going through life without it. I knew, from the depths of my being, that this faith had always lived inside me, a true gift from God, and now that I had finally acknowledged its presence in my life, I wasn't about to surrender it—not for my parents, not for my brother, not for him. It would have been false and contradictory of me to deny what I truly believed. How could I possibly capitulate?

"Through all of my emotional upheaval my spiritual side would simply not allow my temporal side to surrender this faith, much as it ached for me to acknowledge that by standing firm on this point I was giving up something else I wanted, or thought I wanted. It may have taken me a long time but, little by little, by the grace of God, I rekindled the fire that first began to burn in my soul right here in this very place, Amalfi, when I was a little girl. Now I am ready, and wish fervently to do so if you will allow me, to return here and make certain that fire is never extinguished again."

Father Di Pina, rarely speechless, was deeply moved. He listened to Camilla's tremulous voice with eyes closed, elbows on the table, his head supported between cupped hands. He couldn't help but think to himself: *Why is it that converts almost invariably make the most fervent Catholics?* He looked up at Camilla. Tears ran down her cheeks. Before he was about to comment, Camilla reached across the table to take his hand in hers, and in a quavering voice said: "Now please, Father, hear my confession."

"I just did," he whispered. Then laying his left hand gently on her head, he raised his right hand and made the sign of the cross, all the while reciting quietly in Latin the words of forgiveness every penitent craves to hear: "I absolve you of your sins."

Then he said: "For your penance, Camilla . . . you must make me a promise."

"Anything, Father," Camilla answered, a catch in her voice. "To remain at our school for no less than five years."

"I promise," Camilla said without hesitation.

As if words alone, even sacred ones, were not enough to consummate the deal, the young woman leaned across the table and kissed the prelate on the cheek. The gesture caught Father Marco by surprise. But it was not unwelcome.

# Chapter 8

The hiring of Camilla McDonough proved to be propitious. Almost immediately, she brought new life and a breath of fresh air into the moribund school. Through the strength of her intellect, the depth of her knowledge and the soundness of her vision, together with her highly charged dedication and motivation, she convinced teachers, parents and Father Di Pina as well, that the reputation the school had once enjoyed in years past would soon be restored. Within three years time, it was.

First, she completely overhauled the curriculum. Emboldened by Sister Carolina's enthusiastic support, she introduced teaching methods and practices that, while commonplace in most English speaking countries, were quite revolutionary in Italian education at the time. These included tougher work assignments, more stringent testing, group study and greater emphasis on written and oral communication skills. And for children who had reached the age of nine, beginning study in English as a second language, an especially bold undertaking. If that were not enough, she took it upon herself to start a modest library with books she purchased from funds out of her own pocket for the children to use as reference as well as for their personal reading enjoyment, which she heartily encouraged. Using to advantage her greatest skill—an affinity for being able to relate to each individual student on a personal level—she was able to coax out of students in all grade levels a noticeable improvement in test scores and, more important, in learning aptitude.

To her students, as well as to herself, every day was a celebration of teaching and learning. School was fun, and "the best fun-giver in the whole wide world," they enjoyed saying, was none other than the pretty, pale-faced, golden-haired twenty-seven-year-old Scottish lady, Signorina Camilla McDonough. School, parents and at least one exceedingly grateful grandmother could not have been happier.

*     *     *

The dramatic changes taking place in the school had also the effect of producing dramatic changes in personal relationships that might have once seemed impervious to change. For Giuliana, now ten, a gradual but definitely noticeable shift in allegiance from grandmother to teacher began to take hold. One might have thought this new relationship between teacher and student would threaten or, at the very least, taint the tight blood bond that had been forged between grandmother and granddaughter these past five years. But it had just the opposite effect. Being the wise, discerning woman she was, Donatella recognized early on the benefits that Giuliana would enjoy by having close ties with someone who, after all, was all the things she herself, and most people in her immediate circle including Giuliana's parents, were not: educated, wealthy, sophisticated.

So there was never a hint of resentment on Donatella's part toward the young schoolteacher for usurping her role as Giuliana's mentor. If anything, Donatella encouraged it. The time had come for the torch to be passed. And she made it known to both Giuliana and Camilla McDonough that this is how it should be.

Giuliana thrived in this new, exciting environment. For the first time, school became the challenge she had always hoped it would be. And if she wasn't necessarily learning all that she wanted to in the classroom per se, since there were no accelerated courses for exceptionally gifted students like Giuliana in a school the size of Santa Croce, she reveled in the instruction she was receiving outside of class, after school, from Camilla who, impressed with Giuliana's thirst for learning, took the child under her wing.

Proceeding slowly at first, then more aggressively as she came to know her driven, curious star pupil better, she was able to assess Giuliana's capacity for taking on a heavier workload, and to judge how quickly and with what degree of command she was able to absorb and process information. When she became satisfied that Giuliana met the test on both scores, Camilla had her doing an ever increasing number of extracurricular assignments that few students in her class were either inclined to undertake, or capable of doing. In effect, Giuliana had Camilla all to herself. Hardly a day went by that she didn't learn something new from her generous, learned teacher. Camilla, in turn, was herself fascinated by Giuliana's far-ranging interests and sweeping curiosity: it was a *quid pro quo* made in academic heaven.

The study of history, a particular passion of Camilla's, was the initial leap Giuliana took into a world of wonders she hardly knew existed. Giuliana voraciously drank in every last detail that poured from the seemingly limitless fount of knowledge Camilla had on western cultures, a perfect companion to her major area of study, Medieval English Literature.

One fascinating fact Giuliana learned was how present-day Italy came into existence. She was told that the unification of Italy in1861 into a democratic republic was the result of the dissolution of Papal States lorded over for centuries by corrupt, power-hungry popes. And as she studied more thoroughly the history and mores of her native land, Giuliana began asking questions about other countries. This, in turn, led Camilla to ponder just how far her pupil was prepared to delve into history, not just as a school exercise but as a bona fide intellectual discipline.

And that is when Giuliana first became familiar with the word *revolution*. Over the course of several weeks, Camilla touched on the history of revolutions, in France in 1850 and in Franco Spain, concluded only a year ago in 1939. Then she turned her attention to what she considered "perhaps the greatest, most profound revolution the world has known to this point, the American Revolution" and the birth of the United States.

Giuliana had only recently developed what one might describe as a fascination with America. Almost a year had passed since her uncle and aunt had settled there, and like everybody in the family who received word from them, Giuliana was more than curious to learn how they were faring in their new environment. Aside from describing personal experiences and observations—how they liked where they were living, what they were doing, whether they'd made new friends—there was, however, little to be gleaned from these accounts in the way of substantive historical data about the United States.

That job was left to Camilla. She described in colorful detail her impressions of America made from a trip the family took to the United States one summer when she and her brother were in college, describing first the exciting voyage across the Atlantic on the stately Queen Mary, then her experiences during her month-long stay in New York, where her father was sent by his company to learn and study America's banking system. She told of excursions that she, her mother and brother made to Philadelphia, Boston and Chicago, all meticulously recorded in a diary she kept to preserve her impressions.

"That was as far west as we were able to go in the time we had," Camilla explained. "When I returned to Scotland after that trip, I couldn't get the United States out of my head. I wanted to learn everything I could about this fascinating place. So I started studying its incredible history. I vowed that I would one day go there to live for a time to experience firsthand its culture and mores."

"Have you been back since then?" asked Giuliana.

"No," Camilla answered, "but in due course while I'm still young enough I plan on going there and spend some real quality time."

"Does this mean you won't be staying in Amalfi permanently?" her student asked.

"I have no intention of leaving . . . I've been here only two years . . . so any thought of taking up stakes and moving to yet another country so soon after leaving my own isn't something I'm contemplating doing at the moment."

"Do you mind, Camilla, if I ask you a personal question?"

"Of course not, you're free to ask me anything you'd like."

"Why did you come here in the first place?"

This was certainly not a question Camilla expected. She rose from her desk and turning her back went to the blackboard, looking for all the world like a lost soul stranded in a strange place struggling hard to find a way out.

"Does it really matter?" Camilla said, unnerved by the question and uncertain as to how to answer her wily inquisitor.

"Oh, no," said Giuliana. "I was just wondering why someone like you would decide to live in a place that is so different from where you come from, and with people you have so little in common."

"That is a very good and sensible question, Giuliana, and one day when you are a little older, I will tell you."

# Chapter 9

Giuliana's crash course in the history of the United States—highlighted by the American Revolution, the country's seminal event—continued unabated past the school year and well into the summer of 1940. She told her family that what she was learning about America from Camilla was far more exciting than anything she was being taught in her regular classes at school.

Camilla began by covering briefly the discovery of America in 1492 by the Italian explorer Christopher Columbus, whom Giuliana, of course, had heard of, before going on to explain, chronologically, the relevant historical data extant on the birth and growth of the new nation. She told of the first Pilgrim crossing of the Atlantic on the famous ship the *Mayflower* in November 1620 by 102 intrepid English souls intent on living in a land where they would be free to practice their faith as they pleased, and then watching helplessly as their number dwindled by more than half, due to pestilence and disease, by the time they established the first permanent settlement in Plymouth, Massachusetts. (Not to confuse the child, Camilla steered away from discussing the settlement at Jamestown, which occurred some four years earlier.) She described the brutal, bloody wars fought all over New England during the rest of the 1600s and a good part of the 1700s between Native American tribes, and told how Pilgrim and English Puritans began settling in ever greater numbers in northeastern regions of America.

Camilla spent the most time on what she opined was "undoubtedly one of the most important events in all of world history, the American Revolution."

"Isn't that about George Washington?" Giuliana asked.

"Yes," said Camilla, "but it's about more than just one man, important as he is in the history of America. It's about an entire people coming together to fight bravely for their independence from the mother country, in this case England, and then becoming in a rather short time the single most powerful and influential nation on earth. It's quite a story, and it keeps getting better as time goes on."

She got up from her desk and walked to the back of the room where she took a book from the small case that stood against the wall. "I wish you were old enough to read this account of World War I," Camilla said, holding up the book and pointing to an area on the world map that hung above the bookcase. "Germany at the time threatened to take over the entire European continent. They probably would have succeeded had it not been for the United States coming into the war and calling on their powerful army to defeat the Germans. We owe an enormous debt of gratitude to the United States for our freedom—Italy's, England's, Scotland's—every country on this side of the Atlantic. You may be too young to realize this," Camilla continued, "but there are ominous signs at this very moment that may portend the same thing happening again."

"Yes, I am aware of this," said Giuliana. "Nonna keeps talking about it all the time. Only last night at dinner she told us how happy she was that my uncle Umberto had left Italy and gone to America to live. Now she's worried about my brothers being drafted into the army. And so am I."

"Maybe if we're lucky that won't happen," said Camilla, "but in the meantime I wouldn't worry your pretty little head over it . . . you have too much else to think about."

*     *     *

Now and again Camilla would have Giuliana and Donatella over to her apartment for afternoon tea. She explained to them, in a humorous aside, that she had no intention of abandoning the custom of serving tea even to Italian friends she knew had an aversion to any beverage not espresso or cappuccino. On one such occasion she also invited Maddalena to join them. While the three older women were out on the balcony enjoying their tea and scones, Giuliana remained inside paging through books, which she liked to do whenever she visited her mentor. The women were engaged in animated discussion about the gathering storm blowing through much of Western Europe: Nazi Germany had already taken over Poland in September 1939 (the last year of peace in Europe) and Hitler and Mussolini, less than a year later, had declared war on England and France.

Donatella was appalled by what was happening, as were the other women, but she was more vocal in her condemnation of Italy's complicity in the war. "I wonder if we will ever be able to live down in the eyes of the world Italy's switching over from a peace-loving country to a belligerent partner of this madman Hitler," Donatella fretted.

"I think you are right," said Maddalena. "But what concerns me even more is that once America enters the war, which appears likely from everything I hear, the young sons of Italians who migrated to the United States not so long ago might one day soon be actually fighting, and killing, and being killed by their Italian brothers right here on their own native soil. I find this disgraceful and appalling . . ."

". . . and sinful," Camilla interjected. "Italians of good conscience have every right to feel betrayed and repelled by Hitler's and Mussolini's reprehensible conduct, but we mustn't lose sight of the unconscionable suffering being inflicted on the rest of Europe as well, only a quarter of a century since World War I ended."

"Yes, that is true, Camilla, but I still believe we Italians have the added burden of shame for being, how should I put it, turncoats, in addition to suffering actual physical loss—of people, our sacred land, everything," Donatella said.

Perhaps we need to pray harder," said Maddalena.

"That may be so," said Donatella, "but I can't help but wonder sometimes how such evil can be allowed to exist in a land like ours where people for centuries, and still to this very day, have only wanted to be left alone so that they could go about their business of trying to live what is for them a simple, uncomplicated life."

"You are much too pessimistic, Donatella," Camilla countered. "Italy is a great country. Not too long from now Italy's appeal to a totalitarian ideology will fade and the country will emerge from this nightmare better off than before. I further predict the United States will help make that happen."

"But as much as I hate to say it, they'll be our enemy," Maddalena offered.

"No, Maddalena," Camilla explained, "the United States will be Hitler's and Mussolini's enemy, not the Italian people's. You just wait and see . . . they're going to come into the war soon and crush Nazism and Fascism and bring harmony and equilibrium back into our lives. Of this, I am absolutely confident."

"How can you be so sure about a country you hardly know?" asked Maddalena.

"I have been fascinated by the United States for a long time, and have spent a fair amount of time learning its history and mores. Admittedly, I've only been there once, so much of what I know about America has been gleaned from books and newspapers. But next spring at the end of the school term, God willing, I expect to spend the entire summer in New York with a friend who has been studying there for the last two years. She's been sending me material on America ever since she got there.

"As you may know, I have been giving Giuliana after-school lessons on a variety of subjects, including the history of the United States. She is as fascinated with the country as I am. Some of the other kids seem interested, too. That's why I was able to convince Sister Carolina on the importance of the older children learning a little bit of American history, and teaching them some English. They have all taken to it quite nicely, especially Giuliana—that shouldn't come as a surprise to either one of you, I'm sure."

Several days later, Donatella made an appointment to meet privately with Camilla mid-afternoon at a coffee shop in the piazza. She dropped Giuliana off at the rectory after school so that she and Camilla could conduct their business in private for an hour or so.

"Last week when we met at your apartment," Donatella said, immediately getting to the point, "you went on quite a bit about America. I would have mentioned it then, but I didn't want to say anything in front of Maddalena, much as I love her, because I haven't discussed what I am about to tell you with anyone, not even my daughter and son-in-law.

"From the moment she was born, Giuliana has been special to me, and not just because she is my only granddaughter. When my husband died and I went to live with my daughter Maria and her family, that's when I came to realize just how really special she is. I suppose some of it has to do with her being so much like me . . . at least that's what Maria and a lot of other people, including Maddalena, keep telling me all the time."

Donatella then spent several minutes describing her family background and what her life was like growing up, from the time she was a child until just before she married. "I have always said, as much to convince myself as anyone else I suppose, that I never regretted not having a real education . . . I only completed the eighth grade. After all, I kept telling myself, didn't I have an incredible education, but of a different kind? I became a businesswoman, and at an early age . . . something not very many people in this country, least of all women, can possibly say. Didn't that count for something . . . wasn't that better than any school book learning? But now, when I think of my granddaughter, and look at someone like you, I realize how much I've missed out on by not having continued my studies, even if it meant at the time that I would have had to leave Amalfi, which my parents were prepared to have me do." Quickly switching gears, she added: "But that, as they say, is water under the bridge. It's way too late for me. Furthermore, it is not my life I'm concerned about . . . it's Giuliana's."

As more people kept coming into the shop, the two women decided to continue their conversation on a quiet bench near the wharf. Donatella admitted to Camilla that what she had been teaching Giuliana about America had peaked her own interest, to the point where she wondered what it would be like—even how wonderful it would be, despite how painful for her—if Giuliana were to go to the United States to live and go to school. She was certain, based on reports from friends who had emigrated there over the years, and now from her own son and daughter-in-law these last two years, that opportunities to get ahead were bountiful, especially for people who were educated.

"In America, anyone who wants to get ahead, male or female, can do it, I'm told." Donatella kept waiting for Camilla to respond, but she didn't say anything. "The more I think about it," Donatella continued, "the more I'm convinced that we should seriously think about sending Giuliana to America. It would be a shame, even a sin, to deprive someone as talented as my dear granddaughter the chance in life she deserves. She certainly won't get it here." She hesitated for a moment.

"But it may not be easy. First I have to convince my daughter and son-in-law to give up their daughter, in effect, and then convince my son and daughter-in-law in America to take her in."

"Then, of course, there's Giuliana herself to consider," Camilla interjected.

"That's where you come in, Camilla. I don't think you would have much trouble convincing Giuliana that what we're proposing is in her best interest, especially in view of all that you've been teaching her about the United States . . . she's kept me abreast of everything. If I were forty years younger, I'd happily go there myself."

"I'm so happy you see the matter as I do," Camilla said enthusiastically, "but I've always been hesitant to bring it up with you or anyone else . . . certainly not with Giuliana. Frankly, I've been waiting for her to say something to me along the same lines. But then again, why would she? She's still only a child, and any thoughts of leaving her family to go live somewhere else would seem unlikely to be something she would entertain at this stage of her life. Yet, with Giuliana, you never know."

"So you agree with me, this is worth pursuing, do you?" Donatella asked.

"Absolutely," said Camilla, "and I'm thrilled we're thinking along the same lines. We might also consider broaching the subject with Father Marco and Sister Carolina to see what they have to say. In the meantime, as I continue to meet with Giuliana these next few weeks before school starts, I'm going to see if I can draw out of her any thoughts she might have about living in America. Of course, I shall be very subtle in how I go about it. Don't worry . . . I will be careful not to influence her thinking in any way. If you and I know Giuliana as well as we think we do, she will do all the deciding herself."

# Chapter 10

On the 15th of August, a Friday, one week later, a huge crowd was gathered in the town square to celebrate the feast of the Assumption of the Virgin Mary, a holy day of obligation for Catholics. A seven-foot statue of the Mother of God, anchored on a ten-foot-long wood platform regaled in colorful bunting, was carried by ten male members of the Sodality of Mary, who led the parade of worshipers that commenced from the hilly main road just outside of town and ended within sight of the Cathedral of Sant'Andrea and within ear shot of pealing bells that reverberated throughout the piazza.

Walking directly behind the statue were Fathers Gaetano and Di Pina and six altar boys in their red and white cassocks, two abreast. A dozen school children, six to ten in age—five boys in white suits and seven girls in white dresses, veils and shoes, each carrying a single red rose in her white-gloved hand—paraded behind, followed by a band of twenty-four musicians in navy blue uniforms, their heads covered in handsome white soldier caps with gold piping. Several dozen townsfolk took up the rear. In the front of this group were the Gallardos, the Montones, Donatella Fassano and the Landini family. The statue was carried up the steps of the church and placed at the foot of the altar. Fathers Gaetano and Di Pina plus three priests from churches in the surrounding area were present in the cathedral to con-celebrate High Mass.

Midway through the service, a limousine drove slowly into the deserted piazza and stopped in front of a café across the square from the church. Grace and Liam McDonough stepped out of the car and took a seat at one of the outdoor tables that formed a perimeter in front of the café. They waited for Mass to be let out.

Among the parishioners who came streaming out of the church some minutes later was Camilla, chatting animatedly with relatives of two of her students. At first, she did not see her parents from across the way as she descended the steps. Suddenly, her eyes fell on the pale arm of a woman waving a small flag. As it came closer into view, Camilla recognized it to be, unmistakably, the colors of the Scottish flag, and the person waving it wildly, her mother. She gave out a shrill shriek that pierced the air, startling several people adjacent to her. Then snaking and slithering her way to get through the crowd to her mother, Camilla nudged neighbors, acquaintances and strangers alike out of the way.

When they finally came together, Camilla fell deliriously into her mother's waiting arms, smothering her face with kisses, all the while tenderly rubbing her back. Liam McDonough looked on with delight. When it came his turn, he embraced his daughter, hugging her tightly, every so often pushing her gently away, repeating over and over: "Let me look at you."

It had been a year since they had last seen each other. Camilla couldn't keep from sobbing. Neither could her parents. "What ever are you two doing here?" Camilla asked.

"We thought we'd give you a bit of a surprise," said Grace, a delighted, mischievous look spread across her pallid face.

"My God, I should say so."

"Father has meetings all week in the Naples office. When I was certain I'd be able to make the trip, we arranged it so we would start off by first spending a long weekend with our favorite daughter, in our favorite spot on earth. We're staying with the Gallardos the next few days. We warned them not to utter a word to you of our coming . . . we plan to drive back to Naples early Monday morning . . . we have the company car at our disposal."

After this brief and breathless explanation, the McDonoughs exchanged greetings with several acquaintances from bygone days. With the Gallardos and Montones in tow, they retraced their steps back to the base of the church where Father Di Pina was holding court, much as he did every Sunday after Mass. When he looked up and spied the McDonoughs inching slowly through the crowd toward him, the shock of seeing friends he hadn't seen in ages gave him a start. He made the sign of the cross, then instinctively placed a shaking hand over his heart. The joy in his eyes, the broad smile on his face, were like those of a child handed his favorite toy.

In the ten years since they'd last seen each other, the relationship between Father Marco and the McDonoughs had been strictly epistolary: he chose to write, purposely, at Easter and Christmas, the two most sacred days in the Catholic liturgical calendar; his Scottish friends wrote twice a year as well, but made certain their letters were penned at non-religious holiday times. Would the needling between them ever cease?

"As I live and breathe, you are certainly a sight for sore eyes," said Father Marco, smacking his lips and embracing his friends warmly, kissing their cheeks not once but three times. They told the priest they planned to spend the rest of the day with Camilla, visit with him at the rectory the next afternoon, if that was convenient, then meet up with him again that evening at the Gallardos' for dinner, an invitation he had already been extended without having any idea at the time that the mystery guests he was told would also be in attendance were none other than the estimable Mr. and Mrs. Liam McDonough.

\* \* \*

Though they hadn't seen each other in years, Grace McDonough and Maria Landini had remained in touch, as friends as well as purchaser and seller, respectively, of Maria's linens, the best that money could buy. Maria's business was in its infancy when the two women first met. At the recommendation of the Montones, Grace was introduced to Maria Landini and her exquisite linens when it came time for the McDonoughs to furnish their new summer residence.

Working alone at the time Maria still managed to fill a fair amount of orders, including those placed by Mrs. McDonough, who waited patiently and never pressured Maria for early delivery, especially now that the linen maker was six months pregnant with her fourth child, the soon to be born Giuliana. Given her daughter's condition, Donatella lent a helping hand whenever she could. Very often the three women could be found chatting in Maria's shop while daughter and mother went about their work.

*       *       *

The McDonoughs and the Landinis were at the monument in the main square renewing acquaintances when Camilla ushered Giuliana, only six-months old when the McDonoughs had last seen her, over to them. Grace was delighted. Standing in front of her was this beautiful 10-year-old child whom she felt she knew from Camilla's and Maria's letters. It was agreed on the spot that the McDonoughs would dine at the Landinis' on Sunday. "We won't take no for an answer," Maria insisted

The welcoming dinner hosted by the Gallardos was one of the highlights of the McDonoughs' memorable whirlwind, seventy-two-hour weekend in Amalfi. Besides the guests of honor, and daughter Camilla, the other invitees included the Montones; Father Di Pina; the Landinis; Donatella; the mayor of Amalfi, Massimo Iovine and wife,

Sophia; and the head of the carabinieri, Nicola Di Lieto and his wife, Mena. Maddalena was there, too, but not as a guest; she was hired by the Gallardos to assist their live-in housekeeper in preparing and serving the sumptuous meal.

After an hour of drinks and hors d'oeuvres, the fifteen diners took their seats at a long table under a canopy on the travertine patio that looked across a long line of cypress trees dotting the lush landscape stretching valley-like into the distance of the Gallardos' expansive property. It was an absolutely gorgeous August night, mild rather than hot for that time of year. The setting sun in the distant orange, yellow and red sky cast the brightest glow and covered the earth like a warm blanket. Father Marco said grace, after which Dr. Gallardo stood and welcomed his guests, then toasted the McDonoughs at length. Dinner lasted well into the starlit Mediterranean night.

Early in the evening, conversation, as expected, centered mainly on Liam and Grace. Guests wanted to know how they had been faring these past years; the McDonoughs were more than pleased to tell them. Midway through the meal talk turned, as it did around most tables in Europe at the time, to a more somber subject—the war.

"I hope it won't be long before America enters the war," said Antonio Landini.

"I agree," said Massimo Iovine, the Amalfi mayor, who had fought against the Germans in World War 1. "Even though they won't be on our side . . . at least not yet."

"I had pretty much the same conversation with Donatella and Maddalena just the other day," Camilla said. "What I told them then and what I say now is that I believe that with America's intervention Italy will come out of this intact, and Hitler and Mussolini, will quickly disappear from the world scene."

"What do you mean, disappear?" asked Nicola Di Lieto, head of the local carabinieri, whose modest police force was already seriously depleted, the Italian army having drafted several of its men.

"I'm of the opinion that this alliance between Hitler and Mussolini won't hold for very long," Camilla answered. "The rest of the world and most especially the United States, with all its power, will simply not allow this axis of evil to take over the whole of Europe. You mark my words, America is going to come in just as it did in the First World War, crush the Third Reich and destroy Hitler's Germany once and for all. This will result in Mussolini's fall, and Italy will revert back to being a free democracy."

"I pray that you are right, Camilla," said Father Di Pina. "In the meantime we are going to remain on pins and needles until what you have predicted becomes a reality."

". . . and sooner rather than later," offered Donatella.

"I appreciate what you say about Mussolini, Camilla, but there are certain indisputable facts about his brand of fascism that you may not be totally aware of," the priest offered. "For example, when Mussolini came into power in 1922 Italy was at a very low point. The country was in disarray, north and south completely divided, stymied by a government unable, or unwilling, to provide adequate schooling and thwarted by an intractable economy; there were no jobs, unemployment the highest in our history.

"Over these past twenty years or so, Mussolini has almost singlehandedly turned things around. He united north and south and began a series of economic reforms that put us back on our feet. He introduced a spate of state sponsored public work programs: he constructed new roads, built new railroads, put people back to work and made school compulsory for all children, poor or otherwise. He had a vision for Italy, with social democracy the overriding theme of his administration. And he delivered on his promises. He even instituted workers' retirement pension funds, so a family wouldn't go hungry when the principal breadwinner retired. He also introduced medical insurance, unheard of in Italy at the time, as well as insurance to cover lost possessions. On a local note, he brought back to Amalfi the book of maritime laws, absent for almost four centuries."

"Well, then, Father, how do you explain Italy's rapid descent into moral decay under Mussolini?" a surprised Camilla asked, having been presented with a litany of Il Duce's accomplishments she had hitherto not been familiar with.

"The problem was that Italy's hands were tied. England and France had ceased trade with Italy when we started flexing our own expansionist muscles in Africa . . . our goal was to establish colonies there to protect oil interests. The only one we could turn to for help was Hitler, who gave it to us. Mussolini had no intention of joining in his cause . . . he considered Hitler a madman like everybody else. In fact, he waited a full year before joining in the war because Italy had no military power whatsoever, then or now.

"The Italian Foreign Minister at the time, Galeazzo Ciano, noted in his diary 'that Italian divisions had merely the strength of regiments, that there was a shortage of ammunition, that the artillery was obsolete and that antiaircraft and antitank weapons were lacking.' It was a joke among those who were in the know that Mussolini kept flying the same small fleet of planes over one country after another, hoping the enemy would think we had a major air force instead of no more than a meager few dozen fighter aircraft. Mussolini's biggest mistake, though, was in believing the war would be over in six months. He miscalculated badly on two fronts—he never dreamed Hitler would invade Poland, which he did, and he didn't foresee the United States entering the war which, I agree, seems inevitable. Yet despite all this, even in the poor areas of

Italy especially, Mussolini to this very day can do no wrong . . . he's still considered, may the one true God forgive me for saying it, a god."

Having expended a good deal of conversation on the war, and its possible tragic consequences, the guests then turned to more personal matters. Everyone was pleased to hear from Donatella that her son, Umberto, and his wife, Concetta, had adjusted nicely to their new life in America and that, to quote her son, "economic opportunities are everywhere to be found, if you work hard enough."

Francesco Montone chimed in that he learned that to be precisely the case: several of his relatives over the last two decades had left the Amalfi coast and settled in America in and around New Haven, Connecticut (Amalfi's sister city) just as the Fassanos had done. He told about one of his nephew's sons who had just been granted a full scholarship to attend Yale University, one of the elite bastions of higher education in the United States, located most obligingly in the heart of New Haven. All of the guests, in one way or another, had something to say regarding the educational system in America; they were surprisingly knowledgeable, even aware of the law, non-existent in Italy, which mandated that young adults were not allowed to leave school before their sixteenth birthday.

"My friends in America tell me much the same thing," said the prelate. "One of the priests with whom I was in the seminary has been pastor of St. Michael's Church in New Haven for the past eight years. The spiritual needs of the huge Catholic population in the area, many of whose members were born here, are being nicely taken care of. One way is through the neighborhood's excellent parish elementary school run by dedicated Sacred Heart nuns who recognize the sacrifices parents are making to give their children opportunities they never had."

"I am so pleased you brought that up, Father," said Camilla. "I expect to spend next summer in the States; perhaps you could make an introduction for me to your friend. I'm anxious to learn about some of the teaching methods Americans employ. Obviously, I'm conversant with how Scotland teaches its young people and with the school system here in Amalfi, of course, but from all I read I wouldn't be surprised if schools in America were doing some things that our own children might find quite beneficial."

# Chapter 11

When Camilla and her parents arrived at the Landinis' for dinner the next day it did not take long for the conversation to return to the previous evening's topic on education. "I take it from some of the things you said last night that you don't think our schools measure up very well," said Donatella.

"No, that isn't it at all," Camilla answered. "In fact, instruction is quite good in the five-year primary grades as well as in the three-year secondary gymnasium grades. In the classic lyceum and scientific lyceum the teaching is superb, quite vigorous I might add."

"Then what, exactly, is the problem?" asked Donatella.

"It has to do with attitude more than anything. There doesn't appear to be a burning desire on the part of parents for their children to learn more than the compulsory, bare requirements, mainly I believe because they're not educated themselves. Dare I say that to most of them education is a luxury, not a necessity. For reasons that are not fully known to me, education is not taken all that seriously here as it is in other countries I'm familiar with . . . certainly not in mine anyway. And of course the children reflect pretty much the attitude of their parents."

"What can we do about it?" Antonio Landini asked. "Or is the situation hopeless?"

"No, not by any means. But from what I have seen, now that I have been here almost two years, the problem is really a cultural one. It's ingrained in the southern Italian psyche. People here struggle to make ends meet, that's what occupies their minds, not education. And you know what . . . they are absolutely right to think this way. What good, really, is an education if one doesn't know where one's next meal is coming from? But having said that, the argument is valid only up to a point," Camilla continued, speaking with increasing passion. "You, Maria, and you, Antonio . . . I don't believe you are in this category of Italians. I think . . ."

Liam McDonough cut his daughter off before she could continue her psychoanalysis of the Italian mind, and her assessment of the Landinis' state of affairs. "Come, come Camilla," he said reproachfully, "why do you persist in making such presumptions? Aren't you being a mite too personal here?"

"No, I'm not, father. I merely would like to point out that the Landinis don't appear to be burdened by the same constraints that keep many families in this part of Italy from considering education a worthwhile end in itself. From what I can see, Giuliana doesn't have to worry about pitching in to help insure her family's well-being."

"What possible concerns are these of yours?" asked an exasperated Grace McDonough, shifting uneasily in her chair, embarrassed by her daughter's uncharacteristic impertinence. The room fell silent. Hearing her name for the first time in the conversation, Giuliana rose from her place and asked to be excused. Her brothers followed her out of the dining room into the courtyard.

Donatella, sitting between her daughter and son-in-law, did not say a word and before either one of them had a chance to speak up, she placed a hand on Maria's arm and the other on Antonio's knee, as much as to say: "Let her have her say, and don't be offended by what you hear."

"Where is all this leading to?" Liam asked.

"I realize how terribly presumptuous of me this must all sound, but you have to believe me when I say my only concern is Giuliana."

"Please feel free to say anything you wish, Camilla," Maria said curtly, "but you must explain yourself more clearly."

"Here is the point I'm attempting to make, rather badly I suppose. I'm glad Giuliana isn't in the room to hear it." She took a sip of water and cleared her throat. "All of you are aware of the high regard in which I hold Giuliana. She is a most unusual young girl . . . enormously talented . . . with an appetite for learning that can only be described as voracious. I've never seen anything like it in my six years of teaching young children. The way I view it is that with her, school isn't merely a matter of advancing grade by grade in order to meet certain standard requirements. With Giuliana it is something way above that . . . something even transcendent. It's loving knowledge for its own sake. She realizes that with education comes discovery. Young people blessed with this sensibility are special, and those of us in the teaching business who come in contact with someone who possesses this rare gift have a moral obligation, it seems to me, to do everything we can to see to it that that individual is provided every opportunity under the sun to reach her full potential, which in Giuliana's case is limitless in my opinion.

"And it starts with giving her the best and most challenging schooling. If I may be so bold, I believe it behooves you, Maria and Antonio, to see to it that Giuliana is given such an opportunity. Since there isn't a school here in Amalfi that meets her needs, I'm suggesting you send her someplace where she will find one."

"You have spoken glowingly about the United States these past two days," said Donatella, no longer able to hold her tongue; what she was about to say only Camilla had hitherto been privy to. "Could you be suggesting"—she held her breath a split second for emphasis—"that we send Giuliana to America to get educated?"

"As much as I know it must hurt all of you to even contemplate such a prospect, that is precisely what I am suggesting. And more to the point, strongly urging."

"But she is our only daughter," Maria gasped.

"I know."

"How could we give her up?"

"I dare say it won't be easy."

"We all love her so . . . I simply couldn't."

Back and forth it went, argument and counterargument, Maria and Antonio with great emotion stating their case as parents, Camilla single-minded and, on the surface, a seemingly dispassionate outsider, presenting hers.

"I could never have let you leave your mother and me," Liam said emphatically.

"But that's precisely the point, isn't it, Father . . . you never had to."

Donatella rose and went to the sideboard and poured herself a cup of coffee, neglecting the tempting ricotta cheesecake she had baked just hours before, and returned to her place at the table. One by one, the McDonoughs and Landinis also got up and worked their way to the dessert table. The interlude provided a much needed pause in the weighty and what had become increasingly contentious conversation. But before anyone had finished dessert Donatella resumed her probing cross examination, hoping to bring, if not a final resolution of the matter itself, at least an end to its discussion before the night was over.

"Have you talked this over with Giuliana?"

"No, not really," Camilla answered.

"But all she talks of lately is the United States. You have filled her head with an enormous amount of information. It has made a great impression on her. If you ask me, I believe she is already predisposed to the United States."

"That doesn't necessarily mean she's ready to move there, Mama," said Antonio.

"Perhaps not, but at some point if we are to be fair to the child, and to ourselves, we need to learn what Giuliana herself thinks of all this."

"I'm not certain I want to do that," said Antonio. "I don't think this is something we should leave in our daughter's hands. As parents, we have an obligation to do what's best for her . . . she's not old enough right now to decide for herself."

Donatella had all to do to hold back from commenting, for she understood fully what her son-in-law was intimating. She thought of the time her own parents were faced with a similar agonizing dilemma when she was but a little older than her precious granddaughter—she herself had brought the matter to a head, not her parents. As of yet, Giuliana hadn't committed herself one way or the other to the idea of going to live in another country. If anything, she was oblivious to the fact that there was even a commitment that had to be made on her part in the first place.

"You certainly have every right to make that choice," Camilla said, "but if I may, I should like to suggest that you think seriously about this. As I've already pointed out, there simply are no schools anywhere in this immediate area, and I've visited every one of them since I've been here, that frankly can accommodate Giuliana's needs once she leaves Santa Croce. Furthermore, and this is a big issue as far as I'm concerned, there's this awful war to consider. Who knows what might possibly happen, what with Hitler intent on world domination and a complicit Mussolini at his side to do his bidding here in Italy. It's conceivable, perhaps even likely, war will come to these shores and then . . ."

Donatella did not hold back this time. "With the gloomy picture you paint of how things in Italy are at this time, I don't think you leave us much choice," she said.

"My only intention is to paint a realistic picture, not to sound like an alarmist," Camilla answered. "At the sake of repeating myself, let's consider the salient facts again, objectively and dispassionately.

"Number one: You have a brilliant ten-year-old child who, if not given the opportunity, might wither unless challenged. Agreed? Yes. Two: You Maria, you Antonio, you Donatella—you're all sympathetic to Giuliana's needs, and to her ultimate happiness, which involves helping her realize her full potential. Three: From what I can see, you are blessed with sufficient means so you need not look to your daughter to abandon her schooling in order to help support the family like so many other children in this part of Italy are required to do. Four: The war going on here could very possibly jeopardize everything. Five: You have family with established roots in the United States. Finally six, and perhaps most important: In the United States we are speaking of a country that to my way of thinking is the best hope for mankind in the world. Besides, it has arguably the best institutions of higher learning in the world. Its colleges and universities are first rate . . . most of those in Europe can't come close to them.

"The difference between Italy—all of Europe, for that matter— and the United States is that we continue to live and cherish the past whereas America, being so young in comparison, lives in the world of today and is confident only of its future. And you know why?" Camilla asked rhetorically. "Because the United States is the world's most welcoming country to immigrants. Unlike here or in my own country, they embrace people of all ethnic, cultural and religious backgrounds. Such diversity, together with an innate thirst for liberty and self-expression is what has made the United States great, the envy of the world. Plus, it's a true democracy, espousing, above all else, freedom, of every kind, for all its citizens. And need I remind you that women, unlike here in Italy I'm afraid, are most definitely included."

# Chapter 12

The Landinis welcomed the arrival of the new school year. It helped take their minds off, even if only for a little while, the troubling but inevitable decision they would be forced to make regarding their daughter's future. For the next several months, Maria and Antonio went back and forth over what they should do: one day they agreed to send their daughter to America, the next day they both said they would never do it. Then maybe. Then one yes, the other no. And on and on it went. There was no use consulting with Donatella—they knew where she stood on the matter. And after discussions with Father Marco and Sister Carolina, the Landinis had little doubt on which side of the question the church pastor and school principal came down: as much as they regretted seeing Giuliana leave, they believed it to be the best and most sensible course of action.

So there it was: the Landinis, Antonio and Maria, left on their own to decide Giuliana's future, a decision they had so far been reluctant to make. If not for Donatella's persistent but gentle prodding it likely would never have been made. Once the matter had been settled just before Christmas, the cloud of uncertainty that hung over the household these past days and months, dissolved. So did the tension. But not the unhappiness.

While at first everyone tried valiantly to put the best face on things, as time drew closer to the end of the school year there was a palpable change in demeanor amongst all members of the family, no longer hesitant to let their true feelings be known: Maria and Antonio lamented that they were losing their only daughter, the boys their only sister. The one person who would be most affected by Giuliana's leaving said little. If keeping it inside was Donatella's way of coping with having instigated the departure of her beloved granddaughter, "one of God's perfect little creatures," she called her, Maria found her mother's seemingly indifference disconcerting, even puzzling. And she called her on it.

"Don't think for a moment I'm not dying a thousand deaths," Donatella said to Maria when she delivered lunch to her one day at work: Donatella had grown increasingly concerned that Maria's work habits over the last several weeks had become terribly erratic. "I don't know what I'm going to do with myself when Giuliana leaves. You and Antonio and the boys have your work . . . I'm going to miss her so. I thought I would never have to say this to another person, even to my own daughter, being the proud fool I've been for so much of my life, but I'm going to need you to lean on even more as time goes by. I'm an old woman, Maria, and you're all I've got."

Just under eleven months after Giuliana left for America, Donatella Teresa Fassano, a few days shy of her sixty-seventh birthday, was dead. Much of Amalfi mourned her passing. But none more than a twelve-year-old girl recently arrived in New Haven Connecticut.

# PART TWO

# NEW HAVEN

# Chapter 13

On June 15, 1941, the giant oceanliner *SS Italia* eased out of its slip into the Mediterranean. Standing motionless from its bow, Giuliana gazed longingly over her shoulder at the Bay of Naples shimmering resplendently in the bright afternoon sunlight as the boat got farther away from the pier. She nestled up against the ship's protective railing, her arm tightly around the waist of her stalwart companion on this life-altering trip, Camilla McDonough. Teacher and mentor to Giuliana, Camilla was sailing to New York to spend the first of five summer school breaks in the city of her dreams.

The trip across the Atlantic took twelve days. On the boat Giuliana met a number of Italians traveling to America for the first time. A few, like herself, were planning to settle there permanently. One day at lunch, Giuliana and Camilla were seated next to a pretty young American woman returning home after spending several weeks touring the continent with friends. The trip was a college graduation gift from her parents. She had noticed Giuliana when she first appeared on deck in her new dress.

Over the next several days, Jennifer Kirby, who spoke passable Italian, proved to be an amiable companion. When Miss Kirby learned that Giuliana would be living permanently in New Haven, and that Camilla was spending the summer in New York, the three made plans to meet in New Haven sometime during the next two months. Jennifer knew the city well, having spent a good deal of time there visiting her boyfriend, a graduate of Yale, its medical school and now in his first year of residency at New Haven Hospital. The chance meeting between

Giuliana and Jennifer Kirby would one day prove to be propitious for the transplanted young Amalfitan.

Waiting patiently at New York's west side pier to greet Giuliana and take her into his care was her uncle, Umberto Fassano, her mother's younger brother. He had emigrated to the United States in November 1938, six months before the military alliance known as the Rome Berlin Axis (the Pact of Steel) was established between Mussolini and Hitler the following May. Umberto and Concetta, his wife of a year, had settled in New Haven, Connecticut, home to thousands of Amalfitani—peasants, fishermen, unskilled laborers—who, beginning in the late nineteenth and early twentieth centuries, had fled their homeland to escape poverty, unemployment, heavy taxation and an implacable class system in the hope of seeking a better life for themselves and their families.

Umberto, who hadn't seen his niece in over three years, was accompanied by his boyhood Amalfi friend, Paolo Giordano, in whose Model A Ford they would be driving back to New Haven; Concetta had remained at home making final preparations for Giuliana's arrival. Also at the dock were Camilla's childhood friend from Scotland, Margaret Dawson, with whom she would be staying in New York for the summer, as well as Jennifer Kirby's parents; they were there to pick her up and drive her back to their home in Philadelphia.

After the passengers had been processed through customs, they were ushered into the waiting lounge where family and friends stood ready to meet the new arrivals. Introductions were made all around. Just before the group dispersed Camilla took Giuliana off to the side and handed her a package that she took out of a large cloth carrying bag. She told the young girl to open it when she arrived home (to Giuliana the word home sounded so strange). Giuliana, in turn, gave her friend a small manila envelope. Inside was a perfectly rendered pen and ink sketch in an ornate frame, a self-portrait Giuliana had drawn as a going-away present for her friend. At the bottom of the picture was the inscription: *To Camilla, the best friend and school teacher I will ever have, Love, Giuliana.* Tears in their eyes, the two embraced, bid farewell to the others, then departed.

\* \* \*

The 75-mile drive from New York to New Haven—about an hour-and-a-half today but more than twice as long 60-plus years ago driving the highway-less Connecticut roads—was a revelation. After having glimpsed, if only for a moment, the sheer massiveness of the New York skyline—it took her breath away—Giuliana was not thrilled by what she saw on the rest of her journey. More to the point, she was saddened by what she didn't see: there were no stunning views of the soaring, craggy Lattari Mountains. Nor were there tiered rows of white-washed houses with colorful clay roofs carved like shelves into the sides of massive rock formations and, nestled between the shelves, long rows of lush bougainvillea, cypress trees, olive trees and lemon groves from whose branches hung the most delicious lemons, some the size of grapefruits. Nor was there a shimmering emerald blue sea at which to endlessly gaze.

Umberto pointed out that a large body of water, the Long Island Sound, lay just beyond, but it was shielded from the old Post Road they were driving. Instead, what passed in view was a flat uninspiring landscape dotted with nondescript buildings and stores that revealed little of the attractive landscape that lay just beyond the road in quaint coastline towns and villages. When they reached the outskirts of New Haven Giuliana saw for the first time the dimmed silhouette of what a typical American city looked like. Her first impression was that it was drab and colorless and would take some time getting used to. *"Why would anyone want to leave Amalfi to come live here?"* she asked herself.

As she looked out the window her mind kept drifting back to the beautiful town she had just left, and to the weathered plaque hanging under the arched entrance to Duomo Square. It carried the inscription that perfectly expressed the sentiment of its people: *Il giorno del giudizio, per gli Amalfitani che andranno in Paradiso, sara` un giorno come tutti gli altri.* ("Judgment Day for the Amalfitani who go to Paradise will be a day like all the others.") No such sign expressing a similar sentiment was evident to Giuliana as the trio—Paolo at the wheel, Giuliana in the middle, Umberto in the passenger seat—drove into busy downtown New Haven.

# Chapter 14

Like his sister Maria, his parents and grandparents, Umberto Fassano had inherited the family's entrepreneurial spirit. But it would be several years before he realized the dream he had long entertained of owning his own business. For the time being, he was content just to have escaped the stultifying life he led in Italy and grateful to have settled in the United States, in the state of Connecticut, in the city of New Haven. But not necessarily in the "Little Italy" neighborhood, the largest Italian enclave in the city, where a flat had been secured for him by his boyhood friend, Paolo Giordano, whose family property in Amalfi lay just above the Fassano's place. Paolo had come to America five years earlier.

Only recently married to an Italian-American seamstress, Paolo was fortunate to have found a four-room flat for his friend that had become available on the third floor of a row house three doors down from his own on Wooster Street, the main drag in the densely populated Wooster Square area. The Fassanos were grateful to have a roof over their heads when they arrived in November 1938, but when they first got a look at the cold water flat they would be living in, and the street they'd be living on, their spirits sank.

Made up of mostly tenements interspersed with small shops, grocery stores, restaurants and a few free-standing individual dwellings, the street was uniformly drab except for two buildings that had miraculously survived its once glorious past. On the corner of Wooster and Warren Streets, only steps away from where the Fassanos took up residence, was the Joseph Porter House, a three-story, brick Italianate style mansion built in 1879-80 by the well-to-do manufacturer and philanthropist Joseph Porter, a partner in Sperry & Barnes, the largest meat-packing plant in the state.

Occupying a prominent position on the other side of the street directly across from the Fassano flat was the Captain Elisha Peck House, built in 1800 by the wealthy landowner-businessman Austin Denison around 1800 and now the home of the Neighborhood House, the area's sole supervised recreation center. Save for those two rather imposing, out-of-place structures, the rest of the street was a virtual continuum of dull tenement brown, a patch of green grass or a tree nowhere in sight. You had to walk a block and a half to Chapel Street, where in lovely Columbus Green, smack in the center of Wooster Square, stood a profusion of stately old elms nicely spaced among crisscrossed pathways and mini lawns that surrounded dozens of wooden park benches scattered here and there beckoning strollers to sit a spell.

The Green occupied the middle of mostly conjoined, attractive single-family homes erected around the park's perimeter. On one side was Greene Street, where St. Kazmir's Church, Sacred Heart Convent and Columbus Grammar School lay, and further up the street, a full block off the green, St. Michael's Grammar School. Wooster Place, stretching from Greene to Chapel Streets, was anchored by St. Michael's Church, the mainstay and heart of the Amalfi community in New Haven, with its shiny golden dome visible from all over town; the church was located on the same block with two funeral parlors separated by a lovely Federal-style residence that somehow managed to survive the wrecker's ball when gentrification forever changed the face of the area.

Only later, at the Italian-American Club, which he joined immediately upon arriving in New Haven, did Umberto, much to his and later to Giuliana's astonishment, learn that the area, long before he and his wife arrived there, was at one time the most upscale part of the city. Wooster Square, known in the mid-nineteenth century as New Township, had, by 1850, become the city's preeminent fashionable neighborhood, and easily the most beautiful. Three short blocks were all that separated it from the calm Long Island Sound. Attractive white clapboard houses lined streets around the square, complementing its harmonious landscape. Sea captains, industrialists, wealthy philanthropists all lived there in stately homes, including the Revolutionary War hero General David Wooster, after whom the area was named, and on whose site on Wooster Street now stands the renowned Libby's Pastry Shop. Also, Benedict Arnold—yes, that Benedict Arnold—once slept here, in a beautiful Greek revival home his family owned on Water Street, overlooking the Sound. Only three blocks away was a huge beach and a promenade of trees that encircled the magnificent Pavilion Hotel where rich out-of-towners whiled away indolent summers. Then came the Industrial Revolution. And with it mass relocation of the well-to-do and drastic changes to the swanky neighborhood soon to be occupied by poor Italian immigrants. Virtually all of the beautiful single-family homes and mansions, including General Wooster's and Benedict Arnold's and those of other notable New Haven natives, gave way to a ring of mills, factories, and a railroad, that made their newly arrived owners wealthy and gave immigrant workers a job, a place to live and, however dim, a glimmer of hope of a better life for themselves and their families. As the ring began to grow ever inward, all of the area's summer residents left for new playgrounds, replaced by an expanding Italian immigrant army of cheap labor turning out "carriages and clocks, corsets and locks," mainstay products manufactured in the area. The posh Pavilion Hotel was razed, replaced by the Sargent's lock-making factory.

Joseph Sargent, more than any other industrialist, was responsible for giving Italian labor a job. It was in fact his Italian-born wife who convinced her husband to import poor destitute workers from her native Naples area; beginning in 1882 he brought thousands to New Haven to work in his factory. To house these workers, Sargent's and a host of other industrialists bought up all of the property in the area, tore down just about every structure that even smacked of another time and culture, and erected row house upon row house. Within a single square mile were some 50,000 Italians, all members of a cheap labor force whose principal motivation was survival, freedom from discrimination and having a place to educate their children in the five grammar schools that had cropped up in the area during the intervening years. By 1915, "New Township" was no more, replaced by what was now famously referred to as "Little Naples."

\* \* \*

The front stoop of the three-story brownstone where the Fassanos took up residence had six creaky steps leading to a six-by-six foot porch with a high-back wooden bench on the attached side of the entrance. A thick, carved mahogany door opened to a tiny vestibule and a smoky half-glass interior door that led to a narrow hallway dimly lit by a single naked light bulb on a string. The condition of the blistered, paint-peeling walls, worn steps and tentative railings were enough to make Umberto and his young wife want to turn around and flee.

The door on the third floor landing opened to the kitchen, the largest room in the apartment. On the right was a black, wrought iron, four-burner stove. Sitting upright attached to the back of the stove was an eight-gallon, thick glass canister that during cold months contained fuel oil, replenished from a tank in the basement every couple of weeks, that heated the kitchen and adjoining bedroom but not very effectively the two front rooms that faced the street. On the left-hand wall, just beyond the door that led to the small bedroom that Giuliana would come to occupy, was a large, deep porcelain sink that served all household requirements—cooking, washing, even bathing. A closet-size enclosure in the outside hallway landing had a toilet but no sink or bathtub.

The kitchen had two large windows: one backed onto a fire escape, the other had a pulley attached to the outside window frame that ran a clothesline to a pole at the far corner of the small fenced-in yard. A narrow hall separated the kitchen from the two front rooms; it had hooks on either wall for hanging garments and shelves above for storage. There were no built-in closets in the apartment. The hallway opened to the front bedroom, whose two side-by-side windows looked out on to the street. The small living room parlor was separated from the bedroom by French doors, a refined touch strangely out of place in the otherwise lackluster flat. Two windows in the room faced the street.

By the time Giuliana arrived three years later the flat, not nearly what the Fassanos had envisioned as a place they'd be living in permanently, had been completely redone. Umberto might have turned his back on the family building business but he had inherited enough of his father's skills to have transformed what was once a dreary hovel into a rather attractive, quite livable space.

In addition to finding a place for his Amalfi friends Paolo had also secured a job for Umberto at the restaurant across the street where he worked as a waiter. Randazzi's Ristorante was by far the most popular Italian eatery in a city whose population at the time was predominantly Italian. Judges, doctors, sports personalities, a large segment of the Yale University community and local politicians and power brokers were regular and frequent customers. Waiters lucky enough to work there did exceedingly well, as Umberto soon learned.

# Chapter 15

Despite the nice way he had about him, Umberto Fassano was something of an enigma. No one quite knew what to make of his erratic behavior including his mother, whose forbearance was tested time and time again. He wore responsibility lightly, yet often spoke of doing great things, though he exhibited neither the inclination nor the willingness to make good on his promises, claiming his efforts were always being subsumed by forces outside his control. He was a disappointment, especially to his father. No matter how many times Alfonso sweet-talked and cajoled his son into joining him in the masonry business—and later on in the Fassano Construction Company—Umberto would have none of it.

The life he chose to live instead, while not exactly dissolute, was nevertheless wasteful, the result of willful negligence. From the time he left school after the eighth grade he worked very little, that is until he was old enough to wait tables in a series of restaurants in and around Amalfi. He was good at it, though he never held down a job for more than a few months. Unable or unwilling to help himself from feeling alienated and adrift, he spent many a day and night idling with friends in local cafes and coffee houses.

While he appeared to be, like so many Italian men of like temperament—oblivious and indifferent to success, fatalists who never aspired to anything higher than their meager station in life—he was at the same time disdainful of others, but not of himself, for their lack of ambition. His outspokenness included the constant refrain that Italy was no longer a great country, that it was too corrupt, and now that it was ruled by a dictator, however benevolent, never destined to recapture the greatness it once enjoyed.

"There is no life here. There is no meaningful work. The people are uneducated, illiterate, superstitious and complacent. The first chance I get I will leave this place for good."

There were plenty of reasons for the family to inveigh against Umberto and his pessimistic attitude and aimlessness. Yet no one took on the sad task, including Donatella, who naturally fretted over her son's low spirits. If anything, she tried not to interfere or voice too strenuously her growing concerns, believing, and praying, that he would work out his problems in due course, if left alone. His sister Maria was equally troubled by her only sibling's aimlessness, but concerns for her growing family coupled with those of her nascent linen business left her powerless to do anything except offer Umberto moral support, which he said he appreciated but left him oddly resentful more than anything.

Just when Umberto himself had begun to doubt that life would ever change for the better—he was a prematurely aging twenty-nine by then—the sister of a young waiter he worked with at the time in an excellent restaurant overlooking the sea in Conca dei Marini, a town a few kilometers outside Amalfi, came into his life.

The serendipitous meeting took place one late afternoon just before the restaurant opened for dinner, when Concetta Sabatino stopped by to see her brother Tommaso. Umberto was in the front of the house in the bar area setting up tables when Concetta walked in. During closing time later that evening, while the wait staff went about the business of cleaning up and preparing for the next day, Umberto asked Tommaso about his sister. Subsequently, a meeting was arranged for the two to meet the following Sunday afternoon at the Amalfi dock area on the long pier that jutted out into the sea.

In Concetta Sabatino Umberto found his compass, and his salvation. From the moment they fell in love—they married one year later—Concetta was able to ground the once floundering, unhappy, prematurely aging young man. For the first time in his adult life, Umberto held down a steady job, saving every lira he made for his and his wife's eventual move to America, which Umberto had for years said he would one day do. In the meantime, they lived with Concetta's family, all the while planning and dreaming that something wonderful awaited them in the new world, which they were determined to find just as soon as their nest egg, together with funds from Concetta's family and from Donatella, who happily provided her share, was sufficient to sustain them until they were able to establish a foothold in their new country.

# Chapter 16

Concetta was waiting excitedly at the door for Umberto and Giuliana when she heard footsteps on the stairs leading to their third floor flat. Balloons, signs and banners, in both Italian and English, were festooned about the kitchen, and in the small, neat parlor. Several of the Fassanos' closest friends from the neighborhood, many of whom were themselves Amalfi transplants, were there to greet the new arrival. The kitchen table, set against the wall between the two windows that looked out back, and a small card table placed beside it were loaded down with capacious platters of tempting food that during the long welcoming celebration for Giuliana would all be consumed with gusto by party-goers accustomed to marathon eating.

Giuliana's first hours in America started off with a gala party in her honor. It was a good sign, and it made her exceedingly happy. That night she wrote in her diary of the day's events. (Within weeks, she would be making entries in English). She described the people she met and impressions she made concerning her surroundings. In coming days, much of what she experienced would end up in letters to Donatella, her parents and brothers. She told with amusement about her aunt and uncle—they were no longer Concetta and Umberto, but Connie and Bert to everyone in the area—and about their insistence on speaking English in the house and not the Neapolitan dialect heard on the streets. Giuliana spoke in her native tongue only when conversing with the older Italian-born men and women in the neighborhood.

Over weekends and in lazy summer days to follow Giuliana met most everyone in the close-knit community that was Wooster Street. More often than not neighbors gathered on street corners or sat on stoops—stoop-sitting was a favorite summer pastime—or on bridge chairs in front of their houses to flee cramped, stifling flats on steamy days and even more oppressive nights. Day or night, there was always someone around to talk with and pass the time away. There was something to be said for going from one place where everybody knew everybody else—and everybody knew everybody else's business— to another place an ocean away where the same phenomenon seemed to apply. It led Giuliana to believe that in no time at all she would be feeling very much at home.

When she wasn't out playing with the other kids or otherwise engaged, Giuliana could often be found settled in a chair by the window of the apartment's front bedroom, her eyes glued to the sights while inhaling the sounds of the vibrant street scene below.

She watched with fascination pushcarts wending their way precariously along the cobblestone street, some loaded with fresh vegetables and fruits, others with rag remnants, young mothers with infants in strollers ready to do their bidding alongside middle-aged housewives and octogenarian grandmothers, their aprons pulled up into elongated net-like catch basins tied at either end for storing, in the few minutes it would take until they got back to their immaculately clean flats, their morning purchases.

One of her favorite sights was of old man Arturo Longo, the bread man, belting out at the top of his lungs *Vesti la giubba* from the opera *Pagliacci*, hip-hopping merrily along Wooster Street, a dozen or so freshly baked, still-hot loaves of bread nestled in paper sleeves sticking rod-like out from a burlap bag slung across his bony back. As soon as Giuliana spotted the happy-go-lucky bread man, she bolted down the stairs, caught up with Longo and, as was her custom, bought two loaves, one of which she immediately broke off the top and, before the tiny puffs of vaporous steam from the warm bread had evaporated, devoured the piece with lip-smacking delight. Longo was so loved in the neighborhood that a local bard—it was never determined who—even wrote a ditty in his honor:

He saunters up and down the street
his bag full of bread.
Sings like Caruso,
but it's old man Longo instead.

At other times when she heard the clip-clopping of horse and buggy, she rushed down the stairs with old newspapers and rags, which she sold for a few pennies to the Jewish peddler on his once-a-week drive through the neighborhood or, when her stack was ample enough, a nickel or two. Giuliana remembered that most of the kids made fun of his deep-throated accent, forgetting that their own grandmothers and grandfathers, even some of their own mothers and fathers in truth, and quite a few of their neighbors, spoke not in the Germanic accent that made "newspapers, rags" sound like "haish—paypa—regs," but spoke in a tongue unfamiliar to most non-Italians. She always felt sorry for the man.

She wished she had had a camera and microphone to record every one of these picturesque scenes and send them back home to her family in Amalfi. For now, words dutifully recorded in letters and in her rapidly expanding fact-filled diary, would have to suffice to memorialize them.

As was expected, the older folks in the neighborhood were especially forthcoming and friendly to its newest arrival. But the impression Giuliana came away with was that it was more to learn about how things were in the old country rather than any real interest in her. She had frankly expected a more welcoming reception beyond the party given in her honor on the day of her arrival, believing neighbors were ready to greet her with open arms and make her feel at home, even though home was 5,000 miles away.

Inexplicably, even girls her age but not so much the boys, given her good looks, were hesitant at first to totally befriend the ex-patriate. As far as many of them were concerned Giuliana Landini was just another interloper playing on the affections of older neighbors who felt sorry for her, being as she was separated from her family in Amalfi. Paradoxically, that did not keep them from constantly badgering her with questions as to why she had come to America and the rest of her family had stayed behind.

Giuliana had no intention of telling them, or anyone else for that matter, what the real reason was. While the ambitions she stored protectively in her heart often made her feel self-conscious, she guarded against appearing superior, especially to her contemporaries. As the new kid on the block, that was the last thing she wanted to do. At the same time she was confident that once they got to know her, any suspicions they might have once harbored regarding why she had emigrated would soon vanish.

On Monday morning, Umberto and his wife escorted their niece to the rectory at St. Michael's Church, where a meeting with the pastor, Father Dante Mongillo, and the principal of St. Michael's School, Sister Margaret Mary Cirillo, had been arranged.

Father Di Pina had written on her behalf a letter of introduction to his good friend and former seminary classmate well in advance of her arrival. It was agreed that starting the next day, and every day through the rest of the summer, Giuliana would go to the convent, a block up the street from the church, and spend several hours each day with Sister Brita Swensen, a Swedish-born linguist fluent in several languages, who would teach her English. To compensate the nuns for their generosity,

Giuliana would be required to spend two hours after her lessons ended at 2 p.m. helping the convent cook prepare evening meals for the thirty nuns who resided there. The arrangement was perfectly amenable to all concerned, since the pastor had learned from his good friend Father Di Pina that, in addition to being an excellent student, Giuliana was also a talented cook.

Lessons with Sister Brita were intense. While sympathetic to the child's needs, the nun was nevertheless a firm and demanding taskmaster. She told Giuliana she'd have to work very hard to be ready in a little over two months' time to meet the requirements of seventh grade level work, and in order to do it she would have to learn English quickly, and thoroughly. The nun approached her assignment as if her pupil were entering first grade instead of the seventh, driving home forcefully the rudiments of English grammar: sentence structure; tenses; nouns, pronouns, adjectives and adverbs; active and passive verbs; the entire gamut. The last hour, after lunch, was spent on pronunciation, which Giuliana thoroughly enjoyed; it was a lot easier for her than mastering English grammar.

To speed up the process of learning the new language, Sister Brita had the young student do practice lessons at home, which included standing in front of a mirror, mouthing and repeating words aloud. "This will help with the eventual elimination of your accent," the nun said. She also recommended that Giuliana listen to the radio, read the newspaper every day and go to the movies, which Giuliana did as often as she could, finding the suggestion not in the least distasteful. Umberto and Concetta, who were in their own way still trying mightily after three years to learn to speak and write proper English, were amazed at their niece's progress, and were soon her own enthusiastic pupils. Giuliana's neighbors, too, were impressed. Before the summer was out, a discernible comfort level between herself and her peers had been reached, and before long she was a regular and welcome participant in all group activities.

*   *   *

Giuliana soon learned that unlike in Amalfi, work dominated the lives of Americans. Amalfitani, like most foreigners who came here, fell right in line. Umberto, by now a completely changed man from the one who in bygone days in Italy looked upon work as an intrusion upon his leisure, was no different: he held down a full-time day job, working weekdays from 7 a.m. to 3 p.m. at the Sperry & Barnes meat-packing plant, before going off to his night restaurant job, two hours later, which lasted from 5 p.m. to 10 p.m., and to midnight on Fridays and Saturdays. The restaurant was closed Sundays.

As for Concetta, she had only recently started working at home taking in laundry—washing and ironing men's shirts, ladies' blouses and dresses, as well as curtains, drapes and linens, her specialty—after having left in less than a year a job in one of New Haven's dress and shirt factories that serviced the nearby New York garment industry.

As the Great Depression abated, all over lower-end areas of the impoverished city like Wooster Square, once thriving corset factories that stood empty and abandoned in the face of steady manufacturing decline slowly came back to life. Exploitive garment manufacturers, with an eye toward reviving a once flourishing carriage trade, began snapping up prime properties for next to nothing and populating their newly acquired rundown buildings with women—they represented eighty percent of the garment workforce—desperate enough to toil for starvation wages in deplorable, often hazardous work-shop conditions.

The workers were mostly first generation Italian-American teenage girls, some as young as thirteen or fourteen, toiling alongside their

110

immigrant mothers. Very often they worked fifteen hours a day, plus a half day on Sunday, for $4.50 per week, all to help supplement already meager family incomes while sacrificing their dreams of an education and its concomitant by-product, a more genteel, satisfying career in an office. As a seasoned seamstress, Concetta, and other women on the higher end of the pay scale—sewers, cutters, markers—took home the grand sum of $6.00 per week. Only after several workers came down with a mysterious illness that swept the shop's floors did Concetta quit her job, much to the relief of both Umberto and Giuliana.

This episode, coupled with the fire that took place on Franklin Street a few months earlier killing ten workers in the New Haven Quilt and Pad Company, had a particularly chilling and sobering effect on Umberto's attitude toward work in the United States. He began to question whether everything he had heard about the country's reputation for economic opportunity was all that it was cracked up to be. Or that it ever existed in the first place, given what his wife and others like her had to endure for the sake of earning "a measly few dollars." How lucky that Giuliana would soon be in college, he told himself. It wasn't that he was naïve about how things actually worked in America: money doesn't grow on trees and the streets are not paved with gold, as some may have thought. But he wasn't prepared for just how callous and cold-hearted was the workplace in his adopted city. To begin with, jobs were not all that plentiful, there was always fierce competition for those that did become available, and more often than not the work was physically demanding, boring and low paying.

Umberto also soon learned that since the turn of the century the Irish held a stranglehold over the city of New Haven. Having emigrated to America many years before the Italians began to arrive in waves to its shores in the late 1800s, the emboldened Irish, despite being in the minority to Italians in terms of population, not only controlled city hall, but all of the desirable municipal jobs—in the schools, fire department, police department, post office and other areas where political clout and influence peddling was the coin of the realm. Except for a small number of educated Italians in the professions—doctors, lawyers, engineers— Italians occupied a sizable majority of the blue collar factory jobs that dominated the workplace.

It wouldn't be until 1948 when the first Italian mayor, a Republican, was elected that a changing demographic profile of the New Haven workplace would emerge. (Many Italians in the city were forced to change parties in order to wrest control from the Democrat party-dominated Irish to whom, up to this point, they had had no other recourse than to meekly acquiesce. Only after finally seizing an opportunity to back one of their own candidates for mayor, his Republican Party affiliation notwithstanding, were they able to gain a place at the table of opportunity they felt they rightfully deserved.)

For the time being, however, working class Italians like Umberto Fassano, his friend Paolo Giordano and others like them were compelled to turn not to city hall for economic opportunity but to the Italian mutual aid societies that sprang up around the early 1900s, and after. The societies provided safety, comfort and protection from an unfamiliar and potentially hostile world, while giving the Italian community a sense of identity, social solidarity and empowerment. Most, like the Santa Maria Maddalena and Santa Andrea Societies, were affiliated with churches in the area, like St. Michael's, where the Fassanos and most families in and around Wooster Square worshipped.

By 1930 there were some eighty active groups in New Haven that formed a critical support network for a combined membership of over ten thousand immigrants. More than just social centers for men, and later women, they charged modest club dues that provided death and sickness benefits when needed, since the majority of its members had no insurance of any kind. Also, when a member passed away, his or her family received a burial stipend of fifty dollars from the pool of club dues. The amount, an otherwise major expense for poor families, was sufficient to provide a proper burial, which carried great religious significance for the proud Italians.

While Umberto was more than appreciative of the St. Andrew Society's efforts in helping him secure work in the meat-packing plant, he was certain that neither his day nor his night job was ever going to satisfy his burning ambition and fiercely independent spirit. Being in business for himself, he concluded, was the only possible way to succeed in America. And even then, given the harsh realities outside his control that were likely to ensue, he wasn't absolutely certain whether the sacrifices he would have to make to pursue his dream, whatever form it would take, would in the end translate into success.

Yet he realized that no matter what he wound up doing long term, he would have to seize the opportunity just as soon as the right one came along and be willing to put in the time, effort and dedication required. And do whatever it took for him to be better than he ever thought he could possibly be in order to have any chance of succeeding.

Among other questions uppermost in his mind was whether the place he and his wife had chosen to live was the right one. Was this the America he had bargained for? Putting aside the stark and obvious differences between Amalfi and New Haven, it didn't take long for him to see that there was an unmistakable sameness, a glaring lack of diversity in his new surroundings, which especially bothered him. How could it be, he kept asking himself, that he was still living amongst many of the very same people he had sought so hard in Italy to escape—mostly blue collar, second generation Italian-Americans who, like their brothers and sisters an ocean away, seemed unable or unwilling to dream bigger dreams, to strive for greater accomplishments, to have richer lives than the ones they thought they were living, but had in fact long abandoned any hopes of ever achieving? What he found especially galling was that many of them resisted the need to change anything at all in their lives.

Where were all the other people—Italians and non-Italians alike—with a different perspective on life? These were the people he desperately wanted to meet. Yet if he knew where to find them, did he have even the remotest chance of entering their world?

# Chapter 17

Weekends were special for Giuliana, times for new discoveries, new pleasures. Most Saturdays she and her uncle, to whom she had begun to forge a deep attachment, kept a standing date to do something exciting together. When they both lived in Amalfi, except during family functions, Giuliana and her uncle seldom saw much of each other. But now in America, they were more like father and daughter; they relished each other's company. Umberto was more than happy to oblige his always receptive niece in her desire to do all the things that were second nature to her new friends and classmates. One she particularly enjoyed was a day at the shore. She loved running up and down the pock-marked, dimpled beach area along the edge of the water. The feel of the sand—soft, warm and golden—that sifted through her toes never failed to buoy her spirits: she was as carefree as the sea gulls that always seemed to swoop down beside her. She admitted to friends that "as beautiful as the Amalfi coast is, there are no long stretches of sandy beaches like this back home."

But her favorite part of the outing, even more than the beach itself, was the forty-minute open trolley car ride that took them along tracks that ran from Chapel Street, a block and a half away from their flat, all the way to the public beach at Lighthouse Point. The soothing breezes off the waters of the Long Island Sound as the trolley got closer to its destination delighted Giuliana. It made her think of ferry boat trips her mother took her on to Positano or Salerno to call on shops where Maria sold her linens.

Not long after Giuliana had settled in Umberto took his niece to a place he knew she would love, and to which she would return many times over the years—Savin Rock, the gigantic amusement park on the water in West Haven. They spent the better part of a Saturday on their first outing there. In addition to going on as many rides as she could possibly handle (the Whip and Bumper Cars were her favorites), she happily indulged in the Rock's pre-eminent lure—the food. In the space of six hours or so, she ate a Jimmy's famous split hot dog—with plenty of mustard, relish and sauerkraut—a scrumptious, buttered lobster roll, and one of the park's most popular eating delights, a soft-shell crab sandwich on white toast, all new taste treats for the food-loving girl. The shellfish dishes she had at the shore over the years gave her a treasure trove of recipe ideas.

Sunday afternoons were reserved for family outings, mostly walking trips through other parts of the city; like a majority of the people in the neighborhood, the Fassanos did not as yet own a car. Having been reared in an entirely homogeneous environment, Giuliana marveled at how each neighborhood in this city of some hundred-seventy-five thousand inhabitants—Irish, Jewish, Polish, Italian, Negro—was completely different from every other. With, among other things, its own ethnic flavor in food, which she sampled with enthusiastic pleasure.

But the one attraction she never tired of, where the family outing seemed to almost invariably end, was at the Yale campus in the center of town. This was her initial exposure to an institution of higher learning (even if she got to see it only from the outside), and it left her completely in awe. She couldn't get over Yale's sprawling and dominating presence in the down-town area, nor the massiveness of its Gothic stone buildings with their imposing spires that stretched for blocks around corner after another. One day after entering a portal just off the bustling street, she wrote in her diary, amended to read some years later: "It was like being in another world . . . a field of green, cross-hatched by sidewalks running diagonally from the corners of what I later learned was called the quad . . . a quiet serene place where words in Latin were inscribed over the ivy-covered dormitory entranceways. How I love the place."

The historic New Haven Town Green, the focal point of the downtown area, was another place Giuliana came to love. She learned from a book on New Haven she took out of the public library, that the sixteen-acre bifurcated park was originally the town's major marketplace in the early 1700s and later, during the Revolutionary War, a military training ground as well as the place for the public punishment of criminals.

Before leaving the area Giuliana and Umberto always stopped for an ice cream cone from the Good Humor truck stationed at the neck of the Green before taking in the sights that surrounded its four sides: the retail shops and restaurants on Chapel Street; the architecturally imposing Federal Court House and library on Elm Street; City Hall and the Post Office on Church Street; and the three historic Protestant churches erected during the War of 1812 that dominated the landscape on Temple Street—Trinity Episcopal, Center Church, and United Church. She became attached to each of them, even though they weren't Catholic.

As Giuliana's first summer in America wore on, her letters to Camilla—half in Italian, half in English—became more effusive with each writing: "I'm liking my new surroundings. The people are friendly. Everybody is now very nice to me, but I miss my family and friends so much. I miss you, too. There's always something exciting going on in our neighborhood. I was in New Haven only a few days when I got to experience my first big celebration, Fourth of July. Independence Day is what they call it here. I remember you telling me about it. I was so excited. There was a big neighborhood party, it lasted all day, even through the night. It took place in the big open yard behind the houses on my street and the ones behind the street around the corner. There was so much food, and we played games all day long. Americans eat too much, but I'm ashamed to say I love it. When it got dark we had wonderful fireworks, they lit up and colored the sky. It was really spectacular."

In a glowing letter she wrote to her family about the feast of St. Andrew, celebrated in New Haven every June 27 since 1903 on the very same day the "feast of the miracle" is commemorated with great pomp and ceremony in New Haven's sister town of Amalfi, these were her impressions:

"This is a sacred feast, a festival, just like back home," Giuliana wrote, remembering well how much the feast in Amalfi meant to the entire town. "It lasted four days, Thursday to Sunday, from late afternoon until the night. Colorful lights hung over our street from one end to the other, and a lot of people came from all over Connecticut. There were stands set up in two empty lots, some with food—my favorite were the sausage, pepper and onion sandwiches. Others had games for adults and kids. Some stands had gambling . . . they were always busy. Everybody had a wonderful time. They raised money for the St. Andrew Society and for our church.

"But as much as I enjoyed the feast, the best part took place on Sunday after Mass. It reminded me of Amalfi. Men took the statue of St. Andrew out of the church and carried it on a long platform through the streets. Over 100 men and women of the society marched behind. The women and girls were all dressed in white, the men and boys had on blue pants and white shirts. Behind them was a large band of musicians from Brooklyn, New York. They played beautiful music from famous Italian operas. Behind them marching in the procession were a lot of famous New Haven people, like the mayor and other politicians. The presidents of all the other societies in the city that look after Italians were there, too. Just like in Amalfi, a beautiful silk cape was draped around St. Andrew. The statue was carried through the streets, and people pinned dollar bills to it. As I watched the procession, I couldn't help thinking about what was going on in another place. Will I ever see Amalfi again, Camilla? The thought made me very sad."

In a later letter to Camilla, Giuliana wrote: "We had another big celebration on Labor Day . . . do you know anything about that holiday? I'm told it's always the first Monday of September, it honors the American worker. Everybody's off that day. It marks the end of summer, too. They even closed off the side street around the corner. We all had a wonderful time, especially Uncle Umberto and Aunt Concetta. But my favorite time was when the women "put up" their tomatoes. They did it all outdoors . . . peeled and boiled the tomatoes . . . sterilized the jars. The aroma in the neighborhood lasted for days. It felt like I was back in Italy. It made me very homesick. But then I received a nice long letter from Mama . . . everybody back home is well, thank God. Hope your family is, too. Please let me know when you and Jennifer are coming to New Haven. I can't wait."

Giuliana then added a postscript: "By the way, you're right about baseball, Camilla. It is an exciting game. Hope next summer when you come back to New York, I'll be able to come and visit you and you can take me to a Yankee game. Here in our neighborhood it's all people ever talk about, baseball and the New York Yankees. And now Joe DiMaggio. What did you call him . . . the Yankee Clipper? Everybody talks about his hitting streak, even Uncle Umberto and Paolo Giordano. I think it's more because he's Italian than anything else. Like everybody here, they're both big baseball fans . . . they seem to understand the game pretty well. You stroll through the streets, all you hear are Yankee games blaring on the radio. It reminds me of the soccer games Papa and my brothers used to listen to every weekend. I'm getting to like baseball very much. I enjoy watching the boys play baseball. Girls don't play it . . . I wish they did."

Toward the middle of August, Camilla wrote to say that she and Jennifer would be arriving in New Haven on the 20th. "I plan to stay a week . . . made arrangements to meet with Father Mongillo and Sister Cirillo at St. Michael's . . . love to have you join me. I'll tell you all about my summer when I see you. I've booked passage to Italy September 1. Arrive in Amalfi just in time for school. Can't wait to see you. Love, Camilla."

When the two women met up days later they both were amazed at how different each of them looked since arriving in America only weeks ago, the older woman younger, the young girl older. And both had taken on an air unmistakably American, not only in speech, but in dress, mannerisms, even attitude. Giuliana was uncertain whether Camilla would like or approve of the third-floor flat she and her uncle and aunt were sharing, but she should not have worried. Living as she had for the past two months in her friend Margaret Watson's non-elevator fifth floor walk-up in Greenwich Village, Camilla declared the Fassano "digs" to be more than adequate. Charming, in fact, is how she put it, lack of a proper bathroom aside.

After spending an hour or so with Concetta and Giuliana over morning coffee—Umberto was at his day job at Sperry & Barnes—Camilla, with her young friend in tow, went to Sacred Heart Convent to meet with St. Michael School's principal and teachers, and later with Pastor Mongillo. It was a typical August day—hazy, hot and humid—and as the two women approached the tree-shaded Columbus Green on whose perimeters the church and the convent were located, they chose a bench, Giuliana's favorite, to sit and chat for a few minutes, their appointment a good twenty minutes off.

"I am having the time of my life in New York," Camilla said excitedly. "Sometimes I feel so overwhelmed with how much fun I'm having that I have to rein myself in. A lot of people are away this time of year, especially on weekends, so it's much easier to get around the city. And Margaret, of course, has been absolutely fabulous; she's come to learn the city really well. There isn't anything I want to see or do that she isn't amenable to. She took me one day to where she works part time, the New York Public Library . . . her major in college was library science . . . it's the most fabulous library I've ever been in. I must take you there one day, you'll absolutely love it.

"I spend most days touring the city alone, on foot, and take the underground subway only when a place I want to visit is too far away to walk. I've visited just about all the high spots that have any historical significance: where George Washington was inaugurated the country's first president; Theodore Roosevelt's birthplace; Trinity Church where Alexander Hamilton is buried; City Hall; Battery Park; the Cloisters and a lot of other places you're likely to learn about in your history classes.

"The real highlight of the summer were trips Margaret and I took to Philadelphia and Boston. We got to spend a lot of time with Jennifer, who turned out to be the perfect guide in her hometown. Then we went on to Boston. Someday I hope I'll be able to spend more time in these two absolutely fabulous cities. The United States got its start, for all intents and purposes, in these two famous places so one can't spend enough time learning the significant role each of them played in the birth of the country.

"As you might imagine, Giuliana, I've taken copious notes on what I've seen and learned. You might be interested to know that I've actually written articles—two on each city. I sent them to the Travel Editor at the *Glasgow Times*. You won't believe this, but the paper not only actually published them, they encouraged me to write more of the same. My thought is that over the next four summers, I plan to travel to a different part of the United States and write about my impressions of each area. The *Times* has already given me the go-ahead, even suggested that once I've covered enough cities of historical importance they would gladly assist me in getting the work published in book form. They believe it would make a good travel guide for Europeans traveling to America. They also think it might be a nice companion piece to some of the other significant books written on U.S. history."

Giuliana was duly impressed. She told Camilla how much she was enjoying the four-volume Pictorial History of the USA Camilla gave her the day they arrived in New York. "What I wouldn't give to go with you on one of those trips," Giuliana said.

"Perhaps one day you will," said Camilla.

\*　　\*　　\*

On Sunday, Camilla, Jennifer and her fiancé, Doctor Langdon Davies, arrived at the Fassanos' for a traditional mid-afternoon meal. It had been four years since Camilla had last seen Umberto and Concetta, the summer before they left for America. Warm greetings were exchanged, as well as a number of small but thoughtful gifts. Camilla gave the Fassanos a five by seven inch framed print of the Manhattan skyline, and to Giuliana a book describing the purchase in 1626 of Manhattan Island by the Dutch from the Indians for a bunch of trinkets worth the equivalent of $24. Jennifer presented the Fassanos with a set of four hand-crocheted silk doilies, and Giuliana an accordion set of twelve color postcards, each depicting a famous New York City attraction, which in days to come Giuliana would take great pleasure in studying, hoping that sometime in the near future she would get to see each of them in person. The Fassanos gave Camilla a set of faux pearl rosary beads, and to Jennifer and Langdon each a simple wooden cross, sans icon. To all gathered at the happy table, Giuliana gave her culinary skills.

Giuliana was given free reign by her aunt and uncle to prepare whatever she wanted to for the Sunday dinner without interference, or help, from either of them. They had eaten enough of their niece's meals these last two months to know that whatever she had a mind to cook would be something to savor—dishes one craves, say, after a trying day fighting fatigue at a sewing table on the floor of a crowded garment factory, as in Concetta's case, or working a noisy, dirty assembly line at a meat-packing plant, as in Umberto's.

Shortly after the guests had arrived, settled in, and been seated at the kitchen table—adorned with Concetta's best table linen, silverware and a bouquet of fresh cut flowers immediately removed once the serious matter of dining had gotten underway—a chilled glass of sparkling Prosecco was placed before each guest along with Giuliana's first course: on each plate sat three oval-shaped rounds of Italian bread, lightly toasted. Each piece had been rubbed with olive oil, fresh tomatoes and oregano. The mound of ever-so-finely sliced pieces of roasted eggplant, zucchini and red bell pepper, enhanced with a drizzle of virgin olive oil, a touch of grated pecorino cheese and a sprinkle of pepper flakes, was then lightly broiled. The toasted *bruschetta* surrounded slices of paper thin sirloin carpaccio, coated with a touch of oil, a few caper berries and chopped Vidalia onions. Langdon Davies, who brought two of his best bottles of Amarone from his extensive wine collection, declared that had they stopped right there, what they had just eaten would have constituted a memorable meal in its own right.

With the party engaged in animated conversation, Giuliana excused herself and went to the stove to make ready the next course. On the counter next to the stove sat a flat rectangular baking pan containing what looked to be six pies, square in shape, approximately four by four inches, not flat but slightly raised. The shell was made of wide strips of homemade pasta that covered the top and bottom of the large ravioli, or *tortellone*. Concealed in the perfectly shaped shell was a mound of fresh ricotta, parsley and a single raw egg that, once exposed to the heat, blistered, burst and ran through the interior. A sauce made from veal and pork bones that had been simmering on the stove in a deep pot was then drizzled over the pasta just before the tray was put in the oven. Giuliana ladled a more generous amount of sauce after the *tortellone* had been baked and were ready to be served. Grated pecorino and fresh ground pepper finished off the dish.

The look of delight that spread across the faces of the assembled guests as they took their first bite even surprised the youthful chef. Umberto, the beneficiary of his mother Donatella's and sister Maria's excellent cooking for most of his life, and now his own wife's, had never had anything remotely as imaginative, or delicious, as the stuffed *tortellone* with the oozing raw egg yolk. And he did not hesitate to tell his niece, as did everyone else at the table, all of whom beseeched Giuliana for another taste but were emphatically told that one was all they were getting.

Where had an eleven-year-old, a child really, achieved such enormous cooking skills? The question became even more pertinent with the serving of the entrée, at which time the oohing and aahing that filled the air throughout the meal reached a crescendo. It proved to be Giuliana's piece de resistance: roasted guinea hen with a sage bread stuffing and flecks of hot Italian sausage and slivers of Portobello mushrooms; the dish was accompanied by a wedge of semi-soft polenta. A gravy of reduced veal stock with Marsala sat in a small boat for spooning over the tender, succulent meat. A bowl of spinach, sautéed in virgin olive oil and garlic with roasted pine nuts, was set in the center of the table to be served family style.

When the plating had been completed, Giuliana proposed a toast, having received the nodded approval of her uncle to do the honors. She raised her glass, containing a sip or two of the wonderful Amarone, and exclaimed that today, surrounded by family and friends, was one of the happiest she had experienced so far in America, and that she looked forward to many more with those gathered at table. Langdon Davies quickly followed with his own pronouncement: he said the entire meal was unquestionably the best he had ever had—Camilla and Jennifer heartedly agreed—and offered the promise that if Giuliana ever thought about opening a restaurant, an idea he enthusiastically endorsed, he would definitely be its first delighted patron.

That evening, just before retiring, Umberto told his wife that he had had an epiphany midway through the meal earlier that afternoon: the business they would one day start would not be the dry cleaning laundry they had finally agreed on, but a restaurant. He would be the manager, Concetta would work the front of the house, and the kitchen would be anchored by someone, hopefully, as talented as Giuliana.

# Chapter 18

Giuliana was sad to see her first summer in the United States fly by so quickly. It ended much the same way it had begun a little over two months ago—with a gala neighborhood party, this one to honor the American worker. Along with other neighborhood outdoor celebrations that took place through the summer, what she was going to especially miss were her lessons with Sister Brita learning English, and working in the convent kitchen with kindly Sister Katherine, "the loveliest woman you'll ever meet, but not a very good cook," Giuliana wrote in her diary. "I want so much to cook an entire meal all by myself for the convent just to show her how it's done, but I can't bring myself to suggest it . . . I don't want to hurt her feelings."

All things considered, Giuliana couldn't wait for school to start. She was looking forward to the challenges she had facing her—new school, new teachers, new subjects, new classmates. Above all, being taught in a new language she was only now beginning to feel somewhat comfortable in. Her rosy optimism aside, it took Giuliana all of a week to learn that school in America was radically different than school in Italy. She was tested prior to start of the fall term to determine whether she could do 7th-grade-level work.

Allowing for a still tenuous grasp of English grammar, she did well enough to satisfy the nuns that she'd have little trouble meeting the school's and the state's rigid requirements.

But what she wasn't prepared for was the fierce competition that took place in the classroom. In Italy, she had always been the brightest pupil in her class, but here she found other students to be as smart as, if not smarter than she. They constantly vied for the stars Sister Margarita

Mary James, the young energetic spitfire of a teacher, famously known in the school as "the first name nun," doled out not very liberally to all but those students who met her lofty standards. This made Giuliana, who had issues with being considered less than the best student in the class, work harder than she had ever had to in order to catch up to her American classmates, whom she acknowledged to be much further along in some areas academically than her Italian counterparts.

Before the first half of the year had been completed, Giuliana had not only caught up but had assumed what she considered to be her rightful place in the class. As her grasp of English improved, and her accent became less pronounced, she became more confident about being called upon or raising her hand in class. Before long, not surprisingly, her classmates as well as her teacher had completely warmed up to the young foreigner with the winning smile. Her once shaky confidence had been completely restored, and by the time autumn rolled around, Giuliana Landini was just another seventh grader.

\* \* \*

During the dinner Langdon Davies and his fiancé, Jennifer Kirby, attended at the Fassanos' in late August, the young doctor, just months away from completing his first year of residency at New Haven Hospital, promised that on his first free weekend he and Jennifer would take Giuliana on a tour of the Yale campus, an invitation that thrilled the young girl. As it turned out, the outing was to occur on the last Saturday in September, which meant that she would have to forego her weekly Saturday "date" with her uncle, an obligation Umberto gladly relinquished, knowing how much his niece relished learning about and seeing more of the great university.

As luck would have it, the tour actually took place on Sunday instead, Saturday having been reserved quite unexpectedly for a surprise Giuliana later couldn't stop telling her friends about for weeks: attendance at the football game between arch rivals Yale and Harvard in Yale Bowl. The weekend made for the most lengthy and descriptive entry in the young girl's diary to date:

"I wish I had the right words to describe just how wonderful these two days were. After Uncle Umberto left me off at the New Haven Green with Langdon and Jennifer at 11 a.m., the three of us got on an open trolley car that took us to the Yale Bowl. It's shaped like a bowl, that's why they call it that. We were packed together like sardines on the trolley . . . a lot of the Yale students and their dates hopped on the trolley as it chugged along the tracks. Quite a few of the girls were in fur coats and carried large, beautiful yellow flowers on a stick—pompoms, Langdon called them. (In a letter to her parents she told them she could easily see herself similarly outfitted, la-di-daing all over the Yale campus with some rich undergraduate on her arm.) When we reached the stadium I couldn't believe how big it was. Langdon said it seated over seventy-five-thousand people. The field was a beautiful emerald green, very big, with horizontal white stripes running across it. There were long vertical poles—goalposts Langdon called them—at each end of the field. All through the game, Langdon and Jennifer explained to me what was happening on the field between the two teams. All the players were dressed in uniforms and had helmets on their heads. There were a lot of them—well over fifty on each team, Langdon said.

"But what I loved the most were the marching bands, especially Yale's. All the men were dressed alike, not in a uniform like Harvard's. They wore blue jackets—blazers, Langdon called them—and charcoal gray trousers, white shirts, a blue stripped tie and white buckskin shoes.

They looked terrific. Leading the band that marched on the field before the game and during halftime intermission—Langdon called it—were a bunch of cheerleaders dressed in white. Their sweaters had a big "Y" on the front. One of them had a dog on a leash, a funny-looking, pug-nosed dog—a bulldog Langdon said it was—which was the nickname of the Yale football team. I wondered about that. The band played all these college songs that everyone in the stadium seemed to know, and when one team or the other scored—a touchdown, Langdon said it was—the band would play loudly and the cheerleaders would do all kinds of acrobatics, including summersaults. Yale won the game, which made Langdon happy. The experience of being at an American college football game is one I'll never forget."

Giuliana's Sunday excursion to the Yale campus proved to be just as memorable. There was no one better than Langdon Davies to offer up his services as guide. He knew practically every foot of the three-hundred-ten-acre Yale campus that stretched here, there and everywhere across the city's downtown, having visited the school scores of times from when he was a young boy. His grandfather, father and uncle, all pulmonary specialists in practice together in Wilmington, Delaware, were Yale graduates, and over the years one or the other would take young Langdon to a football game or a reunion.

Those experiences, plus his own ten years in New Haven, made him familiar with every part of the city and the surrounding areas, including Wooster Street, where he and thousands of Yalies regularly went to attend special neighborhood celebrations or eat pizza at Sally's or Pepe's, the most famous pizza parlors in Connecticut. He also knew a good deal about the significant role New Haven played in the American Revolution, as well as the contribution to the city Yale University had made since its founding in 1718.

Within a matter of six hours the doctor, his fiancé and their young companion visited the Sterling Memorial Library, the Payne Whitney Gym, Woolsey Hall, Battell Chapel, Hillhouse Avenue, where the president of the university resided, the Yale Co-op, the Yale Drama School, and the School of Architecture, which Giuliana especially wanted to see.

As an added bonus, Langdon took Giuliana to Calhoun College, where he'd spent his undergraduate days. Langdon pointed out that beginning in 1930 the university was broken up into twelve individual residence colleges patterned after the great British universities, Oxford and Cambridge. He told Giuliana that "each college surrounds a courtyard, occupies up to a city block, and is self-sustaining: students live, eat, socialize and pursue a variety of academic and extracurricular activities there."

After introducing Giuliana to the compact but comfortable suite he and two roommates shared for four years, Langdon took his guests to lunch. There, in the college's spacious and stately Edwardian dining hall, with its oak-paneled walls, vaulted ceilings and wood-burning marble fireplace at either end, Giuliana was served a lunch of turkey croquettes with white gravy, mashed potatoes and peas, Parker House rolls, butter, two glasses of milk and a brownie. She ate with gusto everything on her plate. Sensing her host's surprise, Giuliana explained that it was important that she become accustomed to the American diet. If that meant eating food completely foreign to her . . . well, so be it.

As for what she saw of the university and her overall impression of the campus and its facilities, the girl was smitten. When told that only men attended Yale—women were allowed to pursue degrees only in the graduate school at the time—Giuliana gave out with a groan. However disappointed she may have seemed over this apparent snub, she would nevertheless maintain a life-long love of the famous university.

# Chapter 19

In honor of Columbus Day, which was to take place on Friday, October 12, Sister Margarita spent several history periods reviewing the events that took place in Europe before, during and after Columbus's historic voyage to the new world. While the students in her class were familiar with this period of history, Giuliana was more than happy to have been given a chance to learn about this seminal event, one she had first heard about from Camilla. She was also looking forward with much anticipation to the colorful parade that marched through town and ended up at Columbus Green in Wooster Square. The holiday meant a day off from school for the children and an abbreviated work day for tens of thousands of Italians anxious to show off their ethnic pride in the enormous accomplishments of one of their own.

Giuliana noticed that each day as she and her friends walked through Columbus Green on their way to school men from the city's Public Works Department were sprucing up the grounds and hanging red, white and blue bunting at various intervals along the wrought iron railings that fenced the park and, later that first week in October, erecting a speakers' platform adjacent to the statue of Columbus facing Chapel Street that would accommodate the host of dignitaries thus assembled. Most were politicians, of one stripe or another, who, in their remarks, shamelessly burnished their own image by extolling, by way of the most exaggerated oratory, the great explorer's historic feat, the American way of life and, receiving the most emphasis, the formidable accomplishments of the city's growing Italian population. Giuliana was also told by her friends that after the speeches there would be entertainment, mostly by Italian-American stars. This year Vic Damone and the great Jimmy Durante were slated to perform, along with Tony Martin, who was generally thought to be Italian but was in fact Jewish. Giuliana never heard of any of them, but it didn't matter. She couldn't wait.

But for her, sadly, the experience was not to be. She would have to wait until the following year to take part in her first Columbus Day celebration. For just after dinner on Wednesday evening, less than two days before the parade, a knock at the door brought Antoinette Giordano to the Fassano flat.

"Mother Campion called from the convent a few minutes ago and asked if I would get this message to you," Antoinette explained to Concetta who, like many others in the neighborhood, did not as yet have a telephone. "If possible, she would like to see you and Giuliana at the convent this evening. She said it was nothing to be alarmed about, but she did say she would appreciate it if the two of you could go there as soon as possible. If you'd like, I would be happy to go with you."

When they arrived at the convent, Giuliana and her aunt were ushered into Mother Campion's office; the convent's head nun was standing at the door anxiously waiting to greet them. Antoinette remained in the visitor's lounge.

"Please be seated, Mrs. Fassano . . . you, too, Giuliana" she said from her desk. "Something of a crisis has developed in just the last hours. Sister Katherine, our convent cook, has come down with a severe intestinal virus. The doctor just this minute left . . . he says she won't be back on her feet for at least several days."

The blank stare on the faces of Giuliana and Concetta prompted Mother Campion to say: "I know you both must be wondering what Sister's illness has to do with you, but the fact is there is a tangible connection." (The nun had a penchant for using big words even when speaking to those she knew would be unfamiliar with them.)

"Bishop Serratelli, who heads the archdiocese of Hartford, under whose aegis our parish and school fall, is coming to New Haven on Monday, Columbus Day, to take part in the ceremonies. While in New Haven he plans to visit all the parochial schools in the area the rest of the week. He's coming to St. Michael's on Friday. You see, the Bishop has not had a chance to visit the school since we moved into our new building this past September, and he's been most anxious to do so. He and his assistant, Monsignor Declan Murray, would also like to meet with Father Mongillo, myself and Sister Margaret Mary, our school principal; they asked if we'd give them an update on the progress we have made this past year. Later that evening we plan to have the bishop and monsignor for dinner at the convent. In addition to myself and those mentioned, we've also invited Anthony and Carmela Amatruda, members of St. Andrew's Society, whom I'm sure you know. They were instrumental in helping raise money in the parish for construction of our new school."

Then without a moment's hesitation, she added: "I would like you, Giuliana, with your permission of course, Mrs. Fassano, to prepare and cook this important dinner. I realize full well you have less than two days to begin your preparations," she said, looking directly at the child, "but I believe if anyone can do it, you can."

Concetta shifted uneasily in her chair while casting a sideward glance at her niece. "With all due respect, Mother Campion, don't you think this is a little bit too much responsibility for my niece, and on such short notice?" Concetta pleaded with downcast eyes. "After all, she's only a child."

"But an unusually gifted one, I dare say, Mrs. Fassano," the nun countered, cheerfully. "During the nine or ten weeks this past summer that Giuliana assisted in the convent kitchen, I'm happy to say that our meals—and this is in no way a criticism of Sister Katherine, mind you—improved immeasurably. I'm also aware that her cooking skills are those of someone well beyond her years, beyond those of many an accomplished cook of any age, I might add."

Mother Campion rose from her desk and went to a side table. On it were several books and a stack of papers. She took from the neat pile a folder that sat on top, returned to her desk and from it removed what looked like a neatly written composition paper. She turned the paper around so that both Giuliana and her aunt would have no trouble seeing the A+ in red and the two gold stars at the top, plus a teacher's written commentary, also in red, next to it. Holding the paper high in her hand, Mother Campion explained that the composition was an assignment Giuliana had written for Sister Margarita's 7th grade class. The teacher had asked her students shortly after school started six weeks ago to describe the most memorable experience they had had during the past summer.

"Giuliana wrote about the dinner she prepared for you and Mr. Fassano, the young doctor and his fiancé, and her Scottish friend, the teacher. She described in the most elaborate detail the entire meal, leaving absolutely nothing out," said Mother Campion, grinning from ear to ear, the mischievous glint in her eyes darting from Concetta to Giuliana.

"She also wrote about the two individuals in her life in Italy most responsible for, how should I put it, her reverence for food and its preparation. I must tell you, Mrs. Fassano, in this convent Giuliana is more of a celebrity than you can possibly believe." Concetta brought her hand to her mouth to conceal her obvious delight; Giuliana lowered her head, blushing like the young schoolgirl she was.

That evening, Giuliana asked her aunt for permission to stay up a half hour later than her usual 9:30 p.m. curfew. She sat at the tiny desk in her room flipping through Magdalena Vertucci's recipes, jotting down notes and ruminating on the challenge that lay before her. Just before turning out the light, she had pretty much settled on a menu. The excitement she felt at that moment kept her awake for some time. She realized she'd have to forego the Columbus Day parade and festivities— "there's always next year"—but what really kept her adrenaline flowing was the prospect of cooking for people she didn't know. Up to now, Giuliana had exhibited her culinary skills exclusively for family and friends, never strangers. She told herself she'd have to put forward her best effort. The thought, rather than frightening the unflappable Giuliana, actually excited her. She looked up at the painting on the wall across from her bed and prayed to St. Lucy, knowing that the saint would, as always, "see" her through this newest challenge.

In school the next morning Giuliana acted as though nothing unusual had happened the night before. Or was about to happen a night later. Instead of going home for lunch as she normally did when morning classes concluded, Giuliana went directly to the convent kitchen to begin prepping for Friday night's dinner. She had been excused from her afternoon classes and from a favorite Thursday after-school activity—an hour of volleyball in the gym, a sport she had grown fond of and disliked missing.

When she arrived just before noon, she was met at the door by Celeste Harrington, a nineteen-year-old postulate with whom Giuliana had struck up a friendship during her summer days at the convent. Celeste occasionally assisted Sister Katherine for a half hour or so in the kitchen, though her main responsibility was helping care for children in the orphanage the nuns ran in a separate facility next to the convent. Giuliana had long been fascinated by women like Celeste who renounce their worldly comforts in pursuit of the more transcendent goals of the cloistered life, but was always reluctant to bring up the subject while Sister Catherine was around.

But now that she was alone in the kitchen with Celeste—someone not much older than she and someone with whom she could easily communicate—Giuliana was anxious to find out what it was exactly that attracted mostly young girls to this vocation. She also wanted to learn what it took in time and preparation for a young woman to become a nun.

"I wanted to be a nun as far back as I can remember," Celeste explained, as the two girls went about planning for the big meal the next evening. "My parents, however, especially my father, would have preferred I pursue, how should I put it, a different line of work. He had other ideas for his only daughter: he wanted me to have a brilliant, earthly career." (She couldn't suppress a girlish giggle as she said it.) "But they finally succumbed when they realized I had my mind set. They became completely accepting of my career path once they convinced themselves that my calling was genuine."

Ever the curious one, Giuliana wanted to know more about the Apostles of the Sacred Heart, and why Celeste chose to commit her life to this particular order of nuns.

"From its humble beginnings," Celeste explained, "the order's mission has been to serve the church through charitable works and caring for the needy, children, and adults. This is precisely what I wish to do with my life, now and forever. As far as its history is concerned, the Apostles of the Sacred Heart was founded in May 1894 in the heavily populated town of Viareggio in Tuscany, Italy by a young nun, Clelia Merloni, who, like myself, came from a well-to-do family and who, after much prayer and contemplation, decided to devote her life to helping alleviate the poverty, homelessness and despair that permeated the region. She was thirty-three at the time; two other nuns joined her in the work. Then in 1902, the bishop who oversaw missions in the United States and South America petitioned the young nun, who by now had become Mother Clelia, to dispatch other Sacred Heart nuns to Boston to help serve the needs of the region's growing Italian immigrant population. In the United States alone at this time were more than 5-million Italian immigrants. Six nuns arrived that year in Boston, establishing the first motherhouse in this country. Four years later a group of nuns was sent to New Haven, right here, to this very location. We became the second mission in America, and the first provincial house in the country."

Giuliana continued her interrogation of the young postulant by asking her about St. Michael School. "For many years, there was a dire need for a parochial school in the parish of St. Michael," Celeste explained. "Our pastor recognized the need. So in September of 1936, classes in the primary grades were held here in the convent. But Father had larger ambitions for St. Michael's. In September of last year those ambitions were realized when the doors to our brand new school building were opened wide for every boy and girl in the neighborhood who desired the kind of education we provide."

As the two young women were finishing tidying up the kitchen, Celeste took Giuliana gently by the arm and said with pride: "Do you realize, Giuliana, come next June, you'll be a member of the second class to graduate from our new school."

"Maybe by then you'll be a teacher there," Giuliana said.

"No, that's not possible. I've chosen a different ministry than our sisters who teach in St. Michael and in our high school. My goal is to work with children, but not as a teacher. My job is going to entail taking care of orphans and abandoned children."

Switching gears, Giuliana then asked: "How long will it be before you actually become a nun?"

"Since you've asked, let me tell you how the process works," answered Celeste. "High school graduates who have a desire to consecrate their lives to the Sacred Heart of Jesus enter the convent life as a postulant for a twelve-month period. A postulant, as you may or may not know, is a person applying for candidacy in a religious order. Next month, on November 21, I will have met my obligation. During this time, girls learn the deep meaning of vocation within the religious life to which they've been exposed in the convent. If after that year the postulant continues in her desire to become a nun, she must make a retreat, after which she receives the habit and takes a religious name."

"Have you chosen your new name yet?" Giuliana inquired.

"I have, but I'm not going to tell you what it is. If you want to know my new name you're going to have to come to the ceremony to find out."

"You mean, you're inviting me?" Giuliana said excitedly, clapping her hands.

"Yes, of course. How else will you get to see me all dressed up in my white bridal gown . . . and meet my little cousin Cathy, who's going to be my flower girl. It's quite a beautiful ceremony . . . I believe you'll be impressed.

"But that's really only the beginning. I have to point out to you, Giuliana," Celeste continued, "that the novitiate stage, which is what I'm in right now, is a time of deepening dedication. Through prayer and study, the novice prepares for a life consecrated to the Sacred Heart. This is a life of love, service and reparation. During this time, the Sister pursues religious studies and decides on which facet of the apostolate to which she wishes to consecrate herself, such as teaching, social work, parish ministry, assisting the infirm and elderly, and so forth. As I've just indicated, my goal, when the time comes, is to work with children.

"Is that it?" Giuliana asked anxiously.

"Not quite," said Celeste, matter-of-factly. "After this part of the novitiate's training, she pronounces and takes her temporary vows. It will then be another five years before she actually takes her final or perpetual vows."

"I had no idea it took so long to become a nun," Giuliana said, with a note of surprise mingled with awe.

"Something so important can not be rushed. The process is meant to determine a young woman's true desire to be a nun. As the thirty women in this convent can attest, when that challenge has been successfully met the rewards are worth all of the effort."

\* \* \*

When Giuliana was walking home from the convent that evening in the company of her aunt, it wasn't the dinner she would be preparing the next night that occupied her thoughts but Celeste's delineation of what was required of a woman to become a nun. She couldn't help from wondering how she would react if at some point in the future she were to decide to pursue such a path. She asked herself the requisite questions:

"Do I love Jesus with all my heart and soul? Yes."

"Do I possess the mental, emotional and spiritual makeup necessary to become a nun? I think so."

"Would I be willing to accept completely a commitment to the cloistered life, renouncing all temporal pleasures?"

Here Giuliana paused in her walk, stopping at the rim of the green, near the statue of Columbus and the speaker platforms, and announced in a loud voice, momentarily startling Concetta, "No . . . I can't." When asked by her aunt what it was she was thinking that had prompted such a response, Giuliana said it was nothing, and left it at that.

But Giuliana's ruminations brought into sharp focus thoughts of her own future. She dwelled for some time on the idea of commitment:

to marriage foremost, but also to children and family. She tried to assess as best she could, realizing hers was from a child's perspective, the marriages of the women closest to her—her grandmother's, her mother's, and now her aunt's. From what she knew and could observe firsthand, theirs were all successful marriages. She was certain each of them loved her husband, and that each man in turn loved his wife unconditionally. If Celeste chose to be married to God in the spiritual sense, Giuliana was certain that when the time came she would choose marriage in the temporal sense and enjoy, hopefully forever, the love of a good man—like her grandfather, her father and her uncle. As to the impact these commitments were likely to have on her career, to which she was beginning to give a great deal of thought, she would have to wait and see how things played out in the future.

*   *   *

Mother Campion was aware of how close the two girls had become over the course of the summer, so she lost no time in asking Celeste to assist Giuliana in whatever the latter might need to prepare Friday evening's important dinner. Having the nun-to-be by her side delighted the young culinary prodigy. While hurriedly eating lunch, Giuliana described to Celeste the menu she planned for the bishop's dinner, and then gave her a list, neatly written on a lined sheet of notebook paper, of everything she would need.

"Since it's Friday," Giuliana said, "fish and seafood will be featured."

She then went on to describe in meticulous detail the dinner, which, when it came time, she would go about preparing without the aid of a single note or recipe, just like her mother, grandmother and Maddalena

Vertucci did when cooking, only tasting as she went along, a feat an astounded Celeste said she would not soon forget:

*Antipasti*: Boned fresh anchovies stuffed with mozzarella, dipped in egg and homemade seasoned bread crumbs, fried to a golden brown.

*Primo Piatto*: Pici (homemade or *fatte in casa* tagliatelle) with cuttlefish in a sauce of sautéed olive oil, garlic, peperoncino, parsley, tomato paste and a splash of white wine.

*Insalata*: Radicchio, arugula and shaved fennel in a gorgonzola dressing served with spiced walnuts.

*Secondo Piatto*: Braised sea bass wrapped in Savoy cabbage leaves served in a lemon butter sauce and accompanied by broiled tomatoes topped with freshly seasoned bread crumbs.

*Dolce*: Amaretto and hazelnut chocolate cake served with fresh whipped cream. This dessert was much favored by Maddalena; it had a gold dot affixed to it in the recipe pages she devoted to sweets.

Giuliana told Celeste that if asked, she would suggest to Mother Campion that a nicely chilled white wine, such as Lagrima Christi (The Tears of Christ), be served. This was, in her opinion, the best choice, while making it clear to her friend that it was in no way a concession to the mostly religious makeup of the group; it was simply an appropriate accompaniment to the food on the menu. To top off the meal, limoncello, a gift from her uncle, who made his own aperitif and did it quite well, would be served.

"Are you really going to be able to do all of this by Friday night?" a dubious Celeste asked in amazement.

"Only with your help," Giuliana answered, chuckling.

\*    \*    \*

Celeste left the convent and hurried to Carrano's market on Chapel Street a couple of blocks away to purchase the items on her shopping list. In the meantime, Giuliana set about making the dough for pasta, and a different dough for the dessert. Luckily for her, the convent kitchen was well stocked with plenty of flour.

At the crack of dawn Friday morning Celeste met up with Giuliana, who was waiting on the steps in front of her house. The two young women then made the ten-minute walk in the crisp autumn air to the fishing docks at Waterside Piers, where boats were already unloading their morning's catch. Fishmongers and restaurant cooks from all over the city were lined up like toy soldiers along the pier to snap up whatever fish and seafood struck their fancy. One of those waiting patiently was the fishmonger who owned the store up the street from where Giuliana lived. Every Friday, much to her delight, he loaded up the rear cabin of his flat-bed truck, front to back, side to side, with an enticing array of fish wiggling on a copious bed of ice and, beginning at noon, delivered a just-caught supply directly to the neighborhood, stopping at the same street corner, in the same spot, at virtually the same time of day. (Even along the Amalfi coast, where fish is king, nothing like I just described ever existed, Giuliana wrote in her diary.)

At the first blaring of the fishmonger's horn, women, like flocks of birds frightened out of their nests, swooped down from their flats and lined up alongside the truck, chattering happily among themselves as they waited their turn about how exactly they planned to cook the *merluzzo* or the flounder or the crabs that evening for dinner.

But on this particular Friday, Columbus Day, October 12, Giuliana would not be waiting for the fish truck delivery. For one thing, she couldn't afford the time to walk back home at noon, stand in line at the truck and wait to see whether the fish she was hoping to buy would still be available. Moreover, she felt uncomfortable having to concern herself with what she knew would certainly be questions by neighbors curious to know why she, and not her aunt, was buying fish that day. Nor did she want to have to concern herself with any other questions they might think of bombarding her with.

Though it took Giuliana almost no time at all to select exactly what she wanted, it did not prevent her from examining carefully—she had learned well from her fishermen father and bothers—every single piece of fish she had chosen. Celeste, whose main job was to provide the funds entrusted to her by Mother Campion for whatever Giuliana ordered, looked on in fascinated silence, and in awe, at how adept this child, unlike anyone her age she'd ever met, was in how she went about making her selections. As they were leaving the piers Celeste, who would be serving the guests that evening, turned to her young friend and asked how it was that she had such knowledge of and affinity for food. Giuliana told of how from the age of five she was always at her grandmother's side in the kitchen, "my grandmother was a very good cook," and learned even more from the housekeeper at her parish church in Amalfi, Maddalena Vertucci, "who was an even better cook," the rudiments of fine Italian cooking.

"From the time I was a child, I sensed that food, no matter whatever else I would be involved in later on, would always play an important part in my life." Giuliana went on to explain that it was all part of her fundamental ethos: to prepare food that made people happy, while at the same time preserving the flavors and tastes of the finest Italian cooking she had been brought up with.

"Was food important in your house?" Giuliana asked Celeste.

"Not really," came Celeste's quick reply. "Due to my father's work, he and mother ate out a lot. The housekeeper we had when my brother and I were growing up wasn't much of a cook. To her, food was just a four-letter word," (the girls laughed with glee at the characterization), "so home-cooked meals wasn't a priority. The best food we ever ate at our house was at lavish catered dinners my parents gave for business clients. I realize from being around you these past few months that I may have been missing out on something quite extra-ordinary. Of course, now that I have committed myself to the religious life, worldly pleasures such as fine dining are totally out of the question."

"What a pity," Giuliana said sadly. Celeste merely rolled her eyes.

\*     \*     \*

The dinner could not have gone off any better. While Giuliana worked away in the kitchen preparing each course, Celeste was in the convent's formal dining room serving the guests with the touch of a seasoned hostess. Her responsibilities also extended to the setting of the table. Here again, her touch was impeccable: every glass, plate and eating utensil was perfectly placed. The festive centerpiece, also her doing, consisted of a lovely arrangement of fall flowers jutting out from an exquisite cut-crystal vase, a gift to the convent from a well-to-do parishioner; they matched perfectly the hand-painted porcelain napkin rings Celeste's mother had personally delivered to New Haven the day after her daughter told her about the dinner for the bishop.

"I don't believe I've seen a lovelier table than this one, Sister," Bishop Serratelli said to the young postulate. "You've done a beautiful job. It would appear you've had some practice at such preparations, am I right?"

Celeste went on to tell of the catered dinner parties her very social parents had at their home, and how, even as a child, she would watch with single-minded fascination as the staff, under her mother's watchful eyes, went about their flawless duties.

After the first course was served—the antipasti of fresh, stuffed grilled anchovies with seasoned breadcrumbs—the guests paid much greater attention to the food than to how the table was set.

"This is absolutely delicious," marveled Carmella Amatruda. "I've never had anchovies prepared this way, not even at Randazzi's Restaurant. Do you think I could get the recipe from your cook, Mother Campion?"

"You can ask her yourself after the meal is over," came Mother Campion's quick reply. "I'm sure she'd be happy to give it to you."

"Speaking of the cook, Mother," said Monsignor Murray after he took his first bite, then another of the homemade tagliatelle, "I have to say that the Sacred Heart nuns in this convent have a lot to be thankful for. We certainly don't have a cook of this caliber in our house, do we Your Excellency?"

"Absolutely not," agreed the bishop. "I can't wait to meet her myself."

When dinner had concluded, and coffee and cordials were being served, Mother Campion excused herself and went into the kitchen. She approached the young cook, who was putting away the last of the pots and pans she had cleaned to a gleaming turn, and placed a hand on the child's shoulder. "You certainly did this convent proud tonight, my dear, as well as yourself. Now please remove your apron and cap and come meet our distinguished guests."

Giuliana entered tentatively the large, well-appointed dining room, all the while rubbing both hands gingerly over her school uniform skirt to smooth out the pleats. Her long shiny black hair was pulled back tightly in braids so as to keep it away from her face, and the food, as she prepared dinner. She looked even younger than her age.

"Permit me to introduce the creator of this wonderful meal," Mother Campion said proudly, taking the girl by the hand and revealing, finally, the identity of the one person her guests had been speculating about all through dinner. ". . . Giuliana Landini."

Stunned, incredulous glances were exchanged among the guests. Mother Campion and the school principal Sister Margaret Mary Cirillo, accustomed from time to time to the pleasures of Giuliana's distinctive cooking, relished the moment. The young girl at first stood stiffly at the head of the table next to the seat occupied by Mother Superior before being motioned by the bishop to come closer to where he sat, at the opposite head.

"Did you really cook this meal all by yourself?" asked Bishop Serratelli, with a raised arched eyebrow and a wry smile on his face.

Yes, Your Excellency."

". . . and planned every last detail of it?"

"Yes, Your Excellency."

"How old are you, my child?"

"I'll be twelve next February."

"Would you mind telling us," he said, with one eye trained on Giuliana, the other searching the faces of the other disbelieving guests, "how it is you have come to acquire such skills . . . and at such a young age?"

Bishop Serratelli knew from whence he spoke when it came to food. His family was from Bologna, arguably the food capital of Italy, so he was more than familiar with great Italian cooking, having been raised on it. That and frequent trips to Rome on church business always kept him in proximity to his next great meal. Tonight, in Sacred House Convent of all places, was one of them.

Giuliana reiterated the essentials of her young life including, most elaborately, the cooking aspects of it, which only that very morning she had described in florid detail to Celeste.

"So you learned how to cook in Italy, is that right?" the bishop asked rhetorically. She found he had the irritating habit of asking and answering his own questions.

"Amalfi, your Excellency," shot out Giuliana's instant reply.

"Amalfi . . . of course," the bishop corrected himself. "I'm told you also chose the wine for dinner, am I correct?" said the bishop as he sipped from his brandy snifter a twelve-year-old Madeira Mother Campion reserved only for auspicious occasions.

Giuliana then went on to explain in the most casual way that it was nothing unusual even for a young girl like herself to possess a keen understanding of the proper pairing of wine with food since she had been schooled in the art by the nonpareil pastor of her hometown church, Father Marco Di Pina, her personal mentor.

"Very interesting," said the bishop, now ready to change the subject. "How long have you been in America, Giuliana?"

"Since the end of June . . . I came over alone . . . my family is still in Amalfi . . . I live with my uncle and aunt . . . they came to New Haven from Amalfi three years ago."

"Is that so," said his Excellency.

"Yes, it is," said Giuliana.

"May I ask why you came to this country, and the rest of your family did not?"

"No, not at all," Giuliana said obligingly, staring intently at her grand inquisitor as she formulated her answer, hoping this might be the last of the interrogation. "My family wanted me to, especially my grandmother. My teachers, too, and Father Di Pina . . . they all felt I should come to America to get an education. They said I would be wasting my talents if I stayed in Amalfi. Over there girls go to school only up to a certain age . . . then they're taken out of school and put to work until they're old enough to marry, which most of the time is arranged between families. But here, girls like me can get a very good education if they want . . . they can go to high school, then college and then do anything after that. And they don't have to get married if they don't want to, either. My grandmother says that's what it means to live in a free country like the United States."

Everyone at the table was fascinated by the girl's forthright explanation, but no one more so than Bishop Serratelli. He then took a moment to consider how best to phrase his next question. "Are there by chance any plans in your future for becoming a nun?"

"None that I'm aware of," Giuliana said emphatically and without hesitation, while careful not to seem either intimidated by the question or meaning to sound disrespectful.

A wide grin spread across the bishop's face while a hearty, full-throated guffaw erupted like a lava-spewing volcano from the robust Monsignor Murray, who was seated on the bishop's right. A more subdued response, more in the way of chuckles, emanated from the other guests. Only Mother Campion, who bit her upper lip, and Sister Margaret Mary, with a hand over her mouth, made any attempt to appear indifferent to the levity the bishop's question had unintentionally evoked.

Giuliana shifted her gaze from the bishop to the monsignor, not certain how to react to the reception her latest answer had sparked; she was at once fearful she might lose her composure. Had she committed a faux pas, she wanted to know. "Did I say something wrong?" she asked, blushing a beet red.

"Not at all," the bishop said reassuringly, wishing not to embarrass or make the girl feel any more uncomfortable than she obviously already was. "I was just wondering, since you seem to have all your other priorities well in hand, whether you'd given any thought to your future plans . . . you know, the career you'd like to have, once, I'm almost reluctant to say it, you've grown up?"

"Oh yes, I'm pretty certain I want to be an architect," Giuliana said without hesitation, and with a great deal of conviction.

"Is that so," remarked the bemused bishop, surprised by Giuliana's answer. "That's certainly a fine profession. But may I ask why you've chosen this particular field, especially since there are, as far as I know, very few women in this line of work?"

Before she could answer, Sister Margaret Mary, who, like the others at the table had kept her thoughts to herself throughout the interrogation, interjected: "If you'll permit me, Giuliana, I'd like to answer the bishop's question for you. Is that alright?" she asked, looking first at the girl, then mother superior, then the bishop for approval.

Happy at the chance to stand silent, at least for the moment, Giuliana quickly nodded her assent, as did the bishop.

"Giuliana is much too modest to tell you herself, so I'll do it for her," Sister Margaret Mary explained, wishing to add her imprimatur to the career the child had chosen. "Fact is, Giuliana is extremely talented. Being a first-rate cook is only part of it. She's also a wonderful artist and just about the best math student we've ever had in our school, boy or girl. From my perspective, this should put her in a good stead to become a successful architect, even though it's not generally considered a career for women. Perhaps even more important, she has a fascination for buildings and structures that practically borders on worship. It's something she got from her grandfather, whom I'm told was one of Amalfi's leading builders, certainly its best mason."

Now that someone other than the bishop had spoken up, Monsignor Declan Murray decided this would be as good a time as any to enter the conversation. "So you're an artist?" said the Monsignor approvingly. "I happen to paint myself . . . would you mind telling us about it?"

"I don't paint, Monsignor," Giuliana corrected the priest, shaking her head. "I only draw. I've been doing it since I was five years old.

I use pencil mostly, but sometimes pen and ink and once in a while charcoal. I'm not ready to paint in oils yet."

Sensing the Monsignor was about to inquire as to why, Giuliana quickly continued, "Father Di Pina, the pastor at our church in Amalfi, who knows more about art than anyone I know even though he was never a very good artist himself, said that I should not start painting at least until I'm a little older . . . that I should spend my time drawing. He said that by learning how to draw well, painting with oils or watercolors or in any other medium would be a lot easier when the time came."

"You seem to have great affection for this priest," remarked the bishop. "That is commendable."

"Yes, he taught me so much . . . about art and food and wine (she blushed when she said it), but more than that, about faith, not only faith in God, but faith in myself. I will never be able to repay him. He also gave me the best gift I've ever received from anyone—a famous painting of St. Lucy . . . it hangs on the wall in my bedroom." She briefly recounted the genesis of the painting, and Father Di Pina's role in acquiring it. "St. Lucy is the patron saint of sight, as I'm sure you know," she continued. "Thank God, I don't have any problems with my eyes . . . but I do pray to her every night that I might see clearly how best to lead my life."

The bishop rose from his chair and extended a hand to Giuliana. "You have made this evening one I won't soon forget, my dear, and one I honestly must say I never expected, no slight intended Mother Campion. In appreciation, my child, is there anything I can do for you?"

Giuliana did not hesitate in making a request. "Would you please pray for my family in Amalfi, Your Excellency . . . especially for my two brothers in the army . . . they just got called up into the Italian army. I worry about them a lot."

"You have my word, child, that I will remember them and your entire family in my Masses," said the bishop as he patted her softly on the head.

"Now what about you . . . is there something I can do for you?"

"Please give me your blessing," Giuliana requested as she kissed the sacred ring that graced his right hand.

"Is that all?"

"It's all that I need.

As he was saying his goodbyes at the door a few minutes later, the bishop asked Sister Margaret Mary Cirillo and Mother Campion to keep him apprised of Giuliana's progress. He said he would have to make it a point to meet her again, if possible.

* * *

On Monday, word spread rapidly through the school, and by mid-afternoon everyone in the neighborhood was talking about the dinner Giuliana cooked for the bishop. Much was made of the effusive praise the prelate lavished on the talented young cook. Many of the older women, those born in Italy particularly—who looked upon life chiefly as the daily act of deciding what to cook for dinner that night—considered themselves to be the most qualified ambassadors of their native cuisine. But they were nonetheless intrigued by word of the young girl's formidable feat. Even had they been aware of Giuliana's extensive training in two of Amalfi's best kitchens—her grandmother's and Maddalena Vertucci's—they might still have wanted to know just what it was that could possibly have prompted the good Mother Superior to defer to a veritable neophyte to cook such an important meal, her bravura performance notwithstanding. After all, they told themselves, how good could an eleven-year-old possibly be? The only way to find out, of course, was to taste and sample her food.

But how were they to get that to happen? One novel suggestion was to invite Giuliana to one of the meetings of the St. Andrew Society Women's Group, which met once a month at the club around the corner from St. Michael's Church. At least thirty or more of the 100 or so members normally showed up at each meeting, and before sitting down to business one of the women whose turn it was cooked a full meal for the group, part of the allure to ensure a healthy turnout.

It was thus agreed that their sister member Connie Fassano would do what she could to get Giuliana to accept the group's invitation to come to the club. Connie was told to emphasize to her niece that while cooking something simple for the group was an obligation that went along with the invitation, the real reason for asking her to come to the meeting was to ascertain from Amalfi's newest émigré to New Haven the goings-on in their sister city across the sea. Members especially wanted to know about the recent installation of the magnificent grandfather's clock donated by the women's group to St. Andrew's Cathedral, designed by the father of one of its members in the New Haven Clock Company where he worked. Along with the clock, reported to occupy a prominent place in the cathedral's imposing sacristy, was the magnificent bronze statute of St. Andrew. It resided under lock and key and was made visible to the town just once a year on the saint's feast day. Members were also anxious to learn whether the ornate gold-plated plaque, another gift of the women's group, had been prominently mounted as promised on the wall in one of Sant'Andrea's side altars. Engraved on its frontispiece were names of all the members of New Haven's St. Andrew Women's Society.

Concetta was certain she would have a hard time talking Giuliana into accepting the society's invitation. She was right: neither of her entreaties swayed her niece. She had long ago learned how much Giuliana disdained drawing attention to herself, or having attention drawn to her by others, especially those intent on knocking the young girl off an imagined pedestal she had no hand in erecting.

When Giuliana arrived in America less than five months ago, one of the first things she told her guardians was that all she wanted was to fit as seamlessly as possible into the neighborhood. Anything that made her stand out was to be avoided, even though as far back as she could remember she was always being told how smart she was, how good she was, how talented she was, how pretty she was, how much a credit to her family she was, and on and on.

She also remembered vividly, too, those times her grandmother would expound on how tiresome it was for her when women in her circle sought her counsel, even though she felt neither qualified nor, in many cases, capable of delivering it. So when Concetta approached Giuliana about attending the next St. Andrew Women's Society meeting, Giuliana quickly and emphatically demurred, telling her aunt she was less concerned with hurting their feelings than she was with their duplicity in having invited her to the club under false pretenses. With all the hullabaloo in the neighborhood caused by her star turn in the Sacred Heart Convent kitchen on Columbus Day, she was positive she would be asked to demonstrate her cooking skills for perhaps an even more demanding audience than the bishop, the women of Wooster Square, all the more reason for turning down the invitation. By accepting, not only would she be inviting more undue attention, she would be putting herself in an untenable position: if her cooking did not measure up to their expectations, she would be ridiculed; if it exceeded them, she would be resented. Either way, a no-win situation. And she didn't want any part of it.

# Chapter 20

Fall came and went, but not before Giuliana got to celebrate yet another favorite American tradition, Thanksgiving Day. It started off much as it did every year, with neighborhood fathers and their sports-loving sons and daughters attending the traditional Turkey Day football game played at Yale Bowl between New Haven's two arch-rival high schools, Hillhouse and Commercial. With the game due to be over around noon, Giuliana and Umberto would be home in plenty of time to get ready for the festive dinner party scheduled to start mid-afternoon at the Giordanos' place.

Giuliana had become fascinated with the lore of this quintessential American holiday: Native Americans sharing their food on the first Thanksgiving Day in 1621 with a band of English pilgrims, the first foreigners to have set foot on American soil a year earlier. Excited about taking part in the festivities, she was mostly looking forward to eating turkey for the first time, a food rarely if ever seen on tables in the south of Italy.

"But first there is something important we must do before going home," Umberto said as they boarded the trolley car that took them from the stadium back downtown after the game. Walking in the direction of Wooster Street, they stopped two blocks away at the Episcopal Church on the corner of Olive and Chapel Streets.

"Why are we going here, Zio?" a perplexed Giuliana asked. "This isn't our church."

"You'll see in a minute," answered Umberto as they descended the steps that led to the basement. The large room they entered was occupied by scores of mostly shabbily dressed men, many of them Negroes, sitting at long cafeteria tables eating off tin trays.

Others formed a line in front of a lengthy counter at the far end of the room where half a dozen men and women were dishing out turkey dinners to the indigent diners. As soon as he spotted Umberto, a tall distinguished-looking man dressed in what Giuliana later learned was the traditional Salvation Army uniform came over to greet them. "Thank you for coming, Bert . . . I knew I could count on you." Then looking down at the girl at her uncle's side, he said: "I'm Captain William Sperling. Are you here to help, too?" Giuliana looked at her uncle quizzically.

"This is my niece Giuliana Landini, Captain, and she is definitely here to help," Umberto said emphatically. He took Giuliana to a large sink behind the counter. They washed their hands and each was handed a clean white apron from the woman whose place Umberto would be taking behind the counter, dishing out mashed potatoes and gravy. Giuliana was asked to work the small tables on either side of the room replenishing a fresh supply of plastic tableware, napkins and condiments, and gathering up soiled trays for washing in the scullery. An hour passed in no time.

Umberto, having relinquished his spot to another volunteer, approached Giuliana and tapped her on the shoulder; she was surprised to learn that it was already time for them to go. Back on the street, her silence spoke volumes: Umberto knew the experience of volunteering in a Salvation Army soup kitchen had left a deep and lasting impression on his young niece. She carried the image of that experience well into adulthood.

\*　\*　\*

Paolo Giordano, the native-born Italian, not Antoinette, his American-born wife, was, much to Giuliana's surprise, maestro of the Thanksgiving meal. Midway through the first course, a perfectly executed puree-of-mushroom soup, Paolo checked the large clock over the sink then took the turkey out of the oven to rest. The aroma, coupled with the sight of the golden-brown, glistening bird had Giuliana swooning. When she finally got to taste her first bite of the juicy, tender meat drenched in piping hot giblet gravy, her reaction delighted the eight adult diners at the Giordano table. Two other neighborhood couples, Italian immigrants from the Amalfi area, had also been invited.

Everything served, in fact, Giuliana consumed with gusto: the candied yams, mashed potatoes, creamed onions, Brussels sprouts, giblet stuffing, corn pudding, cranberry sauce. Since this was an all-Italian gathering, stuffed artichokes were also served, which the guests unanimously declared not to be out of place on the festive holiday table; laughingly, they felt certain Cristoforo Columbus himself would have approved. Antoinette Giordano's desserts were a big hit, too: pumpkin pie with fresh whipped cream, pecan pie and what turned out to be Giuliana's favorite, mince meat pie.

The meal lasted for hours. When it became apparent that not another morsel of food could possibly be consumed, the men retreated to the parlor to smoke their cigars and sip grappa, while the women remained in the kitchen to tidy up. Suddenly, an ear-splitting cheer erupted from the kitchen, followed by Giuliana's hurried dash into the front parlor to summon the startled men who were by now engrossed in a heated debate on the merits of American football versus European rugby.

"Come quickly," Giuliana entreated, "there's important news you must hear."

Entering the kitchen, the men found the women hugging each other, their happy sobs rendering speech impossible, and unnecessary. As the only non grown-up not engaged in either the hugging or the crying, and unwilling to wait any longer for the exuberant celebration to subside, Giuliana took it upon herself to quickly seize the role of happy pied piper: "Antoinette is going to have a baby!" she blurted out in a loud voice. The announcement prompted the men to then engage in their own round of revelry. It was only after congratulatory handshakes, hugs, pats on the back and *buona salutes* had been dispensed with that Paolo was able to extricate himself from his overjoyed friends and hurry to the ice box to retrieve two bottles of champagne that had been chilling in preparation of the happy news he and Antoinette had themselves planned on sharing with their friends on this, the day of all days for giving thanks.

Talk throughout the meal had been lighthearted and revolved mostly around family news from across the Atlantic, but word of the forthcoming blessed event now prompted the conversation to take on a more serious and weighty turn. As was the case whenever the friends got together, conversation inevitably gravitated to the one topic most on their minds—work. All eight men and women held down blue-collar jobs, all except American-born Antoinette were in the United States less than five years, all four couples, mostly in their thirties, were childless and all were concerned, worried actually, about one thing, and one thing only—whether they would ever be able to achieve financial independence for themselves and, should they be so blessed, as apparently now were the Giordanos, for their children.

"Thank God for the unions," said mother-to-be Antoinette Giordano, nervously drumming her fingers on the table. "It's the only reason I've stayed in my job at the dress factory. Things have gotten a lot better, Connie, since you were there," she continued, looking directly at her friend. "The Garment Workers Union is strong, and it's made a big difference, so I'm going to stay in my job for as long as my doctor tells me it's safe. I'll even be able to collect unemployment insurance for a while after I have the baby. Thank you, President Roosevelt. Just think: before 1935, we wouldn't have had unemployment or health insurance. Or social security. What would we ever do without these benefits?"

Before anyone else could chime in, Pasquale Apuzzo, who with his wife, Annalisa, were the most recent expatriates, from a small village on the outskirts of Salerno, proclaimed ruefully, "I'm not as lucky as you are, Antoinette. I have none of those benefits. I work in construction. In the two years we've been in this country, all I've ever been able to get are day-labor jobs with contractors who claim they're too small to provide the benefits you speak of. If I'm lucky, I get to work regularly maybe five or six weeks at a time. The money's good, very good, but once the cold weather comes in, like in the next couple of weeks, I'll have almost no work the entire winter. I try to pick up odd jobs here and there to help pay the bills, but it's never enough. Even with Annalisa working full time in Shartenberg's Department Store, we have trouble making ends meet. Between the two of us we have no security, and no unions to protect us."

He paused for a moment, looking soulfully at his wife and said: "We long ago gave up hope of owning our own home. If things don't get better for us, as much as I don't like to think about it, we may have to go back to Italy."

"We feel the same way as Pasquale," offered Gaetano Buonocore. He and his wife, Mary Grace, from the rugged mountain town of Agerola, located above Amalfi, had arrived in New Haven six months before the Fassanos, and were the youngest of the group, both in their mid twenties. After five years in America, their once optimistic outlook had long since dissipated, tempered by the realization that menial jobs like theirs—he was a part-time custodian in a public grammar school, she worked on the assembly line of a soda bottling plant across town—forced them to question their prospects and to think twice about starting a family, which they so much wanted to do. "Unless things improve for us, we're not going to stay either," he said sadly.

"I know what you're both saying," offered Umberto in a grave voice, breaking a silence that had suddenly cast a pall over what had been up to this point a jovial table. "As all of you know, I hold down two jobs. I like working as a waiter at Randazzi's, but sometimes customers can be worse than any boss. As for my job at Sperry & Barnes, the stench from slaughtered pigs I can't ever seem to get out of my nostrils. And if you think I like seeing my wife washing other people's clothes and ironing their curtains, you're sadly mistaken. But here is how I look at it: forget the unions . . . go into business for yourself. That's the only way to fix the problem. That's what I intend to do, maybe not next week, or even next year, but someday. You mark my words."

"That's a pipe dream, Umberto," said Pasquale, derisively.

"No, it's not," shot back Umberto. "Look at Jerry Sacco—didn't he open a dry goods store recently? And what about Vinnie Acri . . . a new convenience store? And . . ."

He was cut off by Paolo, arguing with some conviction: "But they're Americans, not real Italians like us. They know the ropes. To them we're just a bunch of greenhorns."

"You're dead wrong," Umberto challenged. "We have the same opportunities as they have, if we know where to look for them. New businesses are popping up all over the place. If you have a decent idea, banks are more than willing to provide low-interest loans. Joey Garibaldi got money from Polotti's bank on a handshake, and another loan when he bought his house in East Haven. The bank encourages entrepreneurship . . . I know that for a fact . . . Mrs. Randazzi talks about it all the time. I also predict that pretty soon there's going to be a building boom that'll be good for all of us working people. If you're patient and don't give up, experienced construction people like you, Pasquale, are going to do very well . . . and so will the rest of the economy."

Umberto Fassano, thirty-four, in the United States three years, with a formal education that never went beyond eighth grade, saw clearly into the future. His astute analysis of what would shape the new American economy was prescient. But he was a few years off in his predictions. The boom he saw clearly on the horizon would not reach fruition until late in the war, and continue for a good time beyond.

\*　　\*　　\*

That evening, when the Fassanos reached their flat, Giuliana excused herself and went immediately to her room. She did not turn on the light, though it was close to nine o'clock and pitch black. The darkness was soothing and not at all unwelcome. She threw herself on the bed, staring across the room at the wall, making out, but only faintly, the St. Lucy painting from which she always drew comfort. She didn't get up. Ordinarily after a day in which she had experienced so much pleasure and excitement, with sadness mixed in, too, she'd be at her desk transcribing in her diary well into the night the day's events as well as writing letters to family and friends.

For the moment she thought it best to put some distance between how she was feeling at the moment (sullen), and how she hoped she would be feeling in the morning (upbeat), before attempting to formalize thoughts in letters, particularly ones to family.

This did not prevent her, however, from going over, while still fresh in mind, everything she had seen, heard and done that day. And the impressions they had made on her:

The high school football game—fun.
The soup kitchen at St. Paul's Church—sobering.
The Giordano's Thanksgiving dinner—delicious.
The news of Antoinette's pregnancy—joyous.
The long discussion after dinner about work—disturbing.

Very disturbing, in fact. During most of the dinner, except when being asked some innocuous this or that, Giuliana sat ladylike in her place at the table taking in every word being said, careful not to betray how uneasy she felt listening to grown-up men and women she was very fond of voicing their concerns on a subject she had not up to this time given very much thought. But now, lying quietly, she was haunted by thoughts of her family on the other side. How did they feel about their work? How had it affected their lives? What were their aspirations? Were they satisfied or disappointed with their lot? Did they have enough money to get by? All imponderables that prompted Giuliana to engage in the following internal dialogue:

*Whenever Nonna spoke about the cheese business working alongside my great grandparents, she was always so excited. As far as I know all three of them were happy and content. So was Nonno Alfonso, who loved being a mason. He was the pride of Amalfi, the best in his trade. Whenever he took me with him, he'd show me the work he'd done. It was wonderful. He also never failed to point out to me some of the beautiful architecture in our area. I remember one Sunday when he and Nonna Dona took me to Ravello . . . we visited the Villa Cimbrone. He said that if he were capable of creating a building half as beautiful, he would gladly die and go to heaven on the spot. He said I should never forget that. I haven't. I wish I had known him better. Mama is just like him. She loves what she's doing, making linens . . . it's her way of expressing her creativity. Even Papa and my brothers seem to be satisfied in their work . . . all the men on Papa's side of the family were fishermen. That's all they ever knew, and ever wanted to know. Papa says that when he's out on his boat early in the morning, before the sun is even up, he feels a sense of quiet and contentment that no amount of money can buy. I believe him. Only Zio Umberto has always been unhappy, that's why he left Amalfi and came to America. He's become very ambitious . . . stubborn and determined, too. I don't think he will ever be satisfied until he is working for himself. Our family has always been on its own, we've never had to rely on anyone else for a living. I admire him for it. I wish Paolo, Pasquale and Gaetano felt the same way. I worry about them, and about all the other good people in my area who work so hard just to get by. They all seem weighed down by life. I'd give anything to be able to help them.*

Such thoughts gave Giuliana pause to think, more than she had up to now, about the path her own future was likely to take. She had come to the United States to find her way in the world, to take advantage of every opportunity open to her. That meant first and foremost getting a superior education and then, if she were fortunate and talented enough, to become an architect, just like her grandfather wanted her to be. In short, to be happy and successful and, should she be so blessed, married and the mother of as many children as the good Lord bestowed on her.

But what if it turned out that work, and not family, defined who she was? If that were to be the case, wouldn't an over-emphasis on work obscure, even threaten perhaps, her fierce passion for life? She harkened back to the moment she first laid eyes on the majestic Statue of Liberty peeping out of the gray distance as the ship entered the harbor, a dim silhouette in the majestic New York skyline. *How beautiful was the figure of Lady Liberty. It made me feel like the torch in her strong right arm was raised just to greet me . . . to illuminate the way for me to a successful future. But what if I don't realize my dreams? Don't become an architect like I planned? Don't have a good job? Don't marry? Don't have children? Could I still be happy? Or would I spend a lifetime just like my aunt and uncle and their friends fretting over missed opportunities?* Exhausted from dwelling on such disturbing thoughts, Giuliana, fully clothed, fell into a deep sleep, the bed's top blanket her only buffer against the chilly November night.

*       *       *

Giuliana rose the next morning in much better spirits. Today was a day off from school. She thought it would be a good time to spend some part of it across the street at the Neighborhood House. But first there were letters to family and friends she needed to write, narratives replete with happy musings: of the exciting football game, the wonderful Thanksgiving dinner, the thrilling announcement of Antoinette Giordano's pregnancy. Only in her diary, whose entries she penned later that day, was she totally forthcoming, writing sensitively about the emotional experience of helping feed indigent, hungry people in the soup kitchen early in the afternoon, and recreating as best she could remember the disturbing discussion on the subject of work that took place in the evening.

In humorous postscripts to her mother, grandmother and Maddelena Vertucci, she enjoined them to go out and look for a turkey, if ever they were so inclined, and revel in a new taste treat. She would gladly send along cooking instructions, should they need them

# Chapter 21

Having been brought up in the warm, temperate climate of the Mediterranean, Giuliana lived much of her life outdoors. As the cold weather set in, something else she'd have to get used to, Giuliana was now forced to look elsewhere for recreational pleasures. The best place to find them was across the street at the Neighborhood House. Most of the other kids in the community spent a lot of time there. The few times she had gone with friends from school she had enjoyed herself. Especially in the game room, where she liked to play checkers, and in the second-floor reading room, where periodicals and books—mostly novels and biographies for young adults—were available for in-house reading and for borrowing. She had planned to look in on the music and art rooms but had so far not done so. Today, perhaps, would be the time to give it a try.

Walking up the sidewalk leading to the front of the house, Giuliana ran into her best friend and classmate, Phyllis Fiore. Instead of proceeding directly to the front door the two veered off to the right of the building.

"Where are you taking me, Phil?" a puzzled Giuliana asked.

"To Mrs. Lerner's pottery class," her friend answered.

"Pottery?"

"Don't you remember, I told you about it? There's a class every Saturday, and on holidays, from nine to twelve. Why don't you come in and see what it's like."

A half dozen stone steps led to the basement pottery shop, where three girls were putting on smocks while a woman was in the process of firing up the kiln. "So you're the new girl from Amalfi," the woman said, extending her hand. "I'm Rosemary Lerner. My parents are from there, too." She saw that Giuliana appeared confused, so she quickly added: "I'm Italian, my maiden name is Esposito . . . my husband is Jewish . . . we're both teachers . . . we live in the Hill section of the city."

Giuliana looked around the shop. She liked what she saw. Lining three stone shelves were pottery pieces in varying stages of completion: vases, bowls, cups, dishes, candleholders, clay figurines that eventually would be part of a Christmas crèche.

"Would you like to join us?" asked Mrs. Lerner.

"Yes, I think I would, thank you," Giuliana answered.

"Is there something you might want to make?"

Giuliana thought for a second then nodded in the affirmative. "I have a picture in my room of something I think would be perfect. I live directly across the street. It'll take me only a minute to get it. Is it alright if I go?"

"Yes, of course," said Mrs. Lerner, "but try to hurry. I'd like to get started."

Giuliana raced across the street, up the stairs and burst through the kitchen door, brushing past her startled aunt, who had a tub of wash in her arms. She went behind the desk in her room where she kept her bulging art portfolio and retrieved a handful of pictures, then dashed back to the studio. Out of breath, Giuliana handed the teacher a charcoal drawing of a vase. Then she gave her another. And still another. Six renderings in all, each one of the same vase, but from a different angle and perspective.

"Where did you get these?" asked Mrs. Lerner, flipping back and forth from one picture to the next.

"I drew them," Giuliana answered proudly.

"You did?"

"Yes."

"When?"

"Last year, when I lived in Amalfi."

"How long have you been drawing?" asked Mrs. Lerner, obviously impressed.

"Since I was five. That's when my grandmother started giving me art books. She encouraged me to draw, so did our parish priest . . . he knows a lot about art."

"Have you drawn many pictures?" Mrs. Lerner inquired, anxious to gauge as best she could the girl's level of experience.

"Oh, yes. I've done hundreds. Most of them I keep, but there are some I throw away . . . ones I'm not too happy with." Then: "I draw all the time, almost every day."

"Do you think I might see your pictures, sometime?" the teacher asked.

"Of course. If you like, I can bring them over tomorrow," Giuliana offered, happy to accommodate someone she was fast warming up to.

"That would be fine. I'd like Bernice Carroll, our Neighborhood House art teacher, to take a look at your drawings with me, if that's all right with you. Now tell me about the vase. From your drawings, I can tell it's a beautiful piece."

"Was," said the girl wistfully. "It was my mother's favorite vase. She kept it on the stone wall in the yard outside the kitchen window. There were always fresh flowers from my grandmother's garden in it. My father bought it for my mother on her birthday several years ago . . . it's from Vietri, where a lot of beautiful Italian pottery comes from. One day my brother Roberto knocked the vase over by accident. It broke into so many pieces it couldn't be repaired. For days, I kept drawing pictures of the vase from memory, until I was satisfied I had it just right. I'd like to try making it . . . if not the exact same vase, then one I think my mother will like. I'm so happy Phil suggested this place to me."

Over the next two Saturdays, Giuliana worked with singleminded zeal. She mixed the wet clay, added just the right amount of colored shards of stone to achieve the hue she desired, and with hands that had taken to molding the clay around the pottery wheel as deftly as Maddalena Vertucci formed her perfectly shaped gnocchi, produced a piece that, when finished the following Saturday, Mrs. Lerner and the four other girls pronounced to be first rate. Before putting the vase in the kiln, Giuliana added an inscription at the base:

*Mia Cara Mama, Buon Natal, Con Tanto Amore, Giuliana, Decembre 1941.*

When she went back to visit her family years later, Giuliana found the vase she had sent to her mother that Christmas long ago resting on the mantel over the fireplace in the kitchen; it sat proudly all by itself, the only object on the shelf.

# Chapter 22

On Sunday, December 7, 1941, Giuliana woke to snow fluttering outside her bedroom window, the first snow she had ever seen; the first big snowfall of the season was still a few weeks off. She readied herself for the ten o'clock Mass she attended every Sunday with her aunt. Her uncle, a non church-goer like a lot of men she knew in Amalfi and now in America, chose instead to spend his Sunday mornings in the park playing bocce with the boys, weather permitting, and when not, indoors playing cards at the Italian-American Club up the street. When Giuliana asked her uncle one day why he didn't go to church regularly, Umberto told her that he didn't need church to find God: "Christ is in the air we breathe, the ground we walk on, even in the work we do." What's more, he added, he believed more than the so-called believers. Only later in life did Giuliana come to understand what he meant.

Plans for the day called for an early dinner, a movie and then afterward a stop at one of Giuliana's favorite downtown spots, the popular ice cream parlor a few doors from the theater, for "a strawberry milk shake and a slice of yummy banana cream pie." As soon as they reached the porch, they were greeted by a mob scene. Dozens of people were milling about the sidewalk, others gathered in the middle of the street. Within minutes, so many neighbors came pouring out of their buildings that the cobbled street made it impossible for even the occasional automobile to pass.

Suddenly above the buzz of the crowd rang out the high pitched shouts of Billy Pappeo, the 13-year-old paperboy. There he stood, in the center of the throng, in his high-top shoes, knickers, checkered wool coat open at the top, bright red scarf knotted firmly around his neck and a plaid cap cocked sideways on a head hiding a mass of shiny black hair. A dirty gray-white burlap bag was slung over a shoulder, and in his half-gloved right hand he waved a copy of the *New York Daily News*, shouting at the top of his lungs: "EXTRI, EXTRI! READ ALL ABOUT IT! JAPS BOMB PEARL HARBOR!"

*What does this mean*? *And where was Pearl Harbor?* Giuliana asked herself. In almost no time, Billy's supply of papers was gone. But people on the street did not immediately disperse. They were frozen in place, like so many helpless boats caught in a storm. Not Umberto. He grabbed Giuliana by the hand and motioned for Concetta to follow him back into their building. He put the radio on as soon as they were in the house. The dire news was confirmed, but otherwise scant information came over the airwaves. Later on, it was announced that President Roosevelt would address the nation the next evening at eight o'clock.

One by one, friends came knocking at the Fassano door: first Paulo and Antoinette, then Pasquale and his wife, a few minutes later Gaetano and Grace. The same eight friends who only ten days before had been together celebrating Thanksgiving had now reconvened, this time not to party but to comfort and reassure one another. They speculated on what this latest development might mean. Germany, with Italy's compliant and benevolent dictator, Mussolini, at Hitler's side, had already cut a destructive swath through Europe. Now this horrible business in the Pacific. Would America, on the brink of entering one war, have the resources to fight in a second one at the same time? And what about the other concern that had to be faced by Italian-Americans should the United States go to war in Europe: how would America react to them and, most especially, to their Italian-born relatives living permanently in the United States? To whom did their allegiance lie, should they be ever called on to make the painful choice?

The next evening, after work, the eight friends again met, this time at the Giordanos' to listen to the President's address to the nation. Umberto was there, too, Randazzi's Restaurant being shuttered for the night as were most other businesses in town nervously awaiting what the president was about to say regarding the dire events now unfolding. Giuliana did not come; she asked if she could stay home. She wanted to be alone to digest for herself these sad events and to decide what action, if any, would be appropriate for an eleven-year-old to take. Now, more than ever, she yearned to be in Amalfi in the loving care of her parents, and with friends she grew up with. But for now, all she could do was to sit patiently by, like everyone else. And fret.

The next day, December 8, the feast of the Immaculate Conception, President Roosevelt, at 8 p.m. delivered in somber tones his famous "date that will live in infamy" speech. He outlined the details of the attack: at 7:55 on the previous morning, Japanese aircraft in a surprise attack rained bomb after bomb on eight battleships moored in the waters of Pearl Harbor, Hawaii, destroying five of the ships, killing over twenty-four-hundred American servicemen and women and, in virtually a single stroke, obliterating the U.S. Pacific Fleet battleship force. With the approval of Congress, the United States declared war on Japan. Two days later, on Thursday, December 10, in retaliation, Germany and Italy declared war on the United States, thus confirming the dire predictions Camilla McDonough, Maddalena Vertucci and Donatella Fassano had made less than a year ago—that native-born Italians and American-born Italians would soon be killing each other in another dastardly world war.

The sadness that draped the neighborhood like a shroud did not end with the government's official declaration of war. By the end of the week, amidst the steady drumbeat of bad news, a devastating blow, much closer and more personal, was delivered to an already stunned community: Jerome Rispoli, a 19-year-old sailor serving aboard the battleship *Arizona,* who lived up the street from the Fassanos, was killed in the attack; 17-year-old Vincenzo Milani, in whose basement Giuliana, quite unexpectedly, had her first go at spin the bottle, died when the *Pennsylvania* went down. Two sons, not much older than Giuliana, soon coming home dead from the war, forever lost to eternity. And two families and a neighborhood consumed by grief never to be the same again.

Over the course of the next four years, with war being waged on two fronts, such agonizing heartache would be compounded by the deaths of twenty-one soldiers, sailors and Marines from the Wooster Square area, their names forever carved into the World War II Veteran's Memorial Monument honor roll in Columbus Green, erected some years later by The Historic Wooster Square Association in memory of those from the 11th Ward who made the ultimate sacrifice for their country. For the time being gold stars hung in windows to memorialize their deaths. And families and friends of deceased servicemen were going to funerals much in the way elderly people with rotting teeth went to their dentists—with painful regularity.

Giuliana was haunted by the sight of the star-embroidered banners representing servicemen—gold for the dead, silver for the living—that hung from windows all over the neighborhood. Even more disturbing were the frequent air raid warnings and blackouts: the cacophony of whaling sirens reverberating through deserted streets and the eerie, chilling sight of drawn-down shades in every window, rendered New Haven a veritable ghost town. Also contributing to Giuliana's growing unease was the increasingly apocalyptic talk she kept hearing about bomb shelters. Were such ominous war preparations being played out on the other side of the Atlantic in her home town of Amalfi as well, Giuliana worried?

Little by little the neighborhood, and soon the entire city, was drained of young men. Most were called up in the selective service draft. Many others volunteered. Whenever Giuliana passed a poster announcing that UNCLE SAM WANTS YOU, she couldn't help but wonder how many unsuspecting young men the gray-bearded old man in top hat waving his emphatically pointed finger had successfully recruited. She shuddered when Umberto one day announced that if he were younger and an American citizen, he would gladly join the army. Since this wasn't possible, he would do what he could to support the war effort by buying war bonds and adhering to food rationing by planting a truncated version of a victory garden in two orange crates he placed on the fire escape outside the kitchen window.

He also quit his day job at the meat-packing plant and worked the late-night shift, after leaving his restaurant job, at the area's largest manufacturer of rifles and munitions, the Winchester Fire Arms Company, once home to Eli Whitney's Fire Arms Company, which Whitney started long after he had invented the cotton gin. Like so many men and women of Italian extraction who, for whatever reason, were unable to join the armed forces, Umberto wanted to put to rest once and for all any lingering doubts as to his and their loyalty to the American cause. Americans were being asked to make sacrifices, and though he wasn't as yet a citizen, Umberto Fassano felt honor-bound to do his share.

As for what effect the war was having on the people of Amalfi, and on her brothers serving in Mussolini's and, by extension, Hitler's army, Giuliana was not quite certain. Nor was she sure how much credence she should attach to the news she was getting from her family in Italy or, for that matter, from her own neighbors about what was happening across the Atlantic. In either case, she kept her worries and fears to herself. And dove into school work and other activities with fearsome determination that even for her bordered on obsessive.

# Chapter 23

Christmas was Giuliana's favorite holiday. But this year her customary joyful mood was tempered by what was unfolding on the world stage, mostly the war being waged in Europe and on Italian soil. When gut-wrenching word reached New Haven via telegram in late September from Nonna Dona that Alfredo and Roberto Landini, serving together in the same Italian Army infantry unit, had been captured in a small town outside of Paris and were now in the hands of the French, Giuliana's worst fears were realized.

She tried to put the best face on this new development as much as she could by convincing herself that all would turn out right in the end, believing—praying really—that the French, known for their adherence to the rules of war, would treat her brothers and all other prisoners compassionately, Italian and German alike. She put her head down on the desk and petitioned St. Lucy to light the way to safety for her brothers, and prayed to God that He would give all the Landinis and all the Fassanos, here and abroad, the strength they needed to get through this trying time.

*     *     *

The first storm of the season arrived two days after Christmas recess had ended, dumping over a foot of snow on the city. Schools closed for another two days, giving children unaccustomed to the joys of winter a chance at building snowmen or trying out for the first time their shiny new Flexible Flyers. Giuliana marveled at how beautiful everything looked, even the drabbest parts of the area, now cloaked in a mantle of white.

Remarkably, the cold didn't seem to bother her. She liked the feeling of it on her smooth, blemish-free face. She wore less winter clothing, so as not to restrict her movements, than her guardians felt was appropriate during this time of year. In her first real experience with snow she attacked it with gusto, digging the shovel deeply into the undulating sweeps of white stuff that reached high up against the face of the building in the tiny concrete area between her brownstone and the one attached next door. One by one, three of her girl friends came by to lend a hand. Together they built a fort, wide and high enough to protect against the onslaught of snowballs that in minutes would soon be tossed in their direction by devilish boys eager to show off their powerful pitching arms before proceeding to the best spot for sledding—down the long driveway that separated the block of tenements where Giuliana lived from the one around the corner.

At this stage of her life, exposure to a typical New England winter was more an experience to be relished, not dreaded. But two days after her twelfth birthday on February 16—the date in 304 A.D. of St. Juliana's birth, the patron saint of pregnant women, after whom Giuliana was named—the winter of 1942 became the winter of her deepest discontent. When she walked in the door from school a few minutes after three, she found her uncle sitting at the kitchen table, her aunt at the stove making coffee. Immediately she sensed something was wrong: Umberto was never up at this hour. His usual regimen was to sleep the morning and most of the afternoon away—having arrived home around 8:00 am from his 11-7 job at Winchester's—then rise about 4:30 to go to his job across the street waiting tables at Randazzi's. What was he doing up so early?

He rose from his chair and went to Giuliana, drawing her tightly to him. "Come sit, my dear," he said with downcast eyes, his shoulders sagging under the weight of what he was about to tell his niece. "I have some bad news."

When Giuliana learned of her grandmother's death she handled her grief not by retreating into a shell but by writing long letters to her parents and Maddalena, pleading for every detail of Nonna's passing and wanting to know how it was affecting those in Amalfi who had been closest to her. It would be several weeks before she learned the facts. They came in a lengthy letter from Father Di Pina: Donatella Teresa Mancuso Fassano, he wrote, did not die from having been struck by a wayward automobile or an omnibus negotiating the treacherous hairpin turns of the Amalfi drive, as Giuliana had feared, and where far too many Amalfitani over the years, mostly on foot, had met their terrible fate. Nor had she died from a sudden stroke. Her death, it was determined, was slow and insidious, the result of an almost lifelong fight she waged with a rheumatic, enlarged, diseased heart that finally gave out. The frequent trips she made to Salerno were not on family business as she told everyone, but for medical check-ups; Doctor Vito Graziano, her Sicilian-born cardiologist, had been treating her for years. Besides the doctor, the only other person privy to the nature of Donatella's condition was Father Marco; he never uttered a word to another soul, family or friend.

How could it be? Giuliana kept asking herself. Everyone in Amalfi who knew her never failed to remark how wonderful she looked, always beautifully composed, even regal in her bearing. Never sickly. It surprised Giuliana, shocked might be more accurate, that her grandmother had had a heart problem. Except for her being out of breath from time to time from climbing the steep stone steps from the street to the house, Donatella never exhibited any symptoms that would lead family or friends to believe she had anything more seriously wrong with her than, perhaps, a case of creeping old age.

Giuliana slumped in her chair, at first stunned into silence by the devastating news. She then began to whimper like a lost abandoned pup, surrendering any attempt at being brave. She couldn't stop the torrent of tears running down her face, even as her aunt bent over her, hugging her around the shoulders, trying to console her any way she knew how.

"Why didn't she tell anyone?" Giuliana said, in a voice reeking of despair as she rose from her chair and paced about, in meaningless circles, the kitchen floor. "How long had she been sick? Why didn't she go to a hospital? Why didn't she have an operation?" Rhetorical, unanswerable questions asked more of herself than of her aunt and uncle. As her mood vacillated between rueful remorse, for ever having left home in the first place, and unmitigated anger, for Nonna Dona dying before she had a chance to see her one last time, Giuliana tried to convince herself that she was somehow responsible for her grandmother's death, which conceivably might have been prevented from happening had she known of Nonna Dona's condition. "I should never have left Amalfi," she said. She sat silent for a moment, then rose and went to her uncle, her face a mask of sadness and fatigue. In a voice wilted by exhaustion, she said softly: "I want to go home."

Details of Nonna Dona's elaborate funeral in Amalfi came in a long letter Dr. Gallardo wrote to Giuliana. That letter would be as close as she would get for some time before setting foot again on her native soil. All of the Landini and Fassano families—save Giuliana, her two brothers away at war, and uncle Umberto and wife Concetta— were at her funeral. Plus scores of admirers and acquaintances from in and around Amalfi, who came to celebrate her life and mourn her death. So many people, in fact, that the funeral Mass had to be held in Sant'Andrea Cathedral instead of Donatella's own Santa Croce parish church; special permission had to be given for Father Di Pina to celebrate the high Mass of burial for his dearly departed friend. In a heartfelt eulogy, he paid tribute "to a truly remarkable woman who devoted her entire life to her God, to her family and, unselfishly, to those less fortunate than she."

Donatella Teresa Mancuso Fassano, 1886-1942, devoted wife of Alfonso Fassano; loving mother of daughter Maria and son Umberto; grandmother to Alfredo, Roberto, Luigi and Giuliana Landini; mother-in-law to Antonio Landini and Concetta Fassano . . . was interred in the Fassano family plot next to her husband in the cemetery behind Santa Croce Church where she had worshiped practically her entire life.

*   *   *

Giuliana did not spend the next sixteen months pining over the death of Nonna Dona, but not a day went by that she didn't have her grandmother in her thoughts—and in her heart. She compensated for her loss by committing herself even more to the goal of getting the education Donatella, and Camilla McDonough, among others, convinced her she deserved. She dove into school work with a vengeance—studying and studying, writing and writing, working on her vocabulary and verbal skills until they became second nature. It paid off: at St. Michael's School eighth grade graduation ceremony in the church in June of 1943, Giuliana Landini was awarded, along with her diploma, a special certificate for having achieved the highest grades in her class which, under normal circumstances, would have automatically won for her a full scholarship to Sacred Heart High School for Girls, around the corner from the convent up the street.

But because Giuliana had been in St. Michael's for only two years, together with her not having as yet attained American citizenship, it was felt by both the principal and the pastor that, as regrettable as it might be, she would have to be disqualified; the second-best student in her class, another girl, received the scholarship in her place.

Truth be told, Giuliana was not upset. She had decided some time back that she wanted to attend New Haven's excellent public high school, Hillhouse, not the convent school, as most everyone thought she would, including her aunt and uncle, who remained fixed in the notion that it would be best for Giuliana to stay close by in the neighborhood, in an all-girls environment, under the watchful eyes of nuns. The Fassanos had also counted on the scholarship they knew Giuliana was likely to be awarded as the academically highest ranking eighth-grader. This meant, of course, that they wouldn't have to pay a tuition that would seriously eat into their meager savings earmarked for starting a business.

Up to now, Donatella had provided most of the funds supporting Giuliana, and it was generally assumed by Umberto that when his mother passed on, there would be enough money to sustain the young girl at least through high school. Whatever Maria and Antonio Landini had earmarked for their daughter went regularly into a fund, as the family had agreed, for her college education. It was also generally assumed that the inheritance Donatella had received from her parents' cheese business (more modest than expected), together with what her husband had left from his masonry and building business (also less than anticipated), would be more than enough to provide for her comfort later in life. Even with that, there would still be ample funds in the estate for her two children and four grandchildren, the largest share going to Giuliana, when she died.

But that turned out not to be the case. Donatella's affairs had for years been handled by her lawyer and good friend, Francesco Montone. Shortly after his client died he delivered the unfortunate news to each of her heirs that they had been left only a small sum from the proceeds of her will. He went on to explain, in person to Maria and her family, and in separate letters to Umberto and Giuliana, that Donatella for years had literally been giving her money away—to poor farmers in the mountainous cheese-making region of Scala, where she originally was from prior to her move to the seaside village of Amalfi after her marriage to Alfonso Fassano, as well as to fishermen in hamlets and villages along the coast whose prospects were very often threatened by too much competition and too many mouths to feed. She found in Father Di Pina a kindred spirit who shared her concerns for the poor and needy and, together, they doled out food, clothing and other necessities—most of which they payed for themselves—plus what else they could lay their hands on, to people who had become more and more dependent on their largesse.

When Donatella died, practically every grateful beneficiary she had ever helped came to pay his or her last respects and offer their condolences. In the midst of their grieving, they fretted over what would happen to them now that this saint of a woman, who was always there to help, would no longer be around to come to their aid.

One would have thought such circumstances would render it more palatable for Umberto to accept the reality of having Giuliana attend the public high school, especially in light of his now having to assume more of the financial burden of caring for his niece.

Being a proud man, he was unhappy with not having a choice in the matter. But being also a sensible man, he recognized that these were forces well outside his control.

Giuliana herself made the compelling case that if she were ever to completely assimilate and come to understand what the United States was really all about, she would have to broaden her horizons—leave the comforts of the safe, insular, homogeneous environment that was

Wooster Square and enter a world made up of people of different racial, ethnic and religious backgrounds. Had not Umberto himself made much the same argument time and time again? America, she had always been told, was the great melting pot—now was the time, at age thirteen, for her to find out just how successful she was going to be in mixing in with different classes of people, and in more diversified places.

Giuliana made the adjustment seamlessly. In practically no time at all, she had a wide stable of friends, no longer exclusively Italian-American girls and boys from one part of town, but Irish and Poles, Jews and Hispanics, Blacks and Greeks—also a very smart Chinese boy both of whose parents were professors at Yale—from all over the city. Even the faculty was different. Where once she had been taught by female teachers exclusively, there were now male teachers, too, teaching some of her courses. She found the experience exhilarating. And totally liberating.

All four years of high school, in fact, were academically positive ones. But her first two years, though harder than the last two, gave her the most satisfaction. By sophomore year she had really begun to hit her stride. Always self assured, she was now in every way a mature, preternaturally self confident young woman. Her grasp of English was as good as, if not better than, most young people her age. And her accent was practically gone. At five feet, eight inches, with one more inch to grow, she was taller than most of the girls, and her winning smile—the kind that lit up a person's soul—together with her Mediterranean good looks and a body that had begun to fill in nicely, elicited constant attention from boys in her class and those in the upper grades, as well.

Though she was flattered, Giuliana neither encouraged nor sought such attention. She wanted no part of boy-girl entanglements, at least not now, and not at this age. She simply had too much else going on in her life to let in complicated distractions, boys being at the top of the list. Her art, for one, under the benign encouragement of her Neighborhood House mentors, had taken on an entirely new and what was for her an ambitious turn of direction: she started painting in oils, the creative fruits of which she reveled in. But she also found that painting was infinitely harder than drawing, not to mention that it demanded a greater time commitment on her part.

Always an inveterate reader of fiction and history primarily, she now added to her ever expanding and eclectic reading list an entirely new genre—cookbooks. Her home economics teacher made the initial introduction, *Fannie Farmer and The Joy of Cooking* being the first of a steady stream of cooking guides she would be using for reference through the years. As soon as she discovered a new book or manual, she took those recipes she considered the best candidates for her style of innovative cooking, reworked them and, in so doing, concocted totally new dishes, calling on her fertile imagination and an Italian touch for inspiration and guidance. When the results pleased her, she made a meticulous step-by-step recording of the recipes and then tested her culinary experiments on her most willing subjects—her aunt and uncle and their tight circle of friends.

Besides a penchant for writing recipes, Giuliana kept up with daily diary entries (she was already well into a second journal), and remained faithful to the obligatory writing of letters back home. How she found the time, while trying to lead some semblance the life of a normal high school teenager, was a constant marvel to her family and the small circle of close friends she allowed into her extraordinarily hectic but productive life.

# Chapter 24

Giuliana loved school. But summer was her favorite time of year since coming to the United States. That was when she got to see Camilla. The relationship that had first surfaced between student and teacher when they were in Amalfi had now blossomed into a full-blown friendship. And as time went by each woman came to play an increasingly important role in the other person's life. There was little Giuliana did not discuss with Camilla, and vise versa. Separated most of the year, the women nurtured their friendship through a steady stream of letters, writing openly about whatever was on their minds.

When they did get to see each other during the summer for a week or two, either in New Haven or New York, they spent hours on end reprising what they had covered in their lengthy correspondence. With her grandmother gone, Giuliana looked to Camilla to fill the role of surrogate, that indispensable someone with whom she could share her innermost concerns—school, her art, her writing, her career aspirations. As much as she would have liked she didn't feel her aunt, whom she adored as well as respected, was the person she could turn to for guidance since Concetta's narrow interests nowhere approximated those of her precocious, more worldly niece. Nor, for that matter, her mother, who was thousands of miles away and obviously not readily available to counsel her daughter when she most needed it. Conversely, Camilla, despite being more than twice as old as Giuliana, held her in such high regard that she readily acknowledged the younger woman to be as much a sounding board for her own concerns as she was for her young friend's.

As soon as Camilla arrived in New York for her annual summer stay, she phoned Giuliana (the Fassanos finally had telephone service, a three-party line), and the two made arrangements for Giuliana, with Umberto's and Concetta's blessings, to spend a week in Manhattan prior to the young Scottish woman's going off to Washington to write a travel piece on the nation's capital for the *Glasgow Times*. Since Margaret Watson, Camilla's college friend at whose apartment she was staying while in New York, planned to be away that same week in July, Jennifer Kirby was also invited to come up from Philadelphia the latter part of the week to make it a happy threesome. Jennifer timed her arrival to coincide with Giuliana's last two days in New York; together they would take the train to New Haven, Jennifer having made plans to visit her fiancé for a few days.

The week turned out to be one of the most exciting in Giuliana's young life. Playing the role of host and tour guide, Camilla took Giuliana everywhere: to the top of the Empire State Building—"what an incredible view!"; Rockefeller Center; St. Patrick's Cathedral—"for a church that's been around only since 1858 it's quite impressive, but nowhere near as grand as our Sant'Andrea;" Radio City Music Hall, for a performance of *The Little Prince*, Giuliana's attendance at her first live stage show, which she loved. An entire day was reserved for a trip on the ferry to the Statue of Liberty: they went all the way up to the observation deck nestled in Lady Liberty's crown: "an even more incredible view than the one from the Empire State Building," and then to Ellis Island, the entrance point to America for thousands upon thousands of Italian immigrants. That visit moved the young girl in ways she hadn't expected.

Since cooking was not high on Camilla's list of priorities but eating was, the two friends dined out all week long. This delighted Giuliana since it gave her an opportunity to taste foods she hadn't eaten before.

Ironically, one of the most enjoyable meals she had was at an elegant northern Italian restaurant whose food, while new to her, she found much to her liking. All during the meal she asked the waiter to elaborate on each dish, making mental notes, which she transcribed later that evening with an eye toward replicating the dishes, and adding them to her growing collection of recipes.

There were other surprises during the week, such as the wonderful meal she had at a West Side French bistro: Giuliana declared the coq au vin to be divine and the *tarte tatin* to be out of this world. The fiery Mexican food was another treat, and the Peking duck, with its succulent crackling skin, eaten at a nondescript place in Chinatown, was also something the young gourmet savored and celebrated.

But what turned out to be, not surprisingly, one of her favorite spots in the city, more for the novelty than for the food, "although the food wasn't bad either," she later wrote, was the famous Horn & Hardart Automat on 42nd Street. It wasn't hard to fathom why Giuliana was attracted to the place. She had never seen anything like it, and was totally captivated by the concept: "Imagine seeing different plates of food appear behind little glass windows and then, after placing coins in the slots, taking whatever you selected from out behind the tiny compartment doors."

The two women ate lunch there twice. On each occasion Giuliana had what she called a "pie lunch"—chicken pot pie for the main course, lemon meringue pie for dessert. In recounting the experience to her aunt and uncle, she told them that on her next visit to New York she would have to try the macaroni and cheese and the Automat's famous rice pudding, both of which Camilla declared to be excellent choices.

While relaxing in the apartment one evening after a full day of sightseeing followed by another satisfying dinner, Giuliana went into her suitcase and took out a thick stack of papers held together by two thick rubber bands. "I'd like you to take a look at this, Camilla. I've been waiting a long time to get your reaction."

"Is this the diary you've been writing since coming to the United States?" asked Camilla, examining the parcel and its blank top page. She removed the rubber bands and began leafing through the stack of pages, pausing here and there to read some of the text. It was not a diary, but eighty-five typed pages of recipes. Before Camilla had a chance to react, Giuliana said, "This isn't complete yet . . . I'd like to include at least another twenty-five recipes, which I'm working on. What do you think, Camilla?"

"I have to say I'm impressed, Jules," said Camilla, using the pet nickname she'd recently come to calling the girl. Giuliana loved it; it made her feel special. But there was the slightest hint of irritation in the older woman's voice for not having been made privy sooner to the latest undertaking of her always surprisingly resourceful young friend.

"I realize you've been cooking up a storm practically your entire life, and doing it magnificently I might add, but you never once gave me an inkling you were working on anything as ambitious as a cookbook." Then: "I didn't think you were keeping secrets from me, you naughty girl," she said, playfully slapping Giuliana on the knee.

"I wanted it to be a surprise. Every time I picked up a pen to write to you about it I had all to do . . . what's that expression you taught me . . . to keep from spilling the beans," Giuliana said, laughing a laugh that to Camilla was no longer childlike.

"My God, this is bloody impressive," Camilla said as she flipped through the pages raising her distinctive Scottish accent an octave, while resorting to the use of a word she was striving mightily to erase from her vocabulary. "How long have you been at it?"

"I started compiling notes on dishes my mother prepared as soon as I learned how to write. I always loved being in the kitchen with her. Then when grandma came to live with us . . . she did most of the cooking . . . she saw how interested I was in what she was doing and encouraged me to keep a record of the recipes for when I got older. Then there was all that time I spent with Maddalena at the church rectory, the best cook of all.

"But it was never my intention to try my hand at putting together a cookbook . . . I didn't know such a thing even existed until I showed some of what I had written to my home economics teacher. She's the one who really encouraged me . . . and gave me a couple of cookbooks to study. I'd never seen one before, since there aren't many cookbooks around. I suppose that's why she suggested I start thinking seriously about doing an Italian cookbook . . . she said it might be the first of its kind in America. I don't know if that's true, but I can tell you that no cook I know in Italy or in New Haven uses anything but her own two eyes for measuring ingredients in a dish. And they certainly didn't write anything down, as far as I know. To them cooking is strictly instinctive."

She then added: "Do you think I'm at a point where I need to get some professional advice on what to do next?"

"Let me see what I can do," Camilla offered. "Since I've been writing these travel pieces I've gotten to know several people in newspapers and publishing. I'll ask around to see if there is any such thing as publishing devoted exclusively to food, either in book form or in general interest publications, like magazines. In the meantime, I suggest you continue doing what you're doing."

"There's something else related to this project I've been working on," said Giuliana as she reached again into her suitcase and pulled out a cylinder perhaps a dozen inches in length. A piece of tightly wound wax paper held down by masking tape covered the roll, which she gently removed. One by one, she unfurled a series of delicately rendered eight by ten inch paintings, in oil, on linen, of different food groups, and handed them to Camilla. "What I'm thinking of doing is reproducing these paintings and placing them throughout the book. From the few cookbooks I've seen there are very few pictures, mostly text. When I showed these to Mrs. Lerner and Miss Carroll at the Neighborhood House they both thought it was a good idea. What do you think, Camilla?" An approving smile and nod was exactly what Giuliana was hoping for.

The next morning the young ladies set out for the Metropolitan Museum of Art.

They took a subway to 53rd and Fifth Avenue and walked the rest of the way to 84th Street, where the museum was located, stopping here and there along the way to allow Giuliana all the time she needed to admire the tall buildings and different architecture that made up part of the city's spectacular skyline. Giuliana loved strolling the city, so walking long distances was never a problem for her or her friend. If anything, Giuliana, new to the delights of Manhattan, relished gazing up at the massive skyscrapers all over town, dreaming that one day she'd design something as noteworthy—in New York, of course. When in midtown, particularly, she also liked to watch—gawk at really— the bevy of striking women in their fashionable outfits and expensive jewelry parading up and down Fifth Avenue. To her, the street was like a runway for models.

Camilla tried to prepare her young friend for what she was about to see in the museum: a treasure trove of art, sculpture and ancient artifacts, the likes of which would make her head spin. But it was the paintings that left Giuliana breathless, lavishing most of her attention on the French and Dutch masters. One she couldn't take her eyes off and spent minutes studying—up close, from either side, straight on, and from a distance—was a portrait of a certain Madame Leblanc by the great French painter, Jean Auguste Dominique Ingres.

When she caught sight of the painting as she entered the small side room off the main gallery where many great French Impressionist paintings were hung, Giuliana came up short. She whispered to Camilla that she was puzzled to learn the exquisite picture was done by a Frenchman, not an Italian, as she first suspected. Even to the girl's relatively untrained eye it looked Italian. Its subject, how she was dressed, the bold colors, the beautiful simplicity of line, its overall composition bore a striking resemblance to the St. Lucy painting hanging in her bedroom. It ran chills up and down her spine.

When she ventured closer to study it more thoroughly and read the notes on the wall next to it describing the painting's provenance, she gave out a sigh loud enough to make the handful of other gallery viewers turn and cast an irritated and disapproving glance in her direction. I'm right, she said to herself. True, the work is indeed that of a non-Italian, but the picture had actually been painted in Florence long before Ingres, who spent many years in Rome, became prominent among French artists of his day, the early and mid 1800s. He was even awarded the prestigious Prix de Rome soon thereafter.

In acquainting Camilla with these facts after leaving the Metropolitan on the way to their next stop, the Hayden Planetarium at the American Museum of Natural History, Giuliana had Camilla promise that on her next visit to New Haven she would take a closer look at the St. Lucy painting to see for herself how similar it was to the Ingres.

"By the way, have you showed the St. Lucy painting to your friends at the Neighborhood House?" Camilla inquired.

"As a matter of fact, they saw it last week when I showed them some of my drawings. They both liked the painting very much. Especially

Miss Carroll . . . she was an art history major in college. She thinks it might be valuable. She told me she was going to have the head of Yale's Fine Arts Department, a friend of hers, take a look at it."

"That's excellent," exclaimed Camilla. "I'd love to know what he says. If the painting is as valuable as everybody says it is, we'll bring it to New York to get it properly appraised. I'm thinking Christie's or Sotheby's . . . they're two of the best art auction houses in the world. I realize the painting's worth is not why you love it so, but learning that it might be really worth something would be a nice thing for you to know. I'm happy I brought you here."

"So am I," Giuliana said, taking Camilla affectionately by the hand. They walked down Fifth Avenue to the mouth of Central Park and decided to rest a minute or two at the fountain outside the Plaza Hotel, an ideal vantage point for viewing the passing parade. *Who are all these people, and where are they going?* Giuliana thought to herself. As she was absorbed in these and other thoughts, Camilla, out of the blue, announced in the most blasé tone of voice, "I had my first date in America last week."

Giuliana could not restrain herself: "Tell me all about it, Camilla, everything," she yelped, folding her legs under her torso, then crossing her arms across the chest so as to assume just the right pose needed for absorbing such startling news.

"He's a beat reporter covering City Hall for the *New York Herald Tribune*. I met him at a press gathering at the Roosevelt Hotel. We happened to sit next to each other and got into a conversation about the war. When we were about to leave he asked if I was interested in continuing our rather heated discussion over dinner sometime. He asked for my number and I gave it to him. A few days later he called, and last week we went out. We had a most enjoyable evening, partly I think because we discussed practically everything but the horrible bloody war. He's very nice. He's from a town outside of Cleveland, Shaker Heights I believe he said. He went to the Columbia School of Journalism . . . I'm told it's the best journalism school in this country. He has a regular byline in the *Trib*. He's a very good writer. When I return from Washington we're going to have another tete a tete. By the way, his name is Gordon deVries."

Giuliana took all of this in with mounting excitement. "How wonderful, Camilla. Do you think it could develop into something . . ." she paused dutifully for emphasis before adding, "meaningful?"

"Don't let's get ahead of ourselves . . . I've only been on a proper date with the man once," Camilla allowed, trying unsuccessfully to ward off Giuliana's further inquiries. "My only purpose in telling you about him in the first place, Jules, is to get you to stop your constant badgering regarding my love life." (Camilla had told Giuliana of her first love interest, the essential parts only.)

"So now you know. Yes, smarty pants, I've started dating again. I haven't given a moment's thought to whether this relationship has a chance of developing into anything meaningful, as you put it, only time will tell. Meanwhile, I plan to get on with life, which you may be interested to know is soon to take on a whole new direction: I've decided to give up teaching. Once I've met my five-year commitment to remain at Santa Croce School as I promised Father Marco, the year after next, I've decided to move to New York permanently. I believe this is where my future lies. Besides, I love the place."

Giuliana found it hard to digest all the news: Camilla dating again, giving up teaching, moving to New York. What else was likely to come next? "Oh, that's marvelous," Giuliana exclaimed, throwing her arms around Camilla. "That means I'll get to see you more often."

"Very true, but that's not the reason I want to live here," Camilla chuckled playfully. "I'm going to devote my entire time to writing.

Since doing these travel pieces for the *Glasgow Times*, I've discovered that I really love the work—the travel, the research, everything. But what I find most rewarding is the shear writing of the words. When they come together the way I think they should, there's no feeling quite like it. It's a rush I can't explain, and I never want to lose it. As much as I love teaching, I think you know that, I've never experienced quite the same feeling I do as when I'm stringing sentences together. I've got the *Glasgow Times* to thank for that . . . they've given me the opportunity of a lifetime. And they've opened doors for me I couldn't possibly have done on my own, like meeting new people in the business . . . Gordon for instance. I'm pretty sure these contacts are going to be helpful in my landing a permanent job, hopefully at either *Life* or *Look* or some other prestigious magazine."

Topping off the exciting week in New York—as if what they had done for the five previous days hadn't all been special—was the trip Giuliana, Camilla and Jennifer, who had arrived the night before, made to the Bronx. And to Yankee Stadium. When they walked through the portal that led to the excellent box seats behind first base, a gift from Mr. Kirby to his daughter and her two friends, Giuliana was dazzled, much as she'd been on her first visit to Yale Bowl. But here even more so. To be in a major league baseball park, especially this hallowed one, was an experience she had no idea would be so memorable, and what she saw cemented her life-long love affair with baseball: a perfectly manicured, plush pea-green outfield surrounding a brownish-red clay dirt infield; gleaming white bases; players in immaculate uniforms, their knickers rolled up just under the knees; four authoritative-looking men in blue (the umpires). Plus a raucous crowd of almost 70,000 die-hard baseball fans. All part of the mise'en scene that made up thrilling Yankee Stadium (the house that Babe Ruth built, it was explained). That sight alone would have been enough to turn even the most casual observer into a baseball fan. But what happened next permanently solidified baseball's place in Giuliana's heart: in the bottom of the ninth inning Frankie Crosetti, the Yankees' popular shortstop and a particular favorite of the all-things-Italian, baseball-crazy, predominantly-Yankee-rooting Wooster Street neighborhood, hit a bases-clearing double in the gap in left-center field to secure a come-from-behind, last-at-bat, walk-off win against the Philadelphia Athletics.

Giuliana's initiation to major league baseball—the national pastime, Camilla told her it was called—was duly recorded in her memory bank of unforgettable experiences. Her only regret was not getting to see Joe DiMaggio play; he was serving in the army and wouldn't be back in a Yankee uniform until 1946. She couldn't wait.

# Chapter 25

Umberto was at Union Station in New Haven to greet Giuliana and Jennifer Kirby when they came in from the city. After the latter hopped a cab to her fiancé's apartment, Giuliana fell into her uncle's warm embrace, all atwitter as she started to recount what had transpired during her memorable week in New York. But she was cut off just as quickly by Umberto's own recitation of events that had occurred during her absence: that very morning Radio Free Europe confirmed that Allied Forces in Sicily had defeated Mussolini's army, toppling his Fascist government; the dictator was rescued by the Germans and sent to Fascist northern Italy. (He would remain there until he and his mistress were later assassinated). In due course all captured Italian POWs were to be released. "You wait and see, Alfredo and Roberto will soon be home."

The news was so overwhelming that an "Oh my God," repeated over and over, was all Giuliana could manage in response. But no sooner had she learned such good news, she had to steel herself against the bad: while Giuliana was away, Concetta had suffered a miscarriage. Giuliana wasn't even aware her aunt was pregnant; the Fassanos planned on springing the happy surprise when she got back from New York. Now she learned this was in fact the third time her aunt had miscarried, all since she and Umberto arrived in the United States.

"The doctor says this one was very serious. He told me it would be too dangerous for your aunt to become pregnant again. Next week she will be in the hospital having a hysterectomy. We will never have children . . . ever." Umberto made the declaration with such sadness and finality that his face contorted into the most painful frown. Giuliana's body quaked, her legs quivered, the suitcase and parcels she carried felt like weights. But she did not cry. Instead she held his hand so tightly that her long, thin, delicate fingers seemed in danger of crumbling in her uncle's powerful palm. They made the fifteen-minute walk from the station to their flat in stony silence.

Giuliana tore up the stairs, leaving her uncle alone at the stoop to carry up her suitcase and a shopping bag of gifts she had purchased for herself and her guardians. Turning quickly into the hallway leading to her aunt and uncle's front bedroom all she saw was an empty bed. She let out a muffled, plaintive moan and rushed back into the kitchen, then into her bedroom. Concetta lay motionless on the narrow twin bed, her deep-set eyes closed, sunken into dark blue pockets, her ashen face clammy from the humid July air. The only audible sound in the room emanated from a hissing portable desktop fan too weak to throw off anything but not-so-cool breezes. Concetta had the appearance of a woman twice her age.

Momentarily recoiled by the sight, Giuliana immediately pictured her grandmother: how much younger than her aunt had Nonna Dona looked, even at sixty-six, the age she had just turned the last time Giuliana saw her. She knelt beside the bed. Concetta let slip to the floor the rosary in her limp hand. "Please get a damp cloth and wipe my forehead, Giuliana," Concetta whispered, opening her eyes while straining to put a smile on a face now drained of much of its prettiness. "I'm so happy to have you home."

The next days and weeks of Concetta's convalescence was a period of nonstop work for Giuliana. Accustomed to putting responsibility before pleasure, she accepted her role as de facto head of the household. She let slide her own activities to see to her uncle, take care of the house, do the shopping and cooking—and tend to her aunt, who by now was imprisoned in an emotional netherworld. She even tried for a time doing customers' laundry that had piled up since Concetta's miscarriage. At first, they were understanding of the child's plight, but when they learned that Concetta was going into the hospital for an operation that would render her incapacitated for at best a couple of weeks, perhaps longer, all but a few came to retrieve what they had left with the laundress. Giuliana knew full well they wouldn't be returning anytime soon to enlist her aunt's services.

How easy it is for a slide to turn into an avalanche. It would take months before Concetta got back any semblance of her former self. Even then Giuliana, as much concerned now about her aunt's health as she once had been about the safety of her two brothers fighting in the war, wasn't sure her aunt was over the bitter disappointment she felt at the thought of never being able to have children. What Giuliana could only hope for was that her aunt's inner strength and fortitude would be enough to see her through this trying ordeal. After all, wasn't she the one, the only one, who had been able to tackle the job of grounding Umberto and getting him going in a new, positive direction? Wasn't she the one who convinced her husband, much to his initial reluctance, to allow her to work to help with building the nest egg they would eventually need to start a business together? Hadn't she, more than her husband, been the one who had made their niece feel completely at home in her new surroundings?

So it wasn't altogether a surprise to Giuliana, and Umberto, too, that as soon as Concetta felt well enough to quit her bed after a few weeks and resume some of the normal activities associated with running the house, she actually came out of her funk looking better than they could possibly have expected: color was now rouged back into her high-boned cheeks, her face had recaptured its prettiness, and the few pounds she had put on during her sedentary post-operative convalescence added an attractive touch of voluptuousness to her former too-thin, petite silhouette.

And yet, whatever positive physical changes were evident in her appearance, they did not seem to make up for the obvious torment Concetta was suffering, psychologically and emotionally, deep down inside: the pangs of a woman unfulfilled. In the grand scheme of things, she would often tell Giuliana, women were meant to have children. And healthy Italian women, as so many non-Italian people liked to remark rather derisively, were meant to have a lot of children. Just like her mother and grandmother before her. The undeniable realization that this was not now possible led her into previously unexplored areas of reflection, resulting in her having to spend more time than she should have searching for answers as to why an otherwise healthy woman, at the height of her fecund years, had become victim to an intractable uterus unable to bear the weight of a tiny fetus for no more than three months. The only reasonable conclusion she could come to, sadly, was that working practically night and day six days a week since coming to America—exactly what her husband most feared when he questioned whether she should be working at all—had worn her out.

There were other concerns Concetta felt she had to face up to, her husband being her principal worry. She saw how painful it was for Umberto to see her like this. Of even more concern to her was how he might be dealing with the thought of having a wife who was barren. Would the deep love they had for one another be enough to sustain a marriage now bereft of one of its potentially greatest gifts? She tried to reconstruct every conversation they had ever had, either before or after they were married, on the subject of children. Umberto inevitably shied away from such a discussion, admitting only that he wanted his children to be born in the United States. Concetta was always skeptical of this argument. For while he said he wanted kids, American kids, Concetta was never quite certain he meant it. That is until Giuliana came to live with them. The way he doted on the young girl, the amount of time he spent with her despite his work-consumed schedule, led Concetta to believe that he would indeed embrace fatherhood, that he even welcomed it. He said as much only months after settling into their flat on Wooster Street, once the place had been renovated to their mutual liking, and well before the couple had time to get used to the idea that their niece would soon be permanently moving in with them.

*   *   *

Giuliana later learned that try as she might, it took Concetta over a year to conceive. Umberto's unbounded excitement over the announcement filled Concetta with joy: finally, she was the expectant mother she always wanted to be. But their euphoria was short lived. Entering her second trimester, she inexplicably suffered a miscarriage, throwing her husband into alternate stages of stoic resignation and bouts of crushing despondency, and herself into a state of bottomless depression. The cycle was repeated with her second pregnancy just before Giuliana arrived from Italy, and now with this final, life-threatening episode. The Fassanos were inconsolable, and their young ward, Giuliana, sadder than she could ever remember being, including the days and weeks following her separation from family and from the life she once knew in Amalfi. This posed yet another worry that preyed on Concetta's fragile state of mind: how Giuliana was dealing with her aunt's emotional crisis.

Giuliana had grown quite comfortable in the short time she had been with her extended family, one might say even like a daughter discovering a new mother and father. In every aspect, she had adapted well to new surroundings. But all that now threatened to become unhinged. With the daunting burden of having to care for a sick aunt—for how long was anyone's guess—as well as for the concomitant responsibilities attendant to running the house, Giuliana would have to forestall, perhaps even eliminate altogether, one or more of her passionate pursuits: her art, her writing, the recipe book. That thought alone was enough to propel Concetta into an even deeper depression.

Giuliana was determined not to let that happen. She told herself she would have to reassess her priorities. Coming to America had been at the urging of others—parents, teachers, spiritual advisers, friends of the family—who felt that taking up citizenship in America would give her a better chance at reaching her full potential. Her primary job, it was continually emphasized, was for her to get the best education possible, do well and take advantage of opportunities. In short, become a success. If, in the bargain, she also proved to be more of a comfort to her aunt and uncle than anyone in the family might have possibly hoped for, so much the better.

That, ironically, was now precisely the case. Giuliana saw herself not as the temporary ward of relatives standing in *loco parentis*, but as an integral and equal member of the Fassano family trinity. As such, the well-being of her aunt and uncle, short—and long-term, became her paramount concern. Everything else would have to remain on hold until such time as conditions got back to normal. She was thus compelled to go to Umberto soon after and discuss with him how best she might be able to help out even more than she was already doing in order to put her uncle's mind at ease now that the other breadwinner in the family was incapacitated, and might be for some time.

During the two weeks Concetta was in the hospital recuperating from her operation, Giuliana was by her side every day until the end of visiting hours. As for Umberto, he curtailed his hours at the factory to be with his wife as much as he could, leaving at 3:30 a.m. instead of 7:30, sleeping until 8, then spending most of the day at the hospital before going off to his restaurant job, which all three agreed he ought not jeopardize by asking the Randazzis for time off he could ill afford to take. Every day Concetta was in the hospital Umberto brought her a single red rose, and his gentleness and caring were a great comfort to his bed-ridden wife, who sorely hoped her husband's present attentiveness would continue to manifest itself once she got home. While bolstered by the attention being lavished on her, she needed, now more than ever, an understanding husband as well as a sympathetic niece to help assuage the guilt she was feeling over the irreversible turn her life had taken, and, by extension, that of the family.

For a time after she got home Concetta felt vaguely outside herself, as if what was happening to her was happening to some stranger she might have met only the day before, say in the park, or on the trolley taking her uptown. But then little things would jolt her back to reality— the children's cup and saucer an aunt had given to her when she was a little girl; she kept them in the cupboard next to the stove. Or the two crocheted finger towels her mother made for her with her name embroidered on the front: all little reminders that it was she, Concetta Fassano, who was the one going through hell and not someone else.

And yet, as the days passed, she began to draw, little by little, from the reservoir of pluck she was famously known for and was able to put to rest the sense of futility she herself and others who loved her had feared would consume her. She was able to get back on her feet by each day doing a little bit more around the house, but not laundering, a job she said she would never under any circumstances do again. While all of this had a salutary effect on her frame of mind, what in the end proved to be the catalyst that permanently snapped her out of her lethargy was, ironically, the birth of a baby, even if it was not hers but someone else's.

On the last day of July, two weeks after Concetta returned home from the hospital, her good friend and neighbor Antoinette Giordano gave birth to a son, Lorenzo, eight pounds five ounces, perfectly healthy as was his petite mother, according to the midwife who delivered the infant in the Giordano second-floor flat two doors away. The baby was hardly out of its mother's womb when Antoinette and Paolo called the Fassanos and asked if they would do them the honor of standing in as godparents at their son's christening. They also asked Concetta if she would help with the baby while Antoinette recovered from her rather difficult delivery, given Lorenzo's size. Not certain how Concetta would react to the request (was it more a kind overture out of pity for their friend?), Umberto and Giuliana held their collective breath.

Try as they might, the two of them as well as their other friends had serious reservations as to how Concetta, whatever the Giordanos' motivation, would be able to handle being around the new baby given all she had gone through, and likely was still going through. But without consulting her husband, Concetta promptly accepted the invitation, telling everyone she was thrilled at the prospect of becoming a godmother, and savoring the notion of helping the new mother and new baby any way she could.

At first the thought of Concetta putting herself even further in a potentially harmful position, emotionally—of being around a newborn infant not her own—made Giuliana uneasy and left Umberto a nervous wreck. But for Concetta, having a place to go every day where she felt wanted, and of use, was crucial to her eventual recovery. Moreover, after witnessing how perfectly comfortable she was around the baby, and the tender, loving way she handled the infant, any reservations Giuliana and her uncle and their friends may have had initially began to dissipate. As did slowly but surely Concetta's mournful state and the perilous emotional abyss she had fallen into.

# Chapter 26

In all the turmoil of the last several weeks, Giuliana had not had a chance to get in touch with Camilla and inform her about the unsettling changes that had taken place in her life. By the time she got around to picking up the phone to call her friend she realized it was much too late, Camilla having several days earlier departed for Washington to assume her travel writing assignment for the *Glasgow Times*. She asked Margaret Dawson to have Camilla get in touch with her as soon as Margaret heard from her roommate. Giuliana couldn't wait to bare her soul to her friend, and when she learned she would possibly not be hearing from Camilla anytime soon, or getting together with her in New Haven as they customarily had done before Camilla returned to Italy at the end of every summer, Giuliana was bitterly disappointed. When given an explanation as to why Camilla had little choice in the matter, Giuliana was somewhat placated, but not much.

In the week between Giuliana's trip to New York and her friend's assignment in Washington, Camilla had had a second date with her newspaper friend, Gordon deVries. Having gotten along so well with him up to this point, she decided to show him the travel pieces she had written for the *Glasgow Times*. Two days later—three days before she was to depart for the nation's capital—Gordon called to inform Camilla that he had read the articles, liked them, and had the editor of the *Tribune's* Sunday travel supplement take a look at them. The editor was equally impressed; he said they were reporting of high quality and extremely well written, which prompted him to have other members of the editorial staff, always on the lookout for new writers with fresh ideas, assess the work.

The consensus was that Camilla had talent. Perhaps she might consider doing a piece for its winter travel edition on a subject she was very likely intimately familiar with, the Scottish Highlands. A call went out to Camilla, thrilled at the chance to come in and discuss the assignment, which she accepted on the spot. Because of the tight but not impossible deadline, it was suggested that upon completing her work in Washington she leave directly for Scotland, which the *Tribune* would arrange, and not return to New York. That would give Camilla three or four weeks to do research and manage a first draft before returning to Amalfi to resume her teaching duties at Santa Croce in the new school year.

Happy on the one hand for her friend's good fortune but disappointed they would not be seeing each other at the end of the summer as they always had, Giuliana was hoping at least that Camilla would call before leaving the United States. The call came through as soon as Camilla arrived at Idlewild Airport.

"You must think me awful for not getting in touch with you sooner, Jules," Camilla said apologetically, "but I hope Margaret explained why I was unable to. Things have moved so fast I've hardly had time to breathe. Even my family doesn't know I'm on my way home. It should be quite a surprise when they see me walk through the door."

Just hearing Camilla's voice made Giuliana feel better. She then went on to recount the events of the last few weeks. Camilla was genuinely saddened to hear the disturbing news about Connie. Giuliana then went into an elaborate explanation about wanting to find work to help her uncle out while her aunt recovered. She asked her older friend's advice on how she should go about getting Umberto's permission to do so.

The idea of Giuliana working did not sit well with Camilla, but said nothing to betray her unease. She was glad they were on the phone having this delicate discussion; had they been face to face her young friend would have detected immediately how lukewarm Camilla really was on the whole idea.

"I suppose if you feel confident enough that you can handle all of the responsibilities you've just described, then by all means do it. My only concern is that once school starts a few weeks from now, you won't get so overburdened that your studies will suffer at the expense of some mundane, meaningless work. You realize of course, Jules, that school gets progressively harder as you go along."

"I'm not worried about school," Giuliana said confidently. "My only real concern is my aunt's condition, and how it's affecting the family. The last thing I want is to have her feel that by not working we're going to have a tough time making ends meet. And that's another thing . . . Umberto is already working himself to the bone. Now this situation with my aunt. I've been wanting to write to my parents for help but every time I think I will, I decide not to just as quickly . . . they have enough to worry about, what with my brothers away, and my mother's business having fallen off quite a bit since the war started. How I wish Nonna Dona were around."

There was little Camilla could say to assuage Giuliana's concerns. In less than an hour she'd be leaving for an assignment that would preclude her from getting in touch with her young friend for at least a couple of weeks to offer any sage advice. It saddened her at the thought of not having the time to be of greater help, or to provide a comforting shoulder for Giuliana to cry on, so she returned to the subject of a job. "Have you given any thought to the kind of work you'd like to do?"

"All I can think of at the moment is a job in one of the neighborhood grocery stores. Otherwise, there isn't much else close by except the dress factories."

"Which I'm certain your uncle would never agree to," Camilla said, completing Giuliana's thought. "Given your aunt's past experience and what a lot of other women went through in those sweatshops, I'm fairly certain that would be the last place your uncle would allow you to work."

There were moments of silence before Camilla made a suggestion she thought was, if not the perfect solution, at least one that might make some sense. "I've an idea that might work . . . what about asking Umberto if he can get you a job in the restaurant? It would be a natural for you. Of course I don't mean you'd likely be cooking or anything like that, although we both know you could and do it splendidly, but Randazzi's might be able to find plenty other things for you to do, like cleaning up the kitchen, washing dishes, setting tables—you know, that sort of thing."

In late afternoon one week later, as she went about preparing a light supper for her uncle—he was now back on his regular schedule and would be rising soon—she felt the time was right to spring Camilla's suggestion on him. She had gone over and over in her mind the essential points of her argument; the more she thought about it the more she found the prospect of holding down a part-time job sensible. Concetta was next door helping with the Giordano baby so they'd be alone and not have to concern themselves with drawing her into a discussion she might find unsettling. All Giuliana permitted herself to think about now was how her uncle would handle the subject of her working in the first place.

She did not hesitate getting right to the point. Hardly had she placed a lovely zucchini and onion *frittata,* small salad and slices of toasted bread in front of her uncle, before taking up the issue that had been uppermost on her mind the past several days. "I have something very important I want to say to you, Uncle . . . I hope you will hear me out," Giuliana said with all the deference she could muster.

"What is it, my dear?" Umberto said, resting his fork on his plate, a look of concern clearly visible in his still sleepy eyes. "Nothing bad, I hope?"

"Not bad, uncle, but serious," answered Giuliana. "I would like you to give me permission . . . to look for a job. A part-time job, of course."

He stopped eating and fixed Giuliana with a riveting, intense stare, his mouth tightening. "A job . . . why in heaven would you want a job. Don't you have enough to do already, more than anyone your age should ever be required?"

Giuliana did not reply; she wanted her uncle to take all the time he needed to digest her out-of-the-blue request and state his objections, even if it meant his blowing off steam at her, which he never did.

"You're only thirteen, much too young to start working. Believe me, you're going to have plenty of time for that. You came here to go to school, not to work and go to school." He took a bite, then resumed. "And the neighbors . . . what will they think? . . . that I can't support my own family . . . that I have to send my niece out to work?"

Giuliana, who had been standing at the other end of the kitchen table, went to the stove and poured a cup of strong coffee mixed with milk that had been simmering in a small pot. She gently placed it next to Umberto's salad, then took a chair next to his.

"There are several reasons why I believe my having a part-time job would be good for the family," Giuliana said quietly and with great deference. "First of all, it makes me sad, even though you may not see it in my face, knowing that you're working two full jobs. You have so little time for anything else but work. I know why you're doing it, of course, and I couldn't be prouder of you, Zio. I realize you're not going to be truly happy until you're working for yourself, and to do that you're going to need a good deal of money to start a business. Well, I want to help. I feel I must help, not just because Zia isn't working right now, but because I believe it's the right thing for me to do."

"But your age . . . and your schooling?" Umberto said, his irritation evident in the way he pushed aside his half-finished plate of food.

Giuliana did not address directly those issues but continued the arguments she had carefully rehearsed in her mind to counter her uncle's. "America is no different from Italy when it comes to work. When girls reach a certain age, they're taken out of school and go to work to help their families. Look at all the girls from the neighborhood who work in the garment factories, many as young as thirteen, my age. A lot of them will be working in places like that forever, or at least until they get married. Fortunately, I won't be one of them. This is only a part-time, temporary job I'm talking about. I have every intention of remaining in school and getting the education I came here to get. Besides, I'm only suggesting this until Zia is ready to go back to work. Which is another reason I think my having a job would be beneficial— that's to help Zia get back to where she was before she got sick."

"How do you mean?" Umberto asked, uncertain of the new twist Giuliana's argument had now taken.

"Zia needs to take over running the house again, doing the things she knows are her responsibility, not mine, or yours. I believe she needs this for her own peace of mind. The more she waits, the less she'll want to get back to the way things were before. I worry that she might give up wanting to start that business you've been working so hard for. I pray that won't happen. Even worse, she might lose her confidence altogether. It's been a good thing for her to have Antoinette and the baby . . . helping them has given her a purpose. But how long can that last? Besides, I fear she's using the time she's spending at the Giordanos' as an excuse to shirk her responsibilities—to you, the house and, if you don't mind my saying it, to me."

By not immediately responding, Umberto tacitly acknowledged the truth of what his niece was saying. He, too, of course, was worried about his wife's continuing malaise. Could it be that by not having Giuliana so readily available to lean on she would almost certainly have to try to get back to her former self? That reason alone, not the few dollars Giuliana was likely to earn from a part-time job, was what led Umberto to believe he should seriously consider his niece's request, even if it meant putting aside his aversion to having his niece work, even though so many girls her age were already doing so.

"What sort of work are you thinking of? I'm not sure the dress factories on Franklin Street hire part-time help. In any case, I'd have to see for myself whether they've improved conditions since your aunt left."

"I'm not thinking about the dress factories."

"Then, what?"

Without hesitating Giuliana said: "Randazzi's."

"Randazzi's?" Umberto shouted out with alarm.

"Yes, Randazzi's."

"That's out of the question," Umberto said rising suddenly from his chair, beside himself at the mere suggestion. "How would it look, my own niece working in the same place I work in?"

"You keep saying, how would it look," Giuliana said calmly, "first at the idea of my working at all, and now at the thought of my working in the same place you do."

When her uncle, trying hard to calm himself, offered no immediate rebuttal, Giuliana continued. "Mrs. Randazzi likes me. I know it. Every time she sees me, she always has nice things to say. Why just the other day while going across the street to the market to pick up some things for the house, I saw her standing in the doorway of the restaurant like she always does; she invited me in. I told her it was my first time in Randazzi's. I complimented her on it.

"Then she took me back into the kitchen. It wasn't quite noon, so we were alone. The aroma in the kitchen made my stomach growl. She had a huge pot of sauce gurgling on the stove. Without even asking me, she took a plate and scooped out a huge meatball, a fat sausage link and a meaty spare rib, and cut the end of a crusty loaf of bread. She told me to sit in the dining room at the table closest to the kitchen. 'Now *mangia, figlia mia*, you look famished,' she said. 'I wish I could offer you a nice glass of wine, but I can't, even though you look practically old enough to have it.'

"All of our conversation was in Italian. I had almost forgotten how beautiful our native language is. While I was eating the delicious lunch, Mrs. Randazzi and I had a very nice talk. 'I hear from some of the ladies around here that you're quite a cook yourself . . . is that right?' she said. I told her the truth, that I did like to cook, and that I'd been doing it a long time, which made her laugh really hard. We had a wonderful half-hour together. Just as I was leaving she told me that you were the best waiter she ever had. And that included her son. She made me promise not to tell you that."

The remark broke the somber spell that had permeated the conversation. Umberto smiled an appreciative smile, Giuliana gave out with a hearty laugh. Both uncle and niece felt considerably better.

It was not the next day, nor the one after that, but the following Monday—Giuliana had been right: Umberto did need time to digest the notion of his niece working, and even more time to ponder the possibility that Mrs. Randazzi might actually say yes to his request— before he could muster enough nerve to approach his employer. She did in fact say yes. Immediately. With that little matter out of the way, the two agreed that Giuliana would work a very limited schedule, week days only, from noon to three only and, after school started in three weeks, from three to six, no later. Since she wouldn't have to work Saturdays or Sundays (the restaurant was closed Sundays) Giuliana would have an entire weekend free to pursue her other interests.

# Chapter 27

From the moment Giuliana started working at Randazzi's she knew she had found another home. Mrs. Randazzi, but no less her two cooking assistants, even the dishwasher, all made her feel welcome. As she went about her chores, mostly keeping the kitchen spotlessly clean, she found time to pay close attention to how the eponymous restaurant's chef/owner went about preparing the food that fed a hundred or so diners almost every weekday night, and double that on Fridays and Saturdays. It was quite a revelation.

In almost no time at all, Giuliana came to realize that in the person of Mrs. Randazzi she had been blessed with yet another kindred spirit, joining as mentor the other exceptional women in her life—her mother, her grandmother and Maddalena Vertucci. To Mrs. Randazzi, the feeling was mutual. Like so many others, she too found the young girl to be exceptional and, as she was soon to learn, inspirational. In Giuliana she also saw a mirror image of herself, and her long-departed youth. She loved having Giuliana around and wished she could work in the restaurant for longer stretches. While she tried hard to maintain a professional relationship with the girl, she found it difficult. With six grandchildren of her own, all much older than Giuliana, it was her natural motherly (or was it grandmotherly?) inclinations that made her want to nurture and keep the girl close to her. But it wasn't entirely Giuliana's youth that made Mrs. Randazzi feel about her as she did; the child's maturity and intelligence were what she found so fascinating. All in all, she had never met anyone quite like her.

It was Mrs. Randazzi's every intention from the moment she brought Giuliana into her kitchen to have the girl do only the work she had been hired to do: scrub pots and pans, wash down the kitchen floors and tile walls, scour the ovens and stove. And take out the garbage. Beyond that, maybe a neighborhood errand now and again, say to the grocery store to pick up an item or two the restaurant may have run out of.

Giuliana dispatched her work with such meticulous effortlessness that it soon became evident to Mrs. Randazzi that she'd have to find additional chores for the young girl to do to keep her happy and fully engaged. While trying to think of something, the matter was resolved in a totally unexpected way. Giuliana herself, having thought for some time along the same lines, approached the proprietress one early afternoon with a seemingly off-handed suggestion; it was couched in such a way so as not to give the good woman any reason to believe that she, Giuliana, was dissatisfied, or that she was working her guile in order to be given restaurant kitchen duties of a more substantial nature than the ones the two women originally had agreed upon.

"I can't help notice, Mrs. Randazzi, that you never have anything to eat while you're working," Giuliana said, gathering up a pile of empty tomato cans she was about to take out to the trash bin in the yard behind the restaurant. "Don't you ever get hungry, what with all this wonderful food around?"

"I have a big breakfast before I come to work," the lady answered. "Haven't you noticed that as the day goes along, I'm always picking on this or that? Look at me, do I look like somebody who's ever skipped a meal?" At an even five feet tall, and with the handshake of a longshoreman, piercing eyes and an apron that wound around her portly body just barely ("my way of getting at all those women who give up the joy of eating so they can be thin"), Mrs. Randazzi made it a habit of indulging in self-deprecating humor. "Besides, if you really want the truth, I can't bring myself to eat food I cook day after day, no matter how good it is. When I sit down to eat, I like to have something completely different."

Giuliana was surprised to hear this but at the same time encouraged that the woman might find appealing the suggestion she was about to make to her. "I was wondering if you'd let me cook you something?" Giuliana asked diffidently. "Just this past Sunday I made homemade pasta in a sauce my aunt and uncle never had before. They loved it. Please let me make it for you . . . it will only take a few minutes." Giuliana made the request with such pleading in her voice that Mrs. Randazzi didn't have the heart to refuse.

Within thirty minutes Giuliana had fresh strips of thin noodles swimming in a boiling pot of water and a sauce simmering in a pan. Mrs. Randazzi was asked to stay out of the kitchen while the young girl prepared lunch for her boss. The older woman was thankful for the break; it gave her a chance to sit a spell, which she seldom did during her busy day, and read the Italian newspaper, which she enjoyed doing whenever she had the chance. Before she knew it, Giuliana came through the swinging kitchen door carrying a plate of pasta which she placed before the woman. She grated fresh *Parmigiano Reggiano* on the pasta and added some freshly ground pepper; the woman said she wouldn't dream of eating pasta without either.

"*Basta*," said Mrs. Randazzi.

"*Buon appetito,*" said Giuliana, keeping her fingers crossed that Mrs. Randazzi would enjoy the dish she prepared for her.

The plate of pasta with peas, *guanciale*, onions, porcini mushrooms and cream disappeared in the blink of an eye. Mrs. Randazzi may have had her customary hearty breakfast that morning but one would never have known it given the ravenous way she attacked the dish and savored every bite.

"This is really *delicioso*," she said as she twirled the last forkful of pasta, then scooped up the remaining peas, prosciutto and onions with a soup spoon, careful not to let a single morsel escape. "I never had anything like this before. Southern Italians never use cream. We use ricotta cheese instead. You're from the south, too . . . how did you come up with this recipe? And by the way, the pasta was cooked perfectly, *al dente*, just the way I like it."

"I made it up . . . well, part of it, anyway," a delighted Giuliana answered, relishing the compliment. "I got it from my friend in Amalfi, the housekeeper at my parish church. She makes the dish with peas, prosciutto, and fresh pasta, but I experimented a little by substituting *guanciale* for the prosciutto and adding onions and mushrooms. The cream is to bind the pasta a bit more.

"I liked the way it tasted the first time I had it, so I've been making it this way ever since. But you're right about southern Italians eating pasta with red sauce almost all the time. My friend Maddalena's family was originally from the north, in the Torino region . . . she introduced me to many dishes southern Italians don't eat, like pasta in brown sauces. She also taught me a trick when cooking certain pasta—not to cook it all the way, but finish it off in the sauce instead of draining the pasta first and then adding the sauce. In pasta dishes like this one, I find it makes a big difference."

The two women sat over coffee longer than they had intended, each curious to learn more about the other. After Giuliana finished delineating the particulars of her brief life, the older woman went on to paint a much fuller picture of hers.

Letizia Coppola was born in a small village in the region of Calabria, as was her husband, Giancarlo Randazzi, whom she married when she was seventeen, he twenty. Both families, hers and his, farmed the land for sustenance and livelihood. A year after their son Silvio was born in 1896, the Randazzis joined the growing exodus of Italian immigrants to the United States and took up residence in New Haven in a flat in a row house above where the restaurant was now located. At the time, the street-level space housed a shoemaker's shop in front and a two-and-a-half-room apartment in the back, where the shoemaker and his wife lived.

The Randazzis, like so many Italians at the turn of the century, were brought over by the enterprising entrepreneur John Bradford Sargent to work the production lines of his booming lock-making factory. Fifteen years later, with enough money saved, the ambitious Giancarlo took over the shoe shop and converted the space into a luncheonette. How that came to be was the subject of a colorful story.

"With all the food available on Wooster Street, would you believe there was only one sandwich shop in the area at the time," Mrs. Randazzi explained, "Salvatore Monelli's Sub Shop, a few blocks away from here. For a long time it did a booming business. Men from the factories, and truck drivers on their way north to New England were steady customers." She then went on to describe the sad demise of the luncheonette after Monelli retired and handed the place over to his son Leopold.

It seems Leo Monelli, twenty-three at the time, didn't much like slinging hash, as the saying goes; the young man preferred going out on the toot rather than running a business that had grown more successful with each passing year. Before long, his lack of attention to practically every aspect of a once thriving restaurant proved fatal. Customers started complaining. What they found especially intolerable was the luncheonette's serious disregard for cleanliness. One disgruntled patron even went so far as to notify the New Haven Board of Health about it. (Randazzi told Giuliana she didn't want to describe to her what the inspector found.)

Within the space of two years, the health department shut down Monelli's not once but twice for what they described as "egregious food safety violations." The second closing came on the heels of what everyone in the food service business knows is the worst thing that could possibly befall a restaurant: a customer came down with food poisoning. Henceforth, Salvatore Monelli's became known as "Sal-monella's." Once that damning sobriquet—coined by some nameless customer's penchant for imaginative linguistic hyperbole—gained traction, business, already in the doldrums, sank to a new low. Despite every effort Leo attempted to restore the place's once stellar reputation—he even got his father to come out of retirement—nothing worked. Out of disgust, and disgrace, the Monellis finally closed the luncheonette, sold the building and left the area for good: Salvatore Monelli's Sub Shop, now forever known as Sal-monella's in the annals of Wooster Street, and New Haven lore, was no more.

Isn't it amazing how one man's misfortune often proves to be another man's opportunity? As soon as Monelli's went out of business, the enterprising Giancarlo Randazzi seized the moment and shortly thereafter opened his own sub shop, even though it was not the business he had originally contemplated starting. But as someone who kept a sharp eye on which direction the political winds in New Haven were blowing, he learned well in advance before it ever happened that the entire stretch of Wooster Street, one end to the other, would soon be teeming with new construction activity. He was right.

For well over a year carloads of burly laborers made their way into the neighborhood to take up the job of tearing down what few houses remained from Wooster Street's golden past and building nondescript three-story tenements up and down the street to house the growing number of immigrants working in the area's factories. Every day at the sound of the noon whistle, workers hi-tailed it to Randazzi's SubShop to sate their enormous appetites by feasting on Letizia Randazzi's delectable Italian hot and cold hero sandwiches and, on Fridays, steaming plates of *pasta fagioli* and *calamari fra diavolo*. "God bless America," Mrs. Randazzi intoned, with her arms outstretched and eyes cast upward to heaven in prayerful thanks.

Business was so good that their son Silvio—known to everyone in the neighborhood as Sil (except to his parents)—quit school after the eighth grade to work full time in the shop. His parents were more than happy to have him but sad that he was giving up school for good. He, on the other hand, made the career choice with little reservation since school to him was boring and unnecessary.

"By this time the family had grown so large—we now had six children," Mrs. Randazzi explained. "Once in a while one of the older kids would come in to help, but the only one who stayed with us from the beginning was my Silvio. He's still with me, as you can see. He was a good boy, always looking after the others, he never a complained. After my Francesca was born—she's my youngest—we had to rearrange our living conditions. So we moved all the kids upstairs, and me and my husband went to live downstairs in the rooms in back of the store. That arrangement lasted until everybody was grown up and out of the house."

Giuliana wanted to know more about Mr. Randazzi. "He was quite a man, my husband. But the Good Lord took him from me too soon. He was only fifty-eight when he died, massive heart attack," she said, tears swimming in the corners of her eyes. "Only Americans are supposed to die from heart attacks, not Italians. I guess he worked too hard, just like a lot of people in this country. In Italy we work to live; here we live to work. Look at me. I'm still working. I promised my family next year, when I'm seventy, that's it . . . I had enough . . . the place becomes Silvio's."

"Do you mind telling me how you turned a sandwich shop into this restaurant?" Giuliana wanted to know.

"Oh, that," the lady said in an off-handed manner, since just about everyone in the neighborhood was familiar with the story of how the restaurant got started. "As I said before, my husband was very ambitious. It wasn't enough for him just to own a luncheonette, no matter how successful it was . . . and believe me, we were doing very, very good. He had bigger ideas. He was a smart man, not a greenhorn like some. He could have been anything he wanted to be if he had the schooling.

"But it was a real restaurant he wanted. He loved people . . . he loved serving them. You know, making them happy. So right after the First World War ended in November of 1918 we opened Randazzi's. It was early December, a few days after Thanksgiving. That year we had the best Christmas and New Year's we ever had in our lives. Giancarlo had it planned all along. He said that as soon as the kids were out of the house we'd make our move. And that's what happened. First Silvio got married and was out of the house. Then our eldest daughter, Linda, got married eight months later. Our two middle boys, Tony and Andrew, were in the army—thank God they both made it back safely. The only ones left at home were Louis, our youngest son, and Francesca.

"So now we were free to move back upstairs. As soon as we were settled in, we made the entire first floor, including the apartment in the back, into a restaurant. With only a few changes here and there it's the same as it's always been. We put everything we had into this place, every drop of sweat and every cent we could get our hands on. We got a nice loan from Polotti's bank . . . they even gave us money to buy the building, too. Everything worked like my husband said it would. We were so happy, even though we were working like slaves. Our lives were complete . . . until 1929 came along. People remember that year because of the stock market crash and the start of the great Depression. I remember it as the year I lost my beautiful Giancarlo."

Before leaving the restaurant, Giuliana gave Mrs. Randazzi a big hug and a kiss.

# Chapter 28

Giuliana strode happily into the kitchen, dropped her books and donned a clean apron from the linen bin. "How was the first day of school?" Mrs. Randazzi was anxious to know.

"It went very well. I met my new teachers, and a lot of nice kids," Giuliana said as she headed for the pantry where the cleaning supplies were stored, but was stopped by Mrs. Randazzi. "Remember a week ago you made that wonderful pasta dish for me?" Mrs. Randazzi said. Giuliana nodded. "Well, I've been thinking: maybe we should put it on the menu as a special and see what happens. What do you think?"

At first, Giuliana wasn't certain she'd heard right, never believing for a moment that something as wonderful as having her dish on the menu was even remotely possible, at least not this early in her working relationship with the restaurant. "Gee, I think it's a great idea," was all she could muster. "When do you want to try it?"

"How about tonight . . . maybe five or six orders, no more . . . I want to start out slow. Anyway, tonight's lasagna night, the Wednesday special . . . it's very popular . . . I have regular customers come every week like clockwork for my lasagna."

"That won't be a problem," Giuliana said matter-of-factly, once she realized Mrs. Randazzi was serious. She did a good job outwardly acting cool, while inside she was tingling with excitement, dying to let out a girlish whoop. "I already know how much pasta and sauce it takes to make six orders. What doesn't sell, you can use any leftover vegetables for your minestrone soup. But what about my other work?"

"Let's not worry about that for now. I've already asked Sammy" (the restaurant's loyal dishwasher) "to come in an hour early to give us a hand."

Just four orders of the pasta were served that first night. All four diners who had it told Mrs. Randazzi, as she made her customary rounds in the dining room later in the evening, that it was the best plate of pasta they ever had. That was all the proprietress needed to hear to decide then and there that henceforth the dish would remain permanently on the menu, but served as a Thursday night special initially. It would be given a distinctive name—*Pasta Giuliana*. When informed of this wonderful turn of events, the young girl told Mrs. Randazzi how much she appreciated her confidence, but as flattered as she was to have a dish named after her she did what she could to dissuade the restaurant owner from calling it that. To no avail; Letizia Randazzi insisted on it. "I'm the boss, and that's what we're calling it. "*Capische?*"

\*     \*     \*

All through the remainder of the school year, Giuliana maintained her strict schedule of working in the restaurant three hours a day, no more. Her kitchen-cleaning duties were permanently suspended, turned over to the dishwasher, who said he was grateful for the extra work. Giuliana was ecstatic: she finally had a chance to cook professionally, and in a first-class restaurant at that, which was what she had all along been hoping, if not out and out scheming, for.

With the success of *Pasta Giuliana*, the restaurant owner soon came to realize the wisdom of considering some of the young cook's other menu suggestions, which Giuliana was no longer hesitant to offer. "I was telling Zia just the other night that you make the best manicotti," Giuliana said to Mrs. Randazzi one afternoon while preparing her homemade pasta as the older woman looked on, fascinated at how deftly and perfectly the child cut every pasta strip.

"Are you giving me a hint?" asked the older woman, with a teasing look in her eye, believing the girl was scheming for another taste of a dish she loved. "You'll have to wait until tomorrow when I make a fresh new batch for you to have some."

"I can wait, Letizia," a smiling Giuliana said. (Mrs. Randazzi insisted that Giuliana call her by her first name; in the beginning the young girl found it hard to do even though everyone in the neighborhood, even the elderly, was called by his or her first name.) "I was wondering the other night about the kind of customers who come here. Aren't a lot of them non-Italian, sophisticated, well-educated people?"

"So? What's that got to do with what they eat?"

"Well, I have a feeling that those kinds of customers might be more open to trying new dishes. I know they love your southern Italian cooking, but seeing how they've taken to our Thursday-night pasta"—she couldn't bring herself to mouth the name of the dish newly christened in her honor—"I thought maybe we might consider other specials."

"What did you have in mind?"

"Take your manicotti, for example. Why don't we try serving a different version of the dish?"

"And what's that?" asked Mrs. Randazzi dubiously, as she stood at a table whisking eggs in a large bowl.

"Cannelloni," Giuliana answered. "It looks like manicotti, but it's completely different. It's a tubular shell like the one you make, but it's stuffed with spinach, ricotta, and ground pork, veal and beef, then covered in a white sauce called béchamel, made from milk, butter, flour and nutmeg. Then it's topped with grated Parmesan cheese and baked in the oven for twenty minutes. It's so-o-o delicious . . . I know you'd love it."

Letizia did. So did her customers. Which astounded the older woman. She had well over forty years in the food business but still couldn't get over how prescient the girl was in gauging how far customers were willing to go to try new dishes. And what new dishes they were.

From then on, whenever Giuliana came to her brimming with excitement over a new dish she had concocted, Mrs. Randazzi did not hesitate in giving the "child cook" a careful hearing. Always respectful of the older woman, of whom she had grown increasingly fond, Giuliana had Letizia participate fully in the preparation of any new dish she recommended. Then instead of having the older woman alone taste and judge the results, the entire restaurant crew—waiters, line cook, prep cook, even the dishwasher—got to sample the dish at the staff meal served every afternoon promptly at five, well before customers started coming in. That way, Giuliana told Randazzi, she'd have a broader consensus as to how the dish might be received by the public. Equally as important, the waiters would be familiar enough with the dish to be able to answer any questions customers might have regarding its ingredients or preparation.

Little by little, one after another, tantalizing new dishes kept cropping up, first as a dinner special, then as a permanent fixture on the expanded menu. By the end of Giuliana's senior year in high school Randazzi's had become more a reflection of her singular vision than that of the restaurant's owner/chef. To a large extent it was a restaurant transformed: whereas Randazzi's had long been known exclusively for its traditional rustic southern Italian *casa cucina*—featuring mostly red sauces and heaping portions—the restaurant now offered, in addition, a new style of cooking that was more refined, eclectic, imaginative. No other Italian restaurant in the city at the time had taken such a bold step away from its culinary roots. Even neighborhood locals, who almost never went out to fancy restaurants and did not as a rule eat cooking other than their own, started frequenting the place. As did more and more diners outside the immediate New Haven area as word spread extolling the restaurant's new approach to cooking.

Among the endless waves of encomiums was a steady stream of laudatory press. The *New Haven Register*, the city's evening paper, and the *Journal Courier*, the morning edition, both had glowing reviews of the restaurant, the latter newspaper going so far as to send a writer to interview Mrs. Randazzi for a feature article. More than happy to give credit where credit was due, the owner introduced Giuliana as the source of Randazzi's new creative style of cooking. On the strength of such notoriety, coupled with the buzz created from lavish word-of-mouth reports, new customers started eating regularly at the restaurant. Together with its loyal base, Randazzi's soon had more business than it was sometimes capable of handling, especially on weekends.

The symbiotic relationship that had developed between the two women, at opposite poles in age, resulted in a restaurant that eschewed playing it safe. Instead of resting on its laurels it grew in stature commensurate with the excellent product it was serving up to an increasingly appreciative clientele. The restaurant's burgeoning success brought about other changes, some inevitable, others totally unexpected. A notable one was that Letizia Randazzi gave up any thought of retiring in the new year as she promised her family she would: "I have to be honest, I'm having more fun than I ever thought possible at my age."

As for Giuliana, she reveled in the freedom Randazzi's gave her. She had earned Letizia's trust, confidence and respect, so she was allowed to create, experiment and implement to her heart's desire. Moreover, despite her age and working inexperience, and due in large part to her carefree upbringing, she hardly seemed touched by pressures normally associated with neurotic restaurant kitchens; everyone working with her marveled at her cool insouciance. And she did not deflate like a fallen soufflé as those envious of her growing stature as a cook predicted she would.

Now that she was a permanent fixture and major player in the Randazzi Restaurant kitchen, Giuliana was forced to expand her work schedule. This did not please Umberto. Yet he seemed at a loss as to what he could do about it except acquiesce to his niece's and Letizia's wishes. From now on during summers, holiday vacations and Saturdays, Giuliana would work a full shift from 12 noon to 8 p.m.; during the school year she would put in an extra hour, Monday through Thursday, and two hours on Friday. She convinced her guardians that even with this heavy work schedule she would still have ample time during the week to complete her homework assignments, and on Sundays, her one day off, she would also be able to work on the cookbook, her art, and keep up entries in her diaries. As for maintaining any semblance of a social life, well, that was another story.

Even Silvio Randazzi, whose work in the front of the house was sometimes perfunctory and distracted (for reasons soon to be made clear), was a model of professionalism. He was quick to acknowledge that new life had been breathed into the restaurant. This made him especially thankful to be part of a seasoned waitstaff that left happy customers of a mind to tip even more generously than they ever did before.

One other significant change took place in early January. Connie Fassano, her convalescence a thing of the past, went back to work—in the kitchen at Randazzi's alongside her niece, and a mere shout away from her husband, working on the floor waiting tables in the front of the house. Now that business was booming, the restaurant sorely needed the extra hand. And Connie needed the work. It soon became apparent that she was a natural for the job. Not only was she familiar with her niece's innovative cooking, she loved the food the restaurant served: she had grown up on it. Besides, she was a very good cook in her own right, which made Mrs. Randazzi feel confident in her hiring, and Connie thankful for the opportunity.

All in all, Randazzi's, an anomaly in the business at a time when prejudice against women in restaurant kitchens was still widespread, continued to hum as evidenced by the way New Haven's dining public had so completely taken to the place. And as far as the Fassano family was concerned, 1944 was shaping up as a banner year.

# Chapter 29

At 6:00 a.m. on June 6, 1944, a Tuesday, Giuliana was awakened a half hour earlier than normal to a cacophony of sounds that within minutes coalesced into a deafening crescendo. Neighbors on Wooster and Warren Streets had gathered in the backyard and were tooting horns, setting off fireworks and behaving the way they normally did when celebrating a holiday—loudly and with great enthusiasm.

She opened the door to the kitchen to find her aunt and uncle glued to the RCA-VICTOR, their ears pressed against the radio's receiver, hanging on famed newscaster H.V. Kaltenborn's every word. A major allied offensive, known as Operation Overlord, was taking place at that very moment on the beaches of Normandy in France. D-Day had arrived. Between June 6 and August 19, 1944, more than three million allied troops—American, English, French, Russian—would cross the English Channel from England to Normandy, driving out the German army and, in a final push eastward on August 25, liberate Paris, thus foreshadowing, it was fervently hoped by peace-loving citizens on both sides of the Atlantic, the end of the bloodiest war in history.

Like everyone else affected by life during wartime, Giuliana was caught up in the heightened anticipation of the war's conclusion. Of course she wanted to see hostilities ended and peace restored to her homeland as well as to the rest of Europe. She also fervently prayed there would be some measure of solace for families here and abroad, including her own, anguishing over the loss, or potential loss, of sons, husbands, brothers.

But for Giuliana there was a more personal, one might even say selfish, reason for her wanting to see the war end. Not a day went by in the last three years that she didn't talk of returning home to Amalfi for an extended visit. The most logical time for her to do so, she calculated, would be the summer of 1947, between high school graduation in June and the start of college in September. Umberto and Concetta had by now grown used to the idea of her making the trip back home. In fact, they were all for it; they felt a visit would boost their niece's spirits and be a boon to her overall peace of mind, thus enabling her, when she returned, to expend all her energies on matters more aligned with her personal goals—school, cooking, her writing—and not on those she had little control over, like the war and the well being of her family and country an ocean away.

As much as she dreaded having the young girl away from the restaurant for such an extended period of time, Mrs. Randazzi, too, believed a vacation would do Giuliana a world of good, since she almost never stopped talking about her family and friends across the sea. Giuliana had certainly earned the right. How many people her age could have accomplished as much as she had in such a short time, and in a strange country at that? Not to mention all she had done, and was doing, for her aunt and uncle and her employer. To all of them, she was like an angel dropped down from heaven into their lives.

Thankful for the miracle, they unanimously agreed, without Giuliana ever finding out, to start putting aside funds out of their own pockets for her Amalfi holiday. They even decided that the trip should be made by air rather than boat, the less expensive mode of trans-Atlantic transportation but one that took almost three weeks to make. Flying to Italy would give Giuliana more time to spend with family instead of whiling away endless idle hours at sea. (The first trans-Atlantic flight available to the public was flown by Pan-Am in 1939, Baltimore to Dublin, Ireland. Flight time: just over 29 hours.)

Meantime, Giuliana was anxiously awaiting Camilla's arrival in New York for her annual summer stay. She longed to see her friend and mentor so they could take up where they had left off the previous summer. Giuliana also wanted badly to learn news of her family and whatever goings-on in Amalfi Camilla thought might be of interest to her. As was her custom, as soon as Camilla returned to Amalfi for the start of each new school year she made it a point to visit the Landinis to give them an update on their daughter, and on Umberto and Concetta as well. She never failed to bring with her a slew of snapshots taken of Giuliana so that her parents could see for themselves how much their daughter had grown from the previous summer and to judge for themselves, if only through pictures, how even more beautiful and mature looking she had become as she blossomed into womanhood.

Whenever he saw photos of his daughter Antonio never failed to remark to his wife, or anyone within earshot, a worried frown spread across his tanned, leathery, handsome face: "I hope she's watching out for the boys." Maria, on the other hand, gave into her motherly instincts the only way she knew how, by gathering up the handful of snapshots and clutching them to her bosom, rocking and sighing in perfect unison as tears trickled down her once beautiful but now drawn, ashen face.

These were trying times for Maria Landini. The loss of her mother, the loss of her daughter—temporarily, she prayed—the constant worry over the safety and well-being of her two sons in a prisoner of war camp and now, as though this weren't enough to break a mother's heart, the recent call-up of her youngest son Luigi into the Italian army, deployed God only knows where, had taken a toll on a woman once every bit as attractive as Donatella (in her heyday) and her daughter (just on the cusp of womanhood). She looked wan, shriveled, the cares of the world almost too much for her to bear. Even work, always a source of pleasure—not to mention needed income—was no longer a buffer against the sorrows, worries, disappointments she now had to endure. She lost almost all interest in her linen business and had for some time taken on no new orders, which put a serious crimp in the family's finances, Maria being a bigger wage earner than her husband, who, by now, having to work completely on his own, had all to do to keep his fishing business afloat. The strain took a toll on him, too.

Camilla was careful not to mention any of this in a letter she wrote to Giuliana in June. But she could not avoid communicating news Giuliana found most distressing—Camilla would not be coming to America this summer. The war in Europe, and the allied invasion of Italy, restricted all foreign travel; she would have to remain in Amalfi. She wouldn't even be able to make a trip to Scotland to spend time with her family.

She did, however, elaborate on one bit of good news that managed to emerge out of this otherwise disturbing scenario: she had recommended, and *The New York Times* had accepted, based on the excellent work she had turned in on her Scotland piece, an idea for a lengthy travel article on the Amalfi coast. In her pitch to the newspaper she described the high points she would concentrate on in the more popular destinations—Amalfi, Positano, Ravello—but not neglect writing about the as yet undiscovered, lovely little villages and hamlets (thirteen of them) that dotted the landscape along the eastern shore of the Mediterranean. She said that by not having to travel to America and staying put in Amalfi, she would have the luxury of devoting an entire summer to exploring every nook and cranny of the coast, much of which she was familiar with, and studying the entire region's colorful history, which she admitted she needed to know more about.

Giuliana was thrilled to learn how well her journalist friend's writing career was going. But it was hard for her to hide the disappointment she felt at having to wait an entire year, if not more, depending on the progress of the war, before she and Camilla would be able to get together again to indulge their greatest mutual pleasure, happy story swapping.

Meantime in New Haven, the talk of war, not baseball, had become the area's *lingua franca*—in school, at home, in the workplace, everywhere. And as more young soldiers, sailors and marines from the neighborhood were returning home from the war in body bags— while others came back missing an arm or a leg or, as in the case of Sonny Giannelli, scion of the street's sole jewelry store family, with a colostomy bag—a sense of helpless resignation coursed through the area's tight-knit community.

To help lessen some of the pain and sadness, residents from around the city and beyond, looked to Wooster Street as a sanctuary of stability and pleasure, pushing the war, if even for an hour or so, out of their collective consciousness the best way they knew how: by spending hard-earned dollars (wartime jobs were starting to make them flush with cash) as though there was no tomorrow. Which, for many of them, sadly, there was none, having already lost a loved one in the war, or were about to.

So every Friday and Saturday night that summer of '44 was like New Year's Eve in the neighborhood. Revelers happy in the moment strolled unhurriedly up and down the street, cutting through a cacophony of blaring music and happy chatter emanating from bars and restaurants jammed block after block, eating, drinking and buying their way up from one food shop, saloon and restaurant to the next, if not Randazzi's, where the cognoscenti and well-heeled came to dine, then to one of the half dozen other popular restaurants where serious quantities of home-style cooking at less weighty prices drew appreciative crowds. Not to be outdone when it came to eating destinations were the street's pastry shops, coffee houses, *gelaterie* and, of course, at the top of just about everybody's list, Pepe's and Sally's, the two shining gems in the pantheon of pizza parlors.

Once these two New Haven institutions opened their doors a block away from each other, Pepe's in 1925, Sally's in 1938, it didn't take long for either place to rise to cult status. Generations of Yale students and pizza lovers from all over the city, state and beyond, formed long lines and waited patiently, sometimes for hours, to scoff down this newest food craze, the "best *'abeetz'* in the whole wide world." (Frank Sinatra had pies from Sally's shipped regularly to his home in California.)

Giuliana Landini heartily agreed, she of the Neopolitan area where pizza presumably was born. She wrote home, to doubting parents and friends, that nothing in Amalfi, where practically every restaurant had pizza on its menu to go along with a regular bill of fare, came close to duplicating the tomato pies—a name used to define this ethnic oddity for Americans—that popped out of Sally's and Pepe's 850-degree, coal-driven brick ovens, served unceremoniously on white waxed paper in long metal silver trays. The pies were irregular-shaped, thin, flat sheets of dough with charred crisp bottoms, and blistered tops bubbling like lava, redolent with the finest imported ingredients, and a luscious sauce—rich, red and savory.

The first time Giuliana bit into one of Sally's anchovy pizzas she was hooked. One night a week she'd walk across the street, one time to Sally's, next time to Pepe's, with a fifty-cent piece in hand, to pick up a small pie for dinner that she and her aunt shared, Concetta washing down the pizza with a Schlitz beer right out of the bottle, a sight that never ceased to bring a smile to Giuliana's face. When she went to work full time that summer at Randazzi's she saw no reason to give up her weekly and necessary ration of pizza. She convinced Mrs. Randazzi, who herself needed very little urging when it came to *'abeetz,'* that "wouldn't it be nice to have a couple of pies brought in every Wednesday evening around 7:30 for the entire staff, waiters included, to munch on while we all worked."

*   *   *

On the morning of the last day before Giuliana was to start her junior year in high school, she purposefully got to work a few minutes earlier than normal. She wanted to be alone with Letizia so that she could present to her boss another menu idea. She started the conversation with a qualifier the older woman had become familiar with: "I hope you don't think this a crazy idea, Letizia," Giuliana said demurely, "but a thought popped into my head while we were eating pizza the other night, and . . ."

Before Giuliana had a chance to finish the thought, Mrs. Randazzi looked up at her and, in a tone of voice the young girl had not heard before, said, "If you think this restaurant is going to start making pizza, you can forget it. We're a restaurant, not a pizza parlor. Besides, nobody makes pizza better than Sally's and Pepe's. They're successful because that's all they do . . . they don't serve nothin' but pizza, not a blessed thing."

"That's not what I had in mind," Giuliana said, momentarily taken aback by Letizia's unaccustomed harsh tone. "If you don't want me to discuss this any further, I won't," she added, hurtfully.

"No, no, child," a flushed Mrs. Randazzi said almost immediately, unhappy with herself for not holding her tongue and for having made the girl, whom she had come to love and respect like one of her own, twice as unhappy. She had never once denied Giuliana a hearing whenever she came to her with an idea; she wasn't about to start now. Recovering quickly her usual ebullient, sunny demeanor, Letizia added,

"Maybe I jumped too fast to the wrong conclusion . . . please tell me your idea."

"I wouldn't dream of us competing with Sally's or Pepe's," Giuliana stated emphatically. "But when I think of how they make their living I have to say that they've basically built an unbelievable business on nothing more than making and selling bread . . . with a little fresh tomato sauce and other simple but delicious ingredients on top."

She waited for the thought to sink in before continuing: "You're absolutely right, Letizia . . . we're not in that business, we're a restaurant . . . our job is preparing and selling all kinds of wonderful food," here she paused for emphasis, "while giving the bread away for free. I've been thinking about this for weeks . . . I finally figured out what I think is a way to turn some of the bread we serve into a nice money-maker for the restaurant. It's really very simple. Do you want to hear about it?"

"Of course," Letizia said. "Tell me."

"What I have in mind is for us to use leftover bread to make delicious appetizers I'm sure our customers would gladly pay for. I can't believe we didn't think of it sooner."

"How do you mean?" A puzzled Randazzi asked.

"As you know, Letizia," Giuliana said, excitedly, "I've been collecting recipes for a long time. Someday they'll be part of a recipe book on Italian food I hope to get published. Well, some of the recipes in my book call for stale bread as the main ingredient . . . you know, *bruschetta* and *crostini*. They've been around for centuries in Italy. I don't have to tell you that to Italians wasting bread is a cardinal sin. It's a sacred food, the most basic we have. I remember the pastor of our church in Amalfi always referring to my father as '*lui e' buono come il pane.*'

"Just think . . . we could put all that day-old bread to good use, making little toasts and topping them with all sorts of wonderful food, like chopped tomatoes and basil, chickpea spread, caponata, sautéed chicken livers, bits of sweet peppers and olives—there are so many delicious toppings we could make for this appetizer. They'd be perfect to serve with antipasti or before the soup course. Speaking of soup, there's another wonderful recipe I've come across—tomato bread soup; it's a terrific winter dish. And there's *panzanella* . . . a delicious bread salad that's very popular in summer. All these bread-based appetizers and others we could think of are easily made . . . with leftover bread. It's all part of finding ways to make your restaurant" (she could never bring herself to refer to it as our restaurant) "even better than it already is . . . to give customers more than they expected when they come to Randazzi's."

For a minute or so Letizia did not respond. But it was obvious she was mulling over what she had just heard.

"You're absolutely right," Giuliana continued, "we're certainly not going to start making pizza, not the traditional kind, anyway. But think of all the bread dishes we could prepare . . . and make them pay off."

"I never heard of an Italian restaurant doing it," Mrs. Randazzi said.

"That's one reason I think it could really work," exclaimed Giuliana.

# Chapter 30

While Giuliana in New Haven was devoting her singular talents to narrowing the gap between the food she preferred cooking versus the more traditional food Randazzi's customers were accustomed to eating, Camilla in Amalfi was channeling her own considerable energies to upgrading Santa Croce's curriculum and restoring the school's once exemplary reputation. How well she had succeeded in accomplishing both made it all the more painful for Sister Carolina, the principal, and Father Di Pina, the school's de facto head—who tried without success from growing too attached to this lovely, warm, talented woman—to contemplate such time as when the teacher would be leaving the school for good in June 1946, a year and a half away. Camilla was well aware of the disruption her departure from the now smooth-running school was likely to cause, so she had for more than a year been making preparations by writing a manual describing the teaching methods she employed (more important, her philosophy of education) to leave with the staff and for new teachers joining the school in the future.

As she was formulating notes compiled during almost ten years of teaching in Scotland and Italy, the exercise crystallized in her mind, more acutely than ever before, the deep attachment and love she had for the noble profession she had prepared virtually her entire life for but would, sadly, soon be abandoning. How could she possibly think of walking away from what was for her not a job but a calling, much like the calling that had prompted Sister Carolina and the other dedicated women charged with educating Santa Croce's 165 school children to become teaching nuns in the first place? Wasn't this the career she had chosen as the best means she could find to be actively engaged in one of life's most essential and important tasks—molding young minds? Of course it was. Why, then, was she discarding it like a dress suddenly gone out of style?

The short answer, she told herself, was that it wasn't teaching per se that had lost its allure; she had simply discovered another outlet, a much more powerful one, to channel her creative impulses. Even though each new class, each new semester, each new year held out the promise of new and different challenges, the inescapable truth, the stark reality, was that she would be teaching virtually the same material she had taught the year before, and the year before that, and no matter how hard she strove to be as fresh and innovative as her talents permitted her to be, there was just so much one could do to make it original and engaging—not only for the students but, selfishly perhaps, though no less important, for the teacher as well.

Writing, on the other hand, was different. Each story, every article, was *sui generis,* completely different, never the same. "Every piece I write opens up new terrain . . . takes me to places I've never been . . . people I've never met . . . creative muscles I've never flexed, or even knew I had." This is how she described it to Father Di Pina just before leaving the school she loved, the people she loved, the town she loved, her rationale for giving up teaching. She put it all down in a letter to Giuliana in late November.

There was something else she needed to tell her friend; she wrote about that, too, though it was more of a hint than a concrete avowal. It came couched in an off-handed way, almost as an aside, so as not to raise too high her young friend's hopes concerning her relationship with the *Herald Tribune* newspaperman, Gordon deVries. She mentioned a pending overseas trip in mid-December the newspaperman would be making with the press corps accompanying New York's Mayor Fiorello LaGuardia on the latter's three-day visit to meet with Rome's mayor.

(The international travel ban would have been lifted by then.) She said she and Gordon had decided to spend a few days together prior to Gordon's flying back to New York, after which she would continue on to Scotland to spend the holidays and Christmas break with her family. "And yes, oh yes, I shall indeed be coming back to New York in June."

Reading between the lines, Giuliana concluded that everything was progressing just as she had hoped it would between the soon-to-be ex-school teacher and her peripatetic journalist friend, Gordon deVries.

# Chapter 31

May 1945, a month Giuliana would not soon forget. First came the exhilarating moment the whole world had been waiting for—V.E. Day, Tuesday the eighth. She could hardly believe the celebrations that took place, not just on the day immediately following the announcement of the end of the war in Europe, but all through the summer as more and more servicemen were returning home for good, and a sense of normalcy, however fragile, was returning to the neighborhood, the city and the nation.

In the midst of all the joy, another momentous occasion in the young girl's life arrived quite unexpectedly: on Friday the seventeenth, Giuliana had her first official, not-part-of-a-crowd, un-chaperoned date. None other than Hillhouse High's most popular senior and star athlete invited the beautiful, mature sophomore to his senior prom. Concetta Fassano deemed the occasion to be of such importance that instead of going out and buying a prom dress for her niece—"Who knows if some other girl might be wearing the same dress?"—she had Antoinette Giordano, easily the most talented seamstress in Connie's circle of friends, make a dress she was certain no other girl at the prom would be wearing. It took eight coupons of the war-rationed yearly allotment of thirty-six permitted each family to purchase enough fabric to make the dress that, come the evening of the prom, was voted the most beautiful.

An hour before the prom, when Giuliana walked out of her room into the kitchen regaled in her beautiful gown, her aunt, who for weeks had been waiting like an expectant mother for that precious moment to arrive, gave out with a muffled sound that all but made the young girl's knees buckle. "How do I look, Zia?" she asked, as if she didn't know.

Concetta brought a hand to her mouth as she stepped away from Giuliana, unable to mutter a word as crystal-like tears welled in her sparkling eyes. Not once but twice she whirled Giuliana around, taking in every inch of the pink, flowery taffeta gown draped over her stunning niece's shapely body. Giuliana's long black hair was swept up into a tight knot held firmly in place by Concetta's favorite hair pin, a gold plated butterfly pendant given to her by her mother on her confirmation day.

"You look absolutely lovely, my dear, and so much like Nonna Dona I can't begin to tell you. I would gladly give up a week's pay if your mother and father could see you."

A few minutes later Rick DeGoia got a first glimpse of his date. He fell into a stunned silence. She was more beautiful than he'd ever seen her. Not able for a second to tear his eyes away from Giuliana, he greeted Connie vacantly, uttering hardly a word as he fumbled with the box containing the corsage Giuliana would be wearing on her wrist. At the sidewalk, Giuliana, Rick and Concetta greeted the limousine driver taking the handsome couple to the prom. He snapped to attention. But they did not get into the car. Connie, who had asked for a few hours off from work to help her niece get ready for her special first date, accompanied the two prom goers across the street to Randazzi's as planned so that Umberto, Letizia and the rest of the restaurant staff could get a look at their enchanting co-worker and her handsome date. The restaurant was crowded, every table occupied, when the couple walked in.

Umberto was taking an order from a customer when murmurs from some of the diners prompted him to turn toward the door. The first thing he saw was his wife weaving through tables on her way to the kitchen, almost knocking over Silvio Randazzi, to beckon Letizia and the others. He then froze as he caught a glimpse of his niece. The entire room of diners, at first whispering and stealing glances between bites, then began to clap in unison at the sight of the stunning young woman, whom Randazzi regulars acknowledged as the source of many of their memorable meals, resplendent in her beautiful prom dress, her escort standing like an irrelevant wooden statue several steps removed from the radiant star of the evening.

When Letizia caught sight of Giuliana, she had all to do to keep her balance. The girl started to advance toward her but was met by an outstretched hand that as much as said: "My apron is splattered, I smell of food, I mustn't dare touch you, even though I ache to gather you in my arms and smother you with kisses." She stood gazing at the girl for as long as she was able to maintain her composure, every customer taking in the touching scene. Finally, she threw Giuliana a kiss, turned and started toward the kitchen, all the while rubbing her eyes as she disappeared through the swinging door.

# Chapter 32

Ricky DeGoia was the best athlete ever to come out of Wooster Street. Arguably the best athlete in all of New Haven. A senior at Hillhouse High, he was captain of both the basketball and baseball teams and for two years running made all-state in each sport. It could easily have been a third were it not for his father, who forbade the gifted athlete from playing football, fearful an injury might derail him from the professional baseball career everyone who saw him play, including major league scouts, said he was destined for. A shade over six feet tall and a wiry 175 pounds, Ricky was not particularly big except for his hands: large as shovels, with fingers the length of clothes pins, they enabled him to grip a football like an orange and toss a perfect spiral, laces up, more than sixty yards downfield, an otherwise wasted talent if not for after-school pickup touch-football games the boys played in the street or on sandlots. He was far and away the most popular, and envied, kid in the neighborhood. His peers and even some of the older boys looked up to him. To them and a legion of admirers in and around New Haven, if he wasn't quite yet Joe D, he was the next best thing, Ricky D. The sobriquet stuck.

For all his prowess on the athletic field, Ricky was an indifferent student in the classroom. He expended just enough effort to get by, which confounded his teachers but didn't seem to bother him or his parents. In the DeGoia household, there was never a clash of family values when it came to their son's future: they had long determined he was destined for the big leagues. All other career paths, professional or otherwise—including college—were deemed a last resort in the improbable event he was not offered a major league contract.

Though the epicenter of Ricky DeGoia's universe was the baseball diamond, he excelled at another popular pastime—girls. Coeds and townies alike swooned over the muscular, good-looking athlete, whose perfectly accented facial features included deep dimples that stood out like well-placed comas in a lyric poem. He played the dating field as flawlessly as he flagged down fly balls from his center field position, with a single notable exception: the tall, dark-haired, olive-skinned, foreign-born beauty Giuliana Landini was the one girl, the only girl, he could not marshal the courage to ask out, much as he wanted to. Why that was, he couldn't quite understand. At least not at first. When he finally came around to accepting the truth, the admission made him uneasy.

In a word, he found the girl intimidating: she was refined, she was an excellent student, she had worldly interests and artistic talent. Plus, her uncommon good looks set her apart. None of the girls he dated from school or from town came close to matching any of those qualities. If that weren't enough, she was also star chef of one of the city's best restaurants which happened to be smack in the close-knit neighborhood where the limelight that once shone exclusively on himself was now fixated on someone else. An interloper. And a fifteen-year-old girl, no less.

All of which made his attraction to Giuliana even more intense. And thus more painful. Yet because he was powerless to act on his desires the only real time he got to spend with the girl was when they were together in a group of neighborhood kids, most often walking to school in the morning or sometimes back home after school. When it came to outwardly expressing feelings he had for Giuliana, he found it nigh impossible; simple, obsequious acts were all he was capable of managing, such as carrying her books or holding open a classroom door.

As for Giuliana's indifference to the young man, apparent or otherwise, her friends never stopped reminding her of it. No matter, she refrained from making any encouraging overtures her smitten admirer might misinterpret, except to be as cordial and as nice to him as she was to all the other neighborhood kids, male or female. To her mind their interests were far too disparate for them to be anything other than casual friends, so there wasn't much point in trying to engage the boy in anything but the most trivial, innocuous conversation. That being the case, it turned out to be quite a shock when word got out that Ricky DeGoia had asked Giuliana Landini to the senior prom. And even more surprising to learn the girl had accepted the invitation. Would miracles never cease?

It so happened that divine intervention had nothing to do with it. As is the case in certain boy-girl relationships, there always seem to be lurking in the background other *dramatis personae*, usually relatives of the young couple in question, who are dead set on making a match—in this instance one between the DeGoias' son and the Fassanos' niece—and more than willing to provide the nudge to get the proverbial ball rolling. Playing the principal roles of amorous intermediary were Agnes DeGoia, Rick's mother, and Concetta Fassano, Giuliana's aunt.

The two women were good friends and enjoyed each other's company. Loyal members of the St. Andrew Women's Society, they attended church together and on at least one Sunday afternoon a month they went out, just the two of them, usually to a movie or to catch a live performance at the Shubert Theater whenever a musical, often destined for Broadway, was playing. Though Agnes was a second-generation Italian born in America, she spoke the Neopolitan dialect fluently, which put Concetta at ease whenever she had something important she wanted to share with her American-born friend and found in her native language a more comfortable way of saying it. Another reason the women were close was that Agnes's parents, who lived two blocks away from her, were originally from Conca dei Marini on the Amalfi coast, not more than a few kilometers from where Concetta's family lived and not far from the restaurant where she met her husband Umberto.

One Sunday early in April the two friends, having just seen the thrilling movie classic, *To Have and Have Not,* starring Humphrey Bogart and Lauren Bacall, decided to stop for a snack before going home. While chatting over coffee and pastry, Agnes casually mentioned that she had recently run into Giuliana, whom she hadn't seen for a while, at the grocery store.

"My God, Connie, Giuliana has really grown since I last saw her," Agnes said cheerfully. "She's so beautiful and mature looking. And to think she's just a sophomore."

"She is quite lovely, isn't she," Concetta said.

"I should say so. Just the other day my Ricky remarked how nice Giuliana is . . . always so beautifully dressed . . . well-mannered and respectful. He says she's one of the best students in her class and really talented, but not a bit stuck up like some of the other girls. You and Bert must be very proud." Concetta glowed. "We've been blessed, that's for sure," she acknowledged. "Giuliana's made our lives very happy. She's like a daughter to us. I can't imagine what we're going to do when she goes off to college."

"Well, you have plenty of time before that happens."

"That's true, but time flies. Before you know it, she'll be gone . . . for good, I'm afraid. You know what they say: once a child leaves home and goes off on her own to college she's already halfway out the door . . . sometimes all the way out. In the meantime, we're going to enjoy her as much as we can while she's still under our roof. All three of us working together at the restaurant has brought us even closer. It's been wonderful."

"Speaking of the restaurant," Agnes remarked, "if you don't mind my saying it, don't you think Giuliana might be putting in a little bit too much time there when she should be out enjoying herself, having a good time like any normal teenager? You know, Con, there's a lot more to life besides school and work."

Connie had a ready answer: "I know what it may look like to some people, but Giuliana doesn't seem to mind. She thrives on doing things she loves . . . that's when she's the happiest. School, the restaurant, they're not work to her. Besides, she does have a lot of other interests that make her feel like she's not missing out on anything."

Agnes decided to cut to the chase. "But what about boys?" she inquired. "Isn't it about time Giuliana started dating?"

"To be honest, Agnes, I agree. Giuliana should be spreading her wings like all her friends. Umberto and I talk about it a lot. But whenever we bring up the subject she always gives us the same answer—she just doesn't have the time. She says it's not a priority right now . . . that she'll get around to it in due time. When you come right down to it she may be right, the only free time she has for herself to do the other things she's involved in are Saturday mornings and Sundays. So when would she have time for dating? We've even had to give up those nice Sunday outings we used to take as a family when she was younger. As much as she regrets not being more social, she says that as soon as she's a little older and in college she'll have plenty of time for a social life. Till then, we're going to have to go along with what she thinks is best for her." She took a sip of her coffee then asked: "Why all the sudden interest in my niece, Agnes?"

This was the opening Agnes was waiting for. "You know, Connie, May is the busiest and most exciting month of the school year for the kids . . . there are so many activities going on. I was thinking this might be as good a time as any for Giuliana to kind of get her feet wet . . . you know, become a part of the social scene . . . even though she may think she doesn't want to just yet."

"How do you mean?" asked Connie.

"Maybe she should think about attending one of those functions. What I personally had in mind was the senior prom. From what I hear, the kids really have a good time . . . it's always exciting to attend a formal dance, like a prom. I wish I had the chance when I was younger. How I regret never having gone to one."

"Doesn't a boy have to ask her first?"

"Of course, that's the whole point," Agnes said cheerfully.

"Giuliana has never had an actual date, Ag, and . . ."

"I can help fix that in a minute, Connie."

"You can?"

"My Ricky . . . he would love to take Giuliana to the prom."

"How do you know?" Connie asked, caught by surprise by such an admission.

"He told me so."

"Really?"

"He's wanted to ask her out for the longest time but he says he hasn't found the right opportunity. To tell you the truth, I think he's shy," Agnes said, lowering her eyes.

"Are . . . are you saying your Ricky wants to take my Giuliana out but he's too shy to ask her?" an incredulous Connie asked. "From what I hear, Ricky's never been shy about asking girls out."

Both women laughed. "You're absolutely right, Con, but for some reason he's never seemed comfortable approaching Giuliana . . . directly."

"So why doesn't he just ask her, and let it go at that?"

"You have to remember, Con, my Ricky is a very proud boy, with a big ego . . . I'll be the first one to admit it. But at heart he's a good kid, a wonderful kid. To be honest with you, I don't think he wants to risk Giuliana turning him down . . . it would hurt his pride. He would be miserable if that were to happen."

"So let me understand, Ag," a perplexed Connie said, setting her cup down, "are you asking me to go to Giuliana and get her to agree to be Ricky's prom date . . . before he's even asked her himself?"

"All I'm saying is for you to sort of pave the way so that when he does get around to formally asking her, she won't turn him down." While Concetta was staring off in space trying to digest what she'd just heard, Agnes quickly followed up with: "Do you have any problem with that, Con?"

"Let me see what I can do," Concetta answered.

# Chapter 33

The relatively sedate, laid-back life Giuliana had led in Amalfi was far removed from the one she was now leading in New Haven. And she reveled in every new experience that came her way. But nothing came close to rivaling the excitement and sheer joy of prom night. Not only was it her first real date, the event itself far exceeded her expectations. Beginning with her prom dress. The moment she put it on she felt transported. The only other time she felt quite as exhilarated was on the boat crossing the Atlantic four years ago when she wore for the first time the dress Nonna Dona had made for her. She still had that dress and kept it stored in the cedar chest at the foot of the bed. From time to time Giuliana would take it out, lay it neatly on the bed and run her hand across its soft pleats before putting it back in the same plastic bag her grandmother gave her the night before she left for America. She often thought about giving the dress away, but she could never bring herself to part with it. *How could I even think of it . . . I'm saving the dress for my daughter when she comes of age,* she told herself. The very same thought crossed her mind when she put on her prom dress for the first time.

Prom night was everything her friends said it would be. Looking back, Giuliana was thankful Concetta had talked her into accepting Ricky's invitation; without actually saying it, she let her aunt know that she was indebted to Agnes DeGoia as well.

To begin with, there was the memorable reception she and Ricky were accorded the moment they swept into the auditorium. Given the sustained clapping and cheering, one would have thought they were prom king and queen—not the senior class president and his date—so handsome was the couple, Giuliana shimmering in her gorgeous body-hugging, full-length formal dress, unlike any other in the room, Ricky the picture of suave sophistication in a rented cut-a-way tuxedo one would have expected to find at a high-society ball, not at a school prom. He even wore white gloves.

The school auditorium was hardly recognizable. *I can't believe this is where we take gym every day and play volleyball twice a week,* Giuliana thought to herself. It was decorated with such flair, a faithful replica of what Mardi Gras in New Orleans looked like from pictures she had seen. Only this time it was "Mardi Gras in May," the theme of Hillhouse High's 1945 Senior Prom. Candlelit tables three deep formed an arc rimming the shiny hardwood floor that had been installed for dancing, and the stage was festooned with swaying ersatz palm trees and strings of colorful beads that hung from make-believe balconies similar to the kind found in profusion in the Crescent City's famous Latin Quarter. Dozens of exotic masks were pinned to a scrim that stretched across the back of the stage and were illuminated by tiny lights that bounced a warm glow off the gleaming musical instruments played by members of New Haven's favorite prom band, Tony Vittola and His Seven Sensations. Freshmen and sophomores, acting as waiters and outfitted in colorful costumes, served cake and soft drinks to the exuberant partygoers.

All in all, the gym had the look of an intimate nightclub. The girls in beautiful gowns, the boys in rented tuxedos, they waltzed and jitterbugged the night away, including Giuliana. She loved to dance and came well prepared to meet the prom's exhausting demands. In the Fassano house, as in most Italian homes on the street, music was constantly playing. Oftentimes, when Giuliana and her aunt were alone in the flat, Concetta would turn on the radio, usually to Martin Block's *Make Believe Ballroom Time,* move the kitchen table and chairs against the wall out of the way and the two women would shimmy and shake to the latest American dance craze, stopping only when their legs were in danger of giving out.

It was no coincidence that the prom band played many of the same top one-hundred songs and Broadway show tunes Giuliana was familiar with, so she felt quite at ease spending half the night on the dance floor. And not always in the arms of her date. All through the evening so many boys lined up to take the beautiful young sophomore for a "spin around the pines" that Ricky at one point had to bring to a halt the intrusion on his own dance-floor time with the radiant Giuliana.

The evening was a shining moment for the high school sophomore, one she would cherish long after dreams of proms had long faded. (It took up quite a few pages in her diary.) What made it all the more memorable, and to her mind the most pleasant surprise of all, was her date himself. The boy who took her to the prom wasn't anything like Ricky DeGoia the megawatt high school star athlete. He may have looked the same, but away from the playing field and fawning friends and admirers he was a totally different person from the one she thought she knew, or the one she knew largely through hearsay.

Over the course of the seven hours they were in each other's company—the prom ended at midnight; they spent the remaining time together over breakfast at an all-night diner—she learned that most of her previous assumptions were erroneous. The huge ego he was famously known for was nowhere in evidence, replaced instead by an engaging personality, an incisive intelligence and a sensitive side she never expected he had. True, he did speak openly of the excitement he felt at the prospect of playing professional baseball, but only because Giuliana herself—whom he discovered, much to his amazement, to be quite an ardent, knowledgeable baseball fan—brought it up. It wasn't a subject he wanted to get into, having promised himself not to let an occasion that had been so long in coming devolve into another one of his typical solipsistic moments. He set out determined to get to know more about this intriguing, elusive (in his mind) young woman, and at every chance during the evening he attempted to turn the conversation, the only real one he had ever had in the four years he was acquainted with the girl, toward her and away from him.

But Giuliana kept pushing back, resisting, for her own reasons, his entreaties. Like him, she was also prospecting, scoping out, so to speak, new territory: if this were to be the first and only date she would ever have with Ricky DeGoia, well, then, she had better learn all she could about the young man in the space of these few hours.

"I hope you don't mind my asking, Rick" (she preferred calling him Rick instead of what was to her mind the more athletic sounding Ricky; only later did he tell her that his actual first name was Enrico), "but do you have any interests other than athletics?" Giuliana asked, as soon as the couple had settled into a booth.

The suddenness of the question caught Ricky completely off guard. "Not really," he muttered, shaking his head for added emphasis.

"You mean there isn't anything other than baseball that strikes your fancy?" she said, unwilling to accept his cavalier disavowal.

Ricky again hesitated answering, but he sensed she wouldn't let up until she extracted some sort of concession from him. "That's quite an interesting way of putting it," he said, a smile spread across his handsome face. "Would it matter if there were?"

"Perhaps. It all depends what it was."

"And if I did tell you, what would you say if I asked you to keep it to yourself?"

"Is it that bad?" Giuliana said laughingly.

"No, not at all," Ricky quickly allowed, his face by now a touch this side of beet red. "It's just that not many people, not my friends, anyway, know that . . . well, I like opera. In fact, if you really want to know the truth, I love opera. Everybody in my family does. But I would prefer if you didn't spread that news around."

Giuliana did not want to appear to be shocked at such a revelation, but her interest was now definitely peaked. "I don't think that's anything to be ashamed of," she said; it was the best she could do at the moment to reassure the young man. At the same time she was relieved to learn that Ricky's life was more than an endless field of baseball dreams.

"In fact, my uncle, that's all he listens to, opera and Yankee games," Giuliana assured him. "Every chance he gets when he's in the house reading the Italian newspaper or just relaxing between jobs, he cranks up the Victrola and listens to all the great tenors—Enrico Caruso, Tito Gobbi, Beniamino Gigli, Ferruccio Tagliavini, even John McCormick. He has all their records. Then on Saturday afternoons before going off to work at Randazzi's he listens to *The Texaco Hour*, you know, the Metropolitan Opera broadcasts with Milton Cross. I love that kind of music myself. I would think that wouldn't be something to be ashamed of."

Ricky was impressed at hearing names he knew by heart dropping from Giuliana's lips. But of course there's a simple explanation for that: she's a native-born Italian, they all love opera, to them classical music is as popular as jazz is to Americans.

"To me it's no big deal. It's just something I do . . . like batting right handed . . . you know, sort of second nature. I got it from my grandfather. Ever since I was a little boy, I'd sit for hours with him and listen to classical music and opera. He even had me take notes. He knew every Italian opera by heart. Now I do. I love walking around the house singing famous arias. My mom loves it when I sing." He was quite emotive by now. "It's also how I learned Italian, from him and from the music. Anyway, I don't see that it's something that needs to be advertised all over town." Then in an apparent non sequitur, he added: "Besides, your uncle is a lot older than the guys I hang around with."

Learning that Ricky loved opera was one thing; his knowing Italian was another matter. Not a single kid in the neighborhood, as far as she knew, spoke the language, or ever uttered a word of Italian in her presence. They're Americans through and through, she had soon learned. A lot of them in fact wanted nothing to do with matters of ethnicity, or for a foreign language they had little interest in. And as far as where their ancestors came from, Italy was a country half a world away; it had no relevance to them.

She also found, much to her distress, that even some of her closest friends were actually ashamed of their heritage, and made no bones about it. All they ever wanted was to fit in, to be full-fledged Americans. They were part of the younger generation that found the customs and mores of their foreign-born parents and relatives, and their unshakeable attachment to them, off-putting, even un-American, if truth be told. Could it be this young man, down deep, was different?

"You think people would think less of you if they knew?" Giuliana asked the question in Italian, wondering how her companion would react.

Ricky did not answer at first. But he could not, much as he wanted to, keep from cracking a smile, the kind she found endearing. Also the way his shoulder twitched when hearing something that amused him. Then, also in Italian, he said: "Do you mind if we change the subject?"

Giuliana did not want to, but she knew she would have to steer the conversation in a different direction if she were to learn what she wanted to about someone she was beginning to see in a whole new light. She decided to throw caution to the wind. "I hear you're not much of a student, is that true Rick . . . in one or two of your courses you're barely passing?" She even surprised herself at how forward she must have sounded in posing such an indelicate question.

Ricky bridled. "Who told you that?"

"When someone is as popular as you are, you hear a lot of things. It can't be helped," Giuliana said, attempting to sound more diplomatic. She knew she was entering another sensitive area, one that needed to be handled delicately and with as much tact as she was capable of. While considering how best to pursue this sensitive line of questioning, she reflected on her own ideas about education.

When she was being urged years ago by well-meaning family and friends in Amalfi to come to America to get an education she took it for granted that everyone on this side of the Atlantic was doing just that. But she soon discovered this was not the case. If anything, she found that most of the young people in the neighborhood, the boys especially, had an attitude about school completely at variance with her own: they viewed school as a necessary inconvenience that would be permanently disposed of once they reached the age of sixteen, or as soon as they graduated from high school. Perhaps such an attitude was to be expected, since in her immediate circle none of her friends' parents had graduated from high school, some not even from elementary school.

It also disturbed her that not one person she was acquainted with in the entire neighborhood had gone to college, or that not one of her contemporaries from the Wooster Street area, male or female, contemplated doing so. It couldn't just be a money issue, could it? Many families, while certainly not rich, did not have to look over their shoulders expecting the bailiff at any moment; they could afford to send their sons or daughters to college, if not Yale then certainly the University of Connecticut, where state residents benefited from attractive tuition rates. Then it must be a cultural issue, in her eyes something even worse.

It was hard for her to fathom what exactly it was about Italians, here or in her native country, that made them feel that a proper education was less desirable than, say, bringing home a paycheck from an oftentimes degrading factory job, or one requiring little thinking. Were they mutually exclusive? Why did a certain class of Italians, their claims to have mastered the art of living notwithstanding—love of life itself, love of family, love of tradition, of great art, music, food, their sense of place in history—harbor what amounted to an inherent bias against education? Was it anti intellectualism, or just plain ignorance? Or both? If not, why then were the Jews from the Hill section of town, socio-economically no better off than Italians from the Wooster Street area, and who, by the way, almost universally shunned the athletic field, or the WASPs from other parts of the city, the only contemporaries of hers college bound? Which brought her full circle to Rick DeGoia: was he, too, one of those Italo-Americans determined to carry on the lamentable tradition of turning his back on college for fear of venturing too far out of his comfort zone?

"If you think passing a bunch of high school courses is a sign of intelligence, I'd have to completely disagree," Ricky said without rancor, wishing to lay bare, as far as he was concerned, the mistaken notion that school was the exclusive avenue to success and a lifetime of accomplishment.

"Intelligence has nothing to do with it, Rick. But I find it hard to believe that someone with your interests can't find a single thing about school that is worthwhile."

"You don't seem to understand, Giuliana," Ricky said confidently, making a feeble attempt not to sound too cocky, "I've already found what I'm looking for. It's not that school isn't important, it is . . . for a lot of people. But my focus is on something else right now. Let me put it to you this way. I've been blessed with a talent, a God-given talent, few people have. For whatever reason, I've been put on this earth to be a baseball player, not an opera singer or a musician or even a poet, which is something else you might be interested to know I enjoy doing, writing poetry. Do you realize that in this entire country, the whole world in fact, there are only four-hundred major league baseball players? Imagine, only four-hundred . . . on sixteen major league teams . . . twenty-five players to a team. I'm telling you, you're looking at someone who's going to be part of that group. I don't mean to brag. It's just a fact. If I were to turn my back on the unique talent I've been blessed with, or have anything get in the way of my using this talent to the fullest, I really think down deep I'd be committing a sin.

"The way I look at it, all my other interests I can put off temporarily, or else pursue on my own. And as far as school is concerned I may even give that a shot when the right time comes along. But not now. I have to concentrate completely on achieving my goal. The day I graduate, I'll be free to sign a contract with one of those sixteen teams I just mentioned. Then it's on to the minor leagues, for what I hope is a short stay. Once I reach the majors, well, then, who knows what's liable to come next.

"But the one thing I want you to understand, Giuliana, is that if a person is lucky enough to know what it is he wants . . . not many kids our age can say that . . . and truly loves it and has the talent for it, then I really believe in my heart and soul that a person has an obligation to see it through to the end . . . with no ifs, ands or buts. People take all kinds of different paths to success. That's what I feel. Does any of this make sense to you?"

Giuliana smiled wryly while thinking to herself: *All this time I've listened to what others have said about you. I may have even been influenced by what they've said. Could it be I've misjudged you?* She wished she had the nerve to tell him that, but didn't.

Instead she said: "I suppose from your perspective it makes sense, but . . ."

"Well, what about from yours," Ricky interrupted, not wasting another moment before trying to turn the tables on his wily inquisitor. "What do you want to be when you grow up . . . more than a cook I hope?" he said in a clipped, dismissive tone.

Giuliana did not know whether he was trying to be funny or actually mocking her. "What's wrong with being a cook?" she answered defensively, pulling herself away from the back of the booth and sitting up ram-rod straight as a soldier at attention.

"Absolutely nothing, but as far as I know you don't have to go to college to become one," he said, in a much too-sarcastic tone of voice to suit Giuliana.

"I'm doing this, temporarily, because I love being around food," she said, raising her voice an octave. "I have every intention of going to college. That's why I came here in the first place, to get the best education this country has to offer. And by the way, if you really want to know what I plan on doing with my life . . . well, I'm going to be an architect." Giuliana had come full circle: finally she owned up to the career choice she had made, which heretofore she had not divulged to anyone outside of teachers and family.

Ricky, in a more conciliatory voice, sounded impressed: "That should be quite an undertaking, becoming an architect. How did you develop an interest in that field?"

"As far back as I can remember," Giuliana answered evenly, "I've always loved buildings. I suppose it's in my blood. My grandfather was a builder, actually a stone mason, the best in Amalfi. He and his brother and their sons had a construction company. He used to say to me all the time that every building has a history. Unfortunately, I didn't know him very well because he died when I was only five years old, but my grandmother who came to live with us after he died used to take me on walks in the area where we lived to show me some of his work . . . it's very impressive.

"In fact, most of Italy is an architectural marvel. I haven't seen very much of it, I'm afraid, except in books, but one day I'm definitely going to visit as many places as I can, and see what the rest of Italy is like. Someday you should go there and see for yourself. But what really sold me on the idea of becoming an architect were the beautiful churches up and down the Amalfi coast. Of course, our most spectacular is the Cathedral of Sant'Andrea. You should see it, it's something to behold. I never tired of studying the details found in this incredible place, and in some of our other beautiful but lesser known churches. I have a book of sketches on many of them.

"Like you, I believe in my heart this is what I was destined to do, to design buildings that are living, breathing places for people to use as they see fit, and enjoy. If one of them turns out to be a work of art, all the better. I believe I have the talent for this kind of work, and like you I don't plan on squandering it. So you see, Rick, I have my own dream I'm pursuing, just like you have yours. The only difference is that mine can't be realized unless I continue in school, which I definitely plan on doing."

\* \* \*

When the limo pulled up to the curb in front of Giuliana's house, Umberto and a few of his friends were standing on the corner smoking away and trying, not too successfully, to keep their voices down so as not to wake up neighbors whose street-side bedroom windows were open to the balmy early morning May air. Curfew had been strictly adhered to—it was exactly 2 a.m.

Giuliana knew what Ricky must be thinking when he saw Umberto glancing sideways at them as they exited the car. But if she was annoyed at her uncle for being anywhere in sight when her date dropped her off she did an excellent job of concealing it. The couple bid each other goodbye without so much as a friendly parting kiss, which pleased Umberto but not Giuliana; she frankly had been expecting one, but it never came. Before parting, the couple agreed to get together the following Sunday afternoon. Giuliana was certain she would have no trouble getting her uncle's permission to go on another date with Ricky now that he had observed first hand how well the young man had comported himself with his niece.

Giuliana found herself more excited about her upcoming second date with Ricky than the prom date she had been on with him less than thirty-six hours earlier. For one thing, she felt she had got to know the young man over the course of the long evening and definitely liked what she heard and seen. For another, she was certain he was of a like mind: why would he have asked her out again so soon after the prom had he not been impressed? In parsing the evening's special moments, she kept coming back to the self-assured way he handled himself after they'd broken the ice, and to the sentiment he expressed several times during their long and revealing discussion over breakfast: "Find something you love doing, and stick with it." She never forgot his admonition.

The Sunday date immediately following the prom was not the last of their get-togethers. They saw each other every Sunday thereafter until Ricky left New Haven. The couple roller skated, went bowling— Giuliana had never been bowling before—picnicked in the park at the top of East Rock, attended a movie and a live stage show (a young tenor from Philadelphia by the name of Mario Lanza headlined that portion of the show). Also a semi-pro baseball game at Waterside Park.

On the last of their Sunday dates, the day before Ricky left to play minor league baseball, the young couple, dressed literally in their Sunday best, went to the Shubert Theater to hear the Louie Prima band, and the bandleader's talented wife, the singer Keeley Smith. Later that evening, Ricky and Giuliana dined on prime ribs at George & Harry's Chapel Street restaurant. It had been a glorious day and evening. When they got back to the Fassano flat at 8:45, fifteen minutes under Giuliana's 9 p.m. curfew, they sat on the tiny front porch bench and for the next few minutes talked a little bit about each of their seven dates, beginning with the prom. Ricky then took Giuliana's hand in his. He told her he'd call just as soon he got settled. He promised to write often; Giuliana said she would do the same. Ricky unlocked the front door and led Giuliana into the vestibule. He took out of a pocket a small box and handed it to her. Surprised, and moved by the gesture, she opened the box expectantly. In it was a sterling silver bracelet with a single charm attached—a catcher's mitt; it glistened in the dimly lighted hall.

"I was hoping I'd find an outfielder's glove, but Michael's Jewelers didn't have one," Ricky laughingly explained, taking the bracelet out of the box and sliding it on her left wrist. Giuliana, speechless, fell into Ricky's arms. He kissed her gently on each cheek. The hallway light caught her eyes at just the right angle; Ricky told her they sparkled like jewels. At five feet nine inches and in her three-inch high-heeled shoes, Giuliana was at eye level with Ricky. He tilted her head back slightly. For what seemed much longer, not the actual second it took, Ricky brought his lips to hers and kissed Giuliana hard. She responded with more feeling than she had intended, then pulled away.

But only for an instant. This time Giuliana took the initiative. She slid her right hand gently behind his head and drew him close to her. She kissed Ricky meaningfully, then broke away before the startled young man could himself initiate a move he had been contemplating making the moment he gave Giuliana the bracelet. Without saying a word, she ran up the stairs.

*     *     *

The day after Ricky's graduation from high school, the general manager of the Pittsburgh Pirates was at the DeGoia home to sign the young star to a contract, which called for a $17,000 guaranteed bonus, a hefty amount of money in those days. Two days later he was on a train to Indiana and the Pirates' International League West Division Triple A minor league farm team, the Indianapolis Red Barons. Giuliana never saw the young man again.

In the beginning, Ricky kept his promise and wrote Giuliana at least once a week. Giuliana did likewise. With each letter she wrote, she made her feelings known that she, too, was ready to take up where they left off after the baseball season ended and he returned to New Haven in the fall. But as the summer wore on, his letters became less frequent, giving Giuliana pause to wonder whether their relationship was strong enough to withstand a protracted separation like this one. Or as committed enough on Rick's part for him to temper his need to constantly have a parade of women at his beck and call.

In either case, the only way she kept abreast of her friend's progress from then on was through reports that filtered back into the neighborhood. There was never a dearth of news where Ricky was concerned. He remained the main topic of conversation through the entire summer among the neighborhood's baseball cognoscenti caught up in the doings of Wooster Street's first legitimate big-league prospect.

The chances of Ricky DeGoia ever roaming a major league outfield, unfortunately, never came to fruition. Just seven weeks into the season, Ricky was involved in a bone-chilling collision at second base while

260

trying to break up a double play. He slid hard, upending the shortstop coming across from his position to cover the bag. He fell on Ricky with such force that Ricky's right shoulder, the source of his magnificent throwing arm and the nexus from which he generated his power through the hitting zone, was separated like a cracked walnut, and several muscles torn away from the rotator cuff. Orthopedic specialists determined it would take at least a year, possibly two, perhaps never, before DeGoia might regain his powerful throwing arm. Even at that, it would be diminished power at best.

For all intents and purposes, Ricky DeGoia's promising professional baseball career was over before it started; he had just turned nineteen. But as fate would have it, another life was about to begin for the emotionally wounded, physically damaged once promising athlete. A young nurse, a year older than he, came into his life. She ministered to him in and out of the hospital, helped him find an apartment—Ricky couldn't face going back to New Haven—even got him a job in her father's stationery store. A year later, they married, and with part of his baseball bonus money the young couple bought a house not far from where Ricky's in-laws lived.

Free from the pressure of succeeding in a profession no longer open to him, living for the first time as a young adult in an environment no longer focused almost exclusively on him, Ricky started night school at a local junior college. At the time, he had no specific goal in mind. But it didn't take long before the classroom became the fulcrum of his life. After amassing enough credits, he transferred to Indiana University's Indianapolis branch. Working days full time in the store, going to school at night, it took Rick six years to earn his degree in education. Which allowed him to realize his new-found dream—teaching in the Indianapolis public school system. However, he wasn't quite through with educating himself: while teaching fifth and six-graders, he spent another four years working his way resolutely toward a master's degree.

Before he had turned thirty-six, Rick DeGoia, ex-athlete, ex-easterner, ex-man-about-town—and ex-school agnostic—became one of the youngest high school principals in the state of Indiana. And a devoted husband and father of three children. In the future whenever Giuliana thought of Rick DeGoia, as she often did, she would remind herself how wrong she'd been in judging the boy she originally thought of as just another jock.

He wrote her a long letter, the last she'd ever hear from him, after he'd married and been in night school a year. She did not answer it. He freely admitted the crush he'd had on her, and how he often thought about what it might have been like had fate, of a more positive kind, exerted a stronger hand in their relationship. Giuliana was moved by what he said. Not simply because he was forthcoming and lavish with his affections, which had aroused the first stirrings of womanhood in Giuliana, a feeling she frankly found exhilarating; it was more in how Ricky described navigating this critical turn in his life. None of the superior or self-serving attitude he was once famously known for was apparent in his delineation of events. She found only modesty and maturity in his assessment of how fate had dealt him a new, totally unexpected hand. Much to his credit, he even went so far as to describe movingly how he was able to embrace his new responsibilities with equanimity rather than succumbing to self pity, or allowing circumstances to crush any new dreams he might be entertaining.

In the end Rick DeGoia had been right all along, even prescient, regarding his single-minded devotion to a sport that meant everything to him. Things might not have turned out as originally planned. But in one way or another baseball, finally, had paid off just as he had always imagined it would. "Isn't it ironic when you think of it . . . where would

I be today had it not been for baseball?" were the last words Rick DeGoia penned in his final letter to Giuliana Landini.

In this regard, Giuliana couldn't help but compare Rick with Nonna Dona. The similarities were striking. As a young girl Donatella had turned her back on education, not because it wasn't important to her but because she fell in love with a business at which she became, against all odds, very successful. Rick had made a similar determination, to strive for baseball stardom at the expense of school. But now, unlike Nonna Dona for whom the goal of achieving a formal education had been permanently foreclosed after she married, Rick seized the opportunity to reestablish ties with the classroom after departing one career and taking up another. He came to realize that for him school was the only way to achieve the ultimate goal of living an accomplished, satisfying, full life now that his original goal of baseball immortality had been permanently laid to rest. Had she known Rick DeGoia, her grandmother would have approved of him.

In assessing these two lives, Giuliana considered her own priorities. In doing so, she tried to be as honest as she could regarding her desire to become an architect. She told herself there was grandeur in creating buildings . . . in watching them rise from nothing and come to life . . . in having them breathe and become the fulfillment of dreams for their inhabitants. At least that is how she thought she would feel once her efforts came to fruition. But she really didn't know for certain. After all, she had never designed anything as remotely ambitious as a building. The closest she ever came were less than professional renderings she did of same, as well as some modest paintings she had attempted for her own edification—they were just that, and nothing more. Cooking, on the other hand, was something she had done all her life, young as she was. Through it, she was able to immediately see and touch and smell and taste the fruits of her efforts. To her it was in many ways not unlike architecture, since creating a successful meal also required harmony, balance, proportion. Having prepared for grateful diners over and over again the most delectable dishes, hadn't she already experienced and enjoyed such transcendent pleasures?

Yet, she still had doubts. She asked herself over and over whether a culinary career was enough to fan the flames of her fiery ambitions.

# Chapter 34

Giuliana and Camilla met just once over the summer of 1945. It was toward the end of August, three weeks before Camilla was due to return to Amalfi for her final year of teaching at Santa Croce School. It was a little over two years since they'd last seen each other. Camilla arrived in New Haven not from New York but from Boston, where she had spent a week on the Harvard University campus in Cambridge interviewing college administrators and doing research for an article the *Glasgow Times* had commissioned her to write on America's oldest ivy league colleges in the northeast, Princeton (originally known as the College of New Jersey), Columbia (originally known as Kings College) and Yale, the last stop on her list, being the other three.

The two met Sunday at the train and went immediately to Jennifer and Langdon's—now officially Dr. and Mrs. Davies; the couple had married in May shortly after Langdon completed his residency at New Haven Hospital. Camilla had been invited to stay with them for the week while working on the Yale part of the project. After lunch, Jennifer and her husband went for a walk, leaving Camilla and Giuliana alone to catch up after their extended separation. Camilla handed a passel of letters to Giuliana from family and friends in Amalfi; also several photographs she had accumulated over the last year. One that especially caught her eye was a picture of Father Di Pina.

"My God, he's half the size of what he was when I last saw him," Giuliana exclaimed, delighted to see how well her favorite prelate looked.

"He might very well be," Camilla agreed. "Doctor Gallardo finally convinced him he'd have to lose weight, a lot of weight, if he was to survive another heart episode."

"No one ever wrote to me about a heart condition," Giuliana said, surprised and saddened by the news. "Certainly not Father Marco himself. Even Maddalena hasn't mentioned it in her letters. I feel like everyone in Amalfi is keeping things from me." said Giuliana, a worried look on her face. "Is he going to be alright?"

"Well, according to Armando, he should be okay, that is if he adheres to his present regimen of less food and wine and more exercise. He has been good, I must say. He's taken to going on long walks with greater regularity since his last scare several months ago. When I saw him just before leaving for New York, he told me to tell you he's not ready to die just yet, at least not until he gets to see you one last time. He can't get over how you've grown. Your mom is always good about showing him your latest photographs. He says you look just like Donatella, to him a very good thing. But he did say for you to hurry up and graduate . . . he'll be seventy-six come October."

"And what of Mama and Papa . . . I can't tell much from their pictures. How are they doing? Whenever I hear from them they always tell me the same thing—that they couldn't be better. But I don't believe them."

"To tell you the honest truth, Jules," Camilla allowed, "they miss you terribly. Your absence has definitely affected them. All in all I believe they're well, but I'm afraid I don't see them as often as I probably should to know for sure. I'm afraid I've been terribly neglectful when it comes to your family this past year. I must apologize for that."

Two days later Camilla and the Davies went to Randazzi's for dinner. The young married couple needed to firm up plans, including the menu, for a Sunday dinner at the restaurant they were hosting the following month for New Haven friends who were not in attendance at their lavish wedding in Philadelphia in May. Giuliana and the Fassanos regretted having also missed the affair; work prevented their going.

When Camilla arrived around seven—Jennifer and Langdon were already there—it was obvious she was exhausted from a full day of running from one meeting to the next in the oppressive heat and humidity that hung over the city like an impenetrable fish net.

It was just as well the restaurant had few customers, this being a typical dog day of August when trying to stay cool made eating an afterthought. Letizia was especially anxious to meet the two *Amidigans* and the Scottish schoolteacher she had heard so much about from Giuliana. She wasn't disappointed. Italian flew around the table like confetti as soon as Camilla sat down. Even Langdon was able to get in on the conversation here and there with the few words in Italian he knew, before everyone got back to speaking English.

Letizia said Camilla's Italian was impeccable, "more beautiful to my ears than anything I've heard since coming to America, way better than mine," which pleased the soon-to-be-ex-schoolteacher. While everyone was enjoying dessert and coffee, plans for the Davies' dinner were finalized.

"How I wish I could be here for it," moaned Camilla. "It's a shame, I've already missed the wedding itself."

Mrs. Randazzi then offered a toast of Sambuca to everyone gathered, and looking directly at the beaming young newlyweds, wished them "*tanti auguri e tanti bambini.*" She also told them how much she was looking forward to their party next month.

"I have an announcement I would like to make, if you don't mind," Camilla said, after the toast. "I've been keeping it in so long, I'm practically bursting. I'm so happy all my New Haven friends are here to hear it together: Gordon has asked me to marry him."

There was dead silence for a second, then came a roar that had the few customers in the the house look over. "I know, I know, Jules, what you're going to say, 'Why didn't I tell you sooner?' But the fact is, he asked me only two weeks ago. I didn't want to put the news in a letter, or call either one of you (looking first at Giuliana then Jennifer), knowing I'd be seeing both of you in a couple of weeks. I wanted to tell you in person. Well, here I am . . . the cat's finally out of the bag."

The hugs and the kisses, not to mention the flowing tears—even Letizia couldn't hold back, and she hardly knew the girl—got to the usually non-remonstrative, stiff-upper-lipped Scottish lass. Camilla plopped back down in her seat, and through intermittent clearings of the throat and occasional sobs, explained: "We're thinking it should be next year . . . the end of September, actually . . . in New York. It'll be a lot less hassle to have the ceremony there, since I'll have the entire summer to plan things, plus it will be easier for Gordie's family to get to New York than Glasgow. Of course, Mother, Father and my brother, Connor, and his wife will be in attendance and, hopefully, some of my other relatives. As for the rest of the clan on the other side of the pond, Gordie and I have decided to spend part of our honeymoon in Scotland . . . we'll have a proper bash over there for friends and family unable to make it here." Before anyone had a chance to put in a word, Camilla continued: "Of course, this is all going to come as a shock to Mums and Daddy since we haven't told them yet."

"You mean, your mother and father don't know about this?" Letizia exclaimed. *"Che piccato!"*

"Not yet," Camilla answered. "And we're not going to tell them until we can do it in person . . . unless a certain somebody (she threw a mischievous glance Giuliana's way), has a slip of the tongue. In the meantime, we've worked things out, Gordie and I . . . we'll tell my folks at Christmastime. I've already convinced them to come to Amalfi, since it will be my last holiday there. Gordie will be right alongside me when we break the news. In any event, my beau wants to do the right thing by formally asking father for my hand. Gordie believes it's absolutely necessary if we're to get things off on the right foot."

"What about your fiancé's family?" Concetta wanted to know.

"We've already covered that base, Connie. We told his parents when they came to New York last week for their annual summer visit. In a single stroke, I got to meet them for the very first time: 'How do you do . . . and by the way, I'm marrying your son.' I got it all out in in one fell swoop. It was delicious." To Giuliana, Camilla had lost none of her irreverent playfulness; if anything, at thirty-two, she seemed to have gotten sharper.

"One other important item before we get on to other things: Jules, I would like you to be my maid of honor . . . and you, Jen, to be a bridesmaid. I know full well you two absolutely ravishing beauties will most likely upstage yours truly, even on my wedding day. But who cares. Every one of you here, my entire New Haven contingent, is invited to see for yourself how right I'll be."

# Chapter 35

The heart and soul of Randazzi's Restaurant was Letizia Randazzi. But its face belonged to her son Silvio. It was often said that Silvio Randazzi brought more people into the restaurant on the strength of his charm and good looks than the old lady's cooking. It wasn't just his handsome, porcelain-white, incandescent smile that kept customers coming; he had an aura about him that women, especially, found irresistible. ("Signora, a table by the window for you . . . the light is still at its best." Or, "Signorina, for one as lovely as you, we have the perfect special this evening.") There was little doubt that customers were put immediately into the right frame of mind and ready for an hour or two of uninterrupted pleasure. Silvio—and his mother—did not disappoint. But there was a less attractive side to the young man hidden from the view of most of his devoted public: he had a roving eye and a serious gambling problem. Both hung over his head like the sword of Damocles.

When war broke out after Pearl Harbor Silvio wanted desperately to join the army like most of his friends were doing, but with a wife and kids, plus his age, he was declared 4-F and given a deferment. Which left him feeling bereft, angry, a pariah, and totally ashamed: he was safely at home lying idly about while a lot of young men were laying down their lives for their country. To compensate for his despondency, Silvio would go off after restaurant closing hours into mostly outlying parts of town and stay out late, drinking and carousing. Since women were wildly attracted to him, there were always plenty around to help Silvio drown his sorrows. Young and old, single or married, they found it difficult to resist his importuning when he flashed those come-hither bedroom eyes, and were thus all too eager to have his shoes under their bed. As one of the few "available" men his age left in a city decimated by the war's call, Silvio, not given to bouts of moral introspection, had his delectable pick.

At first, his dalliances were shielded from his wife and family. That is, until one late afternoon when the cuckold husband of a customer the affable Valentino had taken up with stormed into the restaurant and confronted him about the affair he was having with his wife. He threatened Silvio. Had Umberto and Sam the dishwasher not come between the two men, the disgruntled husband might have made good on his promise to break Randazzi's nose. Giuliana happened to witness the ugly scene. Once an ardent admirer of the restaurant's heir apparent, she kept the wayward waiter at arms length from that day forward.

For a time, Silvio was chastened. But it wasn't long before he resumed his customary cheating ways. While the handsome Lothario swore off any future liaisons with restaurant patrons, and made good on his promise, he couldn't help himself from continuing to cultivate the larger population of New Haven women who had never set foot in Randazzi's Restaurant.

But as serious a problem as was Silvio's womanizing, which threatened to undo his marriage, his out-of-control gambling came within a hair of endangering his life. In and around Wooster Street crime wasn't something people ever had to worry about. But gambling was a whole other story. Opportunities for making a quick buck were as commonplace as meatless Fridays.

For the small-time gambler there was the Italian numbers lottery. Silvio declared it to be "for suckers and superstitious older-generation Italians," who were willing to literally bet on their dreams. The way the lottery worked was that a person with a particular dream would approach the neighborhood numbers runner who carried with him a little black book filled with scores of numbers that, according to the bookie, interpreted dreams of every conceivable stripe. A bettor, anxious to cash in on the dream he or she had had the night before, had the bookie look up the dream in his book, which had next to it a corresponding three-digit number. Most bettors waged a dime, quarter or half dollar (more if the bettor was presumably well-heeled like Letizia Randazzi who, herself, from time to time, engaged in numbers playing, more for the sport of it than to see how much she could win, at least that's what she told a dubious Giuliana, who frowned on gambling of any kind). On the rare occasion when a particular number actually came out, the lucky winner was quick to acknowledge the efficacy of the little black book to successfully predict dreams, thus enticing even more gullible bettors, much to the greedy delight of numbers runners.

Silvio Randazzi did not piddle around with such "nonsense." His addiction was of a more serious strain. Always flush with cash from generous tips he earned in the restaurant, hardly a day went by that he didn't gamble heavily on some sort of sporting event, mostly professional and college. His gambling parlor of choice was Cappy's Bar & Grille, run by the Boss of Wooster Square (no one ever referred to him by name). To supplement his insatiable appetite for more serious betting he also indulged in, what according to him, was a "harmless little side hobby"—shooting craps every Friday in the basement of the neighborhood store that sold fresh-killed chickens. This weekly pastime was also Boss-sponsored.

The store was owned and operated by Gennaro Mangione, famously and appropriately nicknamed "Chick" by everyone in the neighborhood. He sanctioned the gambling because he liked to roll the dice himself now and again. But he was not a heavy bettor. The Boss saw to it that he didn't have to be: he got players to agree that Chick was entitled to rake in a share of each day's wagering since he was sticking his neck out ("just like my chickens," Chick laughed) every time the guys got together in his store basement to shoot craps. What shouts and curses emanated from the gambling venue were muffled by hundreds of clucking chickens, alive and well, at least for the moment, in their coops on the floor above, unaware of their eventual fate. Customers in the shop never heard a sound.

Then arose the episode that almost shut the game down for good. When Chick's father passed away, his eighty-seven-year-old mother came to live with her son in the two-story house he owned directly across the street from the store. Philomena Mangione, infirm, frail, with a bent-over wisp of a body riddled with arthritis, possessed a feisty temperament but a mind still as sharp as a barber's razor, if not a bit fanciful. New to the area, she hardly left the flat except on rare occasions, preferring instead to spend her days in a chair by the window observing the comings and goings of shoppers buying chickens from her son's store, and fresh mozzarella or ricotta from the next-door *latteria*. She also never missed a chance to check on the number of mourners who came to pay their last respects at the funeral home on the corner just steps from her house whenever the occasion arose.

She began to notice that on Fridays, all day long, men, sometimes as many as five or six at a time, would approach the store, furtively look up and down the block, then disappear into the alleyway. At first, she thought nothing of it. But as time went on, she became suspicious and started jotting down dates and the number of men who seemed to magically appear every Friday. She noticed that many of the same men showed up week after week. She uttered not a word of this to her son. Then one day, convinced she had figured out what was going on, she called the police department and asked the desk sergeant to send a patrolman right away to investigate suspicious goings-on in her street. She refused to tell him over the phone what those suspicions were.

When two police officers appeared at her door she took them to the window, and before the first words were out of her mouth, sure enough three men showed up in front of the store, shot a glance left and right, then hurried through the alley to the back of the building. In broken but very understandable English, old lady Mangione proceeded to tell the officers that she was convinced there was a brothel behind her son's chicken store that he didn't know about, and that operated on Fridays only: "Because-a those-a days a lotta women buy their fresh-a chickens and-a cheese for the weekend . . . and after they make-a-their purchases, the *putanne* then-a sneak outta the back-a door and meet uppa with-a the men to do you-know-what in the garage my son keeps-a for storage. Only chicken crates in there, no beds. *Mio Dio!*"

The police officers had all to do to contain themselves. But instead of breaking out laughing, they listened attentively to the old woman, pretending to take down every word of her complaint. They explained to her that they wouldn't be able to search the premises without first securing a warrant, which they would obtain just as soon as they returned to precinct headquarters. Philomena thanked them.

The officers immediately sought out the lieutenant in charge. Listening to their story, the big Irish cop let out a roar that shook the precinct. Between gales of laughter he was finally able blurt out: "I'm going to have to get Chick to sit his mother down and let her know what's going on."

"And, lieutenant," said the sergeant, trying hard to sound serious, "you better start wearing a good disguise from now on when you go in there."

When word got out, the incident became a *cause celebre*. Giuliana loved hearing the story so much she wrote long letters about it to everybody she could think of, including Father Di Pina, who wrote back saying that it was the funniest story he had ever heard. He added that he would give anything to meet Philomena Mangione.

# Chapter 36

Except for Silvio Randazzi, splayed like a giant crab in the big round corner booth, his head cradled in arms that extended languidly across the oval table, Cappy's Bar & Grille was deserted. It was ten-thirty in the morning and outside a howling, belligerent wind was blowing icy circles of snow from the previous night's storm and scratching it against the window at the front end of the saloon. Angelo the bartender swung through the kitchen door and went behind the bar. He switched on a light over the mirror, counted out some bills and change he took from a small cloth bag and put the money in the cash register. The sound of coins dropping in the till caused Silvio to shift his position slightly, and as he did he emitted a long, soft sigh. Angelo turned like a flash, his arm catching the tip glass next to the register, sending it crashing to the floor.

"Who the hell's there?" a startled Angelo said in a loud voice, flailing the baseball bat he kept for protection behind the bar. Silvio lifted his head slowly and rubbed his eyes with his fists. But he didn't get up. "Don't be scared Ang, it's only me, Sil."

Angelo lifted the hinged top section of the bar at the far end and walked over to the booth, bat still in hand. "Jesus, Sil, you really gave me a start. What the hell you doin' here at this time?"

"Ralphie let me in about an hour ago," Randazzi said. "He was in the kitchen getting stuff ready for lunch, he let me in the back door. Didn't he tell you?"

"He didn't say nothin' that son-of-a-bitch," Angelo said smiling. "Ya' know him, if you get two words out of the guy you doin' great."

Silvio got up and shook hands with Angelo. The two men walked towards the bar, Angelo stopping to retrieve a broom and dust pan to sweep up the broken glass.

"Wanna drink?" Angelo asked, after cleaning up the mess.

"It's a little early for me, but yeah, I think I will."

Angelo placed a shot glass in front of his friend, then went over to the tap to draw a glass of beer. Coming back, he picked up a bottle of Four Roses and poured out a generous shot of whiskey. He placed the glass of beer beside it. Silvio drained the shot in one gulp, took a sip of beer then lighted a cigarette. Angelo began polishing glasses.

"What you doin' that for . . . there won't be any business today," Silvio said.

"Don't kid yourself, the boozers around here never take a day off. A little snow ain't gonna stop them from juicin' up."

"When's Cappy comin' in," Silvio asked.

"He's usually here by now but with the storm, he called and said he wouldn't be coming in until around one, one thirty. He said you'd be coming by, for you to wait for him. He told me to tell you to be sure to be here when he got in."

"What else did he say?" "That was it."

Silvio took a last swallow of beer. He rose from his stool and turned up his collar. "Tell Cappy I'll be back," he said.

Angelo, who was now wiping the bar mirror with a dry cloth, turned and scooted over to where Silvio had been sitting but was now standing to leave. He hunched himself as far over the bar as he could directly in front of Randazzi and with one hand grabbed him by the arm, forcing Silvio back onto the stool. Angelo's face was now so close to his friend's that Silvio pushed back a little and sat perfectly erect. But Angelo did not let go of his arm. He was leaning so far over the bar that his feet were lifted off the slatted wooden pallet on the floor behind him. The bartender looked left and right as though the place was crowded with customers and he didn't want anyone to hear what he was saying. He began pulling on the man's sleeve, all the while gritting his teeth. He spoke so softly, almost inaudibly, that Silvio had to inch closer.

"We go back a long time, you and me, Sil. I know what's going on. Cappy's into you for plenty . . . you're up to your fuckin' ears and you don't know how to get out of it, do you? I'm tellin' ya, this gambling shit is no good, it's poison. Believe me, I know. I seen suckers like you all my life. I was one myself, remember. I coulda been sittin'nice and easy by now if only I had half a brain, but no" (he lets go of his friend and points an accusing finger at himself, his voice dripping with self-loathing and remorse), "now look at me, a lousy fuckin' bartender working in this dive, without a lousy fuckin' pot to piss in." He stopped hurling invective and abuse at himself long enough to add: "But you wanna know something,' I'm not miserable for the first time in my life. I know I'm a slob, but I'm a contented slob. And I don't owe nobody nothin'."

Randazzi despised being talked to like this, but Angelo was an old friend so he allowed the bartender to press on. "You gonna see the light one of these days, Sil. God willin' it won't be too late. I mean, why do ya gotta gamble in the first place . . . you got a great business, you make good money, ain't that enough? And what about your family, your wife . . ." (Angelo was well aware of Silvio's other major shortcoming, but he wasn't about to bring up that business, too).

"Whadda ya mean, my wife, what's Rosa got to do with it?"

"Don't get excited, Sil, I don't mean nothin' by it. It's just that when someone's got a problem like you got, everybody suffers. Just ask my wife, she'll tell ya . . . in spades."

"Don't you go worryin' about my wife," Silvio said sharply. "I take damn good care of her . . . and my kids, too."

"I know that, Sil, you been a good guy all your life . . . we grew up together, remember?"

Before Angelo could finish, Silvio broke in, his voice dripping with sarcasm. He couldn't hide his annoyance, even from a friend he knew meant well and had his best interests at heart. "How come all of a sudden you're so interested in my gambling, Ang? I been blowin' dough all my life and you never said nothin'. Now after all these years ya' givin' me a sermon . . . and a headache. Tell me Ang, what the fuck you doin' to me?"

Angelo poured Silvio another drink without asking if he wanted one, then himself one. He lit a cigarette and came around from the back of the bar and took a stool next to his friend. "O.K. Sil, I'm gonna give it to ya' straight, and you gonna listen if I have to beat your brains in. The Boss was in here the other night. Cappy and him are in the back room goin' over betting slips. I'm in the kitchen makin' myself a sandwich. I overhear them talk. He wants to know who owes what. They come to your name. Cappy says you owe over twenty gees. I almost fall down when I hear it. The Boss asks Cappy how long he's been carryin' you. Cappy tells him. He tells Cappy to get the money number one, and cut you off number two. He orders Cappy to tell you that if you don't come up with the money, and soon, it's gonna be real bad for you . . . and for Cappy. too."

Before Angelo could utter another cautionary word Silvio got up from the stool and as he was walking out said over his shoulder, "Tell Cappy I'll be back at one thirty." He left his drink on the bar.

# Chapter 37

Caspar Santamoro was another childhood friend of Randazzi's, and a regular customer of the restaurant. But unlike Silvio, Cappy genuinely liked school when they were growing up and was a very good student. His grammar-school teachers, in fact, were all of the opinion that he was a mathematics whiz, destined for great things. Unfortunately, he had to be pulled out of school before he finished the eighth grade and forced to go to work to help support his mother and six brothers and sisters when his father, a New Haven Railroad linesman, was electrocuted and killed instantly by accidentally touching a transformer switch while doing track repairs.

The Boss, who owned the Fair Street Bar & Grille, a front for his myriad gambling activities, recognizing the family's exigent needs, took Cappy under his wing. He had him work in the bar doing odd jobs, but mostly picking up small packages from a half dozen other gambling spots and smoke shops he owned around town. Cappy at first had no idea what was in them.

Over the next several years, Cappy got to learn all he would ever need to know about the bookie business. The Boss took him around, showed him the ropes. "Booking bets is serious business," the Boss warned. "So is bookkeeping. Be sure you keep good records, but out of sight. And remember, don't carry guys too long who owe you money."

Cappy became so good at his job, and the Boss liked him so much, that on Cappy's twenty-first birthday the Boss turned the saloon over to him—lock, stock and barrel. He even renamed the place Cappy's Bar & Grille. To sweeten the pot, the Boss rewarded Cappy with half the bar and grill profits, and a small piece of his thriving gambling operation.

Caspar Santamoro, still in his twenties, had virtually overnight become one of the area's best "business" successes. And the poster boy for young men disinclined toward school or legitimate hard work.

What distinguished Cappy from run-of-the-mill gamblers was his suave, easy-going way. He got what he wanted—gamblers to pay up on time—not by bullying or strong-arm tactics, which he was certainly capable of. He preferred instead a kid-glove approach, one that ran more toward gentle persuasion, which made it hard for "clients" to even think of disappointing him, regardless of the consequences if they did. Consistent with his newfound status, Cappy began to look the part of a professional entrepreneur, not a run-of-the-mill hood. He took to wearing expensive tailor-made, double-breasted suits, driving around in a brand-new Packard and taking his stable of mostly blonde, non-Italian girlfriends to the best night spots in town. Life was good, better than good, for the ex-mathematician turned "businessman." That is, until his friend Silvio Randazzi's problem fell into his lap.

The saloon keeper/ bookie was in the back room standing next to the public telephone booth he used for conducting business—calling in bets to the "office" the Boss maintained in another part of the city— while reading results of the previous night's college and professional basketball games from a ticker-tape machine that click-clacked scores from around the country. He spun around when Silvio walked in.

"There's five grand in the bag, you can count it," Silvio said solemnly, a baleful look in his eyes, as he handed Cappy a brown paper bag.

Cappy stared intently at Silvio. "That's not good enough, Sil," he said, shoving the bag back into the other man's chest without examining its contents. "You're sixteen and change short."

"I need more time, Cap. You know I'll make good," he pleaded. Raising his voice, he said, "When the fuck did I ever try to stiff you . . . never."

"As much as I hate it, Sil, I'm giving you one more week, that's it," Cappy said, his normal basso voice lowered an octave. "I can't carry you no more. My ass is on the line, too. The Boss had no idea you owed him this much. He was plenty pissed when I told him. You're asking for a lot of trouble if you think for one minute he's gonna' let you off the hook. For your own sake, and mine, Sil, you better come up with the dough."

# Chapter 38

When it came to the restaurant, Letizia Randazzi went to bed every night with a clear head, secure in the knowledge that every aspect of the business was on solid footing. On the food side, she had herself, the talented Giuliana Landini and a loyal kitchen and wait staff to keep things humming. On the money side, she had her dedicated son Silvio to thank—he took care of things: he paid bills, handled wages, and every morning promptly at nine he made cash deposits of the previous night's take into the restaurant's always flush account.

At the first sign his gambling debts were far exceeding his tips and the generous salary his mother paid him every week as part-owner of the restaurant, Silvio resorted to an act he hated himself for but couldn't help from committing: he started skimming from restaurant deposits, a little at a time in the beginning but more as his debts grew larger.

Since customers paid their restaurant tabs in cold hard cash, the only currency in vogue in those days, it was easy for Silvio to steal from the till. No one was the wiser to any short-falls, certainly not Letizia, whose sole focus was on cooking great food, not oversight of the restaurant's money matters. There was never any doubt in her mind that the restaurant she and her late husband had built into one of the city's finest was on anything but solid financial footing, thanks mostly to her son.

*　*　*

Silvio slammed the door as he headed out of Cappy's saloon. Trudging up the street, the crunching sound of his boots on the packed-down snow, together with a howling wind that grew louder with every step he took, made him feel as though he was marching to his doom. In seconds his hair, eyebrows and day-old beard were dotted white, the icy snow clinging to his burning reddish-purple face as he maneuvered up, across and finally down deserted Wooster Street.

He spied Giuliana coming down the steps of her building. The last thing he wanted was for her to see him, so he snuck out of sight in an alleyway. It appeared she was heading for Randazzi's, but he was thankful her destination was the grocery store a few doors down. Though the two continued to work together amicably, Giuliana otherwise avoided having anything to do with Silvio since witnessing the incident in the restaurant with the out-of-control cuckold husband.

While waiting for Giuliana to come out of the store, Silvio thought of going to his house and spilling his guts out to his wife. He immediately thought better of it: Rosa had enough on her mind dealing with the hurt his infidelity had caused; to pile gambling woes on top of that was, even for him, unthinkable. Besides, she certainly didn't have the money to bale him out of any danger. And out of his misery.

He next thought of heading for the church to talk with Father Martini. Though Silvio didn't regularly attend Mass, except at Easter and Christmas, he and the priest were good friends. *How is the good Father going take what I did to my own mother, and to the Randazzi name?* Silvio asked himself with trepidation. He thought better of making that call. When the priest did eventually learn of what his friend had done, he angrily confronted Silvio and told him in no uncertain terms that he found his actions soul-numbing.

As a last resort, Silvio turned onto Wooster Street and instead headed for the one place he could always count on to offer him succor, the restaurant. He knew his mother wouldn't be there at this hour so he'd be quiet and alone, with ample time to try to figure out how best to extricate himself from this latest calamity. But as soon as he unlocked the front door he saw light streaming out from under the kitchen door. "Ma, is that you in there?" Silvio called out.

"Who else you think would be here on a day like this," Letizia answered. "I came down to get some chicken wings and backs . . . gonna make a nice pot of soup, with lots of vegetables and *pastina*. Maybe you stay for some?"

"No, Mama, but I could really use a cup-a coffee . . . I'm freezing."

"Then come upstairs, I got a nice fresh pot on the stove."

Silvio sat drinking his coffee, silent as a church mouse, his customary sunny disposition tucked away under his turned-up coat collar, agonizing over whether he should tell his mother the harrowing truth. And if so, how. Sooner or later she was bound to find out. He decided he'd have to tell her right now rather than later. Later, in fact, might be too late. Besides, who else could he go to for money? Not his brothers and sisters—they didn't have any lying around to part with. Not the bank either. Imagine what they'd say when he went to them for a loan: 'Gee, fellas, I'm way over my head in gambling debt, would you please lend me twenty gs so I can pay off my bookie before he takes it out of my hide?'

Letizia went about her business, focused on cutting and dicing vegetables, for the moment immune to the pain her son was about to inflict on her. But after a few minutes of Silvio's deafening silence, and the desperate look she saw on his face, she knew there was something he needed to get off his chest. It was Letizia who broke the silence that was beginning to grate on her nerves: "Maybe it's time I go to Florida, like your sister says I should. Winters are getting too hard for me. I can't take them no more. And I worked long enough. I'm too old."

"Mama, sit down for a minute, please . . . I got something to tell you," Silvio said, softly. "Please, stop what you're doing," he pleaded.

Her son's plaintive tone made her heart flutter. She put down the knife and took a seat next to him at the table. "You not in trouble with another one of your *putanni*, are you?" she asked, her wary eyes narrowing. There was an edge to her voice.

"No Mama . . . it's more serious than that."

Letizia reached into the pocket of her apron and pulled out the rosary she always carried with her, and started thumbing the beads. "Now tell me, my son, what is it that's so bad with you," she asked, trying to sound calm as she studied her hapless son through black-rimmed glasses that framed her soulful gray eyes.

# Chapter 39

Silvio, from the time he was a little boy, was the kind of son who couldn't keep anything from his mother, even his most embarrassing indiscretions. This latest episode, however, was not some childlike prank gone awry. It had all the earmarks of a major catastrophe, even bigger than getting caught cheating on his wife, as egregious a breech of trust as that was. But at the moment he wasn't thinking of himself. He was worried sick about his mother, the one person other than his kids he'd gladly die for. How was she going to deal with this latest ignominious act of his? The excruciating anguish he was experiencing put him very near the edge of breaking down, but he fought to maintain his composure. He unburdened himself and told her everything. Even his stealing of restaurant money. With this admission, Silvio had come full circle: he had not only failed as a husband, he had failed as a son, in his eyes a much graver sin.

Letizia took it all in, not once interrupting her son's confession. There were no admonitions, recriminations, excoriating words or angry, red-faced eruptions on her part. He almost wished there had been. She did not pull her hair or wail against God and man for her son's despicable conduct, his irresponsible actions; he brought this horror on himself, not some vengeful God or man, she told herself. As for damage to the family's reputation once word got out, that would have to be dealt with in good time. For now, all she could think of was her son's fragile state of mind—and safety.

As Silvio recounted one awful fact after the other, and the dire consequences his actions had unleashed, his traumatized mother at one point stopped listening. Her eyes did not glaze over but had a far-away look, those of an unbelieving mother trying to cobble together the pieces of her son's past, once so full of innocence and promise. She looked for anything to try to understand how it had come to this. She began thinking back to when her son was a boy, searching to find whatever might give her a clue to the underlying pathology of his actions, clues that might have foreshadowed his now self-destructive, out-of-control impulses, his craven indifference to all that the Randazzi family held sacred. She may have turned a blind eye to her son's cheating on his wife—Rosa had long suspected it and had voiced her concerns a number of times to her mother-in-law—but what could Letizia do other than reassure Rosa that his infidelity was a phase married men, even the best ones, sometimes go through.

Letizia was also aware that her son gambled a lot, that he was in fact an addict. But this other totally reckless, even obscene, impulse of his had not only driven him far from his ethical, moral center but had him breaking commandments he was brought up to believe in. Especially those that had long governed fealty to his parents: honor thy father and mother, thou shalt not steal, thou shalt not covet thy neighbor's goods— all tenets instructive of a person's true worth. For the first twenty or so years of his life Silvio had lived up to those tenets, a loyal, loving son to parents whose trust he would never think of betraying. In short, the perfect son, the best little boy. What made him all of a sudden succumb to such base instincts?

And yet, no matter what he had done, Letizia would not permit herself to be swayed, to join the chorus of those who, once they had learned the nature of his transgressions, would have without a moment's hesitation thrown her son to the wolves, including his own siblings, who, if truth be told, had long been resentful of their mother's excessive affection for her eldest child. She kept telling herself that of all her children it was Silvio, and only Silvio who had sacrificed his youth for his parents, sublimating what desires and ambitions he may have once harbored to insure first his father's, now his mother's well-being, not his own. Perhaps that was the problem, Letizia told herself, not misplaced values but Silvio's resentment against parents whose interests he always put before his own. She thought of that day, not more than a couple of weeks ago when she and Giuliana were alone in the kitchen: she told the young girl how much she admired her parents for allowing her to leave home, and Giuliana for seizing the opportunity. In the Landinis' case, both parents and daughter made the ultimate sacrifice. In the Randazzis,' only Silvio was the one to have done so, not his parents.

Regardless of what it was that drove him to commit such craven acts, *It's my turn to stand strong for my son,* she vowed. "How much is in the restaurant account?" she asked, her rounded, hunched shoulders accentuating the figure of a mother struggling to steel herself against even more disturbing news, a look of worry now having replaced the look of sadness that had taken up permanent residence in her once sparkling gray eyes.

Silvio gulped hard: "Twenty-five hundred dollars."

Letizia's lips tightened. Even allowing for her *laissez-faire* attitude concerning restaurant finances, she assumed there had to have been at least five times that amount in the bank. But all she managed to say, or was capable of saying, was: "I have forty-six hundred dollars in cash in the jewelry box on the shelf in my bedroom closet. Go get it and take four thousand and leave six hundred dollars . . . that'll be enough for me to live on for a while."

Silvio put his face in his hands and sobbed hard.

"Don't, Silvio, please . . . if it weren't for you there'd be no Randazzi's Restaurant. This is your money, anyway. Now go back to Caspar and tell him I want to see him, first thing in the morning . . . I'm sure he won't deny me this courtesy."

"What you gonna' tell him, Ma?" Silvio asked, hardly able to mouth the words, his face contorted in pain.

"Leave that up to me. You'll find out when he does. Now go, give him the nine thousand, and tell him we'll have more tomorrow."

"But he says the Boss wants it all within a week." "We have time . . . the week just started."

\* \* \*

Cappy came to the restaurant on the dot of ten o'clock the next morning. The weather had considerably improved. The sun was out. Silvio had already been to the bank to withdraw two thousand dollars from the restaurant's account. As soon as the bookie was let in, Silvio ushered him into the kitchen, safely out of sight of any passers-by who might wonder what Cappy was doing in the place at that hour. He kissed Mrs. Randazzi on both cheeks and told her how good she looked. He did not remove his coat, nor was he able to erase the saturnine look visible on his clean-shaven, heavily-lotioned face. For someone who normally sucked the air out of a room by his presence, here in Randazzi's kitchen he found himself breathlessly and totally diminished.

"This is not what I wanted, Letizia, believe me," Cappy said diffidently as he took a seat next to the woman. He spoke in Italian, wanting to make certain she clearly understood every word of their conversation. "But you gotta know, my hands are tied."

"I'm not blaming you, Caspar," Letizia answered. "I'm not blaming your boss. I'm not blaming anyone. I'm not even blaming my son. This is business. You're going to get your money, every penny of it . . . you have my word."

She handed Cappy 20 one-hundred dollar bills. "Take it . . . that makes eleven thousand all-together. I still owe you ten thousand three hundred more." Letizia purposely said I, not we, not Silvio. She repeated what she'd just said; she wanted to assure Cappy that she, Letizia Randazzi, one of the most respected restaurateurs and business women in New Haven, stood behind the I.O.U., thus assuming full responsibility for the debt and, in effect, absolving Silvio from any further obligation.

"And the rest of the money," Cappy asked, sheepishly, the first hint of perspiration visible on his brow, "when can we expect it?"

Letizia shot her son a look, more pitying than reproachful. She in turn held his laser-like stare. When he couldn't stand it any longer, he dropped his eyes and looked away in disgust. Then turning to Cappy she said evenly: "I spoke to my lawyer last night . . . he's drawing up papers right this minute . . . I'm handing over the restaurant to you."

Silvio erupted with all the force of a lava-spewing volcano: "Mama, what are you saying!"

Letizia did not look at her son. "That way, you're guaranteed to have your money, no matter whether we sell the place right away or not. My lawyer also told me to tell you that starting a week from today—you gave me a week, that's what you told Silvio—we'll pay you interest on the rest of the money we owe you because you had to wait so long."

"You can't do that, Mama!" Silvio yelled, thrashing about the kitchen like an enraged, caged animal.

"Sit down and be quiet," Letizia said sternly. Then fixing her steely gaze back at Cappy she said: "My lawyer, Joe Fusco—you know him— thinks we shouldn't have any trouble selling the place. Not with the kind of business we do here, Caspar. Just ask the Boss, he's a regular customer like you. For years, I've been getting offers to sell. Well, now is the time for me to do it. I've been thinking about selling anyway. I'm getting too old. I'm putting the restaurant up for sale immediately."

"Oh my God! I can't take any more of this," Silvio shouted, jumping up out of his chair, shoving it aside and heading for the door leading out back.

"Don't you dare move!" Letizia barked, without looking at her son. She kept her eyes firmly fixed on Cappy who, by now, was in full sweat mode: he had the same nauseating feeling that an athlete or a stage actor feels at the start of a game or a performance. The mortified look on his face told Letizia she had made her point. Without saying another word Santamoro rose from his chair, shook the woman's hand and left.

Mrs. Randzzi did not give her son a chance to try to argue against the painful choice she had been forced to make, on his behalf. The issue was closed. And he knew it.

She walked into the dining room and picked up the phone at the front desk. "Concetta, it's me, Letizia. No, nothing's wrong. I want you and Umberto—and Giuliana, if she can—to come in a little early today, around four thirty. (Pause.) No, no, I said nothing's wrong. I want everybody to be here so we can discuss an important matter before customers start coming in. O.K.? And please call Paolo for me, tell him, too. *Ciao.*"

Nothing about Silvio's problem (now her problem) was mentioned when Letizia addressed the staff. All she said was that time had come for her to take leave of the terribly demanding business that had consumed her life for nearly fifty years so she could live out her remaining days in the relative peace and tranquility, and the warmth, of the Florida sun. She may have said it, but the mere thought of moving permanently to Florida "to live among a bunch of old people waiting to die" had always made her queasy. Buyers would be sought immediately. As for her staff, she would make every effort to have the new owner retain "my wonderful Randazzi team, the best restaurant people in New Haven." Giuliana could not believe her ears. Nor could Umberto or Concetta.

# Chapter 40

Umberto went to his regular factory job that Friday night, but when he arrived home at eight the next morning he did not go to bed after breakfast as he normally did. During his midnight shift he had all to do to keep from thinking about anything but the restaurant and its pending sale. He couldn't wait to get home to discuss the matter with his wife and niece.

"Do you think our jobs are safe if there is a sale, Umberto?" asked a concerned Concetta, placing a cup of coffee and a bowl of hot cereal in front of her husband.

Umberto answered emphatically, "I do not."

"Then what do you propose we do?" an equally concerned Giuliana asked.

"Buy the place!" Umberto said with such emphasis that his wife could not hold back from exclaiming loudly, "You must be kidding!"

"No, I am serious. Haven't I been preaching for years—to ourselves and to our friends—haven't you heard me say it a thousand times—that the only way to succeed in this country is to own a business? Ownership, that's what people in America look up to. Well, here is our chance . . . I don't want to let it pass us by. We may never have another one like it. And besides, we know this business inside out . . . all three of us, and we're all good at it. It's not like getting into something we're going to have to learn, like starting a dry cleaning business. I can't believe this is what we always thought we'd do."

"But the money, Umberto, where are we going to get the money? All the years we've worked, you and I, scrimping every penny since coming to America, all we have managed to save is a few thousand dollars. That's not even enough for a down payment."

"It's true, my dear wife, but we're going to have to find a way to get it, if not all of it, then a good part of it."

"Supposing what Letizia is asking for the restaurant is too much for us to raise?"

"Whatever her asking price, I swear to you as God is my witness, I'm going to come up with the money."

Back and forth, Umberto and Concetta parried: where to get the money, how much and, most important, how soon. Giuliana had kept silent. Umberto was waiting patiently for his niece to offer an opinion; he was much relieved when she finally did.

"First of all, Zia," Giuliana asked calmly, "do you agree with Zio about wanting to own the business to begin with?"

"I am all for it, my dear, even though the suddenness of having to think about it is giving me *agita*. But I am trying to be practical, too. Even if we had the money, or could get the money, there are other considerations. Who is going to replace Letizia, if she's serious about not wanting to work anymore? And if she decides not to go to Florida, would she be willing to work for us until we found someone else? And what about you, Giuliana? You're the most important person in the kitchen right now, more important than even Letizia . . . you know that. What's going to happen when you go off to college . . . who is going to take your place? Customers are used to the food you and Letizia have been cooking. If we can't continue to give them the same high quality food, the business is bound to suffer. If that happens, then we would have taken a big risk for nothing."

"These are legitimate concerns," Umberto said, "but if we worry about them now, the place will be gone before we know it."

"I agree with Uncle," Giuliana offered. "We must first own the restaurant before worrying about those other matters, important as they are. If you don't mind my saying it, Aunt, you don't give yourself enough credit; you're as good a cook as anyone . . . Terri is doing just fine on the line, she is not far from becoming an excellent cook herself, and as for me, I still have several months before I'll be going off to college. By then, I'm sure we'll have everything in place to keep things going as smoothly as they are now."

"But there's still the money." Concetta countered. "Whatever the amount, it will be an awful lot for us to raise in such short a time."

Umberto remained silent: let the women talk it out until they're both convinced this is the course of action the family should take, then we'll be half way home.

"There's no question about that, but I believe I can help in this regard," Giuliana offered, matter-of-factly.

"How?" Umberto asked, no longer able to constrain himself, listening to his niece make such a declaration, and with such confidence.

"I am going to call Camilla and Jennifer and ask them if they would lend us some of the money. Don't you remember that time, Uncle, a couple of years ago, when we had them over for Sunday dinner? Langdon Davies said we should open a restaurant, and if we did he'd be our first customer?"

"I do remember that," said Umberto. "But that's not the same as actually giving us money to do it."

"Well, we're going to find out soon enough whether we can count on them for help," came Giuliana's quick reply.

"It's settled then?" Umberto said. "Does this satisfy you, Connie?"

Before Concetta could answer, Giuliana said: "Please excuse me, Aunt, but hear me out on another suggestion I have in mind."

"Does it concern the money?" Concetta asked.

"Yes." Giuliana said, then hesitated before elaborating further, something she did not normally do, being of a mind, just like her grandmother, to always speak out forthrightly and without hesitation.

"Well, what is it?" her anxious uncle wanted to know.

"I'm prepared to sell my St. Lucy painting."

There was stunned silence in the room for several moments before Concetta exploded: "No, absolutely not, you can't do that!" she argued adamantly. "You love that painting so . . . it's your most treasured possession . . . Father Di Pina gave it to you out of the goodness of his heart . . . what would he think if he knew you got rid of it . . . sold it, sold it to some, some . . ." her voice trailed off.

Umberto was overcome at the mere mention of the generous offer this child he loved so much had made, on his behalf more than on his wife's or even her own. Yet, as much as he appreciated Giuliana's offer he couldn't bring himself to tell her he accepted it. Nor could he utter the words, "No, I will not allow it," which would have put a lid on this delicate matter once and for all. Instead he just sat there, fiddling with his breakfast, hoping that the two most precious women in his life would come to a meeting of the minds on this issue, thus absolving him of the disturbing task of having to disappoint one or the other.

"The head of the art history department at Yale told me when he saw the painting some time ago that the university would definitely be interested in purchasing the picture for their new art gallery. But they first wanted to have it appraised before they agreed on a price. You remember I took it to New York last summer when I went to visit Camilla; she set up appointments for me at two of the best art auction houses. They both informed me that the work of Ottavio Colangelo, the artist who painted my St. Lucy, had come into much favor since his death almost a half century ago. They said the painting could easily be worth twenty thousand dollars, or more, without any problem."

"Oh, my God!" Concetta exclaimed.

"I'm going to bed," Umberto chimed in, "we've had enough excitement for one morning."

*   *   *

Umberto did not wait for five o'clock to go to work that day. At noon, after just three hours or so of fitful, unrestful sleep, he and Concetta shot across the street, and rushed into the restaurant kitchen. "Letizia, we want to buy Randazzi's," an out of breathe Umberto gushed. He told the woman that in his almost ten years working in the restaurant he had come to love the place as if it were his own. Mrs. Randazzi said that she was not shocked. If anything, she was thrilled. She had long believed, and fervently hoped, once she resigned herself to the fact that her son's sole ownership of the restaurant had all but vanished once she learned the harrowing truth of his misdeeds, that it would be her loyal waiter Umberto Fassano who took over the place. Tears of joy, not sorrow, welled in her eyes. The Fassanos did not hold back either.

"But we need a few weeks, Letizia, before we can get the money," Umberto said, "If you could tell us what you are asking for the restaurant, I am certain we can come up with at least the down payment by next Friday at the latest."

He went on to explain where they expected money for the purchase to come from. "Giuliana is calling her friends right now. I'm sure we will have good news by the time she comes to work in a little while," Umberto said confidently. "As for the painting, that might take a little longer." He went on to say, "Hopefully, we'll get the rest of the money from the bank. With a good word from you and the money we will have in hand, plus our putting up the painting as collateral, the bank should look kindly on our request. Is this satisfactory to you, Letizia?"

Wednesday, a little before noon, Concetta handed Letitia two certified bank checks, each for five thousand dollars, made out to Randazzi's Restaurant, one endorsed by Camilla McDonough, the other by Jennifer Kirby Davies. Letizia examined the checks, took off her apron, kissed Concetta warmly, and said she'd be back in a little while. She did not go to the bank. Instead, she headed for Cappy's Bar & Grille. The place was not yet crowded with lunchtime customers, so when Angelo saw Mrs. Randazzi he immediately came out from behind the bar and escorted her to the same booth where only days before he had found Silvio sleeping. He asked the woman if there was anything he could get her.

"Only Caspar, if you don't mind," was her terse reply.

The normally ebullient saloon keeper/bookie emerged from the kitchen stone faced and jittery. He approached the woman's table with a greeting that was deferential but otherwise devoid of intimacy: he did not kiss Letizia as he normally would have done out of respect. She told, not asked, him to take a seat. The mere sight of the one person he least wanted to have to deal with unnerved the usually unflappable Santamoro. She watched the blood drain from his face. He took a seat as far away from her as the booth would allow. Letizia slid the two checks toward him.

She did not explain, and Cappy did not ask, anything about the checks. Nor did she make mention of the pending sale of the restaurant to the Fassanos; none of this was any business of his. She did, however, iterate that it would take a few days for the checks to clear, which Cappy was well aware of even though banks were the last place anyone in his line of business was likely to have put his money. Mrs. Randazzi assured him that she would have cash in hand to pay off the debt in full by no later than Tuesday or Wednesday of next week, "a few days beyond the deadline you gave me, I'm sorry." Were it possible for Cappy to crawl through the woodwork at that moment he would readily and gratefully have done so.

"Now I have a request of you, Caspar . . . I'm going to insist you honor it. You must give me your word that you will not take any more bets from Silvio . . . ever. I also want you to promise me that none of the other bookies in town take my son's bets either. I know that you or the Boss or whoever the others are that control gambling in New Haven can make sure of that. Do I have your word?"

Before he could slink out of the booth, Santamoro nodded his assent.

# Chapter 41

Randazzi's Restaurant changed hands on Sunday, March 1, two weeks after Giuliana's seventeenth birthday and five weeks before she received word that Barnard College in New York City had accepted her application for admission for the fall term. Closing of the sale was far from a happy occasion, not for the Randazzis, who had been forced to surrender a business they loved and spent a lifetime building, nor for the Fassanos, who felt uneasy assuming ownership of an iconic institution run by an iconic woman they were exceedingly fond of and admired.

In a gesture of genuine friendship and respect, as well as practicality, the Fassanos asked Mrs. Randazzis to stay on. But no amount of Umberto's cajoling—nor Concetta's or Giuliana's—could convince the woman to remain in the kitchen while they found a seasoned cook to replace her. She argued that she had had enough of the business and, besides, at almost seventy-five, had overstayed by over four years the time she had intended to remain active in the restaurant.

"No, no I can't . . . it's time for me to leave."

But Letizia's spirits brightened when Umberto asked, "If it's alright with you, we would like to keep the name of the restaurant as it is. It will always be Randazzi's Ristorante, as long as we own the place." In silence she took off her apron for the last time and handed it to Giuliana, who hung it on a hook next to the scullery, never to be used again.

A few days later, Letizia's daughter and son-in-law picked her up and took her to their home in White Plains. "I need to rest for a couple of weeks and collect my thoughts," she said. She stayed until her death, less than two years later. She was buried in a cemetery not far from her daughter's home. One of her last wishes before she died was that her body not be sent back to New Haven for internment in St. Lawrence Cemetery across the street from Yale Bowl, where her husband, other members of the family, and the bodies of most of the city's Italian community, were buried. She told her daughter that she never wanted to go back to New Haven.

Silvio left the restaurant for good a week before the Fassanos took over. He told Umberto he could no longer bring himself to be anywhere near the place now that it was out of his family's hands. Just after Christmas, the down and out waiter moved to Florida, alone. The damage to their marriage proved irreparable: the pain she suffered too much to bear, Rosa took herself and the kids and moved out of New Haven, not far from her parents, but far enough away from wagging tongues on Wooster Street not uncomfortable in dishing dirt regarding the Randazzi affair, as it became famously known. More than enough people in the neighborhood, despite expressing their outrage, seemed not in the least constrained to put to rest the scandal involving Silvio's stealing from his mother and cheating on his wife.

For a while, Silvio did well waiting tables in the restaurant of one of Miami's swankiest hotels. But not so well gambling away his earnings—on horses, on dogs, on anything that moved. One way or the other he was always able to finagle his way out of the most potentially dangerous predicament when it came to paying up debts to bookies and other shady characters who held his markers. But as is the case with nine out ten gamblers who push their luck, incapable of exorcising those feral gambling demons, the odds inevitably run out. As they did, finally, for Silvio Randazzi.

Though never a user of drugs himself, even in his darkest days, Randazzi got involved with Cuban drug dealers who controlled betting parlors Silvio frequented, and to whom he owed a sizable chunk of gambling debt. To pay off his creditors, Silvio was forced to act as "candy man" in the hotel where he worked by supplying drugs to employees, some of whom were heavy users. Things went smoothly for Randazzi right up until the day he took a cache of drugs and attempted to sell them, not to fellow employees, but to users in another part of town he knew were willing to pay a higher price for the goods. It was Randazzi's intent all along to stiff his creditors, pocket the money, skip town and, once and for all, turn over a new leaf. And, hopefully, resuscitate long deferred dreams that now hung by a thread.

It hardly came as a surprise that his bullet-riddled body was found in a ditch after one of his potential buyers ratted on him. Thus ended, violently, the life of Silvio Randazzi, along with his once promising business career. At one time one of Wooster Street's most looked-up-to young men, he was finally done in, not so much by trafficking in drugs but, more than anything, trafficking in false hopes. He was forty-six.

Letizia, always a tower of strength in moments of crises, fell completely apart when she learned of her son's death, and the circumstances surrounding it. She died quietly in her daughter's home a few weeks later.

# Chapter 42

Giuliana's graduation from high school was only three months off but her mind was more on the restaurant than on preparing for college. When word came in early April that she had been accepted into New York City's Barnard College's 1947 freshman class on a full scholarship—room, board and tuition, renewable each year thereafter providing she maintained her class standing—Giuliana was beside herself with excitement. And relief: the pressure of paying for college was off her guardians, her parents, and herself.

Barnard had become her college of choice on the basis of a strong recommendation by the head of Yale's art history department, the person most responsible for the university's purchase of the St. Lucy painting. He convinced Giuliana that a good, solid liberal arts education, with heavy emphasis on the arts, which the college was famous for providing young women, would be the ideal preparation for postgraduate work in the school of architecture at Columbia University (Barnard was affiliated with the university), or at Yale, which also boasted of having one of the best programs in the country. Another reason Giuliana felt her choice of Barnard was an ideal one was because of the school's proximity to Camilla McDonough, soon to become Mrs. Gordon deVries. Camilla lived in Greenwich Village, a mere subway ride away from the school. Could things have fallen any better into place?

A few days later, a group of Giuliana's fellow high school seniors decided that a party that Friday night would be an appropriate way to celebrate their collective good fortune for having each received an acceptance letter to his or her college of choice. Though Fridays were one of the two busiest days of the week at Randazzi's, Umberto and Concetta did not hesitate in telling Giuliana that she should forget about the restaurant for at least one day and be with her friends on this happy occasion. They insisted they'd be able to manage without her.

The party was held at the home of Winston Hsu, the Chinese boy with whom Giuliana had forged a close relationship since freshman year at Hillhouse High. Both his parents were Yale professors. Over time Winston kept hoping, though he never pushed it, that their friendship might develop into something more than innocent hand-holding. But Giuliana was not ready to make a commitment, not to Winston Hsu or to any other male admirer—and there were many—afflicted with a case of love-sickness for the young Italian beauty. As hard as she tried not to admit it, she was still pining over Rick DeGoia. So while she very much wanted to continue being good friends with Winston, she was determined to see that their relationship remained one predicated on the mutual interests of two like-minded people, and nothing more.

Winston Hsu was a brilliant student, valedictorian of his and Giuliana's senior class at Hillhouse High. Besides being one of Giuliana's best school friends, he had become her closest confidant, too. Though mathematics and economics were what drove him—not art, architecture, literature or food, Giuliana's abiding passions—he had a healthy regard for music, politics and, for reasons he said he couldn't for the life of him explain where he got it, an insatiable curiosity about farming and animal husbandry. This surprising side of Hsu's persona fascinated Giuliana. When he learned the particulars of Giuliana's own ancestral history, most notably that farming ran for generations in her family, plus her grandmother's and great grandparents' cheese-making business, Winston was even more taken with his beautiful young friend.

As the son of Yale academics, Winston availed himself of many of the same privileges the university students enjoyed, and had access to a host of cultural activities that regularly took place on the Yale campus. Beginning in the winter of their junior year and continuing through senior year, Winston often invited Giuliana to join him and his parents at Sunday afternoon events he was certain would interest her. She was thrilled at the invitation and accompanied him to many of them. Her favorites were the piano and violin recitals in Woolsey Hall.

At other times, Winston took her to lectures by politicians and journalists, most of whom spoke on the recently concluded war. One topic that particularly interested her, not surprisingly, was Walter Lippmann's analysis of the Marshall Plan, the United States government's policy for European post-war reconstruction. In the Q&A that followed the talk, Giuliana asked the famous *New York Times* columnist to expound specifically on what, if anything, was being done to help Italy. Much to Giuliana's dismay, his response was hopelessly vague.

On a number of these occasions, Winston brought Giuliana back to his house where the Hsus and some of their Yale colleagues gathered for drinks and a lively discussion of what they had just seen and heard. Giuliana said that she learned more about classical music and American politics from those impromptu salon gatherings at the Hsus' than she possibly could have from anywhere else, including the classroom.

The elder Hsus were always delighted to see Giuliana. Having dined often at Randazzi's over the years, they had gotten to know not only the young chef but her uncle, as well; Umberto waited on them regularly. Most of the Hsus' Yale colleagues frequented the restaurant, too. To them, as well as to their hosts, Giuliana was a celebrity, so whenever she was in their company on Sundays at the Hsus, not minutes after Winston walked her through the door Giuliana was bombarded with all manner of questions regarding her cooking. Instead of feeling put out by their inquiries, Giuliana obligingly took the time to conduct a mini food seminar and patiently explain to them anything they wanted to know about a particular dish they had eaten at the restaurant. Since she'd been as accommodating as possible in discussing her work, she felt little hesitancy in then interrogating the erudite group for insights into theirs. As well as getting them to expound on the music recital or lecture they had all just attended.

Being around the Hsus and thus connected, even tangentially, to Yale and a world of culture and sophistication completely foreign to her was a whole new experience for the impressionable young girl. Practically overnight, the city of New Haven had taken on a vibrancy that the world across the Atlantic from whence she came sorely lacked, due principally to the great university's towering presence in the city, just a few walking blocks away from Wooster Street, and its concomitant benefits.

Being part of the Hsu's world also put her face to face for the first time in her young life with the social divide that existed between the haves and have-nots. While she didn't necessarily consider herself one of the latter, she certainly did not consider herself one of the former either. Thus, her abundant self-confidence kept her from feeling intimidated or out of place at the Hsus' Sunday afternoon salons. Nor was she in the least embarrassed for having lived, first in a small, parochial Italian town populated mostly by fishermen and shopkeepers, and now for the last couple of years in a blue-collar, ethnic American neighborhood of predominantly factory and garment workers to whom the simple things in life—family, church, food, sports—was at the root of their being, not the life of the mind. If anything, she was buoyed by her association with the Hsus and the opportunity it gave her to mingle with them and the other exciting, brilliant people in their orbit.

One early Monday morning, while Giuliana was having breakfast before leaving for school, she happened to mention to her aunt and uncle the lecture she had heard at Yale the previous day and the riveting discussion that had taken place later at the Hsus regarding Harry F. Truman's ascendancy to the American presidency after the death of the revered Franklin Delano Roosevelt. That evening, after coming home early from a rare not-so-busy night in the restaurant, Umberto casually mentioned to his niece that it would be fine with him and Concetta if on some Sunday in the near future she invited the Hsus over for dinner. He said it would be a privilege to have such distinguished guests come to their home. Giuliana was overjoyed, and wasted no time the next morning in extending to Winston and his parents an invitation to dine at the Fassanos—not at some time in the future but the following Sunday.

In the four years they'd been friends, Winston Hsu had never been to the Fassano flat. Walking Giuliana home on many a Sunday, as far as he got were the front steps in front of her building. There they'd linger no more than a minute or two before bidding each other a hurried goodnight; they always felt uncomfortable having neighbors around eyeing them as they parted company. After one such occasion, it was reported back to Concetta—via her friend, Agnes DeGoia—that a number of eyebrows were raised at what seemed to be the regular sight of a Chinese boy in their midst dropping off the Landini girl. "Whatsa' matter, our boys aren't good enough for her?" one woman was reported to have said.

When Connie told this to her husband, Umberto exploded. "All the more reason I'm glad they're coming on Sunday," Umberto said angrily, out of earshot of his niece. "Next thing you know, they'll think we're planning a wedding. As a matter of fact, go ahead and tell 'em that, will you please Connie . . . tell 'em they're getting married."

On Sunday at one in the afternoon Winston and his parents, Yao and Ming Hsu, came to dinner. As soon as they entered the first-floor hallway they were met by pungent smells they happily speculated must be emanating from the Fassanos' third-floor flat; they became stronger as they ascended each flight of stairs. Yao Hsu carried a huge basket of specialty Chinese delicacies, his wife Ming a beautiful gardenia plant, Winston a small book of poems, presents for each of their three hosts. Giuliana was at the stove working away when they walked through the kitchen door. She immediately took off her apron, greeted the Hsus warmly then took them to the parlor past her guardians' bedroom, where Umberto and Concetta were placing the last of several dishes of appetizers on the coffee table. Greetings were exchanged, drinks poured and the party of six got down to pleasantries.

Dinner was served an hour later at the kitchen table, impeccably set for the occasion by Concetta. Winston's parents were seated with their backs against the far wall; the stove on the left gave them a perfect vantage point from which they were able to observe with utter fascination (lack of a formal dining room, in this case, proved a blessing), Giuliana's every move as she cooked, and Concetta platted, each dish of Giuliana's memorable meal. The Hsus judged it to be a bravura performance.

But for Giuliana, it was just another day at the office. As so many of her restaurant customers were quick to remark, it wasn't just food she was serving, it was ecstasy itself. Not a single dish was anything the Hsus had had before, not at Randazzi's or at any other New Haven restaurant. Even the bread was different—Giuliana had baked homemade *foccacia*. Dessert proved to be another revelation—a warm chestnut and fig tart topped with a dollop of *crème fraiche*. The Hsus did not leave until well past seven that evening.

During the course of the exquisite, leisurely paced meal, the Hsus and Fassanos exchanged biographical information. The Fassanos, in particular, were riveted by the Hsus' accounts and hung on their every word. Both Yao Hsu and his wife, Ming, came from prominent families in the Zhejiang Province of China that went back generations, Yao's dating to the Ming and Qing dynasties. They met not in China but at England's Cambridge University. Upon graduation from the esteemed British institution, the couple returned briefly to China to marry, and then moved to the states six months later to pursue Phds at Princeton, Yao in bio chemistry, Ming in economics. After three years at Princeton—each taught while pursuing doctorates in their respective fields—the couple accepted teaching positions at Yale and settled in New Haven. Their son Winston, an only child, was born in New Jersey in 1930, the same year as Giuliana. Of the six diners at the Fassano table that memorable Sunday, Winston Hsu was the only native-born American.

"I often wonder what it must be like to be educated like the two of you," said Umberto, looking first at Yao then Ming Hsu. "Here we are, Connie and me, we barely made it out of elementary school."

"Speak for yourself, Umberto," chided Concetta. "I was a good student."

"Don't mistake being educated with having degrees, Bert," Yao said in his clipped, British accent. "We both can tell you that there are plenty of so called educated people right here at Yale, teachers and students alike, who have no right being at this university."

"But tell me Doctor Hsu, aren't people who go to college, whether you think they're educated or not, aren't they the ones who have a better chance of getting ahead in this world than somebody like me who doesn't have any real schooling?"

"Not necessarily," said Ming Hsu. "Take Giuliana, for example. She hasn't even graduated from high school. Yet as far as I'm concerned she's more successful than ninety percent of those who have graduated from college will ever hope to be. And from what we've been able to observe about her since she's been coming regularly to our home, she may also be well on her way to becoming a highly educated person as well."

"Are you telling us that Giuliana shouldn't go to college?"

"No, not at all, Bert," Yao Hsu said. "What I am saying is that in Giuliana's case going to college and becoming an architect—I believe that's the career she said she'd like to pursue—will not necessarily make her either educated or successful."

Giuliana sat quietly taking it all in, not of a mind to make her own feelings known on the subject. She was riveted on what the Hsus, both of whom she greatly admired, had to say about a phenomenon that always intrigued her: how and why people become successful. And education's role in bringing success about.

"What I think my husband is saying," Ming Hsu interjected, "is that Giuliana has already achieved success, if by success one means being able to perform a task consistently brilliantly. I doubt there's anyone in town cooking at her level, or is as good as she is. You may not know or appreciate it, but Giuliana has accomplished something quite rare and remarkable: she's raised the rather mundane job of cooking into an art form. If you ask me, I doubt she needs to look any further to find a more fulfilling career."

\* \* \*

On the day she was required to notify Barnard of her decision, Giuliana called the college from the office of Hillhouse High's guidance counselor and informed the admissions director that she was turning down their offer. She gave as a reason exigent family circumstances that would force her to postpone, but for only a year, matriculating at Barnard. However, she fervently hoped that the college would consider offering her a spot in next year's freshman class and, that if it were possible, to admit her on the basis of its present offer: a full scholarship the first year, and subsequent scholarships for the last three years, contingent on her maintaining the requisite grade point average.

When Giuliana told her aunt and uncle of her decision, they were aghast. They had been steeling themselves against the eventual day Giuliana would be gone for good from Randazzi's. To help lessen the impact of her departure, Umberto, not having to concern himself any longer with a second job, had been coming early to the restaurant to help prep in the kitchen. Concetta did her part, too—she got Antoinette Giordano to agree to pitch in a few hours on Thursdays, Fridays and Saturdays, the restaurant's busiest days, until a permanent cook could be hired.

"Do you realize what you're doing, Giuliana?" a concerned Concetta said when she learned of her niece's decision to forego college . . ."what you're giving up? And what about your parents . . . what are you going to tell them?"

In making her decision, as painful as it was, Giuliana knew very well the sacrifice she was making. But she told herself she needed more time to think through the matter of pursuing a career as an architect. Uppermost in her mind was an uneasy feeling that had been gnawing at her all along: if she went away to college she would be walking away from obligations she felt she owed her guardians especially now, at this critical moment, the early days of their ownership of Randazzi's.

As for being away from the classroom, this was perhaps her biggest regret even though, in her mind, it would only be a temporary, not permanent deprivation. For her, learning had always been a top priority, an end in itself, not a path pursued as a necessary means of making a living. School and cooking had given her the most satisfaction, and joy. To have to abandon one for the other, even if for only a year, would not be something she looked forward to doing. Yet, she felt compelled to do exactly that.

Then there was the matter of what up to now had been a tepid social life. Being as she was a key player in an all-consuming business, time for socializing with friends, or enjoying an active social life, was at a premium. Therefore, longtime relationships with contemporaries in and out of school were always being disrupted, or even permanently damaged. While she had nurtured some wonderful friendships in high school, like the one she had with Winston Hsu, she frankly couldn't wait for college where she was certain she would be hob-knobbing with an even greater number of people from even more diversified backgrounds. Now that, too, would have to be put on hold.

"Yes, of course, I know what I'm sacrificing, dear Aunt," Giuliana said, wishing to allay her guardian's disappointment, while at the same time attempting to put a positive spin on a not altogether happy choice she'd made. "But I'm only putting off college for a year. You have to remember that most of the seniors in my class are already eighteen, so I'll have another year to mature (the broad smile on her face made her aunt smile, too). Barnard's admissions director assured me that it was likely the scholarship they offered would still be available next year. My grades, plus my architectural drawings, impressed the admissions people. She told me that if from time to time I could send along some new drawings or paintings, it might help when I resubmitted an application next spring."

"When are you going to find time," Umberto inquired, "what with all you have to do running a restaurant kitchen?"

"Leave that to me, Uncle," Giuliana said confidently. "As for my parents . . . well, I'm going to have to think carefully about what to tell them."

Outwardly, Umberto appeared to be disappointed that Giuliana would be putting off college for a year; inwardly, he couldn't help but breathe a sigh of relief.

# Chapter 43

On June 15, 1947, three months to the day since taking control of the restaurant, and a week before Giuliana's high school graduation, Umberto hosted a dinner party to honor those who helped make his dream of owning his own business come true.

"First, I thank my wonderful wife, Concetta. Without her none of this would be possible. Next, I want to thank my beautiful niece Giuliana . . . like a daughter to us . . . brilliant, talented . . . the best cook in the world. I thank God, my sister Maria and brother-in-law Antonio for giving us this gift. To you, Camilla and Jennifer, my two generous friends . . . you both are a godsend. I can't tell you how much your help has meant to us. I also want to thank the Giordanos, Antoinette, and you, Paolo, for being my best friend since we were kids. Your dedication to Randazzi's has been an inspiration to me. If it wasn't for you, I would not have a job in the restaurant at all. And, finally, to you Langdon and Gordon, thank you for going along with your wives to help us . . . also for giving us your loyalty and encouragement. Most of all, your money." They all laughed heartily.

"Today is the happiest day in my life, except for the day I married my wife. To be with all of you who helped us, I cannot find words to thank you enough. You are special, every one of you. I always believed that when we came to America ten years ago lots of people would be ready to help me and Concetta. To be honest, I thought they would be Italians who felt obligated to help two struggling immigrants from the old country.

"But today, I am surrounded by new friends, none of them Italian, from places I never heard of before . . . Pennsylvania, Delaware,

Ohio . . . Scotland I heard of (everyone laughed) . . . educated, successful, lovely people. You were once strangers to me and Connie, but no longer. You are our truest, dearest, most loyal friends. As long as I live I will never forget what you have done for us. I love the United States of America."

After the clapping subsided, Umberto continued: "I have another announcement." He opened the top drawer of a tiny cabinet against the wall behind his chair. "This is for you, Giuliana," he said, handing his niece a letter-size envelope. "Please."

Giuliana tore open the envelope. For a second she didn't know what it was. Then she let out what everyone later said was the most delicious scream. She clutched the contents of the envelope to her chest, then held it high for everyone to see—round trip tickets on Pan American Airlines to Rome, departing August 2, returning September 3.

"Your uncle and I know you've waited patiently for the day to come when you would return to Amalfi for a visit," Concetta said, momentarily choked up. "We realize it is not the full summer you had been looking forward to after graduation, but a month should be enough time to reacquaint yourself with family and friends."

"But the restaurant, Aunt?" Giuliana protested, a concerned look on her face. The thought of work responsibilities momentarily pushed aside the anticipated pleasure of her first trip back home in six years.

"You mustn't think of that, my dear, we have everything well in hand," Umberto explained. "August in the United States is like in our country—everybody goes on holiday. We're going to close the restaurant for two weeks anyway so that we can have a little break ourselves, maybe spend a week at the shore, a couple of days in New York. It will be our first time off from work since coming here. The other two weeks, I'm sure we'll manage without you. We're never that busy in August. Besides, your aunt and the others in the kitchen will be able to handle things. God willing, next summer or the one after that, we will be able to go back to Italy for a vacation ourselves . . . we miss our families, too," Umberto said wistfully, throwing a loving look in his wife's direction.

\*　　\*　　\*

For six long years Giuliana had wondered what it would be like to return home to Amalfi to be together again with family, friends and the beautiful town of her birth. In one recurring and disturbing dream, when she arrived in town after her extended absence not a soul recognized who she was—not parents, brothers or friends. People she stopped on the street with a "Hey, it's me, Giuliana Landini!" simply looked away, blank stares their only expressions. Each time she awoke, shaken from the frightening nightmare, she mumbled a silent prayer of thanks.

Now that the time for the trip had finally arrived, she told Camilla in a lengthy phone call that she was more nervous than she'd been on her first day of school in America, or even the night of the prom and her date with Rick DeGoia.

"Don't be surprised if the trip doesn't live up to your expectations," Camilla cautioned her friend.

When Giuliana asked Camilla why she thought that, Camilla described the letdown she experienced every time she went back to Scotland. "Seeing my parents, my brother, Connor, and relatives and friends was wonderful, of course, but somehow every trip home always proved to be terribly disappointing," she told her.

She said she simply had outgrown Glasgow. "New York—chaotic, exciting, stimulating New York—is now my home. Leaving it at the end of every summer to return to Amalfi to teach, or to go on holiday to

Scotland inevitably turned, with each passing year, to be nothing more than an endless string of dashed expectations."

Giuliana kept Camilla's words in mind as she prepared for her trip and was determined that that would not happen to her.

\*　　\*　　\*

During her month in Amalfi Giuliana tried especially hard to put on the happiest of faces. But it wasn't always easy. While Maria and Antonio were beside themselves with joy at having their daughter back home with them—even if it was only a brief visit—knowing that Giuliana would not be going to college in a few weeks when she returned to America put a added damper on their spirits, and no matter what reasoned explanation Giuliana gave for why she was putting off college for a year, nothing she said seemed to lessen their concerns. Antonio went so far as telling his wife, "You mark my words, she won't be going at all."

Her parents concerns aside, Giuliana reveled in her time with family relatives, some of whom she hadn't seen in years. Others—like her three sisters-in-law and three nieces and one nephew whom she was acquainted with only through letters she exchanged with her brothers— she was meeting for the first time. She also relished the long, leisurely hours she spent with former school friends.

Some of Giuliana's fondest memories of her fleeting trip back to Amalfi were of times spent with Maddalena Vertucci in the rectory of Santa Croce Church. She'd first attend early morning Mass, then visit Nonna Dona's gravesite in the cemetery behind the church, talking to her as though she were ready to answer back, telling Nonna about life in the United States, then tidying up the grounds around the headstone and laying a small bouquet of fresh flowers before saying goodbye till next time, God only knows when that would be.

On more than one of those visits with Maddalena, while having the best time reminiscing about the good old days, the two women stood side by side in the kitchen preparing a meal for Father Di Pina, at whose table they were then invited to dine. After a long, leisurely lunch, the pastor and Giuliana would then go to his office and extend their visit well into the afternoon.

Amalfi itself proved to be an unexpected delight for Giuliana; she hadn't realized how much she'd missed the town. Every chance she got, either alone or arm-in-arm with a friend, she walked up and down Flavia Gioia from one end to the other, stopping numerous times along the way to mingle with acquaintances anxious to greet the lovely young lady. Many knew her as a child, and were anxious to inquire about her new life in America. Nothing appeared to have changed since she'd been away: the place was as beautiful as ever, the people were as nice as they'd always been, and the same shops, restaurants, food stalls and other concessions were right where they'd always been, inhabited by the same purveyors dispensing their same wares. If there was a single, defining change in the place, it had to do with ever larger crowds of vacationers from all over the world, having finally discovered this relatively new Mediterranean paradise, flooding its streets.

All in all, apart from Camilla's warnings, it was a joy for Giuliana to be back home in Amalfi. The only disappointment was not having Nona Donna around with whom to share it.

# Chapter 44

In the days and weeks after she returned to New Haven from her trip, Giuliana became consumed by work. The restaurant was the perfect refuge for putting aside concerns she continued to harbor for her parents, still trying to cope with her absence and still troubled by her decision to put off college, even though she kept assuring them it was only for a year. She came early to the restaurant, and stayed late. She didn't wait for the fish man or the fruit man or the vegetable man to deliver to her door. Twice a week she rose at dawn and headed for the docks to select the best fish. On other days she arrived in the market to purchase the freshest produce even before vendors finished setting up their tables.

Part of her rounds also included regular visits to the meat market to order the finest cuts. During her vacation in Amalfi she was lucky to have spent several mornings working with the best butcher in town; he showed Giuliana how to handle a carving knife as delicately as if it were a bow on a perfectly strung Stradivarius. He taught her how to butcher and trim meat so she wouldn't have to cede that important job to her local butcher, who was obligated to charge more when called on to do the cutting and the trimming. She got to love butchering, for it gave her a chance to learn two valuable lessons in running a successful restaurant kitchen: how to get the most out of every food item, especially an expensive one like meat, and how to exercise good portion control.

Giuliana could not have been more content in her work. But there was a noticeable change in her demeanor since returning from Amalfi that the Fassanos immediately picked up on: Giuliana was no longer the happy-go-lucky teenager without a care in the world, but a mature woman with concerns she had been far too long storing up in a deep emotional worry bank. Being with her parents everyday for a month after having been away for six years was a sobering experience. The sadness Giuliana read in their eyes gave her a jolt.

Both Antonio and Maria were still on the sunny side of fifty, yet each appeared years older. Not so much that the attractiveness had been drained from their faces; it was a vacant, beaten-down look that most concerned her. Maria still agonized over Nona's death and Giuliana's absence. Camilla's leaving Amalfi for good the previous June did not help either: the Landinis were fond of the school teacher. Plus, she was their closest link to Giuliana in America. At the end of the summer when Camilla returned from New York, the Landinis could always count on the annual update she gave them on their daughter. To have that connection permanently severed was yet another blow to their already fragile emotional state.

Add to that the departure, one by one, of the Landinis' three sons, now safely home from the war but married, each with his own new family, all living away from Amalfi, none close enough to drop everything they were doing at a moment's notice and rush to their mother's side to give her a consoling hug when she most needed one. Maria lost all desire for work, and what little she managed to do was hardly worth the effort; it brought in little money, and even less satisfaction.

Antonio was no better off; his malaise was as acute as his wife's. He pined for Giuliana as much as Maria did, though less demonstratively, yet his heaviness of heart was compounded by a sense of dislocation: he no longer worked in the only business he ever knew, fishing. He gave up the sea entirely and joined Fassano Construction, work he fell into strictly on the basis of being family. He appreciated his relatives' kind gesture, but he disliked carpentry and masonry work, wasn't very good at it and spent more time away from the job than on it. His not working often enough made it virtually impossible for him to ever bring home a decent pay, and since money had been a prevailing concern from the moment Giuliana left for America the Landinis were forced to go through funds earmarked for their daughter's education in order to supplement their meager income.

The guilt, if not outright embarrassment, of having to dip into Giuliana's college fund and watch it evaporate like soap bubbles into thin air, was a bitter pill for the proud Italian husband and father to swallow. One would have thought Giuliana's not going off to college in the fall would be a load off his back, but it had the opposite effect.

Now that Giuliana had seen for herself how unhappy, and how strapped financially her parents were, she vowed to do something about securing their future. As a full and equal partner in the newly acquired restaurant, she explained to them in a long letter that she was making a very good living, had few expenses, and so it would be no problem at all to wire them a monthly check. She also asked her father to promise, now that he could count on steady money coming in—"consider it a loan, not an outright gift"—that he would go back to fishing, even if it meant doing it for someone else. Maria was asked to make a promise, too—to resume her linen making. "It will take your mind off other concerns. And besides, you're much too good at it to just let that talent go to waste."

But in the back of her mind lurked another, bolder plan. The first step was to have her parents come live permanently with her in America. The chances of that happening were especially promising now that Letizia no longer owned the restaurant. She told Giuliana it was her intention to sell the building, move out of the apartment and go live permanently with her daughter in White Plains. Upon hearing the news

Giuliana, without a moment's hesitation, told the woman she would buy the building. "When you are ready to sell, I am confident I can get my aunt and uncle to go in with me on the purchase. I only ask that you give us the first opportunity to bid on it before you put it up for sale."

In her mind, Giuliana had created the perfect scenario: with the roomy apartment over the restaurant soon to become available once she owned the building, Giuliana would then work on getting her parents to agree to come to America. Just think: the three of them—father, mother and daughter—back together again, living in Mrs. Randazzi's beautiful apartment, one of the nicest on Wooster Street. And Umberto and Concetta, in their own place, with their privacy once again restored, living right across the street.

That settled, she would put into play the other part of her plan, one she had for some time given considerable thought to even before she learned of her parents' shaky finances: she would give up plans for college altogether. In carefully weighing the ramifications of such a bold decision, she kept coming back again and again to an observation the Hsus had made only weeks before at the Fassano kitchen table: Giuliana did not need college to become successful—she already was.

*Hasn't cooking already put me in closer proximity to whatever life-long dreams I might have had for myself? Hadn't I always said, even as a little girl, that I wanted to be the best cook in the world? Well, now I have my chance to prove it . . . and it's time to stop deluding myself that a college education and a career in architecture is what I really want, not the food business: I'm a cook. I have no other choice. That's all there is to it.*

There were other compelling reasons as to why she believed she was making the right decision in giving up college for the kitchen, not the least of which was the war. In her tiny part of the world, in her adopted city, it had for almost five years virtually wiped out the restaurant business. She felt an obligation to help restore it through the unique style of cooking she had pioneered and that had become so popular in New Haven. Food preparation, the kind she was interested in, she believed to be an art form that stretched every creative fiber of her being, taking her to new areas of exploration. It was the centerpiece of her persona, every bit as challenging as either her art or her writing. She found that whenever she was able to achieve in a dish exactly the taste and texture she desired, and then have the fruits of that effort recognized by appreciative diners, the experience was transportive. Having been brought up in a culture where food forged an indelible identity, the sine qua non of Italian family unity and joy, was there work any more satisfying to devote one's life?

She also felt strongly the need to address another important issue—society's lingering bias against women in business. That battle had always been fraught: Italy was famous for it, America no less accepting. For how many Letizia Randazzis (or Giuliana Landinis) were there? At first the notion of speaking out for and helping women forge an identity in business hadn't entered her thinking. But over time, just like her grandmother before her, even her mother, and lately the irrepressible Letizia Randazzi, Giuliana came to embrace her role as a crusader of women's rights, vowing not to allow gender discrimination to dissuade, deter or deny her from fulfilling the goal of succeeding in business, even if it meant competing in a world dominated by men and in an industry traditionally foreclosed to women. As the avatar of a new style of cooking, she had more than met the test, and had no intention of abandoning the pursuit of finding even greater challenges to meet and conquer. As an adjunct to her own ambitions, she wanted to help bring along other women seeking to make their mark in the culinary arts.

Again she turned to the war as the perfect metaphor. She put down her thoughts at length in an impassioned letter to her parents informing them that she would not be going to college.

"The war," she wrote in part, "has a way of sealing up the cracks of prejudice that exist among people in our society. When a soldier is on the battlefield, he doesn't much care if the guy next to him is white, colored, Catholic, Jew or atheist. The same can be said of food: Does it really matter whether a great meal comes out of a kitchen run by a man or a woman?"

Finally, there was, perhaps, the most compelling reason of all— economics. Giuliana found herself in the enviable position of not having to compete for clients the way, say, a doctor, lawyer, engineer—or an architect, for that matter—would out of necessity be required to do to build a practice. Randazzi's Giuliana Landini-inspired restaurant suffered no dearth of customers. If anything, they were frequenting the place in ever greater numbers. At the tender age of seventeen, the supremely confident chef knew she had plenty more years to watch the business grow to secure her financial future.

Rick DeGoia had said it best: "When you find something you love, don't walk away from it."

# Chapter 45

How many times had Donatella Fassano told her granddaughter that life is unpredictable . . . that it could change in the blink of an eye? That sentiment had left an indelible impression on Giuliana.

In May, 1948, on a warm, springlike Saturday night, Joseph Amendola, pastry instructor at the recently founded New Haven Restaurant Institute, walked into Randazzi's Restaurant and, in a little less than two hours, one of those transformative moments occurred.

Having grown up in New Haven, Joe Amendola had heard of Randazzi's. But he had not eaten there, before or since coming back from his service in the war in late 1946. Now that he was an important member of a venture committed to training the next generation of cooks, bakers and food administrators who would hopefully resuscitate the food industry in New Haven, he felt duty bound to visit as many restaurants, food shops and bakeries in town as possible to judge for himself just how well they were doing. And since Randazzi's enjoyed such a stellar reputation, due principally to the cooking of its distaff teenage chef, Joe Amendola had it at the top of his list, anxious to discover for himself what it was about Randazzi's that made it one of the best, if not the best Italian restaurant in the city—the birthplace of *la cucina Italiana moderna*. He came away raving: the food, the presentation, the service, were nothing short of excellent. He went back again and again to make sure it was not a fluke.

Joseph Amendola knew food. It was in his blood. Born in New Haven in 1920, he was one of nine children, all of whom went to work at an early age to help support the family—the boys bagged groceries in a neighborhood store or shined shoes in the corner barber shop, his sisters worked as seamstresses. Joe was the lucky one. Growing up in the pre-depression 20s, he was only nine when he got a job in his Uncle Frank's bakery as an apprentice. He grew to love the bakery business and learned the trade from the ground up from his talented but demanding uncle.

After eight years of working in the bakery seven days a week, including holidays, Joe felt he had learned all he was ever going to learn from his uncle. Craving a desire for greater responsibility, as well as to get out from under his uncle's smothering presence, he left the shop to accept a position in the city's largest bakery. By the time he was nineteen, he was managing the store's twenty-eight bakers. Then came the war. The day after Pearl Harbor, Joe enlisted in the Army, trading spatula and rolling pin for a rifle and a flak jacket. He was assigned to the tanker corps and remained there for two years until his superiors got wind of the young man's real talents: they removed him from tank duty and put him in the kitchen, where he belonged. The last two years of his five-year active service duty were spent catering to the sweet tooth of the army general in charge of all U.S. European-based military personnel. Traveling the continent, he got to learn from some of the finest pastry chefs in the world. By the end of his career, Amendola was generally recognized to be in their peer.

While the war interrupted Joe Amendola's career, it virtually wiped out the food service industry in cities all over the country. New Haven was no exception. Restaurants were in desperate need of workers. The hope was that returning veterans would help fill the void. But how and where they were to be trained were questions that first needed to be answered. Both were, by two enterprising women neither one schooled in the food service business, attorney Francis L. Roth and Katherine Angell, wife of the then president of Yale University. They not only recognized the need, they found the venue. On May 22, 1946 in a side-street storefront in the center of town, the New Haven Restaurant Institute was born. Fifty raw recruits, all matriculating under the recently passed GI BILL, comprised that first class of aspiring culinary workers. The faculty consisted of a chef, a pastry cook and a nutritionist to teach them the ropes.

At the time, who would have thought that New Haven was on the brink of a culinary renaissance and that a school for chefs, hitherto never before imagined, would be the catalyst? But that's exactly what this truly historic day would foreshadow for the food service industry, not only in New Haven but eventually for the entire country.

In less than a year later the school was bursting at the seams, as more and more returning GIs were drawn to an industry that offered stability and excellent career opportunities. To accommodate the rapid growth, NHRI moved into an old carriage house on the edge of Yale's expansive property. It never looked back.

In 1952, in an effort to become more inclusive, the school name was changed to Culinary Institute of Connecticut, forerunner of the Culinary Institute of America, today the country's pre-eminent training ground for the culinary arts. In 1972 CIA relocated to Hyde Park, New York, on a seventy-five-acre campus overlooking the Hudson River, site of a former Jesuit Seminary. In 1995 CIA expanded west, opening a branch at Greystone, in the heart of California's Napa Valley. In 2007, the Center for Foods of the Americas in San Antonio, Texas was added to the college.

More than 2,900 students representing all fifty states and thirty foreign countries are today enrolled in the CIA's degree programs. One of the main buildings on the attractive campus is named after Katherine Angell.

\*     \*     \*

On a cold, raw day in January of 1947 Joe Amendola, only weeks out of the army, walked up the long winding driveway that led to the New Haven Restaurant Institute and asked for a job as a bakery and pastry instructor. Administrators who interviewed him were impressed, but questioned his youth; they were concerned that some of the older returning GIs would have a hard time relating to someone younger in age teaching them. But his resume and experience could not be ignored. Nor his obvious passion and love of food. Still skeptical, the best they could do was offer him a probationary, part time job.

It lasted all of three weeks. His work ethic, not to mention infectious personality, so impressed school administrators that they quickly signed him on to a full time position. It was one of the wisest decisions the school ever made. Amendola spent the next forty-five years at CIA— as an instructor, head of the baking program, and eventually executive vice president and chief spokesman for the institute. He was generally recognized as one of the most influential food service practitioners in the world, as judged by the numerous international awards bestowed on him through the years.

# Chapter 46

Once Joe Amendola, as food professional as well as steady customer, had been won over by Randazzi's, he couldn't get the restaurant out of his head. Or the young, enormously talented chef who, by then, had permanently succeeded the venerable Letizia Randazzi in the kitchen. He started asking around the neighborhood to learn what he could of the young girl's background. Weeks later, while teaching one of his baking classes, an idea, like a thunderclap, came to him out of the blue:

*What if we could get Giuliana Landini to come to the school and teach? Wouldn't that be something. Maybe it's a long shot, but if we could pull it off . . . what a coup, what a public relations dream. And what a possible nightmare. But how will I ever get administration, faculty and a bunch of battle-hardened ex-GIs, in a business almost exclusively reserved for men, to even consider dealing with a woman, and a teenager at that? Even if those issues could be resolved, what about Giuliana herself: would she be willing to take on such a daunting responsibility?*

But first things first. Joe went to what he considered the perfect sounding board—the team of Roth and Angell—with his outrageous idea. He hardly finished making his pitch before the women were on their feet: not only did they not think the suggestion outrageous, they jumped for joy when they heard it. Furthermore, try as they might, they could find little downside risk in the proposal. For one thing, both women were devoted Randazzi patrons, well aware that it was the young female virtuoso in the kitchen responsible for the countless great meals they, their husbands, and the notable guests they entertained, ate there.

"Why hadn't we thought of this brilliant idea ourselves?" they asked excitedly. For another, the school was woefully short of instructors. More important, someone as talented as Giuliana Landini comes along only once in a blue moon. But such a precedent-shattering recommendation needed to be handled with kid gloves, the women admitted. They would pave the way with the powers that be at the school: "A little arm twisting shouldn't hurt too badly," Katherine Angell said gleefully.

It took the school a while to come around. But not a second after it gave the go-ahead, Joe Amendola was at the restaurant making his impassioned pitch to Giuliana. She was intrigued, but not so Umberto; it took him several days to digest what he considered to be a potentially risky idea. Only after listening to Giuliana's reasons for believing it to be a worthwhile endeavor did Umberto reluctantly give in. "Think of all the publicity, the terrific exposure for the restaurant, the new business we're likely to generate," she told her uncle. Plus, she assured him yet again that she could handle the added responsibility and was not in the least bit intimidated at the prospect of teaching a subject that was in her blood and that she knew cold, even if it was to a group of men all considerably older than she. She cited one indisputable fact: Hadn't she made a believer out of Letizia Randazzi?

Before a second meeting had concluded Giuliana, completely on her own, but mostly in consideration of her guardians' concerns for her well being, set down conditions that would have to be met by the school before she would agree to undertake the assignment: she would teach Mondays, Tuesdays and Wednesdays only, not Thursdays, Fridays or Saturdays, the restaurant's busiest days; her hours would be eight in the morning to one in the afternoon, no later; and since the school was some distance from her house, transportation would have to be provided to and from. The conditions were agreed to by all parties concerned.

As predicted, there was extensive newspaper and radio coverage of the hiring and ample praise for the groundbreaking arrangement between the New Haven Restaurant Institute and Giuliana Landini, the teenage head chef and part owner of Randazzi's Restaurant. The school, in its infancy, welcomed every complimentary word it could get and thus benefited greatly from the free publicity.

But no more so than the students themselves: they were the greatest beneficiary of the association. The battle-hardened men, many old enough to be their instructor's father, took to Giuliana almost immediately. Though unsparing in her instruction, she was at the same time understandably patient. From the first day she walked into the classroom she was in total command. Even those who hadn't spent a minute at a stove could easily see that her knowledge, poise, creativity and professionalism made her something special. It did not hurt that she was beautiful, too. Neither naïve nor unaware of the affect she had on the opposite sex, she did not shy away from using her good looks spectacularly to her advantage: the men craved her attention, and bent over backwards to please her. Much like the other reigning star at the school, Joseph Amendola, Giuliana was someone from whom students were inclined to learn far more about food preparation than they'd ever bargained for.

Giuliana, too, got more than she expected out of her time at NHRI. She discovered that teaching on a grand scale very much suited her. She loved preparing lesson plans, interacting with fifty different egos with fifty different approaches to cooking. And she didn't have to teach by the book, since there was no book to teach from, except the one she was creating from the fount of ideas conjured up in her own fertile imagination.

For example, it was her novel idea to take students into the field: they visited markets to learn how to select the best fruits and vegetables, to meat markets and poultry stores, to the docks to examine fish as it was unloaded from the boats. And since the school was brand new, her role as a teacher brand new, her students brand new, she had the freedom to experiment to her heart's desire, so that by the time she left the school several years and hundreds of students later, she had not only helped create the rich gastronomic canon of the place, but had in fact become the exemplar of the school's very core mission: to provide the best culinary education in the country, if not the world.

Randazzi's did just as well during Giuliana's time at the NHRI: the city's continuing love affair with the young chef assured a steady increase of new customers. The association produced another quite unexpected benefit: Randazzi's hired its first male kitchen employee. Vasclav Turchek, a recently discharged Navy Seal and one of NHRI's first enrollees, was also the first student hired by a New Haven restaurant. This resulted in yet another round of publicity for the school and the restaurant.

Giuliana was impressed with Vash's skills and found his work ethic to be exemplary. She decided, with her uncle's approval, to offer him an after-school job in the kitchen. He jumped at the chance. To be a chef in a first-class restaurant was all he ever wanted from the time his Hungarian mother first taught him how to cook, at an age not much older than Giuliana's when she started learning at the knee of her own mother and grandmother. Vash made the most delicious stews and soups, often served at staff dinners. Later on, a few of the dishes he concocted, embellished by the subtlest of Italian touches, found their way onto the menu. Besides exhibiting a real flair for preparing food, he was the hardest worker the hitherto all-woman Randazzi kitchen had ever encountered.

# Chapter 47

The immediate post-war boom in New Haven kept apace throughout the entire latter half of the 1940s. Everywhere one looked construction was going on. Small family-owned retail shops and businesses were sprouting like spring crocuses all over town. The restaurant business especially, once in the doldrums, had come vigorously back to life and now played a pivotal role in the recovery of the city and its environs. What became music to the ears of restaurateurs was the oft heard refrain: "Let's go out for dinner."

Most encouraging, consumers were starting to spend liberally on discretionary items, too. One of the hottest products they were plunking their money down on was television sets. While radio had long been a staple in public broadcasting, the phenomenon of television was just starting to catch hold. In 1946, there were less than 100,000 sets in use nationwide. A year later 180,000 more were added, most along the East Coast, the majority of which sprouted their antennae, still famously known as rabbit ears, in the New York area.

Wooster Street proved to be an eager market for this exciting new technological marvel, television. Prieto Brothers, a family-owned appliance business on State Street that carried big-ticket items—stoves, washing machines and refrigerators being their biggest sellers— had opened a shop two years earlier in modest space next door to Randazzi's. The satellite outlet sold and repaired small appliances— radios, clocks, irons, toasters and the like. Yet some of the first television sets sold in New Haven came not from Prieto's huge State Street store but from their tiny Wooster Street shop. Giuliana talked her aunt and uncle into buying one of the first sets.

Jerry Prieto, who ran the business with his younger brother, Fredo, was a natural born merchant with prescient marketing instincts. As soon as the first shipment of television sets came in, he put one of the RCA Victor consoles in the window of the shop and kept it on day and night, attracting enthusiastic crowds of awed, potential buyers. Late in September, appreciative neighborhood sports fans lined up six deep—not counting kids still young enough to perch on their fathers' shoulders—to watch in fascination a round or two of Joe Louis's world heavyweight boxing match, split decision over Jersey Joe Walcott. A year later, almost to the day, many of those same fans, now in the comfort of their own homes, were glued to newly purchased TVs from Prieto's cheering on their beloved New York Yankees against their hated arch rivals, the Brooklyn Dodgers, in the 1948 World Series.

Eight months later, with television rapidly becoming a staple in more and more households, New Haven launched its own television station, the first in Connecticut. The *New Haven Register*, the city's largest newspaper, recognizing the need for a local outlet, got into the act and founded WNHC-TV; a later affiliate of the ABC Television network, it aired its first broadcast on June 15, 1948. In that momentous first year WNHC broadcast live, from television network feeds, not only the World Series but both national conventions, Democrat and Republican, at which Harry Truman and Thomas Dewey were nominated respectively.

A few months after the station had been in operation, three of the *Register* executives instrumental in starting WNHC, accompanied by the broadcast executive who had been hired away from Philadelphia's number one TV station to run WNHC, had dinner at Randazzi's. After the last of the customers had departed around nine on that early weekday night, the foursome, oblivious to the time and the desire of the Randazzi staff to close the restaurant early for a change, were still engaged in animated conversation when Giuliana stuck her head out of the swinging kitchen door to peer into the dining room. She was spotted by the *Register's* executive vice president, Leon Genet, a frequent customer, who immediately rose from his chair and motioned for the young chef to come over to the table and meet his guests.

Giuliana, whenever she was able to, just as Letizia Randazzi had always done, was more than happy to accommodate customers who wanted to meet her, believing such an obligation to be part of the overall dining experience at Randazzi's. Following brief introductions, the men went on about how much they had enjoyed their meal, making it a point of telling Giuliana that they couldn't wait to be back.

Over the winter and into early spring of 1949 Jake Mulvaney, the Philadelphia broadcast pro brought in to run WNHC-TV, dined frequently at Randazzi's. His family loved going there, too; it was their favorite eating place in town. One evening while they were enjoying their customarily delicious Randazzi dinner, thirteen-year-old, eighth-grader Laurie Mulvaney made what she thought was a simple, offhanded remark:

"You know what I think," she said, having just devoured a mouth watering bite of stuffed veal, "I think Giuliana should be teaching people how to cook." She said it while glancing sideways at her mother who, instead of taking offense at her daughter's sly attempt to denigrate her culinary skills, laughed heartily.

"I wish I were better in the kitchen," Claire Mulvaney allowed, "but if I were, we wouldn't be eating here as often as we do, and that would be a pity."

"You have a point, Mom," fifteen-year-old Fran Mulvaney piped up, "but it would be nice if once and a while we had a dinner at home . . . that we all actually enjoyed. I'm sure Giuliana could teach you a thing or two."

"No doubt," Mrs. Mulvaney chuckled.

Only Jake did not laugh; he was thoughtfully weighing his daughter Laurie's remark. "You know, I found out only recently that Giuliana does teach cooking," he said.

"Where?" his wife wanted to know.

"At the New Haven Restaurant School. The people at the paper told me. They showed me some of the articles they'd written about her and the restaurant over the years. It's quite amazing, isn't it . . . a girl this young being so good at a job you'd hardly think someone like her would be interested in."

"What makes you say that, Dad? Maybe she likes what she's doing." Laurie said.

"Oh, I don't doubt that for a minute," Jake agreed, "but I still find it hard to believe that someone as obviously talented and bright as she is would want to spend half the day in a steamy hot kitchen while she could be in school preparing for a more refined career."

"Do you know how much of a snob you sound like saying that?" Claire Mulvaney chided her husband. "Maybe she's doing this kind of work only temporarily . . . you know, preparing herself for something else down the line."

"Like what?" Jake asked.

"Maybe she'll become a television star someday," Laurie speculated, not waiting for her mother to answer. "She's certainly beautiful enough."

# Chapter 48

The conference in Jake's office lasted through lunch. He had gathered his small production staff together to brain storm ideas for producing live television in broadcast hours not devoted exclusively to network shows like Milton Berle, Dragnet, the Today Show, and national news telecasts among others. If WNHC was to have any kind of impact on the community the station would have to come up with its own stable of programming to meet local needs—news, weather, variety, religion, entertainment, education—shows of interest and importance to New Haven's viewing public, the station's primary audience.

"Does anybody have any bright ideas?" Mulvaney challenged his staff.

A children's morning program for pre-schoolers, broadcasts of high school football and basketball games, a few suggestions for afternoon game shows, news updates at different times of day, a broadcast of religious services for shut-ins—these were some of the recommendations put forth.

"What do you think about a cooking show?" Jake broke in.

"A cooking show? I've never seen one on television," Jake's most senior assistant, whom he had brought with him from the station in Philadelphia, offered. "I wouldn't have the slightest idea how to put one together."

"Do you know anything about cooking?" asked Jake.

"You mean besides loving to eat . . . of course not," came the quick reply.

"Well, then, maybe that's why you wouldn't know how to produce this type of show. But supposing we were to put the idea in the hands of someone who really knows something about cooking . . . a consummate pro who's familiar intimately with all the ins and outs of food preparation . . ."

"Do you have somebody in mind?"

"I do." Then Jake added: "But forgetting for the moment the person or persons who would actually be featured on the show, how do you feel about the idea in the first place? Do you think it would fly?"

"Look, Jake," explained his assistant, "anything is possible. We're in a brand-new business, television broadcasting . . . who's to say what will or won't work, until we try it."

"Then you think it's worth a shot?"

"Absolutely. And if I'm right in believing that no other station in this infant industry is doing a cooking show, then . . ."

"And so what if they were, it wouldn't affect us," piped up one of the other men. "Our main concern is the New Haven market. Remember, we're the only game in town."

On a Monday, two weeks later, a few minutes after Giuliana had come from her teaching classes at New Haven Culinary Institute, the executive vice president of the *New Haven Register*, Leon Genet, the Randazzi's Restaurant regular whom Giuliana knew well, and Jake Mulvaney, whom Giuliana was getting to know better with his every new visit to Randazzi's, arrived at the restaurant. The latter had called the young chef several days earlier to ask if a meeting could be arranged to discuss a new assignment the *Register* was contemplating in conjunction with WNHC-Radio & TV. Giuliana, believing it had to do with making arrangements for a private party they wanted to talk to her about, and much too busy when he telephoned to get more details, willingly agreed to the meeting.

One might have thought Giuliana would be thrown by the suggestion of her appearing on television. But she wasn't. Anything to get viewers to learn the joys of good food and the art of fine dining could not be a bad thing, she told the executives, and not necessarily because she might be the one responsible for dishing out the ideas. Wasn't that precisely why she was writing a cookbook—to make cooking appealing . . . to help housewives achieve better skills . . . to demonstrate to them how pleasurable an everyday occupation cooking could be, not a mundane chore? Most important, how to make memorable meals from modest ingredients?

The only possible drawback she could think of was whether, despite her celebrity amongst an ever-widening circle of food-conscious Randazzi diners, she would be able to engage a much wider audience of viewers throughout New Haven and the state who had no idea who she was, or had ever been to Randazzi's. And, of course, there was that old bug-a-boo to consider when it came to Giuliana's competence as a cook: would older women take a teenager seriously?

"I thought of some of those things, too," said Jake, echoing Giuliana's concerns. His ear was especially attuned to any hint of fear he might detect in the young girl at the prospect of her being the one to blaze this new trail. There was none.

"You have to remember this is all brand new to us, too," Jake continued, "so we won't be able to gauge just how good an idea we have until the show's been on the air for a while. We'd have to see whether we can build an audience and attract advertisers, that part's crucial. Our feeling is that you'll be fine in front of a camera. You're articulate, you know your subject, and you're quite presentable." (Jake made a conscious effort not to pile it on too thick, though he often said, even to his wife, that Giuliana was one of the most strikingly beautiful women he'd ever met.)

"You realize you've already been performing, so to speak, in front of an audience at the restaurant school. We've checked around there . . .

everyone including your students gives you high marks, so we're confident, at least from our point of view, that you'd be a natural. The only question is whether you think so, too."

Whenever Giuliana was confronted with a challenge that appealed to her she invariably reacted the way she normally did—by confidently seizing the moment. While this latest challenge might arguably be the most exciting, and at the same time potentially unnerving one she'd face so far in her young life (short of that first summer preparing for the seventh grade at St. Michael's), as Mulvaney outlined specifics of the assignment, she had already determined that taking the risk would be well worth it.

Jake explained that the thirty-minute show would air just one day a week. Due to Giuliana's schedule, Tuesdays at 2:30 in the afternoon was chosen; this would give her ample time to get back to Randazzi's by no later than 4 p.m. Rehearsal would be kept to a minimum. "We want the show to be spontaneous and real . . . as if you were in your own kitchen preparing a meal," Jake explained. "The only ticklish thing about all this is that you're going to have to come up with a recipe or two each week, and prepare the dish, or dishes, from beginning to end. We want you to go through each and every step, explaining what you're doing in a simple, straightforward way. Think you can do that?"

Giuliana did not get a chance to answer. The *New Haven Register* executive spoke up: "Once we see how well the show is going, it's our intention to run a food column in the Wednesday edition of the paper . . . that's the *Register's* regular food shopping day. The piece will tie in with the recipe described on air and contain a short introductory narrative to go along with the recipe—under your byline, of course. Coming up with new recipes every week might be the only tough part of the job, as Jake said."

"That won't be a problem," Giuliana said matter-of-factly. "I already have well over a hundred recipes that we can use."

"You do. Where did you get them?" the surprised newspaperman wanted to know.

"They're my recipes," Giuliana answered. "I've been collecting them since I was a little girl. In fact, I'm in the throes of writing a cookbook . . . it's almost finished. A close friend of mine in New York—a writer for *Life* magazine, and her husband, a writer for the *New York Herald Tribune*—are trying to help me get it published."

The look of astonishment that was on each man's face prompted Giuliana to immediately follow up with: "I'd be happy to show you the book, if you'd like."

That Saturday, Mulvaney and Genet came to the Fassano flat. Giuliana had told her aunt and uncle about the meeting she had a few days before, explaining the TV station's plans for producing a cooking show she would be hosting. This time, Giuliana did not ask their permission to take the job. The Fassanos were by now resigned to go along with just about anything their niece decided she wanted to do without any longer questioning her or her motives. They'd already stepped back when they allowed Giuliana to accept the teaching position at the culinary school, the first adult decision she ever made on her own; they weren't about to deny her the opportunity to undertake any other assignment in the future they might have considered potentially risky.

Nevertheless, it was still hard for Umberto to accept the fact that Giuliana was no longer a child but a mature woman more than capable of deciding for herself what was best for her. He couldn't help thinking she was just like his mother, whom more and more he came to see living in the body of his niece—Donatella and Giuliana, Giuliana and Donatella, interchangeable women—bold, wise, supremely confident, never doubting any decision they'd made, or were about to make. And both extraordinarily talented. So when the media executives arrived at their flat at nine that morning, Umberto and Concetta had already left, leaving Giuliana unencumbered, completely free to embark on yet another new adventure without having to concern herself with seeking their consent or approval.

The recipe book work Giuliana showed her guests impressed them both, particularly Genet, who'd spent his entire career as an experienced newspaper writer and editor. He couldn't decide what he liked more, the excellent writing or the beautifully executed art. As for determining how good the recipes were, he'd leave that for viewers to decide. In any case, his immediate reaction was to assure the young aspiring cookbook author that his newspaper would see to it that the book got published. In fact, he guaranteed it. But not before the end of the show's first year on television; he said the show needed time to build an audience, likewise the newspaper column, and he didn't want the book to pre-empt or compete with either. He also assured Giuliana that the introductions she had written for each section of the book, and for each recipe, were well done; there would be no need to assign a *Register* staff writer to write the column. Giuliana was happy to hear that since it was the one area that had concerned her.

It was further explained that Giuliana would be required to join the actors guild—anyone appearing on camera needed to—as well as the newspaper writers union. Company lawyers would handle that at the time they submitted contracts to Giuliana explaining in legal terms hers and the media's obligations. Also spelled out would be the salary she would be receiving for each of her two work assignments.

The final item on the agenda regarded the show's set decoration. As executive producer of *Giuliana's Kitchen*, the name of the show the TV production staff came up with—much to the young chef's liking—Mulvaney had already asked Giuliana to submit a list of what she would need on set, including appliances and the like. That done, they next wanted her to present any ideas she might have regarding the set's design. They suggested she visit the station as soon as possible so she could get a feel for the physical layout and dimensions of the space she'd be working in.

Once the location visit had been completed, Giuliana turned her attention to what her studio kitchen would look like. Working with instructors from the restaurant school, principally Joe Amendola, and drawing on her familiarity with the Randazzi kitchen and Maddalena Vertucci's spacious rectory kitchen—nothing had been lost on the young chef—Giuliana did a number of sketches. When satisfied she had captured the look she wanted to achieve, a final rendering, executed in color pastels, was presented to Jake Mulvaney and his staff for final approval. With minor alterations to accommodate placement of cameras, microphones, lighting—technical equipment Giuliana could not possibly have been familiar with—the design was wholeheartedly approved. As a further fillip, Mulvaney indicated that in the list of credits scrolled on screen at the end of the show, Giuliana's name would also appear under the heading of set designer.

# Chapter 49

On a Sunday, two days before the show's premiere, Giuliana left Mass at St. Michael's Church with her aunt and Agnes DeGoia, and instead of walking directly home with them she decided to stop at the convent to see her friend Celeste Harrington, now officially Sister Bridget. The two women had remained close and tried to see each other from time to time, on a Sunday, the one day visitors were permitted in the convent, and Giuliana's one full day off from work. It being well before noon, when lunch in the convent was normally served, the women decided to go across the street and sit for a spell in Columbus Green. It had been a little over a month since they had last seen each other; they had much catching up to do.

Sister Bridget started off by telling her young friend that her parents still couldn't stop talking about the private dinner party they hosted for family and friends in the nun's honor at Randazzi's the Sunday after Celeste had taken her final vows. But she couldn't help mentioning at the same time that they continued to bemoan that on subsequent Sunday afternoon visits to New Haven to see their daughter they were forced to dine elsewhere that evening, Randazzi's being closed Sundays except for private parties.

When it came Giuliana's turn to describe what she had been up to these past weeks most of the talk centered on the soon-to-be-aired *Giuliana's Kitchen* cooking show. Hearing the news for the first time, the nun's excitement was palpable—she was beside herself with joy. "Oh my God, Julie, you're going to be in show business! How I wish the convent had a television set so we could all see you perform," Sister

Bridget exclaimed. Then quickly: "I can't wait to tell Mother Campion and the other sisters about this."

"Be my guest," Giuliana said.

"Wouldn't it be great if Bishop Serratelli knew about it," the young nun said. "I'm sure he'd love to see you on television. Mother tells me he often asks about you. She said he was very surprised to hear that you had abandoned plans for college. You seemed so certain at the time about wanting to become an architect."

"Actually, he can get to see the show . . . WNHC broadcasts are picked up in Hartford as well as New Haven. You might mention that to Mother," Giuliana said, steering clear of the prelate's reference to college and the career plans she had since abandoned. "I'm certain that because of who he is, there are no restrictions for a television set in *his* rectory." The smirk on Sister Bridget's face elicited by the remark had Giuliana grinning from ear to ear.

"You seem so blasé about the whole thing. Aren't you frightened even a little bit at the thought of being on TV . . . and in your own show? I wouldn't blame you if you were."

"I know it might sound strange and maybe even a little cocky, but I'm not," Giuliana answered, hoping she wasn't sounding too full of herself. "My only disappointment is that Mama and Papa and my brothers and some of my friends, like Maddalena and Father Di Pina, won't be here to see me," she added, a shift in mood evident in her voice. "Sometimes I feel as though everything I've been doing these past few years is, well, if not exactly pointless, not very satisfying either. Lately, I've been feeling so lonesome, something I haven't felt in a long time."

Sister Bridget wasn't used to seeing Giuliana quite so somber. "Is everything okay between you and your aunt and uncle?"

"Oh, God, yes," came Giuliana's quick reply. "I don't know what I'd do without them. I really love them to death, but I miss my parents and brothers terribly. That visit with them last year didn't do it for me. And you know something really strange, Celeste (only when they were alone did she permit herself to call the nun by her given first name), I usually get to feel this way mostly when something wonderful is about to happen to me—like when we bought Randazzi's, or when they offered me a teaching position at the culinary school . . . now this, being on television. I can't explain it. Can you?"

"I can only suppose it has to do with your not having loved ones, not just your aunt and uncle, around to share in your good fortune; you said it yourself."

"I think I told you the last time we met that I asked my parents to come to the United States to live with me. I've written them three separate letters about it, and haven't had a single word back from them in all this time."

"I'm sure you can understand this is no small matter for them . . . they're probably mulling it over as we speak, Julie. Coming to grips with a decision like leaving the only place they've ever known can't be an easy one for them to make. And before you say it, I will . . . you were a mere child, not fifty or however old they are, two people set in their ways . . . not like you, with unlimited prospects, when you came here."

"I realize that, but the fact is I can make things so much better for them."

"I have to wonder if you're not thinking more of yourself than you are of them," Celeste said, running the risk of hurting her dear friend's feelings by saying such a thing, which was the last thing on her mind.

"No, not at all," Giuliana countered, trying not to sound defensive. "It's just that, they've never been the same since I left. When I saw them last summer, I got frightened. They seemed so sad almost the whole time I was there, even though they hardly let me out of their sight. Of course, they knew full well it was just a visit and that I'd soon be leaving them again. For Mama and Papa, nothing is the same anymore. I'm gone, my brothers are gone, they don't get to see their grandchildren often enough. Sometimes I wish I'd never left home. Even the month I spent with them, as much as I enjoyed myself, I'm ashamed to admit I couldn't wait to get back to New Haven."

"You're not the only one experiencing possible buyer's remorse . . . are you familiar with that saying?" Celeste said. Giuliana shook her head. "Well, it's sort of like buying something you thought you wanted then realizing after you bought it that you'd made a mistake; for one reason or another it wasn't worth the price," the nun explained. "Don't you think I feel the same way sometimes? It's only natural," Celeste added, trying to console the young girl. "I miss my family and friends, too. And I know they miss me. Believe me, Italians aren't the only ones who have a run on close family ties.

"But it's part of life . . . all part of growing up . . . part of God's divine plan for us, I like to think. As much as we love those nearest and dearest to us, and they reciprocate that love, each one of us, when you come right down to it, is very much alone. Let me put it this way: you're my friend, more than my friend . . . I truly love and admire you. But I really can't get into your head or your heart . . . or your soul . . . any more than you can get into mine. Sure, we share some of our innermost feelings with each other, but not all.

"I suppose that's one reason I decided to give my life over to God. With Him, you can share everything. He's certainly gotten into my being, and I'm struggling every day like a lot of other committed people to get into His. So far, it seems to be working. I'm extraordinarily happy with the path I've chosen in my life . . . I wouldn't change a thing. I'm fairly certain that you wouldn't either, with the direction your life has taken."

'You're absolutely right," Giuliana said. "I am also a great believer in God's providence. As a famous writer had one of his characters remark in a book I've been reading: 'The older I get, I can't help but think that life is a continuing struggle between faith and prayer.'"

With that, the two young women rose from the bench and in silence walked arm in arm back across the street to the convent.

# Chapter 50

That evening, Giuliana sat at her desk going over remarks she would be delivering to open her television show two days away. Also checking recipes for what she'd be serving. It being Easter week, she had decided that roast leg of lamb, preceded by the Neopolitan Easter soup, *minestra maritata,* a richer and less astringent version of the bitter herb soup Israelites ate the night they left Egypt, would be appropriate for this most sacred of holidays. Also, another Italian favorite found on many Easter tables, ricotta pie. It was her way of paying obeisance to Maddalena Vertucci, the culinary muse most directly responsible for her own cooking prominence. Over the years, she had watched closely the church housekeeper's every move in preparing this traditional Easter meal for Father Di Pina. Now it was her turn to adhere meticulously to the same exacting steps her mentor took in turning out such a delicious feast, even if it was for a completely different and, most likely, less demanding constituency—the Connecticut eating public.

While engrossed in such fond memories, Giuliana was transported back in time to her visit with Maddalena one morning during her return to Amalfi the previous August. Father Marco was off on his customary round of house visits to the sick, infirm and lonely in the parish, so the two women were left to spend a quiet morning reminiscing over coffee on the veranda.

In growing older Maddalena seemed to have lost none of her ebullience, or optimism. If anything, she appeared to have taken on a more serene look—a beatific glow, one might even call it. She seemed much happier than when Giuliana had last seen her six years earlier, the start of that summer in 1941 when she first left Amalfi. *"Would that my parents looked as well, and contented,"* the girl thought to herself.

She noticed a similar look in Celeste Harrington since becoming Sister Bridget. The nun said it was because she was married to God. Maddalena attributed her contented life to being married, so to speak, to Father Di Pina. Not in the conjugal sense, but in most every other way: she took care of his house, the rectory; she nursed him when he was not well; she saw to his dietary needs; she provided companionship when he required it. In short, he was her life. Maddalena said she was happier now than she'd ever been because the priest's health had improved considerably since he started losing weight and had not had an attack of gout in more than two years, which she attributed to his eating and drinking less and exercising more, like taking long walks of an evening into town, joining friends and parishioners on their nightly *passeggiata.*

What also kept him going was work he continued to do for the less fortunate, work he undertook the moment he arrived at Santa Croce parish. Abetted early on by Donatella Fassano, they together accomplished much good along the Amalfi coast, which Maddalena went into describing in great detail for Giuliana's edification. In recounting the priest's works of mercy, she made much of the fact that to this day his salary as pastor of the church, such as it was, he gave away a good portion of to the needy.

"The only concern I have," Maddalena admitted, "is when he reaches seventy-five in two years. At that time, he will have to tender a letter of resignation, mandatory for all priests who have reached that age. If the Archdiocese of Naples accepts his resignation, he will have to leave Amalfi and Santa Croce, and take up residence in the priests' retirement home in Naples. A younger priest will then be assigned here, and . . ."

Giuliana immediately changed the subject, wanting to hear no more of the priest's departure from his beloved Amalfi. The mere thought of this ever happening saddened her no end, so she spent the rest of the morning telling Maddalena about New Haven, the restaurant, high school, her friends—in short, her life in the United States, which she said she had come to love a great deal. When the inevitable subject of food, but not college, came up, Giuliana saved the best for last and described the cookbook she had been working on, which delighted the church housekeeper. When told that it would be dedicated to her, and that it contained many of her recipes, Maddalena was overjoyed.

After Father Di Pina returned to the rectory, his priestly duties having been dispensed with, the three of them, just as they had done many an afternoon in times past, had a leisurely lunch outdoors on the patio, where the priest preferred taking his noontime meals rather than indoors in the formal dining room. It was a simple but delicious lunch of grilled fish, vegetables, salad and fruit. And no wine. But this being a special occasion the aging priest, with an approving nod from his benevolent housekeeper, allowed himself a treat—a helping of Maddalena's homemade gelato. When coffee was served, Maddalena excused herself so that the pastor and the girl could engage in another one of their always stimulating post-prandial conversations in private.

Father Di Pina, despite his infirmities, never lost his childlike playfulness, so it thrilled Giuliana to see that he was still in the habit of making eyeglasses from orange rinds. As he was carving the last piece, the one that formed the bridge of the nose, without looking up, he said: "Your parents have kept me abreast of your activities. I actually see quite a lot of them—at church, of course, but also here in the rectory and as a guest at their home. No need to tell you, your mother is a fine cook. Now I know where some of your cooking talent comes from. I'm happy to say, Antonio comes to Mass every Sunday with your mother.

He's become quite devoted. On feast days and other occasions, he even comes in to help our regular sacristan. He's a wonderful man, your father."

"Have you noticed how sad they seem, Father? I'm worried frankly."

"Don't be. They're fine. I know not having you and the boys around, and not seeing their grandchildren as often as they'd like, is a disappointment, but they're managing. I can also assure you that your brothers seem quite happy; all three married lovely women and have wonderful children. Luigi told me the last time I spoke with him that once he's finished with his studies in tourism, he would like to move back to Amalfi to work. It seems that more and more of the world is discovering Amalfi, so Luigi should be kept quite busy if that were to happen. Having him come back home is certain to please your parents enormously. I'm sure you know that his wife, Veronica, is from Atrani."

"Luigi never told me about such plans."

"Maybe he wanted it to be a surprise . . . I hope I didn't say anything out of turn," the priest said, handing the ersatz spectacles to Giuliana and laying his own glasses down on the table.

Her parents' lingering sadness was only one reason Giuliana lamented her years away from home. "It was strange for me to meet my sisters-in-law and nieces and nephew for the first time. Whenever one of my brothers got married, I died a thousand deaths for not being there to share in their happiness." She gave out a long sigh. "I'm happy for my brothers; their wives seem like lovely women. And as you say, my nieces and nephew are a joy. They were thrilled last Sunday when I gave them my collection of children's books that Nonna Dona gave to me when I was a little girl. I saved them for just such an occasion. I hope they get as much pleasure out of them as I did."

"What about your own reading habits . . . are you keeping up with your studies?"

Giuliana skirted the question, arriving at the moment she most dreaded. "You no doubt heard from Mama and Papa that Uncle Umberto and Aunt Concetta bought a restaurant near our house, and because of that, I put off college for a year to help them out." She waited for the priest's reaction—one of outrage, she feared—but there was none.

"Actually, I did hear about it from the Giordanos," the priest said evenly. "I would have preferred hearing it directly from you, but you're not writing as often as you once did. You must rectify this oversight, my dear. It was Paolo who wrote his parents that Umberto bought the restaurant where they both work. I think it's wonderful. Umberto seems to have turned his life completely around. I'm very happy for him. I wish your grandmother were alive to see it . . . she worried so about him. Your mother, too."

"What else did they tell you—the Giordanos I mean?"

"Only that you have become a rather famous person in the food business in New Haven, nothing about college. Your accomplishments have caused a lot of talking here. People are simply amazed. But not Maddalena. She said it was inevitable. As far as your parents are concerned, they are enormously proud of you, as am I." He said it with such enthusiasm that Giuliana felt momentarily less fearful of divulging the other bit of news she was certain he would not enjoy hearing—her selling of the St. Lucy painting.

Her elation was short-lived. "On the other hand, they are puzzled as to why you elected to forego college. They keep saying the same thing to me over and over again: 'Wasn't that the reason she went to live in America—to get an education? If being a cook was all she wanted for herself, well she could have done that right here in Amalfi.'"

"Is that what you're thinking, too?" Crushed by such a characterization, she asked herself: *Is this what my parents actually think, or is it really how you feel about my decision to forego college for a year?*

"Well, the thought has crossed my mind, I must confess," said the priest, "but I choose to look on the bright side of things. I told them it was only for a year, and assured them it was sometimes a good idea for young people to spend some time working before starting college."

"Did you say that to appease them, or is it what you actually believe?"

"Both," the priest did not hesitate to say. "Besides, think of how much good you've done for your aunt and uncle. From what I hear, they might never have entertained the thought of opening a restaurant were it not for you, and for the considerable talents you bring to the enterprise."

"Did the Giordanos tell you anything else about the business?"

"Not really."

"They didn't say anything about how my uncle got the money to buy the restaurant?" asked a disappointed Giuliana, hoping somebody else might have told Father Marco about her selling of the St. Lucy painting so as to be spared the unpleasant task of having to confess the unfortunate matter herself to the person responsible for bestowing upon her the most cherished gift she might likely ever own in her life, but sadly no longer had in her possession.

"I can only suppose they saved up enough money," Father Di Pina offered. "After all, they've been in America for almost ten years, and from what your parents tell me they've worked very hard. They certainly didn't get any money from your family. What precious little was left from your grandmother's will, I'm sorry to say, has long been gone. I have to admit I'm partially to blame for that."

Giuliana could no longer hold back. In a single, uncontrollable run-on litany, she blurted out: "I sold the St. Lucy painting . . . Yale University bought it for their art gallery . . . they gave me twenty two thousand dollars for it . . . I gave all the money to Zio . . . I'm a full partner in the restaurant . . . Camilla and another wealthy friend of ours lent us some money . . . the bank gave us the rest." Momentarily out of breath, her moist eyes fixated on her shoes and not the priest, she finally said without looking up, "Well, now, there you have it. I sold the painting. Please don't hate me for it."

The priest did not drop the penetrating gaze he fixed on Giuliana as he pondered what he had just heard. "You disappoint me, Giuliana."

"I know I have, I would never have sold the painting, but . . ."

"Not because you sold it."

". . . then, why?" asked a puzzled Giuliana.

"Because you would ever think that I would think such a thing about you. I can't bring myself to even repeat that word, so distasteful do I find it. It is not in my lexicon."

"I didn't mean it literally, Father," a quite shaken Giuliana said.

"I know you didn't . . . but you said it nonetheless, and I wish you hadn't. In fact, what you did cannot be construed as hateful in any way. On the contrary. Loving the painting as I know you do, selling it had to have been one of the most painful decisions you've made in your young life." He wanted that part to sink in before continuing: "But consider why you did it. Wasn't it to help your aunt and uncle realize their dream of owning their own business? Isn't this what life, and love, is all about—to empower others . . . sometimes, perhaps even oftentimes . . . at one's own expense? Oh no, my dear, giving up the St. Lucy was the ultimate act of love. I can't think of a more Christ-like sacrifice on your part . . . and that is something that can never be considered anything but noble."

Giuliana was not so much relieved by the priest's understanding and reassuring words as she was moved by his insight as to her motives for doing what she did. Yes, it was strictly out of love for her uncle and aunt that she sold the painting; she was thrilled that someone else, that someone being Father Di Pina above all others, who had understood and sanctioned her action.

"Think of it this way, Giuliana," he continued, "one you might not have thought of. Now, thousands of people over time will get to enjoy this great painting, whereas before you and I and only a handful of other fortunate souls were able to gaze at its beauty. Great art is priceless, it belongs to everybody, the common property of mankind, not just to the artists who possess the God-given talent to explore the mysteries of creation. To paraphrase a very wise Jesuit priest, whom I honestly must admit I never met: 'Art is an indispensable part of the trilogy of a purposeful life—to create art, to create life, to create a bridge between the human and the divine . . . these are the three most important and essential endeavors we human beings have been put on earth to pursue. Put another way, to be artists, to be lovers, to be saints . . . in short, to be God-like.' Never forget it. As for your selling of the St. Lucy, no amount of money can ever replace . . ."

Before the priest could utter another syllable, Giuliana rose from her chair and threw her arms around the neck of the momentarily startled prelate, thanking him effusively. "For this alone, you have made my trip back to Amalfi a complete joy. I can't put into words how relieved you've made me feel."

The priest was not finished. "As for college, you must alone decide whether it is what you truly desire. Or architecture the work you want to devote the rest of your life." (How unbelievably prescient is Father Marco in being able to peer into my soul, she thought.) "It's quite possible you may find that in the end they're not what you really wanted. If that is the case you needn't have to harbor regrets or be made to feel guilty about changing your mind as to what direction your life should take. I say this because I can well imagine how much pressure you must have had to endure for deciding to put off college for a year, not only from your family but especially from Camilla, since she was the chief instigator in the first place, as everyone knows, for your going to America to get an education. Tell me, Giuliana, how did she react?"

"You're right, Father, not very well. She was frankly aghast, and upbraided me; putting off college for a year was the least of it. Like my parents, and I suppose a lot of other people who know me well, she can't understand my fascination with food and my devotion to the restaurant. Hard as I've tried, I can't seem to get through to her when it comes to these matters. It's strange when you think of it: Nonna Dona might have been disappointed, too, in the decisions I've made, but I think she would have totally understood, since she did the same thing when she was even younger than I. Camilla is disappointed in my actions precisely because she doesn't understand. She even went so far as telling me she might not have lent Zio money had she known I'd be working full time in the business, even though I finally convinced her it was only for a year. I know she didn't really mean it, but it hurt me anyway . . . it's so unlike her to be vindictive. I love her so, she's a wonderful person . . . you know that perhaps better than anyone. Besides, she's done so much for me. I'm crushed to know I've disappointed her."

"She's enormously fond of you; something like this isn't going to change that."

"Oh, I know, but it's just that . . ."

"Remember what I've always told you: listen to your inner voice . . . it's your most reliable guide. And as far as a profession is concerned, please understand that the work-a-day world is not an end in itself. It was Aristotle, I believe, who said it best: do something you really love and you won't have to work a day in your life."

"Did he really say that?" a skeptical Giuliana asked.

"Of course not," said the priest, exhibiting the mischievous look he was famously noted for, "but it sounds good."

# Chapter 51

The first televised show of *Giuliana's Kitchen* went off without a hitch. The young chef was in her element. Anyone doubting Giuliana Landini's resolve, or concerned that she might be biting off more than she could chew and would be less than totally professional in her role as a television performer, such fears were immediately dispelled once she appeared on screen. Giuliana was not just good, she was a compelling presence. The camera loved her. Everyone at WNHC said so. More important, so did the viewing public. Dozens of phone calls came into the station after the initial airing of the show, over triple the number after the second week.

With such positive response, the *Register* moved up its timetable and started running the recipe column, *Giuliana's Kitchen Korner,* in its Wednesday edition after just the show's third week on the air. The TV program now carried an announcement at the end of each show reminding viewers to look for Giuliana's recipes every Wednesday in the paper; the *Register* in turn ran a banner at the end of the column asking for readers to tune in to the television program the following Tuesday afternoon. It was perfect advertising synergy, a fact that did not go unnoticed by food advertisers and local business owners who began buying up huge chunks of television time on WNHC-TV.

Once again Giuliana had taken up another new challenge many thought daunting, but which in no time for her became comfortably routine, just as were her other jobs—the restaurant, the culinary school, the television show, now the newspaper column—together, all time-consuming duties. Through shear force of will, she was able to give each the attention it deserved and demanded.

As the *Register* had promised, at the end of the show's first year on television—a second show on Thursdays had since been added to the schedule—*The Giuliana's Kitchen Cookbook* was published to critical acclaim. And with it came a spate of new media attention, even more extensive than previous coverage. Eighteen-year-old Giuliana Landini was featured on the cover of *Connecticut Magazine*; New Haven's two daily newspapers, the *Register* and *Journal Courier,* ran feature articles on the star chef cum television personality; and, to add to her celebrity, she was made grand marshal of the 1949 Columbus Day Parade, the first non-politician and first woman to be so honored.

Giuliana could not believe her good fortune. Good things seemed to always fall in her lap without her having to so much as lift a finger to make them happen. Oh sure, she had talent, plenty of it, she knew it. But she never flaunted her abilities. Yet what was it, really (she wished to God she knew), that made her either twice blessed or unbelievably lucky, while so many others seemed to come up short in achieving anything close to what they either hoped for, or should have, in her view, hoped for? Giuliana was being unduly modest. She learned early in life that success was not only the result of talent or luck—they were a given—but patience and concentration, too. Such lessons she learned from her parents. The mere thought of failure never entered her mind.

"It started the day my father took me out in his fishing boat, just the two of us. It was 5:30 in the morning, the weather was mild, the sun not up yet, dead silence. The only sound came from the gentle waves lapping against the side of the boat. 'To be a fisherman, a good fisherman,' he told me, "you have to be patient.'"

"My mother taught me the other great lesson that has served me well in my work. In her linen work shop, she said the secret was concentration. 'Don't become distracted,' she cautioned."

The first person to come to mind when Giuliana dwelled on the imponderables of success was Silvio Randazzi. He was a shinning example of someone she thought would do great things with his life; a charming, talented person she believed would one day become the pre-eminent restaurateur in the city, based on the marvelous ideas he had for expanding the business once his mother retired. That was until his repugnant behavior—what he'd done to Randazzi's, what he'd done to his wife, not to speak of what he'd done to his mother—crushed, like the unrelenting force of a jackhammer on obdurate stone, every dream he'd ever entertained. But Silvio's was an isolated case, she told herself, a life corrupted by concupiscence, cheating, irresponsibility— he belonged in a separate category of poor souls who epitomized squandered opportunities. In what circle of hell would Dante have assigned him?

There were far too many other acquaintances of hers who had also fallen short of realizing the American promise for reasons having nothing to do with gambling, greed or cheating, spousal or otherwise. A perfect case in point was Phyliss Fiore, Giuliana's first and best friend from the neighborhood. Giuliana was convinced Phyliss had the makings of a first-rate career in one of the professions. But after graduating from grammar school, while Giuliana opted for the academically vigorous Hillhouse High School, from which the vast majority of the ethnically-diverse student population in New Haven prepared for college, Phyliss, on the other hand, an excellent student by any measure, chose Commercial High, a school that prepared predominantly female graduates for careers in business working in offices as secretaries, clerks and back-room personnel.

Phyliss tired of explaining to Giuliana time and again why she wanted none of the frenetic, fast-paced life so many so-called educated Americans were engaged in ("chasing the quick buck," her father described it), preferring instead a simple, less complicated one that consisted of remaining in New Haven close to family; working a steady, secure job at the same Southern New England Telephone Company where her father, a linesman, enjoyed excellent benefits; getting married to her first and only love, a boy she'd known since first grade; raising a family and, hopefully, when she and her husband had saved enough money, buying a nice little house close to the water in East Haven where they would live happily ever after. For Phyliss Fiore, and a lot of other young people like her, *that* was the American dream.

# Chapter 52

Shortly after Letizia Randazzi moved her possessions out of her apartment in the beginning of the year, Giuliana, in partnership with the Fassanos, bought the building, as she promised she would. Within weeks, Giuliana moved into the flat above the restaurant. Her dejected aunt and uncle felt as though they had lost their "daughter" even though she was living right across the street, to be joined shortly by her parents, the thought of which excited Giuliana no end but left the Fassanos even more despondent. That turned out to be wishful thinking on Giuliana's part. Petition after impassioned petition to Amalfi went for naught and produced the same disappointing results: Giuliana could not get Maria and Antonio to agree to move to America—not this year, not next year, not any year. As much as they wanted to be with their daughter, all they promised her was a visit to New Haven now and again.

Another sad moment for Giuliana came in a telegram she received from Maddalena Vertucci. Father Marco Di Pina died peacefully in his sleep the night of June 5, 1949. As Doctor Gallardo stated in his moving eulogy, reported in the Amalfi town newspaper, "his magnanimous heart finally gave out." He was two months past his seventy-fifth birthday. He never left Amalfi or Santa Croce as he and Maddalena, and his parishioners, feared he might. He was buried not in Naples where other members of his family were interred but in the small cemetery behind the church, his real home, in a gravesite not far from his life-long partner in aiding and abetting those most in need, Donatella Teresa Fassano.

Giuliana, beside herself with grief, immediately called Camilla with the devastating news just as Camilla was about to phone Giuliana with the happy announcement that she was expecting. At this sorrowful time, the younger woman yearned to be with her older friend, the only other person in America close to the priest; together they would commiserate with each other and comfort each other and swap stories with each other about the saintly man who had had such an important influence on their lives. Such was their mutual grief that during the call Camilla did not get a chance to mention her pregnancy, so she had to dial Giuliana back not moments later to tell her about the pending birth of her first child. The announcement, momentarily at least, freed them both from the crushing despondency they had been experiencing only minutes before.

Six weeks after Giuliana learned of the priest's death, a large parcel arrived from Amalfi. She had no idea what it possibly might be. When she opened it her initial reaction was total disbelief, which immediately gave way to a torrent of tears. It was an oil painting, mounted in a beautiful gold frame, a portrait of Father Di Pina as a young seminarian, in his black cassock, snow white cleric's collar and a grin that signaled to the world the Lord God's munificence for having chosen this most unworthy young man as one of his representatives on earth. The signature on the painting was that of Ottavio Colangelo. She gasped, brought her hand to her heart, then spent several minutes staring at the picture before taking up the letter that accompanied the parcel, shipped two weeks before the priest died:

*My dearest Giuliana,*

*Here I sit in my study, in the sinfully comfortable chair you were so fond of, contemplating nearly fifty years of my priesthood, not very well prepared, or ready, I'm afraid, to embark on the final chapter of my earthly journey into a retirement I'd just as soon not have been forced to take. How much I will miss Amalfi, and Santa Croce Church above all, I cannot possibly tell you. For it is here in this rectory, my home for lo these many years, that I'm reminded of all the wonderful get-togethers I've been privileged to have had with the good people of our parish, and of all the wonderful talks I've enjoyed, like the ones I had with you when you were growing up. Nor will I soon forget the lengthy visit we had two summers ago when you returned to us as a mature, accomplished, beautiful young woman.*

*What I cherish most about when you and I ever got together were our discussions of art. Figuring prominently in those countless conversations, as you may well remember, was my dear friend and, in many ways, my mentor, Ottavio Colangelo. I can still remember as though it were yesterday the first time you saw the professor's St. Lucy painting . . . and your utter fascination days later when I told you the story of how the picture came into existence; you were completely enthralled. I said it then, and I say it now: one of the most satisfying pleasures I've ever experienced was giving you that painting. I always felt it belonged to you. When you told me you had sold it two years ago, the thought of your not having the picture any longer pained me, if you could believe it, as much as it must have pained you to part with it.*

*But that was not what I told you, I must confess. You may recall that my thoughts at the time ran along the line that in divesting yourself of this precious possession you had performed one of life's noblest acts—surrendering part of yourself for the betterment of others, in this case, your aunt and uncle. I also told you that by your actions you had also managed to accomplish a rather important ancillary benefit: you put the painting in the hands of worthy professionals in the position of exposing the St. Lucy to God knows how many serious lovers of art, no small accomplishment. I still believe you did the right thing, no matter how bittersweet your action may have seemed at the time, and no doubt still do.*

*Now, as I walk about the rooms of the rectory for perhaps the final time before I depart this special place, I am experiencing pangs of sorrow, similar to what you must have felt when you left all of us here in Amalfi and moved to America. Except for a handful of books and some personal belongings important only to me, plus, of course, the clothes on my back, all the paintings in my study you so much love, all my antiques collected over a lifetime, shall remain here, where they belong. That is as it should be. The young priest who has already assumed my duties will, I pray, derive much pleasure and comfort from these possessions, or be free to do with them as he wishes.*

*There is, however, one very important item I am not leaving behind. It is my final gift to you. Call it the second act in the saga of Ottavio Colangelo and his art. It is a portrait Colangelo painted of yours truly when I was a seminarian. You may be interested to know that, as God is my witness, I had no idea at the time he was doing or had done such a painting. Whenever I was in his studio working away at a picture no other person in the world, thankfully, would ever get to see, Colangelo was at the other end of the studio painting away at another wonderful picture of his. I never realized that on many of those days he was painting a picture of me, your humble servant. I was never permitted to see any work of his in progress, so I had no idea whatsoever what the subject matter was. By the time I left his tutelage he had not yet completed the picture, he later informed me; I didn't get to see it until some five years after my ordination. I had newly arrived here at Santa Croce when the painting miraculously arrived at my door.*

*While I most readily admit the subject pales in comparison with that of the other picture Colangelo gave to me, it is, I'm embarrassed to say, something obviously dear to my heart. You also may be interested to know that few people have ever seen it—my altar servers, sacristan and other visiting priests being the only exceptions. Not even Maddalena, for it has hung these many years in the sacristy, on the wall next to the place where each day I change into my sacred vestments for Mass. Looking at that picture for over forty years I have learned more about myself than I otherwise would have ever imagined, not all of it flattering I'm afraid. Pray you do not judge me too harshly whenever you study the humble visage of yours truly.*

*In my lifetime I have owned two Colangelos. Both have been bequeathed to you. Only if absolutely necessary are you permitted to sell this one, too.*

*Keep me in your prayers always, as I shall you in mine.*

*Yours devotedly in Christ,*

*Father Marco*

# PART THREE

# NEW YORK

# Chapter 53

The start of 1950 ushered in an unexpected opportunity for the new owners of Randazzi's Ristorante. The Prietos shuttered their Wooster Street appliance store, moving the business to the company's expanded State Street site. With space now available right next door to the restaurant, Randazzi's took over rental of the store and immediately converted the space into a full bar, an important service hitherto missing in the restaurant's otherwise long standing goal of providing customers with a total dining experience.

As part of the new construction, Randazzi's added a larger entrance and lounge area and made room for half a dozen more tables. A year later, resigned to the ineluctable fact that her parents weren't coming to America, the new owners negotiated their boldest move to date— having already expanded the business horizontally, Randazzi's decided to literally raise the roof and expand vertically. Their growing business warranted it.

Giuliana had been in Letizia's flat less than six months when she moved out of the flat and went back to live temporarily with her aunt and uncle while the entire second floor of the building was being converted into additional restaurant space, with room for up to sixty seats and a mini bar to accommodate private parties. Customers often spoke of Randazzi's as being like a community meeting place, a home away from home—comforting, nurturing, a repository of happy times and memories. For them, now more than ever, it was all of that. The third-floor apartment, once used by Mrs. Randazzi for storage after her last tenant left, was cleaned out and re-converted into an attractive flat that served all of Giuliana's needs, and then some.

\*    \*    \*

The call came a few minutes before Giuliana was leaving for her morning classes at the restaurant school. On the wire was a very excited Camilla McDonough-deVries. The evening before, over dinner, one of her husband's friends, an executive with the American Broadcasting Company in New York, the parent company of WNHC, its affiliate station in New Haven, informed Gordon deVries that the network was contemplating adding a cooking show to its new daytime fall line-up. As part of the plan, ABC was ready to make an offer to the young star of *Giuliana's Kitchen* to bring her cooking show to New York, where it would be produced and aired nationwide to a wider and rapidly growing television audience.

On a Sunday afternoon, two weeks later, in May 1953, four executives from ABC met with Giuliana to present their offer. Giuliana invited her uncle and her lawyer to sit in on the meeting. Representing ABC were the head of programming; the network's most senior executive producer; in-house counsel; and the company's chief accountant. Each presented his respective proposal. Giuliana mostly listened.

Over the next several weeks contact between the parties intensified. At first, Giuliana dismissed any thoughts of leaving Randazzi's. She kept going over and over again in her mind the same compelling reasons why she should turn down the offer: she did not want to leave her aunt and uncle; she had grown enormously fond of Wooster Street; it was less than a year since the restaurant had been expanded; business was booming; there was talk of opening another restaurant; a second cookbook was in the works; and, finally, she had begun, however tentatively, to enjoy something of a social life, albeit one restricted to Sundays, her only full day off from work. Most important, she had lost none of her passion for the restaurant business. If anything, it had intensified with each new success brought on by each new incarnation of Randazzi's. All in all she felt that at twenty-three her best work was still ahead of her, making it hard to even think of separating herself from the reputation she had so assiduously cultivated in New Haven as the city's preeminent restaurant chef.

Yet little by little, over time, with increasing pressure being put on her by various corporate ABC personnel, she began to warm to the idea of a major career change: her penchant for risk taking, coupled with the enticing prospect of working and living in New York, that cathedral on the hill of sorts, intrigued her. Ever since that first week she'd spent with Camilla in the city shortly after arriving in the United States, she was smitten. She knew that at sometime in the future New York was where she needed to be, just as Camilla had herself made a similar decision the first time she set foot in the nation's media, entertainment and financial capital. For Giuliana, the time seemed to have arrived sooner than she had expected.

Whenever she was able, over the years, to sneak a day or a weekend in the city, Giuliana, as soon as she got off the train at Grand Central Station, felt a surge of energy and excitement unlike anything she had ever experienced. As much as she had grown attached to New Haven, the Wooster Street area and, more than anything, to her wonderful friends and neighbors, she knew that if she were to ever reach the level of success she had set for herself, it would eventually have to be in New York City. There, the stakes were higher, opportunities unlimited and despite what Camilla and her husband kept telling her ad infinitum— that competition was fierce, often unyielding, and that talent alone took a person just so far—it was exactly the kind of challenge she craved. Up to this point Giuliana's youth, gender and foreign birth had proved of little hindrance to her steady rise in business. But that was in a much smaller, more insular place. Would the same hold true in New York, where everything was played out on a grander scale?

In accepting the move of her career, Giuliana, as she had proved so many times before, was confident she was up to the challenge of reaching for stars higher up in the firmament. Yet while cooking would forever remain at the center of her creative persona, Giuliana would now be working her culinary magic exclusively on a television sound stage instead of in a restaurant kitchen.

For the second time in her young life Giuliana was leaving home. Just like the time before when she bid her family in Italy goodbye, a part of her wished that loved ones might have put up stronger resistance to her leaving. She was half hoping her aunt and uncle would have asked her not to go, to remain in New Haven, at Randazzi's and with them. But they were mum on the subject. Much as they regretted seeing her go, they were in agreement that her moving to New York and accepting this once-in-a-lifetime challenge was absolutely the right thing to do. Remaining in New Haven much longer, given Giuliana's strong attachment to New York plus her outsize ambition, would only be forestalling the inevitable.

What also colored their thinking were more personal considerations: the Fassanos felt they had come to rely much too heavily on their niece, whose talent, vision and creativity had eclipsed their own contributions to the success of the restaurant. If they were to continue to defer to Giuliana's judgement much longer, they feared that plans they themselves had long entertained for the the future of the business might have to be deferred, or even permanently abandoned. Another factor in their favor was that even with Giuliana's leaving, Umberto felt confident that his wife would be able to assume her duties as head chef and that Antoinette Giordano, along with other members of the kitchen staff, would be more than able to carry their weight, professionally and effortlessly, as they had always done under Giuliana's leadership. So by the time Giuliana left for New York, Randazzi's was still the pacesetter in New Haven's restaurant scene. And the Fassanos, though they missed their niece more than they let on, felt liberated for the first time since coming to America.

\*   \*   \*

In a matter of a few months after Giuliana's leaving, Umberto started looking for a site to open that second restaurant he had long dreamed of owning—a place on the water not unlike the restaurant in Conca dei Marini on the Amalfi coast he waitered in years ago. After months of searching the East Haven shoreline, he found just what he'd been looking for—a two-acre parcel of land that sat on a promontory overlooking the cool, tranquil Long Island Sound. Located at the end of an enormous field where back in the day long rows of corn once grew, it was more than a mile-and-a-half away from the nearest house in the area, which, from the township's point of view, meant that it posed little concern for residents fearful their peace and tranquility would be compromised once a restaurant, even one nowhere near them, appeared on the horizon.

"It's the perfect spot," Umberto exclaimed to Concetta who, once she saw it, concurred that it was indeed the ideal location for the kind of restaurant her husband had always had his heart set on running—a romantic, secluded spot on the water off the beaten path. In less than two years from the time the Town of East Haven issued the Fassanos a commercial zoning permit allowing them to build a restaurant on the premises, Pesce Ristorante opened its doors under executive chef Vash Torchek and his kitchen staff, made up exclusively of graduates from the Connecticut Culinary Institute. Five nights a week, October through

April, and seven nights a week, May through September, tables at the beautiful seaside fish restaurant were filled.

When Giuliana finally got around to seeing the place on a visit to New Haven the weekend before the restaurant was scheduled to open, she couldn't get over how much it resembled the one on the Amalfi coast her uncle once worked in. She told him she almost wished she were the one running its kitchen.

During the next few years, Umberto and Concetta opened three more restaurants. The simultaneous stewardship of owning five successful restaurants made the Fassanos the foremost restaurateurs in the New Haven area. Umberto's life had come full circle. No longer the malcontent, without a steady job, adrift loner he was in Italy, he was now sitting comfortably on top of a growing, prosperous business. Whenever he wrote his family across the sea he never failed to give praise and thanksgiving to "America the Beautiful."

# Chapter 54

Meanwhile in New York, everyone at ABC believed that *Giuliana's Kitchen*, a flat-out success in the modest New Haven television market, would be an even bigger hit on national television, due in no small measure to the vast resources of the parent company. To be sure, almost as soon as it went on the air *Giuliana's Kitchen,* now the beneficiary of a first class production plus heavy promotion and publicity, indispensable staples for successful new television shows, became a bellwether in ABC's daytime weekly program lineup, assuming a top position in ratings and viewer response and, most important, advertising revenue. Before the season was out, ABC re-negotiated the young star's contract for the next three seasons at a substantial increase in salary. To go along with the pay hike, the company convinced Giuliana that now that she had achieved the status of a bona fide television star, she deserved, and could afford, a more suitable apartment in mid-town rather than the modest studio walk-up in Greenwich Village she had been living in since coming to New York. ABC helped her find one not far from the studio.

With a career in full swing, Giuliana now had the time and the wherewithal to indulge the city's myriad pleasures. With nights free from the rigors of a restaurant kitchen that in New Haven had rendered her social life during high school and well after all but impossible, she was finally able to spread her wings and make up for lost time. Very often, she was seen on the arm of New York's most eligible bachelors squiring the young beauty around town to fine restaurants like La Grenouille and La Cote Basque (the best restaurants in New York in the 1950's were indisputably French), to the theater, to art auctions, gallery openings, to fashion shows. Her ubiquity included frequent visits to the Bronx, cheering lustily for the New York Yankees, still her favorite sports team.

She also got to see a lot of Winston Hsu. After high school graduation, he had gone back to Princeton to get his bachelor's, master's and Phd in economics, and to start his teaching career just as his parents had done years before him. On many a weekend Winston either came to the city or Giuliana took the train to Princeton, where they would often attend a football game on Saturday—a wonderful extra treat when Yale was in town—and a play at McCarter Theater on Sunday afternoon.

But with Winston, as with her other beau, she remained constant in shying away from any long-term romantic commitment, though there had been a time or two when she had teetered on the edge of doing just that. Pressure was unrelenting from those most anxious to see her settle down, most especially from her parents and aunt and uncle, but no less from Camilla, Jennifer Kirby and Phyliss Fiore, all three now married and mothers. She emphatically told each of them over and over that she wasn't quite yet ready for marriage. She said she was having too much fun. "And besides," she stressed in a final riposte, "I haven't met the man I'd like to spend the rest of my life with."

# Chapter 55

On the night of September 7, 1957, ABC hosted a gala black-tie affair to mark the fifth anniversary of *Giuliana's Kitchen* and to honor the twenty-seven-year-old cooking star of the show for her outstanding contributions to the food industry. The event was held at the exclusive Metropolitan Club on Fifth Avenue and brought out a slew of notables from the media, entertainment and restaurant industries including, arguably, the most influential food writer and restaurant critic in America at the time, the *New York Times'* Craig Claiborne. Proceeds raised through ticket sales, auction items and a raffle went to fund scholarships to the Manhattan Restaurant School, where Giuliana taught and on whose board of directors she was a recent, and most welcome addition.

One of the attendees that night was McCann-Erickson advertising executive Michael Brady, supervisor of one of the agency's largest and most prestigious accounts, Goodson Cookies. Since the company's billings on *Giuliana's Kitchen* dwarfed that of all other advertisers, Brady was high on the list of invitees. He also happened to be a college friend of Jake Mulvaney, senior executive producer and creator of *Giuliana's Kitchen,* whom ABC had brought in from New Haven to run the show in New York. Mulvaney stood next to the evening's honoree at the head of the receiving line and introduced guests as they were ushered into the dining room. When it came his turn, Brady approached Giuliana tentatively. Not normally shy, he did a double take when he came face to face with the stunning young woman. Momentarily tongue-tied, all he was able to mutter was a sheepish, "Nice to meet you . . . glad to be here." Giuliana merely smiled.

Brady spent much of the rest of the evening trying to think of a way he could get to meet the young woman a second time before the event broke up, confident that by then, fueled by dinner and sufficient drink, he would be able to manage a little more than a muttered hello to the star of the evening, who looked radiant in her spaghetti-strap, form-hugging black gown with hair swept up in a bun, held tightly by the butterfly barrette her aunt Concetta had given her the night Giuliana had gone to the high school senior prom as Ricky DeGoia's date. As chance would have it, just such an occasion presented itself when Giuliana, during the post-dinner raffle, plucked Brady's winning ticket out of a drum and handed the startled though beaming young man two reserved box seat tickets for a Yankees-Red Sox game at the Stadium later in the month.

The next day Brady, sufficiently recovered from his jaw-dropping encounter with the striking Giuliana Landini the night before, had a note hand-delivered to her by messenger at the television studio. He wrote to say how much he enjoyed the evening, especially meeting her. He thanked her for the Yankee tickets, explaining in the note his love of baseball. He went on to say that he was moved by remarks she delivered following an award presented to her by the network's head of television programming—a sterling silver Tiffany bowl appropriately inscribed—in which she lavishly and unselfishly paid tribute to each and every individual, in Italy and in the United States, who had in any way helped her get to where she was today. Her words extolling the food service industry as an exciting career choice worthy of the best and the brightest young talents, also struck the proper note, Brady wrote.

In a final postscript, he inquired whether it would be possible for him to attend a live broadcast of *Giuliana's Kitchen* since he said he was a big fan of the show and never failed to watch it whenever he was able to. He told her that he loved to cook—"a handy talent for a bachelor"—and wanted to stay abreast of what one of the country's best known celebrity chefs, whom the culinary world had come to calling *The Queen of Cuisine*, was concocting in her well-appointed television studio kitchen.

A week after his visit to the set of *Giuliana's Kitchen,* Michael called Giuliana and asked her out. She accepted the invitation, having found Brady, in the short time they were together after the show, charming, knowledgeable about food, and an engrossing conversationalist. In a round-about way he reminded her of Ricky, her first heart-throb.

After work on the day of their date, the couple met at the Russian Tea Room on West Fifty-Seventh Street for an early dinner, then a concert next door at Carnegie Hall featuring the New York Philharmonic Orchestra. Following the performance, it being a beautiful balmy late September evening, the couple decided to forego a cab and instead walk to the east side of town, and to their respective apartments which, they discovered, were within two blocks of each other. While they strolled, Brady went into a lengthy description of his background. He was already acquainted with Giuliana's, having read her biography in the elaborate *Giuliana's Kitchen* media kit.

\*   \*   \*

Michael Brady grew up in Worcester, Massachusetts, the eldest of five children born to immigrant, working class, ethnically diverse parents. His father Sean, head grounds-keeper at Worcester's public municipal golf course, came from a long line of Irishmen from Ennis in County Clare who began settling in and around the Boston area before the turn of the century. His mother, she of the mellifluous, celestial sounding name, Cecelia Celestina, was born in Genoa and came to the United States with her parents and two brothers in 1914, a year before the start of World War 1, joining other members of the extended Celestina family who had settled in Worcester years before and were, like the Irish immigrants on her husband's side, industrious working class Italians clambering their way up America's welcoming economic ladder.

Cecelia and Sean met at a church social in the mixed Irish-Italian, blue-collar section of the city in 1924 and, in a whirlwind courtship, married six months later much to the discomfort in the beginning of members on both sides of their respective families who, in addition to questioning the attenuated length of their children's relationship, held strong ethnocentric views on "mixed marriages" that were right out there for everyone to see and take note of.

But once the marriage was deemed to be a successful co-mingling of cultures, relations between the two families became quite cordial, even harmonious. In fact, whenever relatives from both sides of the family got together, they did so mostly at the Brady's modest three-bedroom Cape Cod—the house on the street luckily sporting the largest backyard—where it wasn't unusual for as many as thirty or forty assorted aunts, uncles and cousins to show up whenever a holiday, first communion, confirmation or birthday was celebrated.

"I can't tell you how much fun we had in those days whenever we got together," Michael told his walking companion. "But there were times when things got a little raucous. One particular occasion I'll never forget started out as a harmless little tease between our two hot-blooded families. Then things suddenly boiled over, and threatened to get out of hand, would you believe all because of baseball."

Michael went on to describe the fierce rivalry between the Italian relatives on his mother's side of the family, staunch Yankees fans, and the Irish on his father's side whose allegiance to the Red Sox bordered on idolatry. He was surprised that Giuliana wasn't shocked by such churlish behavior. She allowed that she had witnessed exactly the same inexplicable phenomenon in New Haven when it came to the subject of baseball. Must be a New England disease, she speculated.

"I'll never forget the Labor Day barbecue we had at our house one year. That's when the most serious family flare-up occurred," Michael recounted, chuckling at the memory. "I was in high school at the time. The Red Sox had just come off a three-game sweep of the Yankees at Fenway Park. As soon as everybody arrived, my cousin Jerry O'Rourke . . . he's my age and one of my best friends . . . started needling my uncle Patsy Bisceglia, a die-hard Yankees fan. But that wasn't the worst of it. It really boiled over and got nasty when Jerry started serenading my uncle with new lyrics he made up to George M. Cohan's famous song, Yankee Doodle Dandy . . . I'm sure you know the tune. Jerry's version went like this: 'I'm a Red Sox doodle dandy, Red Sox doodle do or die, a real live Bo Sox from the old, old sod,' etcetera, etcetera.'

"I thought all hell was going to break loose. The two sides of the family were this close to coming to blows. But cooler heads prevailed, thanks to mom and dad. After that episode my father, in his lilting Irish brogue, laid down the law once and for all: 'no more fightin' and arguin' over baseball or that will be the end of any family get-togethers at our house.' Since ours was the only place on either side of the family big enough to handle big crowds, that pretty much did the trick. No matter how intense the arguing became from that time on, there were no more serious episodes. In the end, family unity, and my mother's terrific cooking, not baseball, prevailed."

"Tell me, Michael, whose side were you on when those fierce rivalries occurred? I suppose, since you carry the family's Irish name, you must be a Red Sox fan."

"You suppose wrong, Giuliana. And that's something I can't seem to live down in the eyes of my Brady relatives."

"Well, don't tell me you're a Yankees fan?" said a disbelieving Giuliana.

"Actually, I'm a Chicago White Sox fan," Michael said proudly and emphatically.

"How did that happen?" a surprised Giuliana said.

"When I was seven, my father took me to Fenway Park to see the Red Sox play the White Sox. The shortstop on the White Sox was a guy by the name of Luke Appling. You probably never heard of him. Well, seeing him play made me a fan of his and the White Sox for life. He was one of the best, and from that day on shortstop was the position I played all through grammar school, high school and college."

As they reached Giuliana's apartment building, Michael asked if she'd like to go to the Yankees-Red Sox game the following Saturday: "Can't waste those precious tickets I won in the raffle the other night," he said.

"After all this talk about baseball, I can't see how I could possibly refuse," Giuliana said, trying to sound nonchalant when in fact she was thrilled at the chance of getting to see her beloved Yankees take on their toughest, most hated foes. "Remember, though, I'll be rooting with your mother's side of the family."

Giuliana found in Michael's obsession with baseball (she couldn't help but think of Ricky DeGoia) a perfect complement to her own obsession—food.

\*   \*   \*

The couple saw each other practically non-stop over the next several months. There was little doubt that Giuliana found the handsome young man charming and smart and what she especially liked was the way he made her laugh. But love—deep, passionate, lasting love, the kind she had long waited and hoped for—was for her less a sock in the kisser than a gentle pat on the head. For Michael, on the other hand, there was no such lack of amorous feelings; he had fallen head over heels for Giuliana the moment he laid eyes on her.

In the early phase of their dating, they went out once or twice a month, usually to a play or a movie or, when it was absolutely necessary because of Michael's work, to a business function which Giuliana found particularly unpleasant since she had to spend half the night warding off tipsy out-of-shape men, many older than her father, from hitting on her. They appeared not in the least put out by the fact that she was already spoken for.

But their most enjoyable times were the ones they spent going to new restaurants recommended by food critics like Claiborne. Then after a particular notable eating experience, they would spend the better part of a Saturday afternoon, sometimes Sunday, too, in Giuliana's apartment kitchen bonding over a home-cooked meal, all the while assuming the role of two lab technicians trying to replicate the terrific restaurant meal they had only hours before eaten. As their relationship grew and intensified, they would often forego going out altogether and instead eat in, creating new dishes—some rustic, some refined, always intensely flavored—that eventually turned up on *Giuliana's Kitchen* television show. And eventually in one of the star's new cookbooks.

Giuliana liked cooking with her beau so much that she was convinced he would be an ideal guest on her show when and if the time came for her to start inviting guest chefs, which the show's producer, Jake Mulvaney, had long been lobbying for but had not as yet received approval from the powers that be at the network; they were reluctant to tamper with a product that was already successful beyond anyone's imagining. Brady said it was one of the nicest compliments he'd ever received, coming as it did from someone with such culinary bona fides.

By the spring of 1958 Giuliana had succumbed to feelings she had long held captive but now could no longer deny: she was in love with the tall, good-looking, sandy-haired, blue-eyed—inherited, paradoxically, from his northern-Italy-born mother not his father—half-Italian, half-Irish ad man, Michael Brady. Certain he was the man with whom she wanted to spend the rest of her life, Giuliana did not hesitate in accepting Michael's invitation in early May to accompany him to Worcester to meet his family and the rest of the Brady-Celestina clan she had heard so much about.

That evening, as soon as she got home from work, she phoned her parents across the sea and, brimming with excitement, gave them the news of her betrothal. When she told them the name of her intended, there was deadening silence on the other end of the line, which did not surprise Giuliana; she knew what that silence implied: "But Mama, Papa, Michael's half Italian!" she protested. She assured them that, professionally, she would always be known as Giuliana Landini, but otherwise she would happily and proudly assume the name of Mrs. Giuliana Brady. "I can't wait for you to meet him."

After the conversation with her parents, she immediately got back on the phone with Michael and told him, almost word for word, her parents' reaction to the news. They laughed lustily. "But first we have to stop in New Haven . . . it's on the way. I'd like you to meet my aunt and uncle," Giuliana declared. "They've been waiting patiently for me to bring you home. Besides, I promised my parents we would." Michael was all for it. He said it was important for him to have the approval of Giuliana's former guardians before he would feel comfortable asking for her hand.

"If only my parents could be here, too, to give you their blessing," she lamented. "In any case, we'll try to cover that piece of business over the phone. Since you know a bit of Italian, I think you'll be able to express the appropriate sentiments. If not, you have your mother to supply you with the right words."

# Chapter 56

Once their relationship had reached the penultimate stage, Michael began to get more involved in Giuliana's career. It wasn't long in fact before he became her principal business advisor, building on and guiding her in those areas she most enjoyed: being on television, demonstrating the art of cooking to receptive homemakers; teaching at the Manhattan Restaurant School, molding the next generation of chefs; and writing cookbooks.

All that aside, she often spoke of how much fun it would be running a restaurant again. Of how she missed the camaraderie and teamwork of a well-run kitchen. Of the ambrosian smells of perfectly prepared food. Of the cacophony of clanging pots and pans, the sounds of whirring knives, sharper than stilettos, chop, chop, chopping purposefully on a cutting board through onions, carrots, celery, herbs. She confessed also to missing the kitchen's blur of frenetic activity, the tension, even its heady rush. Most of all, she missed the customers, and the flattering comments they invariably made about the food she cooked. But while all of that might have been true, she was quick to acknowledge in the same breath that for the first time she knew she couldn't possibly handle, simultaneously, starring in a television show, teaching cooking classes, writing cookbooks and running a New York restaurant—and do justice to each of those demanding tasks.

Michael told Giuliana not to fret, that there were plenty of other challenges to keep her creative juices flowing, and that he was working on a way to bring all of them to fruition, in one neat little package. His extensive advertising and marketing experience told him that up to now she had merely scratched the surface relative to her influence on the food service business. True, she had fashioned an enormously successful career as the first cooking star ever to appear on television, and her second cookbook, just published, was already generating encomiums from serious food lovers as well as from legions of average housewives accustomed to thinking that until now cooking dinner had been nothing more than a perfunctory, thankless duty.

But what he clearly saw on the horizon were enormous opportunities for Giuliana to extend her franchise well beyond cookbooks and a television show. He put it all down in a comprehensive business plan he took weeks formulating. When Giuliana read it her excitement was palpable. And a bit overwhelming, too. For the first time she could remember, she was apprehensive.

The plan's first bold move was to get the network to restructure Giuliana's contract. With her career as star of her own television show in full bloom, Michael approached ABC on her behalf and argued that on the strength of *Giuliana's Kitchen's* enormous success, Giuliana deserved to be made part owner of the show, a perquisite that would make her eligible to participate in syndication rights and all future reruns of the *Giuliana's Kitchen* show. ABC agreed.

Then Michael pulled off his biggest negotiating coup of all: he got the network to sign an agreement stipulating that Giuliana Landini would retain exclusive rights to all products and services spun off from the show. This move, the seminal one of her career, cleared the path for Michael to put into play the vehicle he had been working on for months that would skyrocket the young entrepreneur to the top of the business world, making her, in a very short span of time, a household name and a media powerhouse. The vehicle was christened **Giuliana's Way**.

To oversee its successful implementation, Michael gave up his advertising career and assumed the chief executive reigns of **Giuliana's Way.** In almost no time, a stream of new household products and services catering to the lifestyle needs of marketing's predominant consumer, the American housewife, entered the marketplace: cookware, tableware, glassware—some sold in stores, others through mail order. (Later on, the company would partner with a leading national retailer to introduce a slew of products for bed and bath.) They all carried the soon-to-become-famous *Giuliana' s Way* logo.

Also appearing under the corporation's marketing umbrella was a stable of other inspired spin-offs: a series of cookbooks; elaborate coffee table editions—sumptuously photographed and illustrated—on entertaining, party planning, home decorating, gardening, crafts, Christmas and holiday decorating. And finally what proved to be the flagship product in the fully-branded company's arsenal, a monthly magazine called *GW*, inaugurated in May 1958, under the editorial direction of none other than Camilla McDonough-deVries, hired away from *Life* magazine by her brilliant, young life-long friend, a move that for Camilla proved to be the capstone of her own career. For not long after *Giuliana's Way, Ltd.* went public, Camilla became one of the most powerful women in magazine publishing. And, like Giuliana herself, a very wealthy one, as well.

# Chapter 57

Giuliana woke early to the sound of cocks crowing from behind the wire mesh enclosure at the edge of the Giordano's vegetable patch that hung above the Landini property. She raised herself upright against propped pillows, rubbing her still sleepy eyes as she scanned the room. It looked exactly the same as it did when she left Amalfi for America in the the summer of 1941, the same as it did when she came back to visit after high school graduation six years later.

Every belonging of hers was in its proper place. Rising, she walked over to the closet in the corner and pulled back the flowered curtain; dresses she wore as a little girl still hung neatly on the closet pole like so many colorful flags. On the floor were several pairs of children's shoes in different sizes. She opened the cedar chest her grandfather had made for her just before he died. The drawers were empty but had lost not a whiff of their aromatic scent; Giuliana loved that smell.

In the bookcase under the window next to the desk and chair that faced out to the patio were books from her days as a student at Santa Croce Elementary School. On another wall was a second gift from her grandfather, an eight-foot long, ornately painted wood shelf he had made for her when she was three years old to accommodate the exquisite collection of dolls and stuffed animals accumulated over the years. She never lost track of how many there were; she was happy to see that not a single one was missing, or out of place.

In another corner near the patio door was an arched recessed opening in the stucco wall. There stood a small statue of the Virgin Mary, arms akimbo, palms open with fingers pointing downward, a welcoming pose for those who sought her intercession. A votive candle sat in front of the statue. A kneeler, also made by her grandfather, faced the statue. For the first years of her life, Giuliana said her morning and evening prayers here.

She went into the kitchen. Not yet 6 a.m., there wasn't a sound in the house to be heard. She took a book of matches from the porcelain shelf above the stove and went back to her room. She lit the candle and got down on her knees. For the next several minutes she prayed, not to the Blessed Mother but to her grandmother—she was certain Nonna Dona was in heaven, a saint—to watch over those she loved: relatives, friends, fellow workers, many of whom were in Amalfi at this very moment, all come together to celebrate one of the most important days of her life, her wedding.

Giuliana became wistful, and as she prayed her thoughts gravitated to the special people who, unfortunately, would not be present at this momentous occasion, except in spirit: Nonna Dona, Father Di Pina, Magdalena Vertucci, Letizia and Silvio Randazzi, other family members, all gone to their rest.

She also thought of her dear friend Sister Bridget (Celeste Harrington) who, though thankfully still very much alive, had, sadly, not been permitted under convent rules to travel to Italy for the wedding. Otherwise, there was a fine representative New Haven contingent in Amalfi: her uncle and aunt, Umberto and Concetta Fassano; the Giordanos—Antoinette and Paolo and Lorenzo; Jennifer and Langdon Davies; her closest friend and grammar school classmate, Phyllis Fiore, and her husband; Joseph Amendola of the Culinary Institute and his wife; Rosemary Lerner from the Neighborhood House and her husband; Agnes and Thomas DeGoia; plus *New Haven Register* executive Leon Genet and his wife Sue; and Giuliana's television producer, Jake Mulvaney and his wife Claire.

All of them were comfortably ensconced in Amalfi, poised to celebrate the town's wedding of the year. (Except for the Davies, Mulvaneys and Genets, the other New Haven guests had come to Amalfi to also visit relatives.) A few executives from ABC in New York were there, too, as were several co-workers and employees of ***Giuliana's Way***.

Another guest who made the wedding was Winston Hsu; he came alone. And from Scotland came the McDonoughs, who said they wouldn't have missed the happy event for anything, nor the rare opportunity to see their daughter Camilla, Giuliana's maid-of-honor, and their eight-year-old granddaughter, Julia, the bride-to-be's lovely namesake and flower girl. Finally, from Boston and Worcester, Massachusetts, came a large contingent of Bradys and Celestinas. Giuliana petitioned not her grandmother but the Virgin Mary to protect each one of them, and thanked the Mother of God for bringing all of them into her life.

She slid back the glass door leading to the patio and walked into the cool, clear early morning air. She was still in her nightgown. Having arrived in Amalfi several days earlier, this was the first opportunity she had had to spend a quiet moment by herself. The town was abuzz with excitement. It wasn't every day that an Amalfi native—rich, famous and now an American citizen—came home to get married, so Giuliana had been kept busy night and day, if not attending one function or another in her honor, then having to patiently try whenever she appeared in the bustling town square to extricate herself from pockets of competing locals falling all over themselves to greet her and pummel her with all manner of questions.

But now, thankfully alone, she was enjoying a moment of solitude, taking stock of the charmed life with which she had so far been blessed, while examining every single life-changing decision she had made in the past almost twenty years: leaving Italy, and her family, to live permanently in America; going to a public rather than a parochial high school; deciding not to go to college; abandoning her dream of becoming an architect; leaving New Haven and moving to New York; choosing the food business as a career; marrying Michael Brady. In sum, doing all of it her way.

She sat for several minutes at the long dining table under the arbor. In less than a week the pungent grapes that hung from their knurled and twisting vines would be ready as were they every year at this time for wine making, and for delicious eating and jelly-making as well. She gave out a quiet sigh as she remembered how in early September she'd spend hours picking grapes for her father, placing them ever so gently, so as not to bruise their delicate skins, in straw baskets her three brawny brothers then carried to the wine cave for pressing. She would always remember, once the wine making had been completed days later, the festive celebration that followed. It brought a tear to her eye.

She got up and walked over to the garden, once Donatella's pride and joy, where as a child she stood alongside her grandmother almost every morning marveling at its canvas of colors, breathing in the garden's glorious scents, learning not only about flowers and vegetables but about life, from someone who had lived it to the fullest. She stood for some time staring down on the barren, flower-less beds, then moved, just steps away, to what were at one time straight-as-an-arrow cantilevered rows that in bygone days were the source of so many wonderfully delicious vegetables and flavorful herbs. Not a single bud or sprig was evident on their barren branches.

What a terrible waste, Giuliana thought, not just this pitiable sight but her own abandonment of the soil; she had not had her hands in dirt since she left Amalfi. She told herself that as soon as she moved out of the city and into the country she'd do something about that, promising that when the time came she would impart to her beneficiaries, God willing she were blessed with children, her own considerable knowledge of the earth and its munificence. She also vowed that, one way or another, since her parents were determined to stay put here in Amalfi, she would see to it that the entire property was restored to its former glory. All of it.

She then walked to end of the garden in the direction of the linen shed. First she stopped at the mouth of the cave and peered in. All she saw, standing alone like neglected, homeless waifs, were just two bottles of wine. Otherwise the shelves were naked—of jarred preserves, tomatoes, vegetables, of all that she loved when her grandmother was alive tending the gardens, reaping their rewards. She couldn't bring herself to go in. She found it hard to understand, and would not accept, why it was that her parents, no matter how acute were their sorrows and disappointments, had not seen fit to continue working what had once been to them a sacred trust, the fertile soil of their once beautiful gardens.

She came to the linen shed apprehensively, opening the door ever so slowly. Had Maria been honest about resuming her linen making; Giuliana had admonished her mother to get back to work time and time again. Or was this yet another once glorious endeavor perishing from neglect? She held her breath. The cutting table, except for a few thin strips of soiled material that looked like strands of over-cooked spaghetti, misshapen and limp, showed little evidence of work in progress. The cabinets were empty as well—not a single piece of finished linen was anywhere in the naked room. How odd. How sad.

Shaking her head, she took a seat in Maria's chair. Unnerved, but disappointed more than anything else by what she saw—a once active, busy workshop gone to pot, a magnificent, bountiful garden gone to seed—she laid her head down on the table. In seconds, sadness was replaced by the most serene, comforting feeling that blew over her like a cool breeze. It was as if her mother were actually standing there at that moment caressing her the way she used to do every day after school when she came running into the studio. Giuliana fell into a sound sleep. But only for a few minutes, though it seemed much longer. When she awakened it was to the touch of Maria's hand stroking gently her long, soft, silken hair.

In that one transcendent moment, no longer did it matter that the gardens looked like quaint ancient artifacts, the cave empty, the linen studio bereft. Giuliana was back with family, if not necessarily back home: hers was in another place, in another part of the world; that transition had long ago been made complete. She rose from her slumber and fell into her mother's arms, the two women frozen in place in front of the barren table, holding on to each other for dear life. Neither said a word.

In silence, Maria gently closed the door to the studio. Together, arm in arm, mother and daughter strode tall and deliberately up the path to the house. In a few hours, with Antonio at her side, Giuliana would be walking up the aisle of Santa Croce Church in her grandmother Donatella's wedding dress, ready to embark on the next phase of her already remarkable life.

**THE END**

# Epilogue

Some twenty-five years later Giuliana Landini-Brady found herself sitting comfortably atop a marketing and media empire (owed principally to her artistry as a cook) that had carried her from the tenement-populated streets of New Haven's Wooster Square to a tony Fifth Avenue apartment overlooking Central Park and a grand estate nestled in the rolling hills of posh Greenwich, Connecticut. Wealthy beyond her wildest imagining, she returned one day to the Elm City to meet with the curator of Yale University's art gallery.

Giuliana was responding to a solicitation she had received from the university regarding a major renovation of the gallery that would soon be underway on the site located directly across from the WNHC studios on Chapel Street, the very spot on which much of her present success had been spawned. High net-worth individuals like herself, particularly those with a long affiliation with the gallery and the university, were asked to help underwrite the cost. Forever regretting not having had a chance to study at the school she was so fond of, Giuliana did not hesitate in making a substantial pledge.

She wrote back to the director informing him that her donation, however, came with a single contingency: in exchange for her gift, Yale would have to return the Ottavio Colangelo St. Lucy painting she had sold to the gallery years earlier. In her letter she explained at length the role St. Lucy had played in her life. She referred to several "miracles" she attributed to the saint regarding the business success she now enjoyed, notably her role in Randazzi's Restaurant very early in her career. She said she needed to have the painting back where it belonged—with her.

In a letter Giuliana received some days later from the university Yale not only agreed to the stipulation, but offered to name a wing of the gallery in her honor, so large was her pledge. Though flattered, Giuliana turned down the offer. In its stead, she asked the university to consider an alternative dedication, which the museum's board of directors subsequently agreed to: Italian Renaissance art would henceforth be housed in the Marco Di Pina wing of the gallery.

In a further gesture from a thankful university to one of its most generous benefactors, the following year, at its 258th commencement, Yale University awarded an honorary Doctor of Letters to the previously degree-deprived Giuliana Landini. She was cited for, among her many other accomplishments, her business acumen, her humanitarian work in the area of hunger relief in America and around the globe, and for her unrelenting efforts in helping women achieve a foothold in the workplace. Three months later, a biography of her life, based largely on material found in Giuliana's diaries, was published on her fiftieth birthday to critical acclaim. The book was authored by Camilla McDonough-deVries.

Giuliana now had in her possession both of Father Di Pina's Ottavio Colangelo paintings. The St. Lucy, just as it had once hung on a wall in her tiny bedroom on Wooster Street, now hung on the wall in the spacious master bedroom of her country estate; the portrait of Father Marco looked down from a perfect perch over the desk in her book-lined study.

Would that the Reverend Father Marco Di Pina had gone to his rest having been thus apprised of the exquisite resting place of two of his most precious possessions.

# Acknowledgements

To have undertaken a project of such wide scope required the help of many people on both sides of the Atlantic. To each and every one of you I am deeply indebted.

In Amalfi, my wife and I could not have had a more knowledgeable guide than Lina Fusco, writer and former school teacher, who was more than generous with her time and spent many hours not only delineating the history of the Amalfi coast, but also for giving us a fascinating look into the psyche of its people.

To Professor Guiseppi Gargano for his colorful descriptions of the Italian school system; Ralph Di Pina (Mister Ralph), travel agent and devoted member of the Cathedral of St. Andrew: you gave us a view of the magnificent church, and its sacristy, few visitors will ever experience.

I would also like to thank the Marino family in Agerola: Sabato and Angelina, for their hospitality and a Sunday meal not soon forgotten; daughter Margharita for valuable information on the area's school system; and most especially Pasquale, who spent an entire day driving us here, there and everywhere along the magnificent Amalfi coast, feeding us with nuggets of valuable information.

On our side of the Atlantic, in New Haven, I can't say enough about Theresa Argento, head of the St. Andrew Society in Wooster Square, for all the help she and other members of the society gave to the project. Not only is Theresa a leading voice in New Haven's Italian-American community, and in the Wooster Street area, but the key liaison between New Haven and its Italian sister city, Amalfi. It was she who provided us with our invaluable contacts in Amalfi.

For his insights into the history of Italians in New Haven, no greater authority than Dr. Ralph Macariello was good enough to meet with me twice in his historic antique-filled brownstone in Wooster Square. Our two lengthy conversations were invaluable, Ralph.

To my boyhood friend, neighbor and teammate, Philip (Junie) Scarpellino, my thanks for your time and for taking me on a visit to the St. Maddalena Society, the other Italian/American social club in the Wooster Square area. To have visited with some of the members of the club whom I hadn't seen in years was a particular treat.

I won't soon forget the memorable morning I spent on the hill at Sacred Heart Manor in Hamden, Connecticut, with six wonderful Sacred Heart nuns—Sisters Mary Ann, Bridget, Benigna, Mary Paul, Claudia and Marcella, the latter four teachers of mine at St. Michael's School. Seeing you all after so many years made my heart skip a beat. A further thank you is due for the material you gave me describing how young women become nuns; needless to say it was invaluable, and I could not have written about the fictional Sister Bridget without it.

I would also like to pay a special note of gratitude to the wonderful women who work at the New Haven Historical Society on Whitney Avenue. They kept supplying me with information I didn't even know I needed, many of them gems.

Along those same lines, Mrs. Richard Mazan sent me a trove of pictures and architectural data on practically every home and building in the Wooster Square area. What a find!

The wonderful visit Theresa Argento and I had over coffee with Theresa Amendola McClure, sister of Joseph Amendola of the Culinary Institute of America, in her home on St. John Street was priceless. Theresa's retelling of stories from the past had me laughing out loud. She was also good enough to give me a copy of her brother Joe's book, which proved indispensable in learning about the CIA. I told Theresa on more than one occasion how sorry I was that I never got a chance to meet him.

Now to those readers of an early version of Giuliana's Way, thank you one and all for your comments: cousin Donald Laudano; cousin Ann Sansone; brother Robert and sister-in-law Maria Parillo; sister Grace Gerard; Angelo and Louise Capozzi; George and Janet Balbach, Arthur D'Italia.

Leslie Shumate and Patrick Lo Brutto, were particularly helpful with their editorial suggestions.

To my children, Pam, Susie, Karen (a CIA graduate, who also gave me a birds-eye look into the school) and Michael—thank you for your comments and suggestions. In this regard, a very special thank you is owed to Michael, a magazine writer and editor, for his meticulous line-read of the final manuscript. Maaz, I owe you big time.

A huge thank you must go to my wife Carol. You were with me every step of the way, and got to know Giuliana before anyone else did. It was your encouragement that saw me through the best and the worst of writing times—not to mention that you typed and retyped every version of Giuliana's Way. For all of that, and more, you have my enduring love and gratitude.

Lastly, to my dearly-departed parents, Albert and Barbara Parillo, to whom I dedicate this work. It was your enduring spirit that guided me through every page of this book.